The Chicken Run

Lynne Whelon

Published in 2012 by FeedARead.com Publishing – Arts Council funded

A CIP catalogue record for this title is available from the British Library.

Kate held Shirley's hand tightly as they crossed Green Street. Although everyone was walking quickly, there was no panic as the sirens droned mournfully. Quite a few people were laughing and there was plenty of good-natured banter.

Kate knew that many of the locals, mainly women and children, making their way towards the shelter were beginning to feel invincible after four years of war. Tonight would be uncomfortable and noisy but they would all trudge home in the morning, tired and grumpy, but alive. Kate was never so sure. Her stomach would twist into knots when she heard the sirens and it would stay that way until she was safely back in her own bed. Her mum squeezed her arm.

'It'll be alright love. Doubt if Hitler's got much ammo left now.'

They smiled at each other.

'Kate, stop pulling me,' Shirley whined. 'My shoelace is undone.'

Kate sighed. 'You go on Mum. She'll be tripping over if I don't do it up.'

'Alright love, I'll see you down on the platform. Your Auntie Molly will be there already. She'll be wanting to get to the tea urn first. I've never seen her move so fast.' They laughed and her mum moved on ahead.

'I want to go home,' Shirley wailed. 'I don't like it down there.' She began to cry softly as Kate bent down to do up the laces.

'Hey, come on Shirley. You don't usually cry and for goodness sake keep your feet still.'

Kate pulled the string through on her sister's highly polished but worn out brown shoes. It crossed her mind how daft it was that they still called them laces. There had been a shower of rain and the string was wet and muddy. She struggled to tie them, her fingers felt cold and clumsy.

'Oh Shirley, stop moving around so much. I can't...'

She never finished the sentence.

The searchlights came on, the beams stretching out and lightening up the sky and in the same instant the ground seemed to rumble beneath their feet. There was a noise like an explosion which roared and rolled all around them. Debris rained down on them from the dark skies. For a few seconds Kate could hear no sounds. She looked up and could just see the fear on all the faces around them. Silent screams.

She saw one of their neighbours. She was standing, facing Kate, clutching her baby in her arms. Screaming and screaming. Her coat had flapped open and Kate noticed that she still had her blue, flowery pinny on underneath.

'It'll be that new bloody bomb!' someone shouted. 'We need to get down the shelter quick!'

Kate grabbed Shirley's hand and began to run towards the entrance and the steps that would take them to safety.

The air was filled with the sirens and the screaming and the chaos. Everyone ran. The crowd pushing and swelling, desperate to get off the street. There was a roaring in Kate's ears and then – nothing.

The next thing she remembered was the smell. Bleach. And she could hear water dripping. Apart from that there was no sound. She had no idea where she was but she found herself sitting in a tiny space. White tiled walls. She must be in the station. Why wasn't she downstairs on the platform? Where she was sitting was a tiny recess in the wall. Kate could remember the sirens going off but where was Shirley? Where was her mum? What had happened? Slowly, she stood up. Her body was aching as if she had been sitting there for hours. She moved into the walkway. The ticket office was there, in the distance but it was deserted. There was no-one anywhere. She began to shake. And then she remembered. Everything.

The scream didn't seem to come from her but she knew it must have done. There was no-one else there.

Then she heard footsteps, ringing, echoing, getting closer and closer. There were two of them. ARP wardens. Running towards her. The scream went on. She just couldn't stop it. One of the men held her by the shoulders and shook her. He was an old man and he was sweating. She heard a voice from somewhere else.

'Hey Reg, take it easy.'

'It's the only way wiv hysterics,' Reg shouted breathlessly.

4

He began to slap her cheeks. Once, twice, three times and eventually, she felt herself falling to the floor. The contact with the cold concrete seemed to stop the noises in her head.

'Now love, come on,' the warden was trying to pull her to her feet. 'Get yourself down the shelter. Pete will take you. He's going down there now. It ain't that bad you know. They've had a good singsong tonight. Everything's alright. It's all over, it's all finished.'

'I don't know where Shirley is,' Kate whispered. 'My little sister. Where is she?'

The other warden came over and held her hands. He was only young but he looked kind and sort of sad. He looked as if he had been crying and his tie wasn't done up properly.

'What's your name love?' he asked gently.

'Kate, my name's Kate but you don't understand. She's only six. Only a baby and it's all my fault.'

She began to shake her head from side to side. The older warden put his hands firmly on her shoulders and spoke urgently. 'Don't tell no-one.' His voice boomed and echoed, bouncing off the walls. 'Don't tell no-one what you've seen. We've had our orders. Do you understand? And if any reporters are sniffing around in the morning when you come up, keep it zipped. Alright?'

She nodded. 'I won't tell,' she said. 'I'll never tell anyone.'

'Come on love.' Pete took her arm and walked her slowly towards the ticket office. 'Bet you anything that your Shirley's down there on the platform waiting. She's probably worried about you an' all.'

Kate turned as they passed the stairs. Seven steps up to the landing and then nineteen up to Green Street. They always counted them, her and Shirley. The stairs were wet. They had been cleaned. Everything was washed away.

As if nothing had ever happened.

East London 1955
Chapter 1

Kate heard the siren but her legs wouldn't move. The ground shook and her teeth rattled. She was back in the dark place again. And she couldn't breathe. The bare, grubby walls of the ticket office were closing in and the man was running towards her shouting. 'Don't tell no-one! No-one!'

As he came closer Kate saw that it wasn't him at all. It was Billy, her husband. The station walls began to crumble and she could just see the window, the panes gleaming under the electric light. The familiar old oak table her granny had given her was in the corner of the living room. Billy's cosy brown jacket hanging on the peg. Kate had come home again. Deep breaths. Everything would be alright. Until the next time...

Jimmy, her son, was kneeling in front of the fire, moving the coals around with the poker. Billy was looking at her over the top of his Daily Mirror. His usual, genial face looked tense. Frown lines on his forehead. He ran his hands through his thick, fair hair. 'You're shaking all over again,' he said. 'It's that bloody air raid siren for the nightshift at the factory. That's what sets you off. It's time they stopped using 'em. They must know how much it upsets people. George has written to the council about it you know.'

Kate sighed, gripped the arms of the faded, flowery armchair and took another deep breath. 'They won't do anything Billy,' she said. 'And please don't swear. I'm alright now. I must have just nodded off.' She gazed at her son and smiled. He looked up; his cheeks rosy from being near the fire.

'I was just wondering ...' he began.

'Oh, what are you after now mate?' asked Billy, looking up from his paper again. 'You've got that voice on. The one that's always gonna ask for something.'

Jimmy turned to face Billy. 'Why can't we have a television dad? John Baxter's got one. And it's in colour.'

'They cost too much,' Kate said. 'And there are no such things as colour televisions. John Baxter's telling fibs.'

'His dad's just the same. Always telling porky pies,' said Billy.

6

'Anyway, what's wrong with the wireless?' Kate sighed. 'They'll all end up with square eyes, people who watch television.'

'You'll be able to spot the ones that have got 'em then,' Billy laughed.

There was a knock at the door. 'That'll be for you mate,' he grinned at Jimmy.

Kate looked at the clock on the mantelpiece. Half past six. 'Well, it's very late. Only half-an hour till your bed-time. Go and answer it then.'

Jimmy came back into the room followed by a tiny red-haired girl who was wearing dungarees and a dirty green jumper. At first sight everyone always thought that Josie was a boy. Her face was certainly not pretty or feminine despite her large soulful eyes. It was an old face that she hadn't yet grown into. When she did, Kate thought, she would be stunning.

Kate wrinkled her nose. 'You're not going out now Jimmy ...'

'But mum that ain't fair.'

'It's not 'ain't' Jimmy, it's 'isn't'. How many times do I have to tell you? And it *is* too late.'

Billy looked up. 'Oh Kate, let him go. He ain't a baby. Hey mate,' he laughed. 'You're starting early. Girls calling for you and you ain't even ten yet. That's my boy.'

Jimmy looked down at his feet and shuffled them around a bit. 'It ain't a girl, its Josie,' he muttered.

'Please Mrs. Potter,' Josie spoke. 'We ain't gonna be long. We've only got a week before Bonfire night. We need to get some more pennies for the guy.'

Kate sighed, stood up from the chair and wiped her hands on her pinny. 'Oh, go on then. At least it'll mean I can listen to the Archers in peace. But not a minute later than seven. And don't forget your cap. Your ears'll get cold.'

Jimmy had grabbed his mac and cap almost before she had finished speaking and the two friends ran out of the room.

'Don't bang the ... '

The walls shook as Jimmy slammed the door behind them.

***

7

'Put your cap on, your ears'll get cold,' Josie laughed at Jimmy as they ran out through the front gate.

'Oh, shut up,' he muttered. 'Anyway, what you calling for me this late for?'

'I'll tell you when we've got the others.'

They ran quickly to number 21, next door to Jimmy's. Legs had heard them coming. He was standing in the doorway. Tall and gangly. Freckles and National Health specs.

'Have you seen it?' he asked excitedly.

'Seen what?' Jimmy shouted.

'It's the witch,' Legs whispered. 'She's lit her bonfire!'

'Well that's a bit early,' said Jimmy. 'It ain't bonfire night till next week.'

Josie stood, hands on hips, as the boys discussed the reasons why the witch could have lit her bonfire and what it might mean. 'You two are like gossiping old women,' she said. 'Perhaps we should just get our arses up there. See what's going on.'

The boys giggled. 'Hang on,' said Jimmy. 'We'd best get Del first.'

'Well I'm not knocking,' said Legs. 'I did it last time.'

'You fibber,' said Josie.

'You ain't knocked since years ago,' Jimmy agreed as they walked slowly across the road to number 18.

'Yeah an' look what happened to me then. I nearly died.' The other two laughed.

'She only kissed yer.'

'And she almost squished me to death.'

Legs looked really scared, Jimmy thought. He remembered that day. Leg's dog had just died so Jimmy supposed that Del's mum was trying to be kind but she had hugged him so tightly that he was nearly turning blue. They had all truly believed that Legsy was going to drown in Maggie Tyler's huge, heaving bosoms. It must have been pretty scary for him, Jimmy thought.

'She gets like that when she's drunk, Del's mum,' Josie was saying. 'It ain't *her* we have to worry about.' They all nodded in agreement. There was a long silence.

'Oh, I s'pose I'll have to do it ... as usual,' said Josie. The other two stayed back in the shadows as she knocked on the dilapidated door. It sounded like pandemonium in there. Del had five brothers and sisters. They could hear his mum screaming above the noise. 'Just get up them stairs the lot of you, I've 'ad enough!' The three giggled nervously as the door opened. Del's dad. Scary. The two boys shrank even further back.

'Is ... Is Del in?' Josie asked bravely.

'What do you want him for, this time of night?'

Big Mick Tyler's enormous frame filled the doorway. They could smell the sweat and the booze from his body. It made them all feel sick. He was hanging on to the doorframe now for support.

'We just wanna talk to him.'

'Well, he ain't going out for long.'

As Del slid past his dad to join his friends, his father cuffed him round the head. 'Ow! What was that for?' Del muttered and then ducked as his father went to hit him again.

The four ran down the path and through the gate. They didn't often get to go out in the dark. Even the air smelt different somehow at night. Cleaner and fresher. It held the promise of excitement and danger. Anything could happen. They heard the tugs hooting from the docks. Dogs barking.

Del told them that he had already seen the bonfire from his bedroom window. 'Wish I had a different dad,' he said, as they ran to the end of Churchill Street and turned left into Montgomery Road.

'Wish I did an' all,' said Jimmy

'At least yours don't hit you *all* the time,' said Del. 'I won't have a brain left soon.'

That did make them laugh. Even Del himself joined in.

'Well my dad says I've got to work down the smelly old docks,' said Jimmy.

Josie looked at him strangely. 'You always said you wanted to work wiv your dad,' she said, 'when you was little.'

'Well I'm older now,' Jimmy mumbled, kicking a stone along the pavement. 'I wanna do something exciting.'

'Well, I ain't working down that sugar factory neither,' said Josie. 'It don't half stink in there. I think I'm gonna be a train driver.' The boys laughed.

'Girls can't drive trains,' said Del. 'They get married an' have babies.'

9

Josie glared at them all. 'Well, I ain't getting married,' she said firmly.

Del stared at her, a slight smile on his face. 'Your mum never bothered neither, did ...'

He was cut off mid sentence by a sharp kick on his shins from Jimmy. 'What was that for?'

'We're not allowed to talk about that,' Legs hissed. 'It's not nice.'

'I can hear what you're saying you know,' said Josie. 'I know what you're on about.'

'Listen,' said Jimmy. 'Josie's our mate. I think we should talk about stuff like that. If she don't mind.'

'I don't mind Jimmy, but I'd like to think about the witch now. Alright?'

Josie felt a surge of happiness coursing through her body as they slowed down to a walk. She knew some people didn't talk to her mum because she wasn't married. And the nuns at the convent whispered about her. She knew that the girls at school giggled and called her names behind her back but Jimmy had called her his mate. And Del and Legs hadn't disagreed. She was definitely one of them.

They passed two older girls who were whispering and chuckling. The sound of their high heels echoed in the early evening air. They wore no coats. Full skirts and tight little blouses. Del and Legs gave them a wolf whistle. The girls giggled even louder.

'Cor,' said Del. 'Did you see them tits?'

Womens' bodies were Del's favourite topic of conversation at the moment. 'Ladies titties are for having babies,' he said. 'You get 'em when you're old.' He was staring intently now at Josie's flat chest.

'Piss off Del,' Josie snapped, folding her arms quickly.

'I seen me sisters when she was in the bath,' he added.

'Can I come and see 'em?' Legs asked.

'Not unless you got sixpence. She said I'd have to pay her a tanner to see 'em again.'

Jimmy wondered whether it would be worth two weeks pocket money to see Julie Tyler's titties and decided against it. He could get six bars of chocolate for that.

'Anyway,' said Josie, 'if we don't hurry up the bonfire will have gone out.' They started running again.

The witch lived in a crumbling old house on a lane, just off the estate. The council had tried to buy her out but she had kicked up such a fuss that they had decided to leave her alone. An old house, covered in ivy, even over some of the windows. The rambling garden, overgrown and full of vicious brambles, was dotted with apple trees. Strange, crooked shapes that stretched skywards, searching for escape.

The children had known about the strange reclusive woman for a long time but it was only about a month ago that she had impacted on their lives. The four of them had been casually walking past her house. Del had thrown his bubble gum wrapper on the ground, just outside her gate. She had appeared as if from nowhere and ranted and raved at them all. They had been really scared. She was more frightening than anyone they had ever met. It was her voice. Low and guttural. It just chilled their bones. And then she stared at them and it was as if she could see right into their very souls.

But it was the cats that had convinced them that she was a witch. There were ten. Well, they weren't really sure that was the exact number but they thought it about right. Legs said he had counted them one day when he was on his own. They were all jet black and two of them were always with her. On the odd occasions when they saw her leave the house, those two followed. They kept looking behind them to check that there were no enemies about. Like bodyguards. They had incredibly long whiskers and evil faces. Jimmy had tried to get their cat Precious to follow him but when he had shouted at her to walk to heel she had just looked at him as if he was daft and stayed right where she was.

She kept herself to herself. The witch. There were rumours that she was a secret German. Of course, being a witch, she spent most of her time in the house or the garden probably casting spells. They had followed her up the road once, just to see what she looked like. She was very, very old, wore long, black clothes and had sticky out white hair and an enormous pointed nose. Last week they had seen her sweeping up leaves with her broom.

11

'I s'pose she might as well use it for that,' Del had said. 'As well as flying on it I mean.'

And they *had* seen her flying. Just now and then, usually when it was windy and the clouds were scudding across the sky at dusk.

They had watched the bonfire getting bigger over the last few weeks from their hiding places behind the hedge. They had made lots of spy holes so they could watch the whole garden. And, although people lit bonfires all the time, they hadn't really expected anything before November 5th.

'Perhaps it's a special witches 'do',' said Jimmy. 'There could be loads of 'em coming. Maybe from all over Plaistow.'

'Even all over London,' Josie added.

'Or the world,' said Legs.

'Shut up Legs,' said Del, 'that's just stupid.'

So they were all a bit disappointed as they crouched down behind the hedge to see the witch on her own. Standing beside the blazing fire.

'Well, that's not much of a party,' said Legs, 'only one witch.'

Josie gasped. 'There is loads of 'em!' she whispered, her eyes widening. 'They're all in the shadows.' The crackling flames lit up most of the garden but there were dark corners. Changing and moving.

'Yeah, you're right Jose,' said Del. 'There's hundreds of 'em. Just like I said.'

Their witch put more wood on the fire. She stood back and cackled. The children all held on to each other, hearts thumping.

'I think I'd best get home,' Legs whispered. 'I just remembered something I've got to do.'

'You can't go now Legs,' said Josie. 'Look, they're all dancing. I'll bet they're casting spells.'

Jimmy squinted. Unsure. He looked at the others all nodding their heads. Their faces shining from the glow of the fire and something else. Something he couldn't resist. 'Yeah,' he said. 'Yeah, I can see them an' all.'

They saw dancing witches all over the garden. Dark, misty shapes in the shadows of the fire. The air was alive with their insane laughter and the four friends gazed in wonder and fear. Jimmy felt a knot in his stomach. He needed the toilet but he couldn't tear his eyes away from the sights and sounds. There was a dark witch in the shadow of an apple tree. He could have sworn it was Auntie Molly but what was she doing here? The heat from the fire was making them all hot and uncomfortable.

'I'm burning up,' said Legs.

'Shush!' Josie put her fingers to her lips. 'I think I can hear 'em singing.'

The flames started to die down a little. The shadows moved to different places and the witches all scurried away into the dark corners. Only their witch was left. Singing by the bonfire. She was very out of tune and sang in a strange language that the children did not recognise.

'German. Definitely a bloody German,' said Del. He spat on the ground. The others all nodded in agreement.

'Bet she don't know Shake Rattle and Roll,' Jimmy giggled.

'Shut up you two!' Josie hissed. 'Look at them cats.'

Four black cats were tiptoeing around the dying fire, their coats glistening under the bright full moon.

'That's it,' Josie confirmed. 'That's why she's lit her bonfire. They've all come out to worship the devil cos there's a full moon. That's what witches do ... I think.'

'They wee in puddles an' all,' said Del. They all giggled except Josie.

'Shut up Del,' she said. 'This is serious.'

'But they *do* wee in puddles,' said Del persistently. 'Me mum said that's what makes thunder and lightning. Witches weeing in puddles.' Jimmy and Legs were trying hard not to laugh out loud. They covered their faces with their hands, then Jimmy snorted and all four exploded in uncontrollable laughter.

'Who's that? Who's over there?'

The witch had heard them, heard them laughing. She was coming over now, waving her stick. Her face was flushed; her pointy nose looked even pointier. The hairs on her chin were thick and long and her white hair waved around her face as she strode towards them. She looked wild. Wild and dangerous.

'We've got to get out of here fast,' Legs screamed. They all panicked and fell over each other. Josie caught her

13

leg on a bramble and Jimmy grabbed her hand. 'Quick Jose! Before she puts a spell on us!'

Del was the last to get away. The witch's footsteps seemed to be getting closer and closer. 'I know you're there, whoever you are,' she croaked.

One of the cats brushed against Del's legs. 'Help me! Help me Jimmy! I can't stand cats!'

Jimmy ran back and grabbed his friend by his jacket. 'Come on Del,' he shouted. 'Just run. Run for your life!'

Jimmy glanced back. The witch had stopped. She stood still, under the full moon, hands on her hips and began to laugh. A dreadful, snickering laugh. Jimmy could see right up her nostrils. They were full of long, black hairs. The children ran and ran, lungs bursting, until they collapsed back into Montgomery Road. Their estate. Their patch. She couldn't get them here.

'It was a spell,' Del gasped. 'She set that cat on me. I could turn into somethin' 'orrible.'

They all stared at him in fear and dread. As if they expected him to turn into a frog or a rat or something, right in front of their very eyes but nothing happened. Del just stood, shaking like a jelly but he wasn't a jelly. He was still Del.

'You might be something else by morning then,' said Josie as they walked quietly into Churchill Street. They kept looking at Del and Del kept looking at himself. A front door opened.

'Jimmy Potter! Get in here right now. It's past your bedtime!' Jimmy's mum's voice grated in the cool autumn air. The rest of the gang laughed at him and the spell was broken...

***

She walked slowly back to the bonfire, leaning heavily on her stick. Dealing with mischievous children was nothing to what she had been through in her life but annoying all the same. There was something... when she had been close to them. The smell of the wood-smoke had almost disguised its scent but it had been there, around one of those children. She shivered suddenly and pulled her cloak closer around her shoulders. This gift she had been born with was so often a curse.

The cats followed as she moved closer to the house and, as she turned and looked at the lights from the estate

14

through the gnarled silhouettes of the apple trees, it came to her again. The impossibly sweet aroma of death. One of those children was going to suffer. And, as she opened her back door and let the cats in, she was well aware that the death itself, which was unstoppable, could be her own. She had been here before...

***

Jimmy's mum pulled him in through the door. 'You're late young man. Get in and get to bed now. Another few minutes and your dad would have walloped you.'

'But mum ...'

'Don't you *but mum* me, I've heard all your excuses before. Now just go and say goodnight to your dad and get up those stairs.'

'Alright. Sorry mum.'

His dad was stirring in the chair. He whispered to Jimmy angrily. 'You never think do yer? How your mum worries. I nearly had to organise a search party.' He winked at his son. Their secret sign. 'Now just go to bed,' he shouted as Jimmy's mum came into the room. 'Next time it'll be the slipper!'

'Don't be so hard on him Billy. He did say sorry.'

'But ... you said ... you told me to ... oh, I give up.'

Jimmy left them to it and slipped upstairs.

***

Billy looked at the clock. 'Well, it's time I was down the pub anyway. I'll never understand women as long as I live,' he muttered, pulling himself out of the chair.

Kate watched him as he took his jacket down from the peg. He was a handsome man, Billy. With his warm, dancing eyes. Fair hair, brushed back with Brylcream. Tall and lean. Well, that would all change, she thought. He wasn't thirty yet. Another ten years and he would probably have a beer belly like they all did. He did his little routine of putting the protesting cat out and locking the back door. Then he came back through to wind up the clock on the mantelpiece. Kate suddenly saw the years stretching ahead of her. Nothing changing. Nothing moving. The thought frightened her but there was nothing she could do. Billy was Billy. He would never change and she loved him with every bone in her body, but oh, he was old before his time.

15

He pinched her bottom lightly on his way past. 'Don't put your face cream on tonight love,' he laughed.

Oh no, Kate thought. Not again.

Chapter 2

Billy Potter and his next door neighbour George Pattinson, headed towards the welcoming lights of The King's Head. It was an old pub, built in Victorian times. Before the war it had stood at the end of a row of small, terraced houses. In those days, the smells from the surrounding factories had mingled with the odours from the shared outdoor lavatories. Being close to the docks, the road had been almost bombed out of existence during the Blitz but the King's Head had escaped unscathed. The war weary locals used to laugh and say that maybe Hitler did have a heart after all. He had spared their local. Now it stood on the edge of the newly built grey brick council estate. Street after street of terraced greyness. Even the front doors were grey. Just a darker shade.

'Did you ever hear back from the council about them sirens?' Billy asked George. 'Kate was bad again tonight. I dunno what to do.'

'Oh yes, right snotty letter they sent, I meant to show it to you. Said they can't do anything to stop private companies using them. What they're basically saying Billy is that the war was ten years ago and it's about time people got over it. It's not just your Kate you know. I've lost count of the number of people I've met who turn into shivering wrecks when they hear that sound.' He clapped his friend on the back. 'Don't worry Billy, I won't let it lie. You know me.'

They made their way through the front door and into the bar. It was a very long bar, the whole length of the building. Faded Victoriana. Nicotine stained walls and smells, mixed with laughter, smoke and body odour.

Mick Tyler was trying to hold on to his glass of whisky, eyes almost closed. He was swaying alarmingly from side to side. 'You've took yer time getting 'ere tonight. Where you been?'

'You might be better if you sat down Mick,' said George, lighting his pipe.

'Only ponces sit down in pubs,' Mick muttered. 'An' don't you try and tell *me* what to do George Pattinson. Bloody northerner.'

'Come on George,' said Billy, 'let's get down the other end. He only spoils our night when he's on the whisky.'

17

'Oh, thass right,' Mick slurred. 'Going off wiv your poncy Northern mate. They're all bleedin' ginger beers up there you know.' Billy and George elbowed their way through to the far end of the bar.

'Cor, it's heaving in 'ere tonight,' said Billy.

He looked around and felt a warm glow spreading right through his bones. All the familiar faces. Some he liked, some he didn't, but this was where he belonged. Where he was brought up and where he would probably die. He could put up with his mind-numbing job at the docks and the never ending stream of bills through the letterbox. The King's Head on a weekend and Upton Park on a Saturday made up for all that. He wasn't sure what life was really about, but he thought football must come into it somewhere. He spotted one of his Hammers mates. 'Going to the match tomorrer mate?'

'Yeah. Never know, we might win one day. Might even get into the First Division an' all. Don't wanna miss it when we do.'

Dreams. You had to have 'em, Billy thought. He laughed at himself and turned around to face the landlord.

'Evening Arthur, you're busy tonight.'

'Tell me about it. Usual you two? Oh, who's let that bleeding cat in again?'

A large, black cat was making its way slowly through the pub, skipping between the punters, tail erect. It stopped next to Billy and rubbed himself against his leg.

'Geroff.' He pushed it away, none too gently, with his foot. The cat moved quickly over towards the toilets.

'It keeps getting in,' said Arthur, 'bloody ugly bastard.'

'It'll belong to her off Montgomery Road,' said George. 'All her cats are black.'

'Bloody German,' Arthur muttered, passing them their pints. 'She's a weird one.'

'She's dangerous,' Billy muttered, to no-one in particular. He inhaled deeply on his cigarette.

'What's she done to upset you Billy?' George asked. 'She's just a bit eccentric, that's all.'

Billy picked up his pint and downed half of it in one go. 'I ain't gonna talk about it George, its private,' he said. 'But believe me, she certainly ain't harmless.'

Arthur lowered his voice and moved closer towards them. 'She lived there before the war you know. Wiv a man. They never spoke to no-one an' then they just disappeared, both of 'em. Anyway, when she come back after the war, she was on her own. Just her and them cats. He weren't old or nothing, the man. I reckon she done him in, buried him in the garden an' done a runner. Come back when she thought she'd got away wiv it.'

Billy laughed. 'Bloody hell Arthur. You ain't half got an imagination. I ain't saying she's a murderer. Well, I don't think so anyway.'

'I'm glad I don't live in your world,' said George. 'You're both as daft as brushes.'

'Only saying what I've heard that's all,' Arthur sniffed as he began to serve another punter.

George shrugged his shoulders as he looked across the bar to where Mick was desperately trying to keep his balance. 'Poor Maggie,' he sighed.

'Poor Maggie, my arse,' the landlord replied. 'Did you see the black eye she give him last week? Gives as good as she gets that one.'

'That's not the point,' George replied. 'He's four times her size. And I'll bet she only hits him when he's unconscious.'

'Kids I feel sorry for though,' said Billy. 'What chance 'ave they got?' They all nodded in agreement.

'Anyway,' said George, 'give us a shout when it all goes pear-shaped Arthur, we'll give you a hand.'

'Cheers lads. I'll have to get some of them bouncers in like they've got down the Ilford Palais. There was four fights in here last Saturday. I got quite a sweat on wiv it all. Course it don't help when the Hammers loses.' He glared at Billy.

'Well don't look at me,' Billy laughed. 'Ain't me what picks the team.'

'An' there ain't no point me calling the coppers. By the time they get 'ere it's all over. Anyway, we don't want them nosing about. Puts the punters off.'

A tall, gangly young man with an angry red scar from his mouth to his left ear limped towards the bar. 'Alright Loopy?' Arthur asked. 'You're limping on the wrong leg again by the way.'

Everyone laughed. Loopy smiled. He always forgot which leg was full of shrapnel from the imaginary Nazi ambush in France. It was one of his better stories and he often managed to get a drink from unsuspecting newcomers on the strength of it. Arthur lowered his voice and whispered into his ear.

'Did you get me that stuff mate?'

'Nah, sorry Arthur, ain't dealing in them no more. Got some nice televisions though. Keep the women 'appy. Twenty quid in the shops. Speckled hen to you. Untraceable.'

Arthur laughed. 'Well, I don't need no television to keep *my* woman happy. Know what I mean Loopy? And I ain't got ten quid to waste on something that will be history in a year's time. It won't catch on you know. Wireless is good enough for us. People ain't gonna sit an' watch a poxy box wiv posh people talking on it. They got better things to do wiv their time.'

'He's off,' George laughed and nudged Billy. 'Hey Arthur,' he shouted across the bar. 'I heard they're having a jukebox put in at The Coach and Horses. You know, a bit of rock n' roll. Bill Haley. Keep the punters happy.'

'*Rock n' roll?* I'll give you rock n' roll. That won't catch on neither. Dreadful racket. Won't let my kids listen to it. They'll all be mutt an' jeff by the time they're forty. It's just too loud, it ain't natural.'

Billy laughed. 'Deaf from rock n' roll and square-eyed from television. Can't wait to get old.'

'World won't last that long,' Arthur replied morosely. 'Not wiv America winding up them Russkies all the time. No, this ain't the world I grew up in.'

He looked towards the door. 'Oh no, not women coming in again.'

Wolf whistles filled the air as everyone turned to look. Six girls walked boldly through the door, laughing and giggling. They all wore high heels and full skirts with starched petticoats underneath. Just to the knee. Bright colours. Reds, purples, greens and blues, like a rainbow amongst the dull greys and blacks of the majority of the punters. The girls were all shapes and sizes but all young. The atmosphere in the Kings Head changed as they spotted men they knew and drifted off in different directions.

George Pattinson looked across the pub, a wry smile on his face. 'Isn't that Julie Tyler over there?' he asked.

'Yeah,' Billy answered. 'Hope no-one tries to chat her up, not wiv Mick on a bender. She's the only one of his kids he's got any time for. Boyfriend's off on his training for National Service.'

George frowned and sucked on his pipe thoughtfully. 'Conscription should be finished by now. I was lucky; I was just too old for Hitler.'

The two emptied their glasses and nodded to Arthur for refills.

'Well, by the time I got called up it was nearly all over an' Hitler was on the run,' said Billy. Just wanted to kill a bleedin' German. Just one would 'ave done me.'

'Time you let it go Billy; we won't be fighting them again.'

'You know me George. I ain't a prejudiced man but I still hate 'em. All of 'em.'

Both men stared silently into their glasses for a few seconds. Remembering.

'I ain't serving them gels you know,' Arthur said as he passed them their drinks. 'Can't be more than sixteen. What they doin' in here anyway?'

'They'll have been rock n' rolling down the Palais I expect,' said Billy.

'Oh don't tell me it's got as far as Ilford. Me old mum would be turning in her grave.'

'Knowing your old mum Arthur, she would have bin rock n' rolling in her grave,' Billy laughed.

'I'm only letting you get away wiv that cos I knows yer,' Arthur warned.

They all looked over towards the other side of the bar. 'Oh, 'ere we go,' Arthur exclaimed. 'Knew it would all kick off now. Shouldn't be allowed into pubs. Bloody women.'

They saw Mick Tyler weaving his way through the punters towards his daughter. Carefully, he put his half full glass down on a table. His daughter was talking to a man who looked old enough to be drawing his old age pension. And he was grabbing the left cheek of her bum.

21

'Oooh, this could be nasty,' Billy nudged George. 'I think we might be needed in a minute.'

As they moved towards Mick they saw him tapping Julie on the shoulder. She turned around to face him.

'Hello dad.'

Mick pushed her away roughly. 'Get on home you little tart,' he shouted.

'Hey, leave her alone,' said the man Julie had been chatting to. 'Who do you think ...?'

He got no further. Mick's right fist connected perfectly with the man's jaw. The girls all screamed and a weeping Julie Tyler ran out with two of the others. The rest of them stayed to watch. Everyone stopped drinking, glasses held in mid-air and a circle began to form around the two men, without anyone even realising that they had moved. As drunk as each other, the two adversaries were finding it difficult to stay upright. They swayed and threw punches into the air, rarely connecting.

'Right, that's enough!' Arthur shouted as a chair was hurled across the room. 'You're both barred.' He gave George and Billy an exaggerated nod. 'Come on lads, get him home will yer?'

Fortunately for Billy and George, the chair had hit Mick on the head and, briefly, knocked him out. Billy ploughed into the melee and dragged him away from his opponent. With George's help, he managed to get Mick to his feet and they all stumbled towards the door.

'I'll get our pram,' said Loopy. 'Won't be a tick. You'll never get him home walking.'

'Don't forget to take the baby out first,' George gasped.

The three of them managed to get enough of Mick's body into the pram to push him slowly into Churchill Street. The springs creaked and groaned.

'I'm getting too old for this,' said George. 'Long time since I pushed a pram.'

Billy laughed. 'You wouldn't usually catch me pushing one neither. I ain't soft. Still, I thought that was quite a good night, an' I reckon, when we've dropped 'im off, we'll still be in time for last orders.'

'Mine's a double whisky,' Mick slurred.

'You're barred mate,' Billy laughed as they tipped him out of the pram at his gate.

'Poor Maggie,' George muttered.

Chapter 3

Billy sighed as he heard the front door slam. He squinted at the clock by the bed. Half-past eight. That would be Jimmy, off out to meet the gang.

'Why does he always have to bang that door?' he muttered to himself. God, his head was thumping this morning. He smiled to himself. Wouldn't be as bad as Mick's though. Billy wished for a moment that he was nine again, no worries, no responsibilities. Trouble was, you spent all your childhood waiting to grow up and it was only when you got there you realised life had been much easier when you were a kid. And no-one ever told you. Oh, they taught you how to do long division and all about the Battle of Hastings but they never said nothing about real life. When you were a kid there was always so much to do. Exciting stuff. And then, of course, there was marriage.

'She's too posh for you,' his mum had said. 'It won't work.'

He had met Kate on VE Day, at a street party. She had fallen over when the heel had broken on her shoe and he had picked her up. She was laughing and he had just fallen in love with her right there. Billy had just wanted to look after her forever. She was different to a lot of the girls. Quiet and shy. She had been staying with a friend in their road.

Kate's Auntie Molly hadn't been impressed either when her niece had told her she was marrying Billy. Didn't think he was good enough for her. Well, perhaps she was right. 'And you're both so young,' she had said disapprovingly.

Yes, he *was* only nineteen and Kate seventeen but everyone else seemed to be getting married when the war finished. Most of them in quite a hurry too. Not them though. Kate was a 'nice' girl, certainly too nice to have sex before marriage. Trouble was she didn't seem too keen on it even after the ceremony. Even more so after she had lost the baby. Well, that was best forgotten about. Should have brought them closer together really he supposed but they never talked about it.

Still, sex wasn't everything. All he had known before he had married was a few fumblings in the air raid shelters

24

and then, when he was called up, a few willing girls, some of them prostitutes. Oh, Kate didn't often refuse him but Billy sometimes wondered what it would be like to have married someone who had enjoyed making love. He had never been unfaithful to her; he just tried not to think about it.

He turned over and looked at her now. She was so pretty. Little button nose and huge blue eyes. Light brown hair which should have been allowed to fall on to her shoulders naturally but instead was in a tight, curly perm. He had loved her hair when he could run his fingers through it. Those days had been better, he thought, but there was always the war stuff and everything that had happened. She had lost her mum and her sister. Her dad had been killed in action. In Kate's head she was never free of it all somehow. It hung over her like a threatening grey cloud and then sometimes it just started pouring with rain and they all suffered.

She never talked about it. Bethnal Green. He knew other people who had been there. They never mentioned it either but all those dead kids couldn't have been a pretty sight. Life in the East End had never been easy but Bethnal Green had been the top of the list as far as tragedies were concerned round here.

Kate had moved away from the East End after that. To live in Ilford with her Auntie Molly. Apart from Molly's sister, who lived out in Australia, she was the only family Kate had left. She never ever talked about the bad stuff that had happened and he didn't know how to.

Her eyes were still closed, her breathing even. She could be asleep or she could be pretending. She looked so lovely in the early morning light. Peaceful. Billy could feel his body responding. Demanding. He put his hand on her breast.

'Oh, get off Billy,' she whispered.

He turned away, tears springing to his eyes. Angry tears. He was her husband, he shouldn't have to beg and plead every time. She had promised to worship him with her body or some such words. It was the only bit of the wedding ceremony he had remembered. Chance would be a fine thing. He turned back to her and nibbled her ear. 'Come on Kate love,' he whispered. 'I won't take long.'

25

He didn't notice the tears in her eyes as she turned towards him.

***

Jimmy stood, swinging on the front gate. The street was deserted. It was quite foggy and cold this morning. Everyone who was working down the docks Saturdays had gone already. He took his cap slowly from his pocket and put it on. The door opposite opened suddenly and Del's dad fell out. 'Morning Mr. Tyler,' Jimmy shouted bravely.

'Fuck off, bloody kids. And Del ain't allowed out this morning before you start.'

His eyes were red, his stomach wobbling as he stumbled along Churchill Street. Not in a very straight line. He looked very old and very angry. Last time I say good morning to him, Jimmy thought.

He sauntered across the road and knocked on Del's door. Del opened it. He looked pale and scared. With his dark thatch of hair and his deep-set hazel eyes, he looked like a ghost this morning. Jimmy could hear crying from inside. It wasn't like the kids crying. It was a moaning, hideous sound.

'What's up Del?' he asked.

'Oh, me dad's on a bender.'

Jimmy just grunted and awkwardly clapped his friend on the shoulder. He kept meaning to ask his dad what a bender was. He didn't like to admit to Del that he didn't know. Well, whatever it was, it always lead to the grown-ups whispering and Del's mum getting black eyes. A bender certainly wasn't a good thing.

'He's bin hitting her all night,' Del said. 'Josie's mum's looking after 'er.'

'Well, why ain't you allowed out? Your dad says you ain't.'

'He don't tell *me* what to do no more,' Del said angrily. 'I went to phone the coppers last night. That's why he's mad at me.'

'Oh,' said Jimmy. He was lost for words. How could he have slept through all this excitement? 'So what did they do?'

'Nothing. Said they wouldn't do nothing. They won't help you when it's a domestic.'

26

Jimmy made a mental note to also ask his dad what a domestic was. That didn't sound too good either.

'Who is it Del?'

Josie's mum came into the hallway. She smiled when she saw Jimmy. She had a lovely smile, he thought. When she smiled you didn't even notice the peeling paint, the rubbish on the floor and the stink of Mick Tyler. It was the sort of smile you wanted to wrap up and take out when you were really fed up. Jimmy thought she was lovely. He didn't care what people said about her. Sometimes, he secretly wished that she was *his* mum but he knew that was a bad thing. It wasn't that he didn't love his own mum. She just never seemed to laugh much. Always nagging him about something.

'Is she alright?' Del asked quietly.

'Yeah. She'll be alright love.' She tried to put her arms around him but Del flinched and moved away.

'Well, I'm off out now then,' he said gruffly, 'wiv Jimmy.'

'Right, well off you go but Josie can't go out till I get back. I've left her watching the babies. Go an' see her if you like.'

Del and Jimmy set off across the road. 'She's nice ain't she?' said Jimmy. 'Josie's mum?'

'She's alright,' said Del, wiping his nose on his sleeve. 'Can tell you fancy her. Little blushing boy. You go all soft when she's around,' he laughed

Jimmy could feel his face reddening. He hated it when Del wound him up. It made him feel angry and it wasn't right, feeling like that about someone in your own gang. He would have to really try and be nice to him today. He would hate to have to live with Mick Tyler but he couldn't let Del accuse him of being soft. That was too much to take. 'I just think she's alright that's all. I ain't soft.'

He punched Del lightly in the stomach to prove his point. Any other time Del would have hit him back even though it wasn't allowed in their Code. Today was different.

'Good job Josie didn't see you do that. You'd have been barred from the gang.'

'Only messing Del.'

As they reached Josie's house, Legs came running out of his back door. 'Wait for me,' he shouted. 'What we doing today?'

'Dunno,' said Jimmy. 'Del's dad's on a bender.'

'Oh,' said Legs, 'that means trouble then.' He fell in to step beside them.

'Funny she ain't married,' said Jimmy.

'Who?' Legs asked.

'Josie's mum. We was talking about her before you come.'

'Oh, you mean Sally,' Legs smirked. 'She said I could call her Sally instead of Mrs. Evans. Bet she hasn't said that to you two.' He stuck his tongue out.

Del and Jimmy ignored him. They often discussed Leg's immature attitude between themselves and had decided it was because he had very old parents. It wasn't his fault that his mum and dad were past it. It must be awful for him so they tried to be kind, not always easy though.

'Anyway,' Jimmy glared at Legs, 'I was just saying. Her being quite pretty an' all. Funny she's on her own.'

'Softy boy, softy boy,' Del laughed. 'Anyway, me mum says she likes the men too much to get married.'

'What's that s'posed to mean?' asked Jimmy.

'Dunno. They're all mad. Grown-ups.'

Chapter 4

Sally Evans wondered how on earth Maggie managed living in this small house with six kids and Mick Tyler.

All the houses that had been built on the estate so far were the same size, except for a few maisonettes for old age pensioners. A tiny hall with a sitting room to the left or right and the stairs that led up to the bedrooms. The door from the hall led into the living room and there was a small kitchen off that. There were sliding doors into the kitchens but no-one ever used them so the cooking smells permeated through the house. Upstairs, the great luxury for everyone was the indoor bathroom. No more running outside to the lavvy in freezing weather or having to use potties at night. Sally shivered at the memory. Now they could have a proper bath once a week instead of having to go to the public ones or, like they did, using an old tin bath that had meant having to boil the kettle about a hundred times to fill it up. Most of the residents on the estate agreed that it was wonderful. Not many would have wanted to go back to the damp, crumbling, insect infested houses they had come from. Not really. The old ones always said they missed the community spirit and having a doorstep to scrub while you had a good old gossip. They forgot about the bad bits. The houses were all the same size upstairs; more bedrooms just meant smaller ones.

She looked around the Tylers' kitchen now. This was bad, even for him. Doors were hanging off cupboards, bloodstains on the grimy floor, plates smashed and Maggie. Sitting at the table in the living room, her head in her hands. One of her eyes was black and very swollen where Mick had punched her. There were plenty of other bruises but he had been careful after that, they didn't show. Sally had seen to all the first aid she could do but she couldn't help Maggie and how she thought inside her head. She left the devastation in the kitchen and put her arm around the older woman's shoulder. 'Del's off out,' she said. 'The others are still asleep.'

'I ain't surprised,' Maggie sniffed. 'They all got woke up.'

'Why do you stay with him?' Sally asked, trying to keep the anger out of her voice.

'Oh and where am I supposed to go wiv six kids?'

'Josie's dad hit me once,' Sally confessed, 'but not like this.' She touched the bruise on Maggie's left eye gently.

'And did you leave 'im?' Maggie asked.

'Never got the chance. He hit me when I told him I was pregnant. As if it was all my fault. Then he buggered off, thank God,' she laughed.

'We're bleedin' daft us women,' Maggie began to laugh with her. 'We ain't got the sense we're born wiv.'

'Oh Maggie, how can you laugh when he's ... when he's ...'

'I 'ave to love. We all do. It's how we survive. Just look at them what don't laugh. Miss Prim and Proper over the road for starters.'

'Kate?'

'Yeah. Thinks she's better than us. Don't make her 'appy though does it? Cor, what I couldn't do wiv a man that looked like Billy. *She* don't appreciate him though. Not 'er.'

Sally laughed. She had never really got on with Kate either. Oh, Kate spoke to her which was more than some of them did but Sally knew she disapproved of unmarried mothers. She could see it in her eyes. People thought Sally was hard and didn't care what anyone thought. Well, they were wrong. It did hurt, but there was no point in hiding away. She couldn't undo what was done. 'She's just different that's all Maggie,' she said now. 'She don't fit in round here really and she ain't had an easy life.'

'Oh, I knew you'd make excuses for her. Life *is* hard especially where we live. You have to put stuff behind yer and just get on wiv it. No, I ain't got no time for 'er.' She put her hand over Sally's and squeezed it. 'Thanks love, for all your help. I used to call you some right names you know. When you first moved 'ere.'

'Yeah, well, I've got used to that. Not married wiv three kids. Women think you're a slut and men hang around wiv their tongues hanging out.'

'Not just their tongues neither,' Maggie laughed.

'Well, I'd best get back home and see how long the queue is this morning.'

'Ooh, send me one over love. Long as he's tall, dark and 'andsome, I ain't fussy ... just have another cuppa eh

Sal?' Maggie put her hand on Sally's arm and gripped it tightly. 'Don't go just yet love.'

Sally could see her friend's eyes filling up.

'Seriously Sal,' Maggie was saying, 'why don't you tell 'em your husband died or something? That's what I'd do.'

'Why should I?' Sally said firmly. 'Once you start lying it never ends.' She got up and filled the kettle with water.

'You're a very strong girl,' said Maggie. 'I couldn't stand the ...' she stopped, embarrassed.

'The shame?' Sally finished the sentence for her. She found an unbroken teapot, warmed it with the boiling water then put some tea leaves in.

'Yeah, that's it. I think you're very brave. I couldn't stand the shame of not having a man. And let's face it, who else would have me? Wiv this face.'

Sally sat back down while the tea brewed.

'Don't worry about me Sal. He'll be alright in a couple of days. He's good as gold when he's sober you know.'

'Oh he'll be alright until the next time. And what about the kids? What if he starts beating *them* black and blue?'

'Oh, he don't' it the little 'uns and they're too fast for him when they get to Del's age. Anyway, he never hits them like he hits me.'

Sally looked at her friend. The bruises and the pain in her eyes. Mick had put her in hospital twice. 'Well all I can say Maggie is that you must really love him to let him do this to yer.'

Maggie looked away from Sally's gaze.

'I suppose I must then,' she said, tears sliding down her cheeks silently.

'Well, it's your life I suppose,' said Sally, putting her arms around her friend's shoulders and giving her a squeeze. She poured Maggie a cup of tea and left the pot in front of her on the greasy table. 'I'll have to get going now though. Goodness knows how Josie's managing wiv them babies. Not the most maternal girl in the world. She should have been a boy. Anyway, you know where I am.'

'Ta Sal,' she said. 'And ... you won't tell no-one will yer?'

Sally smiled to herself. The whole of the estate probably knew about it already and they certainly would when they saw her. 'Course I won't Maggie.'

How *can* she stay with him, Sally thought to herself. How *can* she?

***

There was mayhem in the Evans' kitchen when the three boys walked in. Josie and the twins were all covered in porridge, so was the floor. The babies were screaming and trying to get out of their high chairs.

'Ugh!' said Legs. 'Babies are disgusting.'

As if on cue, they stopped crying when they saw the boys and turned on their most devastating smiles. Jimmy thought they looked really sweet even though their hair was full of porridge. He grinned at them and they laughed right back. Josie wasn't too happy though. 'Don't just stand there,' she shouted. 'Give us an 'and cleaning 'em up.'

'One of 'em's done something,' said Del. Legs and Jimmy held their noses.

'You're all the same you boys,' said Josie. 'Bleedin' useless.'

They all giggled. 'I'll clean their faces,' Jimmy volunteered, grabbing a flannel from the sink. 'You can do the other ends Legs.'

'Bugger off,' said Legs. 'I'm not changing any nappies. That's women's work.'

Jimmy laughed. 'Only winding you up mate.'

'Oh, very funny. Ha ha. I might wait outside actually. You coming Del?'

Del nodded. 'Yeah, let's get out of 'ere. It ain't a place for men to be.'

Just then Sally came bustling in through the door. She took one look and burst out laughing. 'I don't know how much porridge you done Josie but there ain't much gone in their mouths.'

Jimmy was amazed that she was laughing. His mum would have gone spare. He couldn't imagine living in a house that was so messy but there was something cosy and warm about it. You never had to be careful not to spill anything and Josie's mum even let them jump on the sofa. There was porridge everywhere. 'It's no good Jose,' her mum smiled. 'You'll never make an 'ousewife.'

Jimmy was desperately trying to remove porridge from one of the baby's ears. Sally Evans smiled at him again. 'What about you Jimmy? You're good wiv babies. You'll make someone a good husband one day.'

'Yeah, they're alright,' he answered, looking down at his feet. 'Might ask me mum if we can have one.'

The babies were crying now, both trying to get their mother's attention. The noise was deafening as Sally lifted them out one at a time and put them into their playpen. She moved over to the sink and began to wash up. 'Go on then all of you,' she laughed. 'Get out from under me feet. Let me know if your mum needs me Del won't you?'

Del nodded, red-faced. Jimmy thought that he looked as if he was going to burst into tears. Legs was ahead of them and swinging on the gate. 'Glad we haven't got babies,' he said.

'I think your mum might like to have another baby. My mum has one every year nearly,' said Del.

'Nah, my mum's too old. I was a mistake,' Legs said cheerily.

'Don't you mind,' Josie asked, 'being a mistake I mean?'

'Nah. Mum says I was a nice mistake.'

'Ugh. Your mum and dad are really wet,' said Del. 'May and George. What sort of names are they anyway? And always walking round holding hands an' stuff. At their age.'

He spat on the pavement. Then Jimmy spat and Legs as well.

'You're disgusting,' said Josie. 'Anyway, perhaps they all hold hands in ... where is it you come from?'

'Blackpool. I've told you hundreds of times.'

'They're all funny up north,' said Del. 'Me dad says.'

'And they talk funny an' all. Like you did.' Josie added.

'No I don't.'

'I ain't saying you do now.'

'No, you're alright now,' said Del grudgingly.

Legs beamed. A compliment from Del. Wow. That made him feel good. He had tried hard to lose his northern accent. The kids at school had been merciless in their teasing. 'Here's new kid from oop north,' they used to say.

33

Well it hadn't taken him long to stop talking northern. He couldn't do cockney though, they laughed at him even more then so he just tried to talk normal. Jimmy had made friends with him first. He had lent him a pencil. His had just broken and he knew he would be in trouble. He remembered sitting at the desk trying hard not to cry. Not being able to write. Jimmy had smiled at him.

'Here you are mate,' he had said, handing him a worn-down but usable red pencil. 'I don't need a spare, I don't write much.'

He looked around at his friends and was glad those horrible times were over. 'So, what are we doing today then?' he asked. 'We need to take the guy out.'

'Let's go to the den,' said Josie. 'We can decide when we get there.'

'If we can find it in this fog,' said Legs. 'At least we didn't get this much fog in Blackpool.'

'And you're in the First Division. And you've got Stanley Matthews. It ain't all bad Legs,' Jimmy laughed. 'Hey, hang on; I'll have to go back. I ain't got me pocket money.'

'I ain't got no chance today,' said Del.

'You can have a penny of mine when I get it,' said Jimmy kindly.

'You're not having any of mine,' said Legs.

'That's mean Legs,' said Josie. 'How would you like it if your dad went on benders and got drunk for days and days?'

'I need it meself,' said Legs, clutching his threepenny bit tightly in his pocket.

Jimmy made his way home, deep in thought. So, that was what a bender was, what Josie had just said. Drinking for days and days.

He slipped in the front door. It was a bad time, they were arguing. What a morning this was turning out to be. He wished these walls weren't so thin. You could hear everything. They were still upstairs and his dad was shouting.

'I'm only human Kate. I've got me needs, it's only natural. You're my wife or 'ad you forgotten?'

'I can't help it Billy. I'm sorry.'

Jimmy could hear his dad stomping around in the bedroom. He didn't get this angry very often. Jimmy didn't have a clue what they were on about but it scared him a bit. Still, pocket money was pocket money. And he needed it. 'Mum!' He shouted up the stairs. He heard frantic whisperings before his dad appeared on the landing.

'What do you want?' he shouted down.

'Me pocket money please dad.'

'Take it out your mum's purse on the mantelpiece. Only threpence mind.'

Jimmy sighed. They would all have to get together and demand a pocket money rise, it was no good. Threpence just wasn't enough. John Baxter got 10 shillings but then Jimmy was beginning to think that he *was* a fibber. His mum had been right. There weren't such things as colour televisions. He might be telling lies about all sorts; they would have to watch him. Jimmy took a threpenny bit from the purse. There were two pennies in there as well. He thought about taking it all but then he remembered the beating he'd got the last time he tried that. He heard the toilet flush. 'Dad!' he shouted.

'What now?'

'Can I have a penny for Del? His dad's on a bender.'

'Yeah, I know all about Mick's bender. Go on then. Take a penny for him. Poor kid.'

He heard his dad laughing.

'Where does he get these words from,' he was saying. 'Bet he ain't got a clue what a bender is.' His mum was laughing now an' all. Well he wouldn't spoil the moment by telling them that he bloody well did know what a bender was. At least it had stopped them rowing.

Chapter 5

The den was on a patch of wasteland at the end of the road. Not quite enough room for more houses so the council had just left it. Littered with old bricks, rubbish and a couple of derelict cars. Tufts of grass and weeds grew where they could. At the top stood the massive bonfire, already at least ten foot tall. Old Bones was standing next to it, poking his walking stick into the bottom. Slim and stooped, hair down to his shoulders, he was as old as the hills.

'Morning Bones,' Jimmy greeted him.

'Morning dustbin lids,' he replied cheerfully. 'Hope this fog clears up soon, ready for the big night.'

Old Bones was a grown-up like no other, he was on their side. He never shouted at them or nagged. Sometimes he talked a load of rubbish but they didn't mind that. Bonfire night was Bone's night. He loved it. Every year he lit the bonfire, it was tradition. The other grown-ups weren't too keen on him. He did smell a bit. Well, a lot actually. Still, if you breathed in through your mouth when he was very close, it wasn't too bad. Every year he donated something for the guy to hold as he got burnt. The children had been amazed when he'd given Del his stuffed owl. It had always taken pride of place on the windowsill.

'You sure you wanna burn Judy?' Josie asked him. 'We don't mind if you don't.'

'Nah, you burn her. Got a ferret now. Real one. Left him at home this mornin'. Don't want 'im running away till he knows where he is. Nice little fella. Smells a bit though.'

'What's his name?' Legs asked.

'Chuck. I've called him Chuck. After Chuck Berry. Rock n' roll kids. It's gonna last for ever. Mark my words. Don't you listen to them old people. They ain't got a clue.'

Del laughed. They should have known that Old Bones would love rock n' roll.

'I'd best be off now anyway, get back to the little fella.'

Old Bones walked slowly with his stick over the uneven ground and on to the pavement.

'Come on, let's get to the den,' said Josie, running ahead.

At the bottom of the waste was a clump of tired looking bushes. There was a gap between them and the wall. They had made the den with old bricks, wood and branches. A notice outside read,

'PRIVAT PROPTY. ENEWUN ENTRIN WIL AV THER GUTS RIPPD OWT'

Legs had written it after they had found the den destroyed a few months ago. The notice had worked so far. And Del had sorted out the perpetrators in such a way that no-one would have dared cross him again.

Jimmy and Del had robbed some bricks from a building site and made crude walls. The roof was made from two sheets of corrugated iron and they had covered it all with branches and sticks for camouflage. The first thing they did now was to check that the equipment was still there. Legs had dug a hole and put all the things they needed into an old biscuit tin. A torch, a thin rope, box of matches and a Swiss army knife. There were also two packets of digestive biscuits for emergency rations and a holy card. The last was Josie's idea. She said that the saints would protect the den better than any of Leg's notices.

'All there,' said Jimmy.

'Can't we just ...?'

'No Legs, you ain't having a biscuit,' said Josie.

'Emergencies only,' said Del quietly. Jimmy looked at him and saw the hunger in his eyes.

'I think Del should be allowed,' he said. 'He ain't had no breakfast.'

Josie handed Del two biscuits.

'Ta Jose.'

'Right then,' said Josie. What we gonna do today?'

'I think we should go an' see what the witch is up to,' said Jimmy.

'What about the guy?' asked Del with his mouth full. 'It's our bonfire night tomorrer.'

'And it's too dangerous,' said Legs. 'Del's been really poorly since the cats got him.'

'I only 'ad a cold. It weren't much of a spell.'

'Well,' said Josie, 'I agree wiv Jimmy. 'We've got to go back sometime. We 'ave to know what she's planning. She could be getting up to all sorts. We need to keep an eye on 'er.'

Del shivered. He didn't look too keen. 'Well,' he said, 'it ain't no good just peering through the hedge. If we're going up there, we've got to go in.'

The others laughed nervously.

'I suppose you'll go first,' Legs laughed.

'Nah. I was thinking it could be Jimmy.'

'Why me?'

'Cos it's your turn for a dare,' Del answered.

Jimmy had forgotten about that. Yes, it was his turn. He came after Legs who had nicked a packet of Spangles from the sweet shop last week. Still, that was nothing like as dangerous as meddling with a witch, Jimmy thought.

'Tell you what,' said Del, 'seeing as you give me a penny, you don't have to go in the house or nothin'. Just do a bit of scrumping. Through the hedge, up the apple tree and out. That'll do.'

'I still think that's a bit much for an ordinary dare,' said Josie doubtfully.

'He'll be alright. We'll be behind the hedge if he gets into bother,' said Del. 'We'll take the knife.'

'Can we take the digestive biscuits?'

'No Legs,' they all chorused.

'Well, do we *have* to wait for him if the witch comes out?'

'Legs!' Josie exclaimed. 'You wouldn't leave him on his own?'

'I bloody would. Its them cats. They do me head in.'

'Don't worry Legs, cos I ain't doing it anyway.'

Del smirked. 'I knew you was yeller Jimmy Potter.'

Be nice to him, Jimmy told himself. Don't let him wind you up. It was hard sometimes though. He breathed deeply and counted to ten, clenching and unclenching his fists.

'No he ain't yeller,' Josie was saying. 'You wouldn't go, would yer?'

'I might,' said Del, 'but it ain't my turn.'

'We could make it a double dare,' said Legs. 'He can miss his next one.'

'Yeah, that's a good idea,' said Josie. 'Let's vote on it then. Hands for yes.'

Del's hand shot up. Last time I give *him* any money out me mum's purse, Jimmy thought angrily.

38

Legs was more hesitant. 'I'm only voting for it if I don't have to go in and get him out.'

'Oh shut up Legs, course you won't,' said Del.

Josie looked at Jimmy's face and kept her hand down. Two to one. 'Sorry Jimmy,' she said, patting him on the back, 'but you'll 'ave to do it.'

They all looked at Jimmy expectantly. 'Yeah, I s'pose so,' he muttered. 'Come on then, let's get it over wiv.'

Del removed the Swiss army knife from the tin and then put the tin back into the hole. They all moved slowly out of the den. The fog was getting thicker. The muted sounds of ships hooters on the river seemed to be getting louder, more insistent. Although it was only nine o'clock in the morning it was eerie and cold.

'Pooh Jimmy,' Del laughed. 'Just cos you're scared you don't 'ave to fart all over the place. You smell worse than Old Bones.'

They all giggled except for Jimmy. 'It ain't me!' he said indignantly, 'must be Legs.'

'No it isn't,' Legs laughed.

They all looked at Josie. 'Well don't look at me,' she said.

'Nah,' said Del, 'girls don't do jam tarts.'

'Why?' Jimmy asked.

'Dunno. Different shaped bums I suppose.'

Josie could feel herself blushing. 'Well, it was me,' she said, walking on huffily, 'so there.'

Del looked amazed. 'Me dad's never gonna believe this.'

They all giggled as they walked up Churchill Street and made their way slowly towards the witch's house.

***

'Thought I'd just pop in,' said May Pattinson, 'and see if you've heard anything. Across the road I mean.' She nodded in the direction of the Tyler's house. 'Oh, come in May,' Kate smiled. 'I'll put the kettle on.'

'Ooh it's a nasty day out there,' said May, wiping her feet on the doormat. 'My George says they'll be stopping coal fires soon. They reckon that's what causes all this fog. Can you imagine what the lecky bills will be like?'

Kate ushered her into the kitchen. May was always amazed at this house. The furniture was old and worn, the

39

lino faded but nothing was ever out of place. The surfaces gleamed. The pots were always washed up. She looked at Kate affectionately. Those stunning but troubled blue eyes and a face that could be so pretty if she just laughed a bit more. Kate always seemed to look worried somehow.

Secrets. That's what did it, May thought. All those things she never talked about.

'Go through into the sitting room May. I've lit the fire. I know you like a comfy chair.'

She brought a tray into the sitting room and set it down on the coffee table. 'Oh, look at me,' she said after pouring out the tea. 'Still got my pinny on in the sitting room.'

'Oh dear,' May laughed, 'that'll never do. What would your Auntie Molly say?'

'She's been very good to me you know May,' Kate snapped. 'She brought me up really.'

'I know love,' said May, settling her plump frame into the blue, flowery armchair. 'I didn't mean any harm. I was only joking. How is she?'

'She's thinking of emigrating to Australia to live near her sister, you know, my Auntie Cathy. She thinks we should go as well.'

'Would you want to love?'

'Oh May, I'd love to get away from here,' Kate sighed and picked her knitting up from the table. The needles clicked reassuringly. 'It's Jimmy really. I just want him to have a good start in life. Do you know what I mean? I was talking to Billy about moving to the country. I mean, just as far as Essex or something but he won't even think about it. I can't imagine what he'd say if I suggested emigrating.'

'It's not all bad round here you know love,' May said. 'Oh I know there's some rough 'uns like the Tylers' but most of them are good as gold. Give you their last penny. You wouldn't get that in Essex.'

'I wish I could see it like that and get on with people like you do May.'

'Well, lass you do have to make an effort you know. And we're lucky. With our men anyway. I mean, look at poor Maggie. I hear the police were there last night.'

May got up and looked out of the front window. She could barely see the Tyler's house through the fog this morning. She shivered. Yes, things could be worse, much

40

worse. 'My George would never do anything like that. Nor would your Billy. We're very lucky with our men. Anyway, did the police do anything?'

'Don't interfere with domestics do they,' Kate replied. 'Don't know why they bothered coming. Billy said they just sat outside for five minutes, then drove off again.'

'Well they bloody well should do something. Sorry Kate, for swearing in your sitting room, but how many women are going to get battered while they sit in their cars eating sandwiches and puffing on their fags? Makes my blood boil. It's been worse since the war you know. It changes people. Changes everything, something like that.' She looked at her friend. 'You're looking a bit peaky,' she said, looking at Kate's pale face.

Kate put down her knitting and helped herself to a ginger biscuit. 'Oh, I'm just tired. That factory takes it out of me. I hate it there May, I really do.' She poured them both another cup of tea. 'The girls are so common. The things they say.'

May laughed and her enormous bosoms wobbled. 'You've got ideas a bit above your station sometimes lass. They don't mean any harm you know. They're all mouth those girls. Just tell them your Billy's got the biggest dick this side of Wapping.'

'May, really!'

'Well, that's what they're always on about isn't it? Do you not work with Sally? She's a nice lass.'

'Oh Sally's alright I suppose but ... '

'You don't approve?'

'It's not that May, it's the way she flaunts it. She's got no shame. I mean three children, two different fathers, no sight or sound of either of them. How are those kids ever going to know where they've come from? It's not fair and, yes, I do think it's wrong. And one day I'll probably have to tell her.'

May raised her eyebrows. Oh, she could see why people didn't like Kate but she only said what a lot of folk were thinking. There were people on the estate who wouldn't even talk to Sally. May sighed. She hoped things would change one day but she doubted it. She watched her friend again now. Counting stitches while she was talking and looking around the room, probably for an odd speck of dust

41

she had missed. Goodness knows what would happen if she ever saw a cobweb.

'Well, I like Sally,' said May, 'but I do agree with you. About the kids anyway.'

'If we all went round doing what we wanted what would happen? There's got to be rules May hasn't there?'

'So you don't talk to her much then?'

'Oh I see her at work sometimes. We're just different that's all.'

'You can say that again,' May laughed. 'Have you seen Maggie this morning?'

Kate shook her head.

'Poor girl,' May sighed. 'I'll call in later. She's going to have her hands full with that Julie as well. As if she's not got enough with *him*.'

'She does seem a bit wild. I don't know if I could have coped with a girl ... '

May saw the tears in her friend's eyes. She really wished that Kate would talk about the baby she had lost. She had given up trying to get her friend to confide in her about it. 'Boys are easier,' she said quickly. 'Maggie says she's in with a gang of Teddy boys. I even heard she's been drinking. And only fifteen.'

'All that make-up as well,' said Kate. 'My mum would never have let me out the house like that.'

'Can't imagine what my old mum would think of Teddy boys and rock n' roll,' May laughed. 'I think she's best off out of it. Do you know she died the day after we heard that Hitler had killed himself? She was so happy she was going at the same time as him. Do you know what her last words were?'

Kate shook her head.

'She said, "*Just wait till I see him, I'll give him a mouthful. He'll wish he'd never been born by the time I've finished with him.*" She liked a bit of a scrap, my mum.'

Kate smiled and May suddenly saw the person she could have been, maybe still could.

The back door slammed. Billy stood at the door grinning. God, he was a good-looking man, May thought. Had the look of a film star about him. That one who had just died. She could never remember his name. She wondered if women ever chased after him. Mind you, George said that there weren't many women went in the King's Head and there certainly weren't any at football or down the docks. The best thing about Billy, she thought, was that he didn't seem to realise how handsome he was.

'Don't you come in here with your muddy shoes,' Kate scolded him.

'Oh, don't worry,' he laughed. 'Wouldn't want to interrupt your gossiping. Thought you'd all be at it this morning.'

May laughed. 'Don't you try and tell me that you're any different. I used to be a barmaid. I know what men talk about when they think you're not listening.'

'Well, just to let you all know. Mick's off out looking for a pub that'll take him. He's barred from the King's Head an' he's got a lifetime ban from The Feathers. There ain't many more in walking distance.'

'Well I think you should all try and sort him out,' said Kate. 'It's no good you all looking out your windows watching what's going on. Someone should have been helping Maggie last night. Not bringing him back to her.' She sighed. 'It wouldn't be like this in Essex.'

Billy laughed. 'Don't you believe it, that's where all the *real* gangsters live. She don't have to stay wiv him. It's 'er choice. Anyway, what's for me lunch? We've got a match today remember, all this gossiping. And where's Jimmy? I'm going without him if he ain't back.' May and Kate looked at each other Men.

43

Chapter 6

It started to drizzle as the children made their way through the estate. There were a few girls playing hopscotch and some boys playing football.

'D'you wanna play Jimmy?' It was John Baxter.

'Nah.'

'Well you ain't never gonna play for West Ham then. Not if you don't practise. My uncle played for the Hammers you know.'

'Yeah. Just like you got a colour television,' Jimmy replied. 'Anyway, we're busy.'

The others looked at him. A warning. John Baxter picked up the football and came running over. 'Why? Where are you going? Can I come?'

'Nah,' Del pushed him away. 'You ain't in our gang. Piss off.'

'That weren't kind Del,' Josie chastised him as John Baxter retreated tearfully.

'Well I ain't kind am I? We don't want no-one knowing about the witch. It's our secret.'

'It's our mission,' Legs added.

You could barely see the witch's house through the fog and drizzle this morning. Tall trees surrounded the garden. The red brick house contrasting sharply with the grey estate. Grey sky. Grey houses. They arrived at their usual position, behind the hedge. Jimmy wouldn't have any trouble squeezing through. Tendrils of fog drifted in the garden making it look quite spooky.

'Get down!' Josie whispered urgently. They all crouched down. 'I can 'ear something in the garden.'

They listened. It was like a munching sound. They peered intently through the gap but they couldn't see anything. 'There's someone in there,' Josie whispered.

Very slowly, as the fog drifted, a weird shape began to appear. They saw two black eyes. Two horns. They all held their breath.

'It's only a goat,' said Del. Relieved.

The goat ambled slowly away back into the fog at the bottom of the garden. They could still hear it munching on the grass.

'She never had a goat before,' said Josie. 'We'll have to try an' get a book about witches so's we know what to expect.' They all nodded in agreement.

'Well, she ain't about nowhere Jimmy,' said Del. 'You might as well get in there.'

'That goat's got horns,' said Jimmy fearfully. 'It could be dangerous y' know.'

'Go on, it's down the bottom of the garden now,' said Josie. 'It ain't gonna hurt yer.'

'There's loads of apples just lying about,' said Jimmy. 'There's hardly none left on the trees. Can't I just pick some up?'

'No,' Del replied, 'that's cheating.'

'You'll be alright,' Legs whispered. 'We've got the knife.'

'Wish we 'ad some more digestive biscuits,' said Del, listening to his rumbling tummy.

Jimmy crawled through the hedge quickly. The nearest apple tree wasn't too far away. If the goat did come after him, he reckoned he could get back through the gap before it caught him. No, it wasn't the goat he was scared of. It was *her*. She could fly. She would be able to get from the house to the apple tree in half a second and he wasn't that fast. The apples on the tree looked really red and juicy. He decided that he was only going to pick one, for himself. *They* didn't deserve any. Making him go in there with a wild animal. 'Watch them windows,' he hissed.

'You're all clear,' Josie whispered.

Jimmy ran, his heart thumping. Across the lawn to the nearest tree. He looked around. So far, so good. He could still hear the goat munching but he couldn't see it. The fog had suddenly come down thicker. It swirled and crept quietly, surrounding him. The silence was really scary. He couldn't even see the gap in the hedge. It was like he was standing in the middle of a ball of cotton wool. He shivered. Best get it over with.

He swung himself up into the lower branches of the tree. It had quite thick branches, easy to climb. He picked a very large apple and stuffed it into his pocket. His cap fell onto the lawn. Never mind, he would get it later. He peered through the branches towards the house but it was just a vague dark shadow in the fog.

45

Jimmy climbed as high up as he could, just to prove that he wasn't a coward. Then he heard the sound of hooves, coming towards him. He turned, quickly, almost losing his balance. Should he get down now and run for the gap? He still couldn't see it. Jimmy felt a panic rising in his stomach, his legs were shaking. They wouldn't move and he didn't know why. It was only a goat. What was he so scared of?

It was like in his nightmares. The mad axe man, chasing him. And his body wouldn't move. Then, just as the axe was about to splinter his brain, he would wake up, sweating and scared. Well, he was sweating and scared now alright but this wasn't a dream. The fog was clearing a bit and the goat's head appeared, only a few yards away. Drifting and floating into his line of vision. It looked like a floating head with no body. As the fog cleared again the goat became a whole goat. It stopped and sniffed the air. It knew he was there and moved purposely towards the bottom of the tree as if it was preparing to attack. As soon as he got out of the tree Jimmy knew that it would be after him. The goat looked up and stared straight into his eyes.

The goat's eyes were wild and dangerous. Jimmy could see the black hairs up its nostrils.

It was the witch!

Why hadn't they thought of that? She had changed herself into a goat. Course she could. She was a witch!

He heard Josie shouting. It sounded far away, in another time. 'Come on Jimmy. The goat won't hurt you. Just get down and run!'

He wanted to cry and he wanted his mum. He even thought he might wet himself. The witch just kept staring at him. 'Alright,' he sobbed. 'You can have your bloody apple back.' As he tried to get the apple out of his pocket his foot slipped off the branch. And he fell, hard, onto the grass. For a few seconds he didn't know where he was or what had happened. Then he was being dragged and bumped over the lawn. They had come to rescue him. Even Legs.

'You alright mate?' asked Del when they were all safe on the other side of the hedge.

'Yeah, yeah, I think so.'

His head was throbbing but the relief of being out of that evil garden was more overwhelming.

'You've got a big lump on yer head,' said Josie, touching his forehead gently.

'Come on,' said Legs. 'Let's get out of here quick before the witch comes.'

'You're all stupid,' Jimmy whispered angrily. 'The witch is already in the garden. She's turned herself into a goat. The witch *is* the goat!'

They all stared at him in horror. Legs went completely white. 'You mean to say,' he gulped, 'that we were in the garden with the witch?' He looked as if he might be about to faint.

'Bugger me,' said Del.

They looked through the gap in the hedge, she was still there. She lowered her horns and then looked over towards them. The witch hadn't moved from the bottom of the tree. In her mouth she was holding Jimmy's cap and chewing it slowly.

As they ran quickly back to the den, Jimmy felt raw excitement replacing his fear. He had really proved himself today. Like a brave warrior. His Nan had told him that once and he had never forgotten. He had fallen off his three wheeler bike and grazed his knee. 'What a brave little warrior you are,' she had said when he hadn't cried. Well, he wasn't little anymore and he had proved himself today.

'So,' said Del as they all sat around in the den eating digestive biscuits, 'tell us what 'appened then.'

Jimmy took a bite from his apple nonchalantly. He had their full attention now. This was his moment.

'Well,' he began. 'It was a bit scary when I realised like. That it was the witch standing at the bottom of the tree. It was her eyes. It was just her, I knew it was. She was scared of me though when I stared back at 'er.'

'You stared back at her?' Legs asked incredulously.

'Course,' said Jimmy, 'an' then I told her to leave us alone.'

'You told her to leave us alone?' repeated Legs again.

'I never 'eard you,' said Del.

'Well, I 'ad to whisper didn't I?'

'So what happened next?' Josie asked excitedly.

'Well, I just told her not to cast no more spells and not to set them cats on us again.'

47

The other three looked at Jimmy with undisguised admiration. 'You're very brave,' said Josie.

Jimmy shrugged his shoulders casually and took another bite from the apple.

'So what did she say after all that?' Legs asked.

'She didn't say nothing. She couldn't could she, being a goat I mean. Anyway I think I've frightened 'er off for now.'

Del laughed. 'Yeah, I'll bet she's really scared of us. Give over Jimmy.'

Jimmy was about to take another bite from the apple when, in one swift movement, Del grabbed it and threw it over the wall. 'Hey!' Jimmy shouted. 'That was my apple!'

'I've probably just saved your bleedin' life,' said Del. 'It'll be poison won't it? Coming from a witch's tree.'

Jimmy felt sick. He hadn't thought about that. Or his lost cap. His mum would go mad. He'd had three bites of that apple. What if he turned into something? What if he died? He didn't want to die, especially on a weekend. Especially when it was Bonfire Night.

Chapter 7

'Josie, is that you? Your dinner's ready.'

'No, sorry Sal, it's only me.' Sally's friend Dianne from the factory stood at the door grinning. 'Cor blimey, ain't you done yer cleaning yet? It's a right tip in 'ere.'

Sally sighed. She looked at her friend all dressed up in her high heels and petticoats. And then she looked at herself. Stockings with ladders in. Cardigan with holes in the elbows and her old woollen skirt still covered in porridge. Oh, she knew she scrubbed up well when she went out but she never had any money for new clothes so she always wore the same ones. Where did I go wrong, she thought.

'Listen Di, when you've got three kids then you can tell me off about me cleaning. I do me best you know. Anyway, what are you doing here? I told you I couldn't get to the wedding.'

'I know that but everyone's going down the King's Head later on. Just thought you might fancy it.'

'Oh, I dunno. I don't think Julie will be up for babysitting tonight. They've 'ad all sorts of dramas over there.'

'Well, just ask 'er. She can only say no.'

One of the babies chose that moment to start screaming. The other one soon joined in. Sally picked Christopher up and plonked him into her friend's arms. Dianne started to protest but it was too late. Sally was heading for the teapot.

'Only come round to see if you was coming out. I ain't a bloody nanny.'

She made a face, threw the baby up into the air and just managed to catch him. He stopped crying immediately. 'Come on darlin,' smile for yer Auntie Di. There you are, look at 'im laughin' now. Shall we do that again?'

'No. I know you; you'll drop him on his head. You got no idea,' Sally sighed lifting a protesting Christopher from Dianne's arms into the safety of his playpen.

'Ooh I don't know,' Dianne laughed. 'Might have to think about babies soon I s'pose. I'm getting on a bit now Sal. Nearly twenty one. Don't wanna get left on the shelf. I think tonight could be the night you know.'

Sally laughed at her friend. Dianne couldn't stand being without a man. Better if it was one she really liked but as the years went by she was getting pretty desperate to find herself a husband. To not have a steady boyfriend at twenty was quite serious in Plaistow. 'You say 'tonight's the night' every time we go out,' Sally laughed.

'Yeah, but I mean it this time. I can feel it in me water.'

'Not sure that's where you're feelin' it Di.' They both giggled.

'It ain't that bad is it Sal? 'avin' kids I mean?'

'Nah. I wouldn't change nothin'. They're good fun. Well, when they're little anyway. Never see Josie no more except at mealtimes. God knows what they get up to.'

'Best not knowing,' said Dianne, having a gulp of her tea. 'Not if it's anything' like we used to do. Cor, I wish I'd bin this age during the war. All them men in uniform. Oops, sorry Sal.'

Sally raised her eyes to the ceiling. Dianne was always putting her foot in it. She had completely forgotten again that Josie's dad had been an American airman.

''Ave you told 'er?' she asked Sally. 'About 'er dad I mean?'

'She's never asked so I ain't said nothing. If she wants to know, I'll tell 'er.'

'Fancy leaving you like that though. An' you only seventeen.'

Sally laughed. 'Well, I grew up fast anyway. Ain't nothin' much can get to me now. The worst thing was mum and dad chucking me out. If your mum hadn't taken me in I don't know what would 'ave happened to me.'

'I can't believe they just did that, just put you out on the street.'

'Saw mum last week in Woolies,' said Sally.

'You never said.'

'She walked straight past me. Like I didn't exist.'

'Cow,' said Dianne. 'I'd bloody tell 'er what I thought if I'd seen her.'

She would too, Sally thought. Dianne had been a good, loyal friend to her. Her whole family had. They were better than hers had ever been anyway. She didn't know what she would have done without them. 'Well, it's 'er that's

50

missing out,' said Sally. 'She won't get no more grandchildren.'

'That served 'er right didn't it eh. After what she done to you? Having a son who was a ginger beer.' They both laughed.

'Poor Kenny,' sighed Sally. 'Still, he's doing alright in Canada. Says they're real men out there.'

'Ooh wouldn't it be lovely eh? All them mounties and lumberjacks. Right, well, I'd best be off. Get to this wedding. She's up the duff of course.'

'I think she loves 'im though. Sort of,' said Sally.

'Ooh, you're such a romantic Sally Evans. You weren't on the hen night were you or you wouldn't be saying that. She was snogging everythin' in trousers.'

'I'll ask Julie to babysit anyway. You never know. Will you be there by eight? I ain't walking in on me own.'

'I'll be there. Never know Sal. This could be the night you meet someone an' all. It's bin a long time. You ain't seen anyone for,' she stopped and thought about it, 'eighteen months.'

'Go on, bugger off,' Sally laughed.

'Ooh mum I heard that,' Josie had just come in.

'Hiya Josie, not that you smell or nothing but I'm just leaving,' said Dianne.

'See you later Sal.'

Sally looked at her eldest child. Hair all over the place and her dungarees covered in mud. She tried not to laugh. 'Where on earth have you been?' she asked.

'Nowhere. Just playing.'

'Well get them dungarees off and you can wash them yourself after dinner. I ain't doing it. Monday's washing day remember.'

Josie let out a long sigh. 'No other kids 'ave to do their own washing,' she grumbled as she stamped out of the room. 'It ain't fair. I might just go and live somewhere else.'

'Well you can go then. I ain't stopping yer.'

The words had just come out, words she hadn't meant to say. Sally desperately wanted to get on with her daughter but sometimes, she could just strangle her. She knew it wasn't easy for Josie. She knew the kids called her bad names at school. And it wasn't fair. It was all her fault.

Please, she whispered to herself, don't let me be a bad mother. Not like my mum was.

***

Jimmy was surprised to see his mum and Mrs. Pattinson sat in the sitting room when he got in. His dad was shouting at him from the kitchen. 'Come on mate. We're gonna be late for the game. Not that our dinner's ready yet,' he muttered. 'Too much to gossip about this morning.'

Jimmy made his way through to the kitchen. His head was hurting now where he had fallen in the witch's garden. 'Oh yeah,' he laughed. 'Gossiping about Del's dad I s'pose. He told me to fuck off.'

Before he knew what was happening his mum was in the back room and had smacked his legs. Hard. 'Don't you be using that word in this house or any house for that matter,' she said in a very quiet voice. She was scary when she spoke quiet. 'I've a good mind to send you to bed. No football for you today young man. That's probably where you get all this bad language from. Upton Park and Del Tyler.'

Jimmy felt tears threatening. He had had a pretty frightening morning all in all. Dead exciting but it had called for a lot of bravery on his part. He could do without all this. And fancy smacking him in front of Mrs.Pattinson. He had only come home to get his dinner. He wouldn't bother next time. 'I ain't swearin'. I was just telling you what he said that's all,' he said defiantly.

'Don't you be answering your mum back Jimmy,' his dad snapped.

'Well', said May, 'I think I'd best be off. Is my Clive home yet Jimmy?

That always made Jimmy laugh. Whenever he heard Leg's real name. 'Yeah,' he spluttered. 'He's just gone in.'

'What you all been up to this morning then?' she asked Jimmy.

'Nothing much.'

'Just what my Clive always says. You must lead very boring lives you kids. See you all,' she called out as she closed the door behind her.

'Well, the ground must have been pretty hard wherever you've bin,' his dad laughed. 'You got yourself a right lump on yer 'ead.'

52

His mum was there in a second. 'Oh Jimmy what have you done? Why didn't you tell me? Look at the state of you.' She ran over to the sink and put a dishcloth under the cold water tap.

'Stop fussing over him Kate, don't want him growing up soft.'

'Dad, what's a domestic?' Jimmy asked, thinking this might be a good opportunity to find out some information.

'Well, a domestic's a cook or a cleaner. Something like that.'

Jimmy thought about this for a moment. This could explain why the coppers wouldn't help Del's mum. She cooked and cleaned but then so did all mums. That meant that they wouldn't help *his* mum either if she was in trouble. Coppers won't have nothing to do with domestics, Del had said. That meant they just didn't like women. Well that was going a bit far, Jimmy thought. That didn't seem right at all. This world needed sorting out.

'What do you want to know about cleaners for love?' his mum asked, holding the cold cloth on Jimmy's head until his teeth chattered.

'Nothing. It don't matter. I just don't think I wanna be a copper when I grow up that's all.'

His mum and dad looked at each other, puzzled. 'Well, I can't say I understand your reasoning there son but I ain't upset about that.' His dad laughed. 'Don't want you nicking me for me smuggled baccy.'

Jimmy noticed that his mum had started cooking their dinner. His dad sighed. 'Don't start,' she said. 'I know it's a bit late but you've still got time. I don't think you should go today love.' She looked at Jimmy's pale face.

Jimmy smiled to himself. She had forgotten already that she had told him he wasn't going.

'Oh he's alright, Kate, stop fussing,' his dad muttered.

'I don't mind not going today dad. Honest. We ain't gonna beat Blackburn. An' we need to take the guy up Plaistow Station. It's our last chance to get some pennies.'

Jimmy sat down at the table, still holding the cloth on his head. The smell of sizzling sausages filled the room. His favourite.

'So where *have* you been then this morning?' his mum asked, trying to avoid the spitting fat.

They were always wanting to know things, grown ups, Jimmy thought. It really pissed him off sometimes. He never asked where they had been. They would tell him off for being nosy if he did. Tell him to mind his own business. And then it was all, 'Oh not like it was in our day. You're all too spoilt now. Younger generation, think you know it all. We had nothing when we was your age.' The nagging just seemed to go on and on. His mum was looking at him, expectantly. He tried to think which bit he could tell her about.

'Went over to Sally's,' he said eventually.

'Mrs. Evans to you,' his mother said sharply.

'She ain't a Mrs, she ain't married,' said Jimmy.

His dad laughed and his mum looked cross. 'And you can stop laughing. It's not funny.'

'Oh, Sally's alright,' said Billy.

'Well, you would say that wouldn't you? Being a man.'

What on earth does that mean, Jimmy wondered.

'I played wiv the babies,' he said. 'They was alright really.'

His dad was giving him a strange look now. Like a sort of warning but he didn't understand it so he just carried on. His mum was putting the sausages on his plate.

'Can we have a baby mum?'

There was silence for a few seconds. Then Jimmy looked at her face and he sort of remembered something. His stomach turned to lead. His mum dropped the plate and his favourite sausages clattered to the floor. 'Now look what you've made me do,' she screamed at Jimmy. 'Just shut up with your stupid questions.'

His dad got up and tried to put his arms around her. She pushed him away forcefully.

'I'm just going upstairs for a minute.'

She walked past Jimmy. He could see she was crying.

'You just don't think do yer?' His dad was shouting at him now. Jimmy's bottom lip trembled.

'Sorry mate.' His dad put his hands up. 'Sorry, I know you was only a little kid when it 'appened.' He sat down opposite Jimmy at the table.

'It was Dawn,' Jimmy whispered. 'I forgot about Dawn.'

'I told you all about it when we was at football. Remember?'

Jimmy took a deep breath. It was sort of foggy in his mind. He just remembered the baby's name. Dawn. It had been a cup game. They'd had to queue for two hours to get in to the chicken run, the old, wooden East Stand where the loudest and most loyal Hammers supporters stood. Well, that was what his dad always said anyway. His dad would never stand anywhere else in the ground. Surrounded by a wire fence, from the other side of Upton Park, it looked just like a chicken run.

Eventually, they had got in. It had been only the second game Jimmy had ever been to and he had sat on his dad's shoulders He could only have been five or six. The sky had been heavy with snow. It had been bitterly cold but no-one cared. They were all laughing. Anticipation. Excitement. He had noticed that his dad had been a bit quiet. His mum had been due out of hospital the next day. Gran had come over to look after them and she had knitted him a bobble hat in claret and blue to go with his scarf. Better than a cap. His ears had been lovely and warm.

His dad interrupted his thoughts. 'And do you not remember me tellin' yer that she can't have no more babies?'

He had forgotten that bit. It had been such a good game. One all at half-time. That's when his dad had told him about his sister Dawn. She had only lived for five minutes. 'Yeah, no. I don't know.' He hung his head. 'Is that why she's crying?'

His dad nodded. He stood up and put his arm awkwardly around Jimmy's shoulders, then turned away quickly, but not before Jimmy could see that he was nearly crying too. His dad cleared his throat. 'You'd best go an' tell her you're sorry son. An' hurry up, I've got a match to get to.'

Jimmy made his way slowly upstairs. This was awful. What could he say? He knocked on their bedroom door.

'What is it?'

His mum was laid on the bed. When she saw Jimmy she sat up and blew her nose.

'I just come to say ... I come to say sorry,' he blurted out. He couldn't look at her. 'I forgot.'

'It's alright love. I'm just being silly. I'll be down in a minute, do you some more sausages.'

Jimmy walked slowly back downstairs. He should have told her that he didn't really want a baby. He should have said that they were noisy and smelly and that he'd only been joking. But the words just hadn't come out. They never did.

***

Kate was polishing an already gleaming hearth. Her stomach was churning. She shouldn't have shouted at Jimmy like that. He couldn't be expected to remember the baby; he had only just started school himself then. Kate never gave the baby her name in her thoughts. She tried it now. Dawn. Dawn. The tears came. Gulping sobs she couldn't control. She threw the duster on the floor and ran upstairs, collapsing on to the bed. What was the matter with her? Why couldn't she be like other people and just get over things? The pills hadn't done any good. They had just seemed to make it worse. No, it had been Auntie Molly and her old friend who had got her through that. Molly with her practical common sense and her friend in the big house with her healing powers. She took the hankie from her pinny pocket and blew her nose loudly. That's enough now, she told herself.

Kate thought back, as she often did, to the happiest days. Before the war. Growing up in Bethnal Green. They were always laughing; at least that's how she remembered it. Her dad pulling his funny faces, his huge raucous laugh that filled the house and almost made it shake. Her mum, always singing the latest songs out of tune. They had no money, but then no one did in those days. Kate had never forgotten lying in bed some nights, her tummy rumbling. Oh, they never starved, there was always bread and dripping but some weeks when her dad had been out of work, there was certainly no meat. Kate could remember holding her mum's hand and being pulled quickly past the butcher's shop, but not fast enough for Kate to miss seeing the lamb chops and the juicy sausages sitting in the window.

'Mum ...'

'No chance Kate, not today love but who knows what could happen tomorrow. You just never know.'

Her mum had smiled sadly as they moved on. One day though there had been a 'meat tomorrow'. She remembered it now as clearly as if it were yesterday.

Her dad had been out of work for months and one day Auntie Molly had called and brought them some steak. Proper steak! Her mum had put it away in the larder until after Molly had gone. Kate remembered having to borrow some vinegar from Mrs. Peacock next door.

'We're having steak for tea Mrs. Peacock. Steak and chips.'

Mrs Peacock had tutted. 'Alright for some.' Then she had softened at Kate's excited face. 'Well, I daresay your mum could do wiv a bit of meat, babby due any time but remember that steak ain't meant for the likes of us. Our digestives can't cope wiv it you know.'

The smell of the hot crunchy chips and the steak came back to Kate often. Sitting round the table, the three of them giggling.

'I think we should say grace,' her dad had said, laughing.

Her mum had slapped his arm playfully. 'Don't be daft,' she had giggled. 'This ain't nothing to do wiv God, he ain't never give us nothin'. No, we'll say thanks to Molly for this feast.'

They had all raised their cups of water and clinked them together just like the posh people did. 'Come on love,' her dad had laughed. 'Dig in.'

It had been one of the very best times that Kate could remember. She often clung to that memory on the bad days and nights. Just kept it there. Waiting for when it was needed.

After the disaster, she thought about it constantly. When she was in Ilford living with Auntie Molly, sometimes at mealtimes her eyes would fill up with tears.

'Come on, eat up,' Auntie Molly would say, not unkindly. 'You never ate meat like this in Bethnal Green did you?'

And then Auntie Molly would bite her lip and turn her head away and, although they never spoke about that night at the underground station, Kate knew that they were thinking the same thing.

Her mum, her dad and little Shirley. There weren't enough steaks in all the world that could have replaced them.

Chapter 8

'I ain't forgot the potatoes May. For the baked jackets tomorrer.' Maggie Tyler stood at May and George's front door. She had tried very hard to cover her face with a large scarf but one eye was now completely closed, the bruises yellowish black.

'Come in love,' said May quickly. 'Come on, you don't need to be worrying about the potatoes.'

'But I always do 'em for the bonfire, it won't be no different this year. Always start 'em off before we put 'em in the ashes. Only trouble is that me cooker's buggered.'

'Don't worry Maggie,' said May, taking the brown bag of potatoes and moving through to the kitchen with them. 'I'll do them tomorrow. Sit down love, we'll have a cuppa.'

Maggie started to protest but sat down at the table anyway. May wondered what excuses she would come up with for Mick today. It was always the same when this happened. She tried so hard not to be judgmental but one day, she knew that she would have to tell Maggie exactly what she thought of her precious husband.

'I sent him out to get more taters,' said Maggie.' He ain't all bad you know. He'll be nice to me now for a bit. Made me a cuppa this morning.'

'Where is he?'

'Sleeping it off. Oh, I know what you all think but he don't do it that often. That bleedin' war's got a lot to answer for.'

May bit her tongue. Everyone seemed to blame everything on the war, she thought, herself included. And especially battered women. Probably the generation before them blamed it on the Great War and so it went on.

'Well, it's none of my business, nor anyone else's Maggie. I'm not here to judge you but if you're ever frightened or you need us, you're welcome to stay. Anytime.'

Tears oozed from Maggie's bruised eye. And then she lit a cigarette, the twentieth of the day. 'Look love,' she said, 'I ain't leavin' him. I've done it before and he just comes after me. Anyway,' she laughed, as May poured the tea into the yellow, flowery cups, 'there's things I'd miss, you know what I mean?' She winked with her good eye. 'He ain't bad in the bedroom department my old man.'

May couldn't imagine anything worse. The thought of that awful, whisky stinking, smelly man on top of you. She tried not to let it show on her face. Looking towards the window she saw George peering in. His face was a picture when he saw Maggie sitting there. It was a look of pure horror. George couldn't cope with Maggie at all. Goodness knows what would happen if she *did* come to stay, divorce probably. Predictably, he waved his arms around in the window and disappeared. He would stay in his shed now, May thought to herself, until she told him it was safe to come out. She smiled.

'Well, as long as you're happy Maggie. Another cup?'

'So is everything sorted for the bonfire then?' Maggie asked.

'I think so. Billy and Bones have got most of the fireworks. We'll have to watch out for the kids with those penny bangers. Nellie Bransome's cat lost its tail last year. Little buggers. Kate's got the sausages.'

'And the big kids have got the beer.' They laughed.

They sat companionably drinking their tea. 'Well, I'd best get back.' Maggie sighed. See what's happening. I've left Julie in charge. The older boys are off up the station wiv the guy.'

May went to the door with Maggie and gave her a hug.

'I'm alright,' Maggie sniffed, 'as long as I've got all of you.'

May watched her friend shuffle over the road like an old woman. She wasn't an old woman though. Maggie was only thirty four. Shaking her head, May walked through the kitchen and out of the back door to George's shed. He was sat on his stool, puffing on his pipe.

'Has she gone?' he asked. May just stood there smiling. 'What are you stood there grinning at me like that for? You know I can't handle Maggie.'

'I'm not cross with you,' she smiled again, as she moved towards him and planted a kiss on his cheek. 'I just wanted to say,' she stood back and looked at the man she could never have lived without, 'that I really love you George Pattinson.'

'Don't talk soft woman,' he muttered and turned away smiling.

***

'So how come you're out on a Saturday?' Billy asked George as they made their way quickly to the King's Head. The fog had come down again and it was a raw night.

'Two words is the answer to that,' George replied. 'Maggie and Tyler. She keeps appearing at the door. It's like a repeating nightmare. I had to hide in the shed most of the afternoon.'

They laughed. Penny bangers were going off in the distance and fireworks lit up the sky from the park, others from back gardens. The smell of cordite filled the air. Families were still rushing down to the park, running late. Crying babies and laughter everywhere.

'These kids should be in bed,' said George. 'May has taken them all down the park and the Tyler kids as well. In my day, six o'clock was bedtime. And then we've got *our* bonfire tomorrow. Too much for me.'

As he spoke a rocket lit up the sky. They both stood watching it. 'Magic though ennit?' Billy laughed.

'Yeah, I suppose so,' George grinned. 'Like Father Christmas. Though he won't be bringing us a television this year now. Joe, you know my eldest, has left his wife. Needs a bit of money to tide him over. Says he might move down here. I'll just have to explain to Clive that Father Christmas ran out of televisions.'

'They ain't believed in 'im for years,' Billy laughed. 'Only when it suits 'em.'

'You mean there's no Father Christmas? You have upset me Billy.'

'Cor, let's get a move on George; it's taters out here tonight.'

The lights of the King's Head loomed into view. Warm and welcoming on this murky night, the two men almost ran through the door. They heard shrieks of laughter and some bad piano playing coming from inside.

'Oh God,' said George. 'Arthur won't be happy. Women in, two nights in a row. He'd rather have ten Mick

61

Tyler's than that. Fancy a game of darts Billy? I could do with the practise. I'm going to try and get into the team.'

They went to their usual spot. The pub was heaving but their spaces were always there. It was understood. 'Evening Arthur. Usual please and two sets of arrows. How are you mate?'

'How do you think I am? All these screeching women. Again.'

'Well, it makes a change from looking at your legs Arthur,' Billy laughed.

Arthur tutted. 'Oh, it's a different lot tonight. A wedding no less, except that somewhere along the way they've lost the bridegroom.'

As Billy and George walked through the packed pub to the dartboard at the other end, Billy glanced over at the crowd of girls surrounding the piano. God, he thought, the bride looked young. Couple of kids would change all that. She had obviously had a bit too much babycham at the reception or whatever it was that women drank. Her long, white dress was stained and torn, the hem a dirty grey. She was hanging on to the piano for support. He saw Sally Evans talking to the young lad who was trying to play. Billy waved when she looked up.

They passed a gang of young lads milling around the bar at the end. Shiny suits and winkle pickers, ties askew. Teddy boys. They wore long jackets with their tapered trousers. Some of them even had velvet collars.

'What do they think they look like?' he muttered to George as he threw his darts for a double off.

'I don't know,' George replied, 'but I find them a bit intimidating. Oh, well done Billy. You haven't lost your touch. One hundred and forty.'

'What does that mean? Intimidating? You talk more posh than our Kate sometimes.'

'Well, you know, a bit frightening. They like smashing things up. Bugger. I can't even hit the board tonight.'

Billy suddenly felt very old. God, he wasn't thirty yet but he had never had this freedom at their age. Flashy clothes and money to spend.

He had been thirteen years old when war had broken out. Evacuated to Essex for a while, he soon ran

62

back to Plaistow. He just wasn't a country boy and, if truth were known, he had missed his mum, though he would never have admitted it. Their playground had been bombed out buildings. Then he was a young man and off to war. Billy tried to concentrate on his darts.

Sixty left. He did it in two throws. Bull's-eye. Double five.

'Good arrows Billy,' George shook his hand. 'I think I've got a long way to go before they'll put me in the team. Let's get back and have another bevy.'

Arthur was still ranting on behind the bar. 'They'll be bloody running for Prime Minister next, women,' he muttered.

'Well, I don't think there'll be a woman Prime Minister in my lifetime,' George laughed. 'Mind you, our lass would make a good one.'

'Oh, your trouble and strifes are alright but then you wouldn't bring them in 'ere would yer? Not nice gels.'

'Alright Loopy? How's the pram?' Billy laughed.

'God, 'er indoors is giving me real grief over that. It's all bent an' buckled. Another dustbin lid on the way now an' all.' Loopy did not look very excited about having another mouth to feed. They all clapped him on the back.

'Get this man a drink,' said George. 'Congratulations Loopy.'

'Between you an' me,' Arthur whispered to Billy, 'he's milking this a bit. Bin doing very well for free booze for the last couple of days. Wouldn't be surprised if he's telling porkies.'

'Cheers lads. Plenty of goals today Billy,' said Loopy, gulping down his pint. 'Just a pity they got more than us.'

'Typical Hammers. We should have won. They played like shit at the end.'

'Language Billy,' Arthur warned seriously. 'Remember there's ladies in.'

All the men at the bar burst out laughing as Arthur moved away.

'Is he bleedin' serious?' Billy laughed. 'I don't believe that man.'

Down at the other end of the room, the bride was dancing on a table. The pianist was trying to play 'Rock

63

Around The Clock', not very successfully. After three pints Billy needed the toilet. Trouble was he would have to walk right past all those girls at the piano.

'I'm off for a Jimmy Riddle,' he said to George.

'I need to go too,' said George, 'but I don't fancy walking past all those girls.'

He put his hands on his hips and wiggled them. 'Shall we go together Billy?'

'Piss off,' Billy laughed. George was funny when he'd had a few.

'You can wait till I get back. I want them all to meself.'

He felt all the girls looking at him as he walked past.

'You all right Billy?' It was Sally.

'Yeah, I'm fine Sal. You?'

He never usually saw Sally dressed up. She looked different tonight somehow. 'Won't be tomorrow,' she laughed.

'Ooh he's nice,' said a plump, blonde girl. 'Looks a bit like James Dean don't he Sal?'

'You must be really pissed,' Billy smiled as he raced into the sanctuary of the gent's toilet. It felt a bit threatening. All them girls, looking at him like that. When he came out, they were all singing. He slipped back quickly to his position at the bar.

'Glad I don't work down that factory,' he said to George. 'They was looking me up an' down over there.'

George smiled. 'Don't tell me you never look *women* up and down Billy Potter.'

'Well, that's different. We all do that, it's normal. Hey George,' Billy laughed, running his hand through his hair, 'D'you think I look like James Dean?'

George looked at him as if for the first time. 'Yeah, I suppose you do a bit. Didn't do him much good though did it?' They laughed.

'Ooh, that blond one's after you,' George whispered. 'She's coming over. Watch out.'

The girls were all leaving. Singing as they went. The blond girl squeezed past George and snuggled up to Billy. He could feel himself blushing and looked around him for help. Arthur, Loopy and George just couldn't stop laughing.

'I think you're lovely,' she said, running her hands over his chest. She reached up to whisper in his ear. 'I'd let you go nearly all the way, you know but don't tell no-one I said that.'

'I think you'd best get home love,' said Billy, flustered. He pushed her gently away.

'Come on Jen,' said Sally, saving Billy from any further embarrassment. She guided his admirer reluctantly away.

'Cheers Sal,' Billy laughed.

She smiled back at him and Billy suddenly saw her as if for the first time. God she was a looker when she was all dressed up. What he wouldn't give ...

He turned and faced the bar, picked up his pint and downed it in one go. 'I'll have another when you're ready Arthur,' he said. He had just had too much to drink that's all. Shit.

Chapter 9

'Are you feeling all right love?'

Jimmy didn't feel too good but he wasn't going to miss the fireworks for anything. 'Yeah, I'm alright. Just going to see Del.' He grabbed his gabardine mac from behind the door.

'You look very pale.'

'Kate, will you stop fussing over 'im.' His dad looked up from his News of The World.

Jimmy knew he wasn't alright. The smell of sausages wafted through the kitchen again. Usually it made him feel really hungry. This year it made him feel sick. He had to get out. Get some fresh air.

'Well, don't forget your cap. Where *is* your cap?'

Jimmy had dreaded this. He had worked out lots of lies he could tell to explain its disappearance but not one that would work. He decided to play for time. 'Left it at Josie's. I'll get it on me way.'

'*My* way Jimmy not 'me' way. Go on then.'

'See you up at the bonfire son. Won't be long now. I could eat a pig's arse. Can I not just have one of them love?'

His mum smacked his dad's arm as he made his way over to the sausages. 'No you can't, you're worse than the kids.'

'Right well, I'd best go an' get the beers sorted then. And Jimmy, don't bang that... '

As Jimmy slammed the door the cold evening air blasted through his body. He shivered violently. He felt better when he saw Del running towards him carrying the box of bangers. 'You alright mate?' Del asked, looking at Jimmy. 'Well, you ain't turned into nothing anyway.'

'Ain't nothing wrong wiv me. Let's get them penny bangers up to the den an' sort 'em out. Where's Jose and Legs?'

'Up the bonfire wiv Old Bones.' They ran up to the end of the road.

The bonfire stood like a sentinel against the darkening sky. Quite a few kids had gathered already. Excitement was in the air.

'Whatcha, dustbin lids.'

Old Bones stood next to the bonfire. His face alive with anticipation. His tin of paraffin stood next to him. 'Great night boys. Look at it, not a cloud in the sky. Not a gasp of wind. Look at them twinkly little stars up there, couldn't be better.' He rubbed his old, gnarled hands together. 'Best night of the year.'

'Bleedin' cold though,' said Jimmy, his teeth chattering.

'Are you alright?' Josie looked at him.

'Stop askin' me if I'm alright will yer.'

'Well ... you know what I mean.' She lowered her voice. 'The witch's apple.'

Legs sauntered over to join them, hands in his pockets. 'Nah, he'll be alright now. That was yesterday morning. Spells work quicker than that.'

'Come on,' said Del. 'Let's share these penny bangers out in the den before everyone comes.'

'I don't want none,' said Legs.

'Nah. Little Legsy don't like bangs,' Del laughed. 'I can see that cotton wool in yer ears you know. I ain't daft.'

'Leave him alone Del,' said Josie. 'An' if I see any of you lot tying 'em to cats and dogs tails I ain't speaking to none of you again.'

'We ain't never done that,' said Jimmy angrily.

When they got back from the den nearly everyone who lived in Churchill Street was crowded around the dark bonfire. Trestle tables had been set up groaning under the weight of all sorts of food. Everyone had brought something. The smell of hot, succulent sausages wafted through the air. Plates of jellied eels, veal and ham pie, pork scratchings, spam sandwiches. Tomato soup in a huge urn and doorstop slices of bread, covered in lashings of butter. And Maggie's baked jacket potatoes, partly cooked, waiting to be finished off in the embers of the fire.

The men had gathered all the fireworks together and were standing around knocking back their bottles of beer. It was almost time for the lighting of the fire. Jimmy felt a warm feeling, deep inside his guts. He didn't know where it came from or what it was about. And even though he didn't feel his normal self, he just knew that he wouldn't have wanted to be anywhere else in the world at that moment. Old Bones stood, holding his lighted taper waiting for his countdown. His face a picture of perfect happiness.

'Ten, nine, eight, seven, six, five ...'

Old Bones moved his taper closer to the bonfire. The guy sat, a bit askew on the top. One of his eyes had fallen off. Jimmy realised that they had left his shoelaces undone. They had tied Judy the stuffed owl to his head. Her eyes looked startled as always.

'four, three, two, one.'

A great roar went up from the residents of Churchill Street as Old Bones pushed the taper into the middle of the bonfire and it erupted in a sea of yellow flames, crackling into the night sky. The men set rockets off and all the little kids were given a sparkler. You only got one until you were seven. Jimmy sighed to himself. He supposed you had to give a few things up when you got old but he missed his sparkler on Bonfire Night. He looked at the faces of the little Tyler kids as they waved them around, eyes wide with delight.

'Who needs sparklers?' said Del. 'Come on Jimmy, let's go an' let off some bangers.'

Jimmy could hardly tear himself away from the bonfire. The warmth made him feel a bit better. Old Bones put his hand on his shoulder. 'You'll never forget nights like this young Jimmy,' he said seriously. 'They come back to you when you're old. Always hold onto them.'

Jimmy moved away. Old Bones was a bit of a nutter really, he thought, but a nice nutter all the same.

After the golden rains, the catherine wheels that never worked, the penny bangers and the rockets, everyone tucked in to the food by the dying embers of the fire. The potatoes were rescued from the ashes and eaten with relish. The excitement and the cold night air had made everyone hungry. Someone started singing. It was Old Bones. For an old man, he had a very clear tuneful voice.

"We'll meet again, don't know where, don't know when, but I know we'll meet again some sunny day ..."

Jimmy looked around. Some of the grown-ups were crying. Crying while they were smiling. He didn't understand that at all. He knew it was an old war song, so he supposed that was it. Grown-ups were weird. He looked at his mum and saw tears sliding down her cheeks. She came over, stood behind him and put her arms round his waist. She hugged him to her, until it almost hurt. This wasn't like her at all. He wanted to run off but, after upsetting her yesterday, he thought he had better just stay where he was.

He looked for his dad and then he saw *her*. The witch. She was here!

Deep in the shadows of the dying flames of the fire. Talking to his dad. She had something in her hand. It was his cap, or what was left of it. He couldn't breathe. He was going to be in real trouble now.

'Are you alright love?' His mum had loosened her grip and was back to being his mum again.

His dad was putting the cap in his pocket and waving his arms around. Jimmy could see that he was angry with the witch. Why would his dad be like that? With all the other noise and the singing, Jimmy couldn't hear what they were saying but he could see that his dad was shouting. Then she disappeared. Back into the shadows. She was gone.

He looked at his mum. Suddenly he felt very poorly indeed and he just couldn't stop shivering. 'I ain't well mum,' he snivelled. 'I wanna go to bed.'

'Come on then,' she said. 'It's late anyway. School tomorrow.'

His legs felt like lead. They walked slowly home, he hadn't even said goodnight to his mates.

He felt a bit better when his mum had tucked him up in bed. She had taken his temperature. A hundred and one degrees. Quite high, she said and she had given him an aspirin. No school tomorrow. Well, that was what he had wanted wasn't it? A couple of days off school like Del did last week.

He was just nodding off when his dad came in. He looked at Jimmy a bit strange, sat on the bed and took the remains of the cap out of his pocket. 'I ain't gonna have a go at yer son,' he said quietly. 'I used to go scrumping for apples when I was a kid an' all but I'm just gonna say this once. Don't never go near that house again. Alright?' Jimmy nodded. Not sure where this was going.

'She's a very ... strange woman. I ain't saying no more than that about her. And tomorrer, after work, I'm getting you a new cap.'

Blimey, Jimmy thought. His dad was going shopping. That had never happened before.

'There ain't no need to tell your mum, alright? This is our secret,' he whispered.

Jimmy tried to fight falling into the black shadows of sleep. His cap kept floating through. He hoped the mad axe man wouldn't come. He was walking along a lane. It was nowhere he knew. There were dark hedges on each side and he knew that the axe man was in there. Then he saw a gap, a small hole but he knew that he could get through it. Then he found himself at the side of a fast flowing river. It was full of goats and alligators, swimming in all directions. Behind him was the hedge and the mad axe man. He would have to jump into the river, he had no choice. As he jumped he sank deeper and deeper. Blacker and blacker.

Jimmy woke up. At least he thought he had. He pinched himself and sighed with relief. That had hurt. His Gran had told him about it. If you're in a nightmare, pinch yourself because most times that you're scared you're really only dreaming. He was hurting all over though, not just where he had pinched himself and he was burning up. He threw off the blankets and put his feet on the floor. His legs were shaking, as he walked slowly over to the window.

There was a pale, watery light rising in the sky. Jimmy looked into the small back garden and almost had to pinch himself again. There, in the middle of his mum's rose bed, was the witch. She was still a goat of course. She must have followed him. She knew he was here and was looking right up at the window. The witch had poisoned him and now she had come to see if it had worked.

'Mum!' he shouted. 'Mum!'

She was there in seconds. 'Jimmy what are you doing out of bed? Come on, you're not well. I'll get you another aspirin and a hot water bottle.'

I'm going to die, Jimmy thought, as he drifted again through the mad axe man in dark hedges and the goats swimming in the river.

He heard his mum calling. Far away. 'Billy! Billy! There's a goat in the garden. It's eating my plants.'

'Don't be daft Kate. How would a goat get in our garden? This ain't Essex.'

Jimmy couldn't stop the heavy darkness coming down. He never heard her reply.

Chapter 10

Kate paced up and down in the small kitchen. She picked up the potato peeler for the tenth time. And then, for the tenth time, put it down again. Where had that doctor got to? Oh, she knew they were always busy this time of year but she had telephoned from May's house over two hours ago. This new National Health Service wasn't right yet. Not by any means. Then she thought back to when she had been a child. There had been children who had died because their parents couldn't afford the doctor. No, she would give him another half hour then she would try him again.

She ran back up the stairs and sat on Jimmy's bed. He was sweating and moaning in his sleep. He was burning up and he had been like this for two days now. His temperature last night had been a hundred and three degrees. She watched him now. Tossing and turning, his face twitching and restless. As always she saw her father in him, Jimmy's granddad. Jimmy had had the look of him from when he was born. Her mind leapt back to the dreadful day of the telegram. Her mother's face just collapsing. Shirley crying because she was too young to understand and Kate herself had just felt numb with the pain. In her eyes he had been and still was, the most wonderful man she had ever known. She would always remember his warmth, his laughter and his love for her. She ached for him sometimes and thought of him dying, away from them, in a strange land. All alone. She still talked to him in times of pain. Especially after Bethnal Green and the baby. And the bad thing that had happened in the park. She knew he still listened to her.

She had been talking to her dad last night while she had sat beside Jimmy, wiping his face with cool towels. Sometimes he had woken up but he was delirious, kept talking about things that made no sense. Witches and axe men. Talking about apples all the time. She thought that he was trying to tell her that he wanted to eat one but when she had brought an apple up to him he had acted really peculiar. He had just gone mad and screamed at her to take it away, to throw it in the bin. 'Please dad,' Kate had whispered out loud. 'Please let him be alright.'

Oh, Billy had told her to stop fretting, that he just had a touch of flu. He would go mad at her tonight when she told him that she had called the doctor out but she didn't care. She would never be able to forgive herself if anything happened to Jimmy. How she wished she could be calm about things. Not worry all the time. Ever since Jimmy had been born she had been like this. It was as if her love for him was just too much to bear. Whenever he walked out of the door she was on pins until he came back. Billy had no idea how difficult it was for her to let him go. Perhaps it was best that their little girl had died. Where would she have found any more love to give to her?

Just then there was a loud knock on the door.

'He'll be fine Mrs Potter,' said Dr. Harris, after examining a sleepy Jimmy thoroughly. 'Keep him in bed for a couple of days, plenty of water to drink. Two spoonfuls of this medicine three times a day and he'll be right as rain. He's young and fit, not like a lot of my patients. It's not been a good week. That smog we had is finishing a lot of the old ones off. I've lost four in the last few days. And Nellie Bransome isn't good. I'm going to see her now.'

'Oh, no,' Kate said. 'She lived near us in Bethnal Green. Mum used to do her shopping. I must pop in and see her. I'm sorry for calling you out Dr. Harris, I just get so ... '

'I know my dear and it's quite understandable with everything that's happened to you but he really will be alright. He'll be back running around in a couple of days, so stop worrying. You know,' he added, looking at her kindly. 'You're very pale. I think you could do with a tonic and a bit of a check-up Kate. If there's anything worrying you ...'

'I'm fine doctor. Thank you.

He patted her awkwardly on the arm and moved towards the bedroom door. 'I can see myself out. And stop worrying Kate.'

She waited until she heard the front door slam before she gave a very groggy Jimmy his medicine. He was asleep in seconds. He actually looked a bit better already, she thought. There was another knock on the door. Kate walked slowly downstairs and opened it.

'Oh, Maggie,' she exclaimed in surprise. 'How are you feeling?'

73

The bruising on her face had gone down, there were yellow patches but she didn't look so bad. She thrust a brown bag into Kate's hands. There was a bottle of National Health orange juice inside.

'Saw the doc comin' in,' she said abruptly. 'Heard your Jimmy was bad an' I just thought he might like some juice. I get loads of it wiv all the kids I got so there's plenty to spare. Good old National Health eh.'

Kate could feel tears threatening to engulf her. She took a deep breath. Alright, so perhaps Maggie wasn't her favourite person but she had a good heart. And she understood. 'Do you ... would you like to come in for a cup of tea Maggie?' She had never asked her in for tea before.

'No, I can't stop. Anyway, hope he'll be alright.'

And she was gone, walking slowly across the road, back to a house that would never give her a minute's peace.

Kate closed the door quickly and went through to stoke the fire. She sat down in Billy's armchair, breathed in the familiar smells of her home. The lavender polish, the burning coals, Billy's tobacco, the slight odour of last night's liver and bacon and she cried. She had no idea why.

***

Jimmy woke up with a start. His pyjamas were soaked but he felt alright. How long had he been in bed? He had no idea. It was still pitch black dark but he didn't have a clue what day it was. Sunday. He had got ill on Sunday. That seemed a long time ago. He must have been sweating buckets for his jamas to be this wet. He would have to get out of bed and change them. He struggled to sit up and put his feet on the lino floor. It felt really cold. Where were his slippers? He felt around in the dark. They were under the bed so he put them on quickly and tried to stand up but he couldn't seem to get his balance, his head was all funny. As he fell backwards on to his bed, the door opened.

'Jimmy, what are you doing?' It was his mum. She switched the light on, came over and sat down beside him.

'Me jamas are all wet mum.'

'*My* jamas Jimmy, not *me* jamas. Come on, sit in the chair and we'll get you some clean ones. Wrap yourself in the blanket and I'll change your sheets first.'

74

She looked at her son and smiled. 'Ooh, you do look better. You've got your colour back. You've been poorly for ages Jimmy but Dr. Harris said you'd be alright.'

The doctor. Yes he did remember the doctor coming and putting that cold thing on his chest and making him say 'aah' all the time. He watched his mum as she busied herself stripping the bed and fetching sheets from the airing cupboard. Other things were coming back to him an' all. His mum had brought him an apple, or was that a dream? There had been lots of dark dreams in his head. The witch. The witch had been in their garden. This would have to be sorted out. He couldn't afford to be ill any longer.

'What's the time mum?' he asked as she settled him back into his bed. He had been washed and changed and his mum had put fresh, crisp sheets on the bed. He felt like he had gone to heaven when he slipped in to them. How could he ever have wanted Sally Evans to be his mum when his was so kind? He shook his head. He was going soft.

'It's three o'clock in the morning,' she kissed him on the forehead. He didn't resist like he normally did. 'Are you hungry love?' she asked. 'What about some toast and jam? Or a nice apple? The old lady in the big house is giving them away. There's a box full of them outside her gate. They're lovely.'

Jimmy felt his whole body going in to shock. He couldn't take this in. It certainly had *not* been a dream. The witch's apples were in this house, 'No.' He said quickly. 'I ain't hungry mum. I need to see Josie.'

His mum laughed. 'You must be feeling better. They have been round to see how you were but I'm not going to let them in at this time in the morning. You can see them after school tomorrow if you're alright. There's nothing that can't wait till then.'

Oh yes there is, Jimmy thought. He couldn't sleep now. Knowing those apples were in the house. He would have to get rid of them. Giving them away? So, that was her plan. That was how she was going to do it. How she was going to poison people. He had had three bites of one of her apples and he knew that he had been very ill, probably quite close to death. Suddenly, the witch seemed seriously real. It had to be her fault. What else could it be? He lay still for what seemed like hours. When he was sure that his mum would be asleep again he put his feet gingerly to the floor. He was still a bit wobbly but if he took it slowly he was sure that he could make it downstairs. He felt dizzy when he stood up but it soon passed and he crept slowly down the stairs. It was dark and he daren't put any lights on but his eyes soon grew accustomed to the lack of light and he could just make out the fruit bowl on the middle of the table. He went closer. Four of them. Four apples. Gloves. He thought. Mustn't touch them with his bare skin. He didn't want to be ill again. Jimmy crept over to where his mac was hanging up behind the door and felt in the pockets. His woolly gloves were there. After unlocking the back door, he picked up the bowl of apples and carried them outside, placing them one by one into the dustbin so that they would make no noise Then he brought the empty bowl back in.

Jimmy was just congratulating himself on a successful mission when he tripped over something soft and furry. It was Precious, who had followed him in and couldn't believe her luck at being inside on such a cold night. Jimmy and the bowl clattered to the floor. Precious howled and Jimmy swore. 'You stupid bloody cat,' he said under his breath. He waited, expecting that any second his mum or dad would rush downstairs to see what was going on. All he could hear was the ticking of the clock. Nothing happened. No-one came, the bowl hadn't broken. He picked Precious up and put her back outside quietly, put the empty bowl back on the table and crept slowly upstairs. He was exhausted but at least it was done, the job he had to do.

He woke up to the sounds of the milkman's float, tinkling up the road. His dad, setting off for work. His mum, as usual, saying 'Don't slam the door Billy' and then his dad slamming the door. The wireless was tuned in to the Light Programme. His mum was singing along to one of those slow, old-fashioned songs. That was unusual, he thought. He hadn't heard her singing for ages. And then her footsteps were coming up the stairs. All the morning sounds that he had missed for so long.

'Here you are love. You must be starving. Porridge and toast. That'll warm you up. I'll light the fire up here for you.'

'I'm alright now mum. I could come downstairs.'

'No, I want you to stay in bed a bit longer. I'll go and get you a couple of comics from the shop and I need some bread. I won't be long. You'll be alright won't you? I'll ask May to keep an eye. I'll only be five minutes.'

Jimmy listened for the front door closing and then got out of bed slowly. He went into his mum and dad's bedroom and looked out of the window. It looked right out on to the street. They would all be going to school soon, he would have to tell them the bad news. It seemed an age before he saw Josie coming out of her house. Being at the convent, she left earlier than the others. He opened the window. The cold air made him gasp for breath. 'Jose!'

Josie looked up and smiled. She came running up to the gate and crossed herself. 'Thank God you're alright,' she said. 'I've been praying for yer. We all 'ave.'

Jimmy thought it highly unlikely that Del and Legs had been praying for him but he said nothing. 'Yeah, I'm all right now,' he shouted, 'but I was really bad. I need to see you Jose. I need to see all of you. There's stuff bin going on. Serious stuff.'

'We'll come round,' Josie shouted back, 'after school. Shut the window, you'll get cold.'

'You sound just like me mum.'

'It ain't *me* mum Jimmy it's *my* mum,' Josie laughed.

'Yeah, now you really *do* sound like me mum.'

Just then his mum appeared from round the corner. He would be in trouble now. She had seen him. 'Jimmy, close that window this instant! You'll be ill again. And you get off to school Josie; you'll miss your bus. Come and see how he is when you get home if you like.'

He heard Josie shout, 'see you later' as he shut the window and ran back into his bedroom. He was starving. Even though the porridge had gone cold he wolfed it down. He heard his mum coming up the stairs and hoped she had got him the Beano as well as the Dandy. She didn't have either. She *did* have the empty fruit bowl in one hand and a new cap in the other.

'Right', she said sternly. 'Seeing as you seem to think you're better, I'll treat you as if you are. There are two mysteries here Jimmy.'

Oh shit, he thought.

77

'Now the apples. I don't mind if you've eaten them. You must be starving. You have eaten them haven't you?'

Jimmy nodded. He hadn't lied. He hadn't spoken so he couldn't have lied. Could he? His mum turned her attention to the, obviously new, cap which his dad must have bought while he was ill. She waited for him to speak.

'And,' she held the cap in front of him. 'What is this?'

'Well, I ...I lost me old one.'

'*My* old one Jimmy. *My* old one'

'Yeah, *my* old one.'

'That doesn't explain this new one though does it? If you've been out stealing Jimmy I will take you to the police station right now. I don't care how ill you are, I will not have a son of mine being a petty thief. And did you really think I wouldn't notice? It's not even the same colour.'

Jimmy gulped. Now what should he say? Alright his dad saying keep it a secret. It wasn't him who was going to be marched down to the cop shop. No, his dad had lost the right to this secret by being stupid enough to buy a different coloured cap. 'Me dad bought it me. Cos I lost the old one.'

'The only shop your dad goes into is the newsagents. Don't talk daft.'

'Well he did, cos he knew you'd be mad.'

His mum looked like she didn't quite believe him.

'Me head's hurting a bit mum, again,' he said hopefully.

'Won't be able to read your Beano then will you? You go back to sleep and I'll bring it up this afternoon.'

She walked towards the door. He had to find something out. 'Mum?'

She turned to face him.

'Did you like them apples?'

'Yes, they were very nice. Mind you, I only managed to get one,' she frowned. 'I'll get you some more if you like.'

'No,' Jimmy said quickly. 'I didn't like 'em much. I was just starving. I've gone off apples.'

'Could have fooled me,' said his mum as she closed the door behind her.

Jimmy sighed. They were nice, that's what she had said. So his mum had eaten an apple an' all. And now he had to wait until four o'clock to see the others and to try and do something. It wasn't easy being a child. Not easy at all.

Chapter 11

Frankie Lymon sang "*Why Do Fools Fall In Love*" on the factory wireless. The girls all joined in, some more in tune than others.

'This is the best hour of the day 'ennit Sal?' Dianne shouted to her friend over the normal factory noises. The screeching of the conveyor belt, the banging and clattering of various bits of machinery and the shouting and banter of five hundred women.

'I'm gonna have to go to the lav Di,' Sally replied. 'I'm desperate. Can you watch me station?' Sally rang a bell on the belt and waited for the nod from the supervisor.

'She's taking her time,' Dianne moaned. ' Bloody cow.'

Sally tried to be patient. The supervisor didn't approve of her, she knew that. Sometimes she made her wait twenty minutes for the lav. There was no point getting angry about it. You just got marked down as a troublemaker. Eventually, she got a cursory nod and made her way to the other side of the factory.

Julie Tyler was stood at the mirror, backcombing her hair. 'Ooh Sal, glad I've seen you. Can I bring my Freddie babysitting tomorrer only he's got some leave an' then I ain't gonna see him for ages.'

'Yeah, course you can Julie. Hang on while I go to the lav.'

'Oh, I'll still be 'ere. I ain't rushing back for no-one.'

No, she'll get away with it, Sally thought. I wouldn't. 'So, how you getting on?' she asked Julie when she came out. 'How's your first week bin?'

'I 'ate it,' said Julie sullenly. 'The noise and the smells, the smells is worst. Makes me feel sick all the time. That's why I ain't bin over to see yer. I'm knackered.'

'Oh you get used to it after a couple of years,' Sally laughed. She glanced at Julie while she washed her hands. She didn't look well. Very pasty and dark, shadows under her eyes. She always seemed lifeless somehow. As if everything was all a bit too much and it was always someone else's fault.

'You ain't looking too good,' said Sally. 'How's your mum now?'

Julie shrugged her thin shoulders. 'Dunno. Alright I s'pose. He ain't hit her again this week.'

'Don't you ever let a man do that to you Julie will yer?'

'Freddie don't hit me,' she said defensively.

'What about ... no, it don't matter. It ain't none of my business.'

Julie was looking away from her now. Staring into the mirror and squeezing a particularly large spot.

'But you've 'ad sex?' Sally asked quietly, 'ain't yer?'

Sally watched Julie's face in the mirror. She saw her swallow, take a deep breath and put her head down. 'I only done it twice,' she whispered, turning now to face Sally. 'Only gone all the way twice. We was careful. Freddie says it'll be alright. You don't understand Sal. He's going away for two years. He said if I loved him I would. He'll finish wiv me if I don't. Anyway,' she stared at Sally defiantly, 'you ain't got no right to lecture me. You got three bloody kids an' you ain't even married.'

'That's *exactly* why I am telling you Julie. I don't want you to end up like me.'

'I wouldn't mind,' she smiled shyly. 'Being you. Well, long as I had a man anyway. And I wouldn't care if I was pregnant. Better than working in this place. I 'ate it.'

Sally sighed. One day, she would get away. Do something with her life. She loved the people round here, despite everything, but most of them were frightened of anything outside their own little world.

There was a knock on the door. The Supervisor came in. 'Come on Sally Evans. You ain't paid to stand around gossiping in the lavs. I'll dock your pay if you do it again.' She winked at Julie.

Julie smirked. 'See you tomorrow then Sal.'

Sally left quickly, her face burning. She glared at the supervisor. Please God, she thought, let my day come soon.

'Trouble?' Dianne asked when she got back to her station.

'Oh just Julie Tyler and that ... that bitch.'

Dianne looked at her friend sympathetically. 'Never mind eh Sal. Tomorrow night we'll be down that Palais, jiving away. We'll forget all this then. Ooh, me second favourite record, Tutti Frutti.'

80

The girls sang along with Little Richard. "*Got a girl named Daisy always drives me crazy, got a girl named Daisy always drives me crazy ...* "

'D'you know Sal, I'm sure they move this belt faster when I've got 'angover. Anyway, it's me that should be pissed off today. I've got to work wiv Julie when you go, now that Kate's off. She might be a toffee nosed bitch but she's a bloody good worker, I'll say that for her. Julie don't know the meaning of the word 'work'. And that supervisor is just trying to get into her knickers. She's definitely a lezzy Sal. She's always in them toilets, trying to catch the young gels sitting on them lavs. Tell you what; I always lock the door when I go in there now. What's up wiv Kate anyway?'

'Jimmy's poorly, he's got a bit of flu I think. He's a nice kid you know.'

'Feel sorry for him. Having a mum like her. Can't be much fun.'

'Well ...'

'I know,' Dianne laughed. 'I ain't a mother. I know nuffin'.'

They both laughed. It was Friday. The weekend started here.

***

Jimmy, Josie and Legs crouched together in the den. It was Saturday morning and Jimmy had been allowed out at last. He had seen Josie yesterday and told her to call an emergency meeting at nine o'clock.

'Where's Del got to?' Legs asked. 'Can't we just start without 'im?'

'No, we can't. This is urgent Legs. Jimmy told me yesterday. We all need to be 'ere.'

'Well,' said Legs, smiling and keeping his voice very low. 'I've got a big secret to tell as well. My dad told me. I know how babies are made.'

Jimmy's eyes opened wide. He had often wondered.

Just at that moment Del burst in. 'You ain't started have yer. I had to clean the boy's bedroom up. It's always me. It ain't fair. So what's this important meeting about anyway?'

'Sex,' said Legs, smiling.

'No it ain't,' said Josie. 'It's about the witch. Tell 'em Jimmy.'

'Well,' said Jimmy, his curiosity getting the better of him. 'Legs can talk about ... sex first if he wants to.'

'It's only about kissing and stuff,' said Josie knowledgeably. 'That's just boring.'

'It's a lot more than that,' said Legs. 'So my dad says.'

'Oh, go on then,' Josie sighed.

Legs took a deep breath. Now he had come to the point of telling them he felt a bit daft. They probably wouldn't believe him anyway. He wasn't sure if he believed it himself. He shifted around uncomfortably on the cold ground. 'Well,' he whispered. 'It's your dick, you know, your willy. That's what sex is.' The boys all looked down at themselves instinctively.

'Don't be daft,' said Jimmy quickly. 'That's just for peeing with.'

'Well, I ain't got one,' Josie said quietly.

'Yeah I know that but you have a ... I can't remember the word now. Anyway, it's like a hole at the front of your bum. Men put their willies into ladies holes and that's sex. And that,' he finished proudly, 'is how babies are made.' They all giggled.

'And then they come out of ladies belly buttons,' said Del.

'Oh no they don't.' Legs was enjoying himself on being the bringer of this massive secret. 'They grow inside their bellies and they come out ...' he paused for dramatic effect, 'of the hole.'

'Must be a bleeding big hole then,' Del laughed.

'That must be where the blood comes from,' said Josie, suddenly becoming more interested.

'What blood?'

'Ladies have blood. It's called the curse.'

'Why?' Del asked.

Josie sighed. She really wished that she hadn't said anything about it now. Her mum had told her when Josie had seen her throwing sanitary towels on the fire. About how you had blood every month. It didn't seem fair to Josie that men didn't have it. Sometimes her mum went to bed with a hot water bottle. Sometimes she even cried. Didn't seem right talking to boys about it though. It made her feel dirty. Still, she had brought it up so now she would have to explain.

82

'Well, when Adam and Eve was in the Garden of Eden ...' she began.

'Where's that?' Legs interrupted.

'Shut up Legs. Don't you know nothing?' said Jimmy. He was fascinated by all this now. Somehow he had known that his willy was destined for more than just weeing.

'Eve was trying to give Adam an apple,' Josie continued, 'and God told him not to take it, but he did. So God cursed Eve and all women. That's why we have blood. It hurts sometimes, me mum says.'

'What did God do to Adam?' Del asked.

'Dunno. Nothing, I don't think.'

'Well, that ain't fair,' said Jimmy. 'Will you have blood Jose?' She nodded.

'Is there a lot of it?' Del asked excitedly. Blood was one of his favourite subjects.

'Yeah, you have to wear special things to stop it running down yer legs.'

'Ugh,' said Legs. 'Well, I ain't putting my willy into that then.'

They all laughed. Except Josie. 'It don't bleed all the time, stupid. Only sometimes.'

'Well, I'm glad I ain't a girl,' Jimmy shivered and smiled sympathetically at Josie. The boys all nodded in agreement.

'Anyway,' said Legs who was a bit put out at Josie taking over his secret, 'let's get on with our meeting. We've done sex now.'

'No we ain't,' laughed Del, 'we ain't old enough.' They all started giggling.

'Can we just stop going on about it,' said Josie crossly. Jimmy's got some big news an' all. And it's much more important than sex. He's bin really poorly, nearly died probably and we all know who done it, so let's get it sorted.'

The boys all stopped laughing. Josie could be quite scary sometimes.

'Well,' Jimmy began. 'The witch has made Del and me ill now an' I think I did nearly die, an' what's worst is that she's giving the apples away,' he took a deep breath, 'in a box outside 'er gate.' They all gasped.

'So Eve must have been the first witch then,' said Legs.

'And them apples *are* cursed,' said Del. 'I told you they was.'

'And look how ill Jimmy's bin,' said Josie, 'and he only had one bite.'

'Three,' Del argued. 'He had three bites. I counted. Before I saved 'is life.'

They all sat looking at one another. 'And, even worse,' Josie took over the story, 'Jimmy's mum had some in the house.'

'She ate one an' all,' said Jimmy, 'before I could chuck 'em in the bin.'

Josie patted him on the shoulder. 'Grown-ups are bigger,' she said. 'It would take a lot more than one apple to make *them* poorly.'

'Anyway,' said Jimmy. 'We've got to get up there an' get rid of 'em. Somehow.'

'I say we go up there now an' tip 'em all out,' said Josie.

They looked through the branches of the den. The early morning sky had suddenly darkened. Clouds scuttered across it and they felt drops of cold rain hitting their skin like needles.

'I'd say it was dark enough,' said Jimmy. 'Better for camouflage. Let's go an' do it now. Put your gloves on everyone, we don't want to touch them apples.'

They walked quickly out of Churchill Street, along the overgrown footpath and into Montgomery Road towards the old house. For a few seconds Jimmy remembered his promise to his dad. That he wouldn't go near the witch's house again. He still didn't know how his dad knew her. Another mystery he would have to solve. It couldn't be anything as important as this though.

The sky seemed to grow darker and darker until it was almost like night. The wind came up from nowhere and Jimmy had to hang on to his new cap. Daren't lose another one. Not up here. Sheets of rain stung their faces as they moved slowly along the side of the big house. It was so dark outside but there were no lights on.

'Perhaps she's on holiday,' said Legs, hopefully.

'She might've won the pools,' said Josie. 'Me mum collects her pools money.'

Jimmy shook his head. Witches doing the pools. That didn't sound right.

They crouched behind the hedge and moved slowly up to the front of the house.

'I wonder if witches do sex,' Legs whispered.

'Don't be stupid,' said Josie. 'They live on their own.'

'Well that explains it then,' said Legs.

'Explains what?'

'Why you never see no baby witches.'

***

'There it is!' Jimmy exclaimed as they knelt down at the corner of the front garden. 'The box of apples.'

Through the gloom and the rain they saw the box standing ominously in front of the gate. As they crept towards it they saw the witch's writing on the side. The rain was making it smudge but they could just make out the words, "*PLEASE HELP YOURSELF.*"

They crouched down behind the box. The house was still in darkness. No sound. No movement. Just the rain lashing down and the wind howling.

'Right,' Jimmy whispered. 'Let's get 'em all tipped out now. One on each corner.'

They moved quickly and tipped the box over. It was quite heavy. The red, rosy apples spilled out and rolled along the pavement. The children watched. Mesmerised. Suddenly, and, without warning, there was a flash of lightning. They were caught in a blaze of light. The witch had appeared from nowhere. She was standing at the gate just watching them. Jimmy gasped. How had she got there without them seeing her? Then he realised. Of course, she had flown.

They all stood transfixed. Terrified. Thunder rumbled through the skies. She stood, sniffing the air. Like a wild animal. Her body bent. Her long, black cloak covering her from head to foot. She leant, heavily on her stick and stared intently at the apples, rolling now, into the gutter. 'What are you doing?' She asked quietly.

Her voice was powerful and paralyzing. It seemed to invade their whole beings. Just like when Del had dropped the chewing gum wrapper outside her gate. It was more scary than Miss Parsons when she heard someone swearing in class. It was a voice that made them all unable to move.

85

Jimmy swallowed hard. His legs wouldn't work. He looked round at the others. It was almost like they were playing a game of musical statues in the pouring rain. Oh God, he thought. She's staring. Straight at me. Her eyes looked dark and dangerous. Then she spoke. 'I'm surprised at you children,' she said, still staring straight into his eyes. Jimmy shivered. How could she know *him*? Perhaps it was from when he had climbed the apple tree. When she had been a goat.

Suddenly she moved towards them. She was so fast they all instinctively jumped back. 'So why,' she hissed, standing next to the empty box. 'Why are you doing this ... eh? Do you have nothing better to do than to spy on me? Invade my privacy? Steal from my garden. Do not imagine for one moment that you can frighten me. Believe me I have suffered much worse things in my lifetime. I spit on you all!'

She spat, and the green, venomous liquid glistened on the pavement in front of them. God, thought Jimmy. Witch's spit. What could that do to you?

As the witch turned her head upwards towards the dark sky, Josie picked up one of the fallen apples and stepped forward. The boys gasped. Jimmy put out his hand to pull her back but she shook him off. 'We done it,' she said, her voice shaking, 'because you can't go round p-p-poisoning people wiv these.' She held the apple up above her head. 'It ain't right.'

There was a deep silence. For a few seconds the wind died down. The rain grew light, like whispers on their skin. Josie stepped back and the boys moved towards her.

'If we're going to die,' Jimmy whispered. 'We all die together.'

'Do we have to?' Legs whimpered. 'I think I want my mum.'

At this, the witch threw her head back and roared with laughter. Black tonsils dangled in her evil mouth. She jumped towards them again pointing a gnarled accusing finger. 'Is that what you really think?' she cackled. 'What a good idea. What a good way to get you all out of my life. Now go away and leave me alone.'

Josie looked up. The clouds seemed to be dropping lower from the sky. The rain lashed down again. She could hardly see. It felt like her eyes were drowning. The witch was still shouting at them. Unintelligible words. She was no longer speaking in English. From all around dogs began to howl. And then the sky lit up in one massive flash of sheet lightning. 'Run!' Josie screamed. 'Run!'

As if woken from a trance the children began to move. They could no longer hear the witch, as they ran around the corner and along Montgomery Road. She made no attempt to follow them.

'We ain't dead!' Legs exclaimed, laughing with relief. 'We ain't dead.'

The four friends collapsed in a heap at the end of the path.

'Did you see that lightning?' said Josie. 'It was coming right out of her finger. She done that. I seen her.' They all nodded.

'And all them warts on her face. Ugh,' said Legs. 'She's horrible.'

'She's a bloody nutter,' Del gasped.

'Look,' said Josie. 'The rain. It's stopped.' The sky was clear. It was almost as if the storm had never happened.

They heard the ambulance bells long before they saw the vehicle itself. It passed them at a ferocious pace and turned left, into Churchill Street. The children ran with the little breath they had left.

'What the hell's happened now?' Josie asked.

The ambulance had stopped outside Nellie Bransome's house. The four children stood at the gate. The ambulance men had gone inside by the time they got there.

'She must be poorly,' said Jimmy.

'Ain't surprised,' said Josie. 'Look in the window.'

In the front window of Nellie Bransome's house, between the china dog and the vase of pink chrysanthemums, was a bowl of rosy, red apples.

Chapter 12

'You're losing weight Billy. She don't feed you proper.'

Billy laughed at his mum. She was sitting in his chair by the fire, darning a pair of Jimmy's socks. 'Don't be daft mum. Kate's a good cook. What was wrong wiv that shepherds pie you just had?'

'Yeah, you're right I s'pose, it was lovely. Don't half make a difference now that meat rationing is finished an' all. Yeah, you could've done worse I suppose.'

She sniffed, as if to convey the effort it had taken to actually say those words. Billy waited for the next remark; it was bound to be a criticism. He grinned to himself.

'Don't know why she still has to take him up to bed though. He's nine years old.'

'He likes her to read to him mum.'

'Can't he read himself?'

'Nah, not much. Don't think none of them can at that school. Takes the teachers all their time to keep 'em quiet I should think. Still, don't matter that much does it. I'm alright as long as I can read me paper, he won't need more than that.'

'Well, I ain't so sure,' his mum said. 'World's changing Billy.'

'Well you can't read mum an' you've always got by.'

'Don't mean to say I wouldn't like to,' she retorted. 'Don't know why I can't. The letters just seem all jumbled up. Never where they was supposed to be.'

'Kate would help you if you asked her. She went to grammar school.'

His mum looked outraged at the suggestion. 'No, I ain't asking no-one to help me. You're right son, it ain't important.'

She sighed and held up the perfectly darned sock. 'He'll be in long trousers soon. Things he comes out wiv,' she laughed. 'He's like a little old man.' She lowered her voice. 'It's a shame though, that she can't have no more. Horrible for him growing up all on his own. Couldn't you adopt one or something?'

Billy sat down at the table and picked up his paper. Here we go again, he thought. 'Don't start all that mum.

Anyway, all I remember when we was kids was having to do without cos there was so many of us. And then when one of us did get something, we all fought over it. I was the youngest, I never got nothing,' he laughed.

'Oh, it weren't like that Billy. You do exaggerate.'

'Just saying what I remember, that's all mum. And when dad buggered off ...'

'Stop that swearing Billy and don't talk about yer dad. You know how it upsets me.'

'Sorry mum but all I'm saying is that it ain't the be all and end all to have more than one kid. Half of us don't talk to each other and the other half have buggered ... sorry mum ... moved away. Anyway,' he stood up suddenly and went to get his coat from behind the door, 'I'm off down the pub.'

'Yeah, you go an' have a drink son. 'You work hard, you deserve it. Wrap up warm now, it's taters out there.'

Billy kissed her on the cheek, shouted goodnight to Jimmy and Kate and made his way out into the street. The fog had come down again. Strange weather at the moment, he thought. That thunderstorm this morning, it had just come out of nowhere. Of course Jimmy had got soaked through and Kate had gone mad at him. Wouldn't let him go to the football again. Still, it was only the reserves and he hadn't missed much. They had played like a load of old women and had been lucky to get a draw. He turned his collar up. No point calling for George. He wouldn't go out in this fog, not after his last bout of bronchitis. A large figure loomed beside him. It was Mick. 'Going down the King's Head Billy?'

'Not wiv you I ain't. You're barred.'

'Nah, it's all right now. I seen Arthur. Apologised like.'

They heard footsteps behind them. High heels. 'That you Sal?' Mick asked.

'Yeah,' Sally came alongside them. 'Just going down Dianne's. Didn't realise it was as thick as this or I'd have stayed in. Anyway,' the tone of her voice changed. 'I want words wiv you Mick Tyler.'

'I know, I know,' Mick put his hands up in the air. 'I ain't gonna do it again.'

'You'd better not cos next time I'll pay for someone to sort you out and see how *you* like it.'

'Oh, shut up woman,' he said without malice. 'I can see why no-one married you.'

Billy held his breath. This could get nasty. He looked sideways at Sal. She didn't seem in the slightest taken aback by Mick's remark. She looked lovely an' all.

'I'd rather be on me own for the rest of me life,' she said, 'than end up wiv someone like you.'

'My Maggie don't go on at me like this you know,' he growled. 'She'd be out that bleeding door if she did.'

'She'd be better off if she was,' Sally snapped.

Billy walked, uncomfortably, between them. If anyone else had talked to Mick like that he would have flattened them. Man or woman. They heard someone shuffling towards them as they turned into Montgomery Road. It was Bones, looking agitated.

'Hey you lot. You ain't seen Chuck anywhere have yer?' They all stopped walking.

'Who the fuck's Chuck?' asked Mick. 'Sorry Sal.'

'Me ferret. He's gone missing. I ain't seen him since teatime.'

Billy laughed. 'I don't blame him Bones. He probably ain't met no-one who smells worse than him before.'

'Oh, very funny Billy Potter. He'll get lost in this fog. I'm just a bit worried about 'im.'

'We'll keep our eyes open,' Sally giggled, 'an' we'll bring him home if we see 'im.'

'You speak for yourself,' Billy laughed.

Bones went shuffling off down the road muttering under his breath.

'He's a weirdo,' Mick laughed. 'He don't even drink.'

They couldn't stop laughing as they walked along. Well at least that's eased the tension a bit, thought Billy. He felt excited being this close to Sal. Until last Saturday in the pub he had never really given her much thought. Maybe he was as bad as the others. She wasn't a 'nice girl'. Nice girls didn't have three illegitimate children. He supposed he had always looked down on her a bit. The smell of her perfume made him excited now though. Roses, that's what she smelt of. Summer days. He was glad Mick was there. Anyway, it wouldn't do any harm having a little fantasy.

'Well, this is where I leave you,' she said as they approached Dianne's road.

'You coming in the pub later on?' Billy asked quickly. Now why had he said that? He was a married man. What was he thinking? He didn't know.

'Yeah. Yeah, we might if the Palais is as rubbish as usual,' she laughed.

'See you then,' he said. His voice had come out all squeaky and funny. Oh, grow up Billy, he told himself.

'An' you behave yerself Mick Tyler,' she shouted as she walked away.

'Bloody women,' Mick muttered under his breath.

The pub was almost empty when they walked in. 'Glad someone's come to join me,' said Arthur wearily. 'Hear Nellie Bransome's not so good.'

'In hospital,' said Mick. 'She'll have croaked by the morning. The usual Arthur please.'

'God she used to terrify me when I was a nipper,' Arthur laughed. 'If she caught you doin' anything you shouldn't she used to box you round the ears an' when I told me mum she used to say, '*Well, you must have done something wrong.*' Lost two sons in the Great War an' all. Well, she's had a good run. Not many of that generation left now.'

'All be bleeding black round here next generation,' said Mick grimly.

'Oh come on,' said Billy. 'One family on the whole estate.'

'Well, that's how it starts ennit? You mark my words Billy. Won't be long an' they'll be everywhere.'

Billy picked up his pint and downed half of it in one go. 'Well,' he said, 'they don't bother me.'

'Ah, you say that now,' said Arthur. 'Just wait till they're after your job an' your 'ouse.'

Billy shrugged his shoulders. He might bring his mate from the docks down here one night. Winston. Black as the ace of spades. Everyone gave him a hard time but he took it on the chin. He could just imagine Arthur's face.

'What you laughing at?' Arthur asked him. 'An where are *you* off to?' he shouted at Mick as he slammed his empty glass on to the counter and made towards the door.

'Dogs at Walthamstow. I feel lucky. See you later.'

'Well, just you an' me then Billy. Hey, did you find out who that goat belonged to?'

91

'Yeah. The old Kraut up on Montgomery Road.'

Arthur lowered his voice even though there was no-one to overhear him. 'All sorts of people go in there so I've 'eard. All times of the day and night. An' all women. Young 'uns and old 'uns. And if she *is* a German...

'Oh, she's a German all right. I can't even pronounce her name and I know strange things go on. I've bloody seen 'em.'

'What do you mean Billy?'

'Oh nothing Arthur. She's just weird. Just preys on vulnerable women.'

'Oooh Billy. That was a long word for you.'

Billy laughed. 'Walter Gabriel said it in The Archers the other night. Knew it would come in 'andy.'

'Well, she shouldn't be 'ere, it ain't right. Germans. After what they done.'

'Anyway,' said Billy, changing the subject. 'Why have you let Mick back in?'

'Oh, he put on his pathetic routine. You know what he's like. No more whisky though. That's our agreement and when all's said an' done,' Arthur leant across the bar, 'he sorts out any bother, you know what I mean?'

Yeah, I do, thought Billy. Last bit of bother Mick had sorted had ended up with two blokes in hospital. Still, he wasn't too bad when he was off the whisky. Even so, everyone was relieved when he took off now and again back to the Merchant Navy. He certainly wasn't the only man round here who hit his wife. You never knew what went on behind closed doors.

A few pints later and the pub was getting busy. Billy found himself watching the door, just in case ... Nah, she wouldn't come in. Not when there was all those blokes up the Ilford Palais drooling over her. He bet *she* never went short of a dance.

Then suddenly, she was there. Stood in the doorway. He could hardly breathe.

'Oh no,' Arthur growled. 'Bleeding tarts again.'

'Sally ain't a tart,' said Billy angrily. A little voice in his head told him to be careful. Arthur was looking at him funny already. She smiled at Billy and her and Dianne walked over towards him.

'D'you wanna a drink girls?' he asked, praying that he would have enough money. Ooh he felt much braver now he had sunk a few beers.

'Well you'd better get a move on, it's last orders,' Arthur said sharply. He picked up the bell from the counter and rang it aggressively.

'I don't think he likes us,' Sally giggled.

'Don't take no notice,' said Billy. 'It ain't you. He just don't like women in pubs.'

'Touch of lavender eh?' Dianne laughed.

'Oh don't let him hear you say that. No, he ain't queer he's married. Just wouldn't let 'er come in 'ere that's all. As far as Arthur is concerned, pubs are for men only.'

'Don't mean they ain't at it just cos they're married Billy,' Dianne laughed. 'Sal's brother only goes out wiv married men don't he Sal?' Sally nodded and laughed. 'Yeah, it don't mean nothin' a wedding ring,' she agreed.

Billy pulled a face as he passed the girls their drinks. A bitter lemon for Sal and a gin and tonic for Dianne.

'Ta Billy. Oh look there's Col, I'm just going to have a word wiv him. Won't be long Sal.'

Sally laughed. 'Won't see her again. She's fancied him for ages.' They both watched as Dianne made her way over to Col and his mates.

'The winkle picker brigade,' Sally laughed.

'Go an' join 'em if you want Sal. I don't mind.'

Sally shook her head. 'No, I'm quite comfy here thanks Billy.' She pulled up a stool .'They're a bit young an' daft for me.'

'Any good down the Palais?'

'The music's getting better. They play a bit of rock n' roll now but it's still that borin' old band most of the time and it's just ... well it's a bit like a cattle market Billy, you know what I mean?'

Billy didn't know. For a start he was a man and he hadn't been to the Palais for years. He shook his head and moved a bit closer to her. She didn't seem to mind.

'I mean all the blokes fall out the bar when the slow stuff comes on an' then they walk round the room, lookin' you up and down. It just ain't me really.'

'Bet you get asked to dance a lot though,' he answered.

'I think it's Dianne they're after more than me,' she laughed. They both looked along the bar. Dianne had obviously impressed Col in a very short space of time. They were having a full on snog, their hands all over each other.

'That'll be enough of that,' Arthur shouted. 'I ain't a brothel you know. This is a respectable pub.'

Billy wished he hadn't had that last pint. Sally was beginning to look like Grace Kelly. He would have to watch himself; his mouth seemed to be two miles in front of his brain. 'I'll walk you home if you like,' he said to her as she finished her drink.

'Yeah, alright Billy. Might get lost on me own in this fog,' she laughed. 'I'll just tell Di that I'm going.'

As they walked towards the door everyone looked at them. Billy should have been embarrassed but he had drunk too much. He was walking Grace Kelly home in the fog. And he didn't care who knew about it.

'Lucky bastard,' he heard someone say as they left.

It was eerie but peaceful outside. Just the muffled sounds of the boats on the river. Like you had cotton wool in your ears.

'This is the blind leading the blind,' Sally laughed as Billy tried hard to walk in a straight line along Montgomery Road. When they turned down the footpath he took her hand. For a few seconds she left it there and then she took it away.

'What are you doing Billy?' she asked him angrily.

'Sorry Sal, I'm just a bit pissed.'

He grabbed her shoulders then and bent his head down towards hers. When he began to kiss her, Sally resisted for a few seconds, before she responded fervently. Passion and desire flooded both their bodies. Billy began to move his hands all over her, pulling her closer towards him. Suddenly she clung to his arm and screamed. 'Billy, Billy. Something's just run up me legs!'

'Well it ain't me,' he slurred, moving back and almost falling over. 'I've only got two hands.' They both looked down and saw a flash of white fur running away from them. 'I think we just found Old Bone's ferret,' Billy laughed.

'Quick, catch him Billy, before he runs into them bushes.'

They were both giggling uncontrollably. The fresh air and seven pints had caught up with Billy now, he was beyond catching anything. He took one step and fell flat on his face. It was Sally who crawled into the undergrowth and came back carrying Chuck tightly in her grip. 'I'll take him home to Old Bones,' she said. 'You go on Billy. If you can walk that is.'

Billy managed to get to his feet. As Sally walked off still giggling in the opposite direction, he took a deep breath. What a prat, he thought to himself. Why had he kissed her like that? Who did he think he was? One of the winkle picker brigade? Free and single? Come on Billy, he told himself as he came through his front gate. Please don't end up like your dad. No, he wasn't like his dad. He wasn't always looking at other women. He had been married for ten years now and it hadn't been easy. Still, it wasn't supposed to be was it?

The landing light was on and their bedroom door open. Billy quickly took his clothes off, got into his pyjamas in the semi-darkness and jumped into the bed.

'Hello love,' he whispered. He heard Kate sigh. He could just pretend now. Pretend she was someone else. He snuggled into Kate's neck and smelt Sally's roses.

'Get off Billy. Your mum's next door.'

'Kate, this is our house and we're married. We're allowed to do it you know.'

'Don't talk so loud, you'll wake her up and I'm sorry but I'm tired and you stink of booze.'

Billy lay on his back. The room was going round and round. He slipped dizzily into sleep. What was Jimmy doing here? He was smiling as he floated above him. And offering him a red, rosy apple. Sprinkled with dew. 'Here dad, I picked this for you meself.' He tried to reach it but he couldn't. It seemed the most important thing in the world. And Jimmy kept laughing at him, laughing and laughing. He woke up suddenly and groaned. He was going to throw up. As he rolled out of bed, Kate stirred.

'Are you alright?' she murmured sleepily.

Don't you be nice to me, he thought. Not now.

Chapter 13

It had been an ordinary sort of day at school. Jimmy had spent most of the time looking out the window thinking about the witch. They had to find out how to stop her hurting people. They couldn't let it just go on.

Miss Parsons was reading them a story. This was the best bit of the day. She was alright really, for a teacher. She never threw chalk at you or shouted and she never sent anyone to the head for a caning. Sometimes she talked about quite exciting stuff. They had even been chatting about rock n' roll yesterday. He wanted to tell her that his Auntie Molly said that it was the devil's music, but when Miss Parsons said that she thought some of it was quite good, he thought he had better not.

She was dark haired like his mum but she put it back in a sort of ponytail. She was quite plump and had big titties as Del kept reminding them all. He wondered if she had a boyfriend and if they did sex. Josie said you could only do it if you were married. Del had told her that if that was true she wouldn't even exist. She had sort of agreed. Maybe it was just another grown up lie, like the Father Christmas one, Jimmy thought.

The story was coming to an end. It had been a long book and he had missed all last week so he really didn't have a clue what it was about. Too many words he didn't understand. Still, it was written in the old days. He wished she would read them The Secret Seven like his mum did but it was quite nice, just listening to her soft voice.

'There,' she said. 'That was The Water Babies. How did you like that ending?'

'Alright I s'pose,' Del yawned.

'Not very exciting,' said another.

Miss Parsons smiled. 'Well, we'll try and find something a bit more riveting next time shall we?'

A small ginger haired boy at the front put his hand up. 'Can we have a book about the war miss?' he asked. 'Us against the Germans?'

'Well Jeffrey, the war did finish ten years ago now. We don't fight the Germans anymore.'

'My dad says there's still some left,' said Del knowledgeably.

'Yes, that's true Derek but we should all try and be friends now shouldn't we?'

Jimmy put his hand up. 'Yes you can go to the toilet Jimmy,' said Miss Parsons.

'No, I don't need to miss. I wanted to ask if we could have a story about witches.'

There was a murmur of approval around the class. Del kicked him sharply under the desk. 'Shut up,' he muttered.

'Well, that's different Jimmy. Are you interested in witches?'

'Yeah, in spells an' stuff mostly miss.'

'Would anyone else be interested?'

Del was the only one who kept his hand down.

'I'll have to see what I can find,' she said.

'And I wondered,' Jimmy put his hand up again. He didn't want to miss this chance. He prayed that the bell wouldn't ring yet. 'How do child ... How do you stop witches doing bad things?' Del kicked him again. Harder this time.

'They used to say that if you were baptised witches could never harm you but that was a long time ago. We don't believe in witches now do we?' She smiled at Jimmy and it made him feel all warm inside. He supposed that she wasn't used to him asking questions. Except when he asked to go to the lavs of course.

'You're not going to tell me that that's why you were off sick last week is it? Were you bewitched Jimmy Potter?' she laughed. The class all began to titter. Jimmy opened and closed his mouth like a goldfish. How could she know?

'Fuckin' shut up now!' Del hissed.

'Miss, miss. Del just said a rude word.'

'Yes Pamela. I heard him. I don't need you to tell tales thank you.'

Miss Parsons didn't like swearing. Her face had changed. It was scary when she got angry. She spoke very softly still, but she sounded hard and cold, it made you shiver. 'Derek, come out here please.' Del glared at Jimmy as he walked out to the front of the class. 'Go and stand outside the door. I'll deal with you after the lesson has finished.' Del walked slowly towards the door.

Jimmy felt a bit guilty but he didn't understand why Del was upset. They had to find out how to stop the witch.

97

Him and Del had both been ill and Mrs. Bransome was very poorly and now he had found out what they had to do. Josie would know because she knew all about God so they could all get baptised. That shouldn't be too difficult.

***

'Here he comes,' said Legs as he and Jimmy waited outside the school gates for Del. Jimmy tried to look confident but Del looked pretty angry. Anyway it wasn't his fault. They had to find out how to make things right.

'Ain't speaking to you Jimmy Potter,' Del growled. 'I got detention now cos of you. You're lucky I don't hit yer.'

'You can't. It's in our Code.'

'Yeah well, I ain't speaking to yer anyway.'

Jimmy shrugged his shoulders. Legs, who had removed himself to a safe distance in case there was violence, rejoined them as they wandered up the road.

'Bet I know what lines you've got to write in detention,' he laughed. 'I bet you've got to write "I must not say fuck" a hundred times.'

'He wouldn't know how to spell it,' Jimmy laughed. They had to hold on to their stomachs they were giggling so much. Eventually Del joined in too. Until he remembered why he was so angry with Jimmy. 'Anyway,' he whispered, looking around to see if they were alone, 'what was you asking her about witches for? She's our witch. Ain't no-one else's.'

'Yeah but,' said Legs hesitantly, 'now we know what to do to stop her making us ill. We have to get christened again. It probably wears off by the time you get to our age.'

'Well I ain't been christened, 'said Del. 'and I don't believe in all that shit.'

'Hope he can't hear you,' Jimmy looked up to the sky, 'up there.'

'So,' said Legs, 'now we just have to find out how to do it.'

'Well,' said Jimmy, 'Josie will know, her being a Catholic. We could go and wait for 'er at the bus stop.'

'She don't like us doing that,' said Del. 'Remember when we met 'er off the bus before an' all them kids started calling her names an' stuff.'

98

'They called her a tart,' said Jimmy. 'I remember now. Said she was a tart like her mum just cos she likes playing with boys. Ain't fair that.'

'We'll go an' call for her later then,' said Legs.

'Yeah I suppose,' said Del. 'Ooh, look, the sambos are out playing.'

They had just come through the other end of the estate. A family of West Indians had moved into the house they were passing. Two little girls stood by the rusting gate, wearing matching yellow frilly frocks and large, pink ribbons in their tightly curled hair. They looked cold and a bit lost. Del and Legs immediately started doing ape impressions, jumping up and down and making the appropriate noises.

'Come on Jimmy,' said Del. 'This is a good laugh.'

Jimmy wasn't so sure but he didn't want to upset Del again today so he joined in. The two little girls were laughing anyway. They didn't seem to mind.

'They're so thick,' said Del. 'They don't even know we're taking the piss.'

'Good job Josie didn't see us,' Legs laughed. 'They're all God's children, she'd have said. She would have gone right off.'

Del laughed. 'Well, my dad says that they're worse than the Germans. And he *hates* them.'

'Your dad hates everyone,' said Jimmy. 'They don't bother me.'

The three boys made their way home and agreed to meet in the den in half an hour. Jimmy knew something was wrong as soon as he opened their back door. His mum and May Pattinson were sat at the table. The cracked blue teapot in the centre. His mum was crying and he knew straight away what had happened. She wiped her eyes with her hankie. 'Sorry Jimmy. We've just had some bad news. Nellie ... Mrs. Bransome has died.'

Jimmy swallowed hard. That was it then. The witch had killed someone.

'Do you want a sugar sandwich love?' His mum got up and sniffed.

'I'd best get in and get something for Clive,' said Leg's mum. 'They're always so hungry when they come in from school. I don't know where they put it all.'

She smiled at Jimmy as she got up to leave.

'I don't want nothing,' said Jimmy, 'I'm off out.'

As he ran through the front gate Del was running towards him. 'Have you heard?' he asked unnecessarily. Jimmy nodded. 'Right, we have to get Legs and go an' meet Jose whether she likes it or not. We 'ave to do something now Del.'

'Yeah, we have to do something but God ain't gonna help.'

It seemed an age waiting at the bus stop for Josie. At last, the old red bus came trundling up the road and hordes of noisy children disembarked.

'Ooh Josie,' teased one of them. 'Your boyfriends are all here again.'

'Shut up Peter,' she snapped and looked angrily at her friends.

'Sorry Jose,' said Jimmy, 'but it's an emergency. We need to get to the den an' sort it out. We can't talk at the bus stop. Someone might 'ear us.'

When they were all sitting comfortably in the den they told Josie everything that had happened.

'So, she's killed someone,' Josie whispered.

'But now we know what to do,' said Legs. 'Well, we hope *you* do.'

They told Josie what Miss Parsons had said about witches and how they all needed to be baptised. She took a deep breath and thought about it for a few seconds.

'Perhaps as it's a special occasion,' said Legs, 'we could have a biscuit. I'm starving.'

'How can you think about food at a time like this?' Josie asked.

'I think we should,' said Jimmy. 'Just to keep our strength up.'

They all munched quietly for a few moments.

'We'll do it in the den,' said Josie finally. 'The baptisms. At night when it's dark. I'll get some holy water an' I'll bring my statue of the Virgin Mary.'

'What's a Virgin Mary?' asked Del.

'She's Jesus' mum,' said Jimmy. 'Don't you know nothing?'

'Do we have to have the whole family?' Del asked. He stood up. 'I think this is a rubbish idea. I don't believe in God. There ain't no-one up there.'

100

'Right,' said Jimmy. 'We'll have a vote then. We've got to do something Del.'

'We could kill one of 'er cats,' said Del.

'No!' Josie shouted. 'We ain't doing that. Come on, let's vote. Hands up if you wanna do a baptism.'

Jimmy and Josie put their hands up straightaway, Legs was more reluctant. He looked at Del who had kept his hands firmly by his side. 'Well, I dunno. I don't want to hurt any animals but if Del doesn't agree...'

'So what *do* you wanna do?' Jimmy asked. 'Just do nothing till she kills someone else?'

Legs raised his hand slowly and glared at Jimmy. 'I'm only voting for it because Miss Parsons says, not because you and Josie do. Sorry Del.'

Del shrugged his shoulders. 'Ain't got much choice then 'ave I?'

They all spat into their hands and shook on it.

'We'd better do it soon, or she'll get us an' all,' said Legs.

'Next Sunday,' said Josie. 'Because it's a holy day. Just after midnight.'

'How are we going to get out then?' Del asked.

'If you bang your head on the pillow twelve times on Saturday night when you go to bed,' she said, 'that'll wake you up at midnight, an' then just creep out. They'll all be asleep then. We could do a communion an' all.'

'What's that?' Legs asked.

'You eat the body of Christ and you drink his blood.'

The boys all pulled faces. 'Well, I ain't eating no dead body you can stuff that for a lark,' said Del. 'Don't mind the blood bit though.'

'It ain't real blood and bodies stupid. We 'ave to use bread and wine.'

'We got sherry,' said Legs.

'That'll do,' said Josie.

'We need to make a list of all the stuff we need,' said Jimmy, 'an' then she'll never ever be able to hurt us again.'

'I'll believe that when it 'appens,' said Del. 'I still think we should ...'

'No Del!' they all shouted in unison.

'Alright, baptism it is then but it won't work.'

101

They all nodded to each other as they made their separate ways home for tea.

Chapter 14

Billy had come home early from work. He wasn't happy. The ship he was supposed to be unloading was late in so he'd been laid off for the day. That meant less money in the kitty this week.

And, he was embarrassed about Saturday night. Two of his so called mates from work had been winding him up all day about leaving the pub with Sally. Oh, of course nothing much had happened but they didn't believe that. How could he have been so stupid? He hoped to God that Kate wouldn't find out. Maybe she had heard something already; perhaps that was why she was crying now. He held his breath as he looked at her.

'I can't stop thinking about Nellie being dead,' she sniffed.

Billy heaved a sigh of relief. 'That was two days ago love. She was your mum's friend not yours. Come on, I'll get you a cuppa.'

Kate wiped her eyes with her hankie and watched Billy put the kettle on.

'I remember her babysitting me once. Mum and dad had gone out to a dance. They hardly ever went out. Mum had looked lovely. She had a beautiful blue velvet dress on. From Auntie Doris of course. She had blue high heels too. No idea how she could have afforded them. I think my dad must have had plenty of work then. He looked really handsome in a double-breasted suit. They looked so happy, so full of life. I just remember feeling so proud. So proud that they were my...'

'Hey, Kate, don't take on. You've still got me an' Jimmy.' Billy put his arm round her shoulders as she began to cry again.

'I'll tell you something that'll make you laugh,' he said, sitting in his chair and lighting up a cigarette. 'George was telling me that he's just had a talk wiv Legs about the birds an' the bees. They'll all know about it now.'

'But they're too young to be thinking about all that Billy. It's not nice. I wonder if that's why ... '

'What?'

'Well, Jimmy's just been acting a bit strange lately. Perhaps it's upset him. He's such a little worrier.'

103

Billy snorted. 'Rubbish. One of the best bits of news I ever had that was.'

Kate blushed and went over to the boiling kettle which Billy had completely forgotten about. 'He's not you Billy, he's different.'

'Oh, it's slagging off Billy time again is it?'

'I'm just saying that he's a sensitive little boy that's all. He's not like the others. They get him into all sorts of trouble especially that Del. He'd be much better away from here.'

He saw tears welling up in her eyes again. 'We ain't moving nowhere Kate. He's fine where he is, and he's quite happy. He's just a normal kid and you just fuss over 'im too much.'

'Molly is thinking about emigrating,' she said quietly, 'to Australia.'

'Well, that's 'er business an' I know you'll miss her but we ain't going wiv her Kate, an' that's final. An' if you don't get a move on you'll be late for your shift. Don't know why you volunteer for overtime, it puts us all out.'

'I hardly ever do lates Billy and your tea's always on the table before I go. It's you that's always moaning about us being broke. Why are you so grumpy? I'd love to be given a day off work.'

'You won't be saying that at the end of the week when me wages are down.'

'Money isn't everything,' she answered as she put her coat on. 'I hope Jimmy gets a job he likes when he grows up.'

'You ain't meant to *enjoy* work,' Billy laughed, 'It's just what you have to do. You ain't in the real world sometimes Kate. You'd still have to work in a factory in Australia. It ain't all lying on beaches an' getting a suntan.'

'I know that but I just think he would have a better chance. He can hardly read Billy.' She made her way to the door. 'And can you have a word with him when he comes in? You know, about the birds and the bees. Make sure he's got it straight. I don't want him to get in a muddle about it.'

Billy shook his paper and opened it. He looked at his wife. She hadn't done her hair properly today and she didn't have any lipstick on. It didn't look as if she had even glanced in the mirror. He hoped she wasn't going to be ill again. That

104

was sometimes how it all started. 'Yeah, yeah,' he said. 'I'll mention it. An' cheer up love, it'll be Christmas soon.'

'Oh well, that makes everything alright then,' she said as she closed the door.

***

It was lunchtime in the factory. The noise in the staff canteen was even louder than on the factory floor, it just smelt a bit better in there.

'Hey I want a word wiv you,' Dianne tapped Sally on the shoulder, 'about Saturday.'

'What about Saturday?' Sally asked quickly.

'We'll go an' sit in a two seater by the window.'

'The two-seaters are full of girls wanting a private gossip Dianne, you know that. I ain't got nothing to hide. Have you?'

Sally knew exactly what her friend was on about. She could feel herself blushing.

'Come on,' Dianne guided Sally towards a spare two seater.

'So,' Dianne started, playing with her shepherds pie, 'what happened wiv you an' Billy then?'

'Nothing happened Di. We just left the pub together that's all. We nearly live next door to each other for goodness sake. Anyway, what about you an' that Col. You was snogging the face off 'im.'

'That's different. He ain't married. Anyway, don't you change the subject. I seen the way you looked at each other.

'I'm surprised you 'ad the time to notice anyone else, you hardly came up for air. You seriously pissed Arthur off an' all.'

'This conversation ain't about me. It's about you. Come on Sal, how long have we known each other? Nearly all our lives. You've always told me everything.'

'There ain't nothin' to tell. How many times do I have to say it?'

'You don't fancy him then?'

Sally shook her head. Dianne was looking at her. *Really* looking at her.

'Well alright, but this is between you an' me. We waited till we got to the little alleyway from Montgomery Street and we made mad passionate love right there. Against the wall. Then we went an' done it again in me

105

garden shed an' then for a third time in me flower bed. You know, the one where I have me busy lizzies. Is that good enough for yer?'

Dianne laughed, and then waited.

'I do fancy 'im. Who wouldn't?' said Sally eventually. He's bloody gorgeous but all he did was snog me. Just the once, that's all. Then Chuck ran up me legs so I had to take him back to Old Bones and Billy went home on his own. That's it. Alright?'

'Who the hell's Chuck?' Dianne asked.

'Chuck is Old Bone's ferret, he'd escaped. Dianne, this ain't something I could make up if I tried.'

Dianne was in fits of laughter, eventually Sally joined in.

'So – So you think Billy Potter fancies me then?'

'Well I doubt if he gets into Kate's knickers very often so I reckon you'd be in wiv a very good chance.'

Across the room they saw Kate making her way towards the tea counter.

'I ain't doing nothing,' said Sally. 'I can't. Nor can he. And ...' she leaned in close to Dianne and whispered angrily. 'There ain't nothing happening so get it out of yer head.'

Dianne stood up as the bell rang. That signalled that they had five minutes left. 'Well I'd best get started early. I'm on wiv Julie again. Can't wait. See you later Sal.'

'Yeah and Dianne ... '

Too late, she'd gone, swinging her hips through the crowded cafe. Laughing at the wolf whistles from the workmen who were in this week fixing the machines. Sally smiled. That was her friend all over. Anything for attention. But she was a good mate. She had been going to ask her not to say anything about Billy to Julie Tyler but it didn't matter. She wouldn't be that daft.

Chapter 15

It was Saturday afternoon and it had felt like a really long day to Sally already. The rain had been relentless. The babies had been grumpy since five this morning. Why did they have to always be cutting a tooth at the same time she wondered. Dianne wouldn't be popping in; she was off for the weekend somewhere with Col.

Josie and her mates had been traipsing in and out all day. It was raining too hard even for them to get up to whatever they usually did. They had been up in Josie's bedroom for ages. When Sally had asked them what they were doing they had all looked really guilty.

'Just talking,' Josie had said quickly. 'Can we have some biscuits mum? Them nice pink ones?'

'Oh, go on then,' Sally had laughed.

No night out to look forward to tonight either, with Dianne away. There was something about Saturday nights in that was really depressing. Just her and the wireless. And she wouldn't see Billy. She was finding it difficult to stop thinking about him. Oh, she knew he had been really pissed when he had kissed her but it wasn't half a nice kiss, she thought. Not all men could kiss like that. She had never really noticed him before. Her and Dianne had only just started going in to the King's Head. She wondered if ... no. Stop it, she told herself. He's married and he lives two doors away. Not only that but she worked with his wife. She had to stop doing these stupid, self-destructive things. No, it was good that she wasn't going out tonight. She would meet someone one day, someone who didn't belong to anyone else.

She sighed and watched Julie Tyler as she played with Christopher on the floor. At least she was keeping him happy and Peter was asleep in the playpen. Julie often called in. She wasn't any trouble and Sally didn't blame her for wanting to get out of that house sometimes. 'Hope them kids ain't playing doctors an' nurses up there,' Sally laughed. Julie didn't even smile. She rarely did. 'I suppose I'll have to have another chat wiv Jose,' said Sally, realising that she was really talking to herself. Julie seemed to be on another planet today.

'They know it all,' said Julie quietly. 'Mr. Pattinson told Legs an' he told the others.'

Sally laughed. 'Oh my gawd. I hate to think what Legsy has told them. I'll definitely have to talk to her now.'

Christopher was beginning to get agitated. Sally lifted him up off the floor, put him in the playpen and gave him his dummy. His eyes had almost closed by the time she sat back down at the table. Julie was looking at her.

'Talking about doctors an' nurses Sal,' she said, looking away from Sally's gaze, 'that Dianne's bin saying stuff at the factory. About you an' Billy.'

Sally felt like someone had slapped her around the face. For a few seconds she found it difficult to breathe.

'I'm telling you because you're a mate. You think she's your best friend but she ain't, she's bin saying bad things. I just thought you'd wanna know.'

Sally took a deep breath. She would rather just ignore what Julie had told her but she couldn't. Not now. She had to find out. 'What exactly 'as she said Julie? Look at me an' tell me the truth.'

'She's just saying that you're at it like rabbits. You an' Billy.'

Sally banged her fist on the table. Christopher stirred and whimpered in his sleep. 'It ain't true Julie,' Sally hissed. 'Are you sure that's what she's saying cos if it is I'll bleedin' kill her.'

Julie smirked. 'That's what she told me Sal, honest.' She stood up. 'Anyway, I'd best be off. Ain't you going out tonight Sal?'

'No, Dianne's away. I'll bloody see her first thing on Monday though. She ain't getting away wiv this.'

'Well, me an' Freddie might pop round later then.'

Oh no, thought Sally. I can't cope with him. 'Actually Julie, I've got a bit of an' 'eadache, I'll probably have an early night.'

She stood up, encouraging Julie to go. Julie slouched towards the back door. 'Didn't mean to upset you Sal,' she said quietly. 'Just tryin' to be a good mate that's all.'

Sally put her arm around Julie's shoulders. She flinched. 'You *are* a good mate Julie an' I am glad you told me but please don't say nothing about it to no-one else. Remember it ain't true.' Julie nodded.

108

'An' you an' Freddie,' she added. 'Just be careful. You know what I mean.'

Julie left by the back door and walked slowly across the road. Sally had a vision in her head of how things would be in twenty years time. Julie with six kids walking home to a brute of a husband. Just like Maggie.

***

'Are you sure you don't mind missing a Saturday night down the pub Billy?'

Kate was putting on her coat. Auntie Molly stood next to her, clucking as she flicked a bit of fluff from Kate's shoulders.

'Course he doesn't mind,' she said. 'Won't do him any harm to let you have a night out once in a while.'

Billy forced a smile. He tried to put up with Molly. She was the only family Kate had left in this country. But it wasn't easy. Still, it was him who had suggested Saturday night when Kate had kept going on about "Oklahoma".

'Molly will go wiv you,' he'd said. 'I'll stay in. Listen to the wireless.' He had said it quickly, before he could change his mind. He had felt guilty somehow after the walk home with Sally. He knew it was only a kiss, but something had happened. In *his* head anyway. That was another reason he didn't want to go to the King's Head tonight. She might be there and he would be really embarrassed.

He had suggested "Oklahoma" to Kate on the Thursday and then, yesterday, as he had opened the front door, he had seen Sally out of the corner of his eye, pushing the pram out of her gate. He had totally panicked.

'That was a quick shift,' said Kate, as he had come back into the house.

'Er ... yeah. I just forgot something.' Flustered, he had opened and shut all the kitchen cupboards noisily.

'Well, what have you lost?'

'Dunno. I think it's upstairs.' He had moved towards the hall.

'You think what's upstairs?'

'Oh shut up nagging Kate. I need to go to the lav now.'

'Oh and that's my fault as well is it?'

Oh God, he had thought, lighting up a cigarette in the safe haven of the locked bathroom. This is ridiculous. A memory had come back to him suddenly. Spotty Susan Crabtree. When he was sixteen. She had pursued him relentlessly for over a year. He had often had to hide in the outside lav that year, even during a bomb raid once. But he wasn't sixteen now. He was a married man with a child but, sometimes he had thought, nothing in life ever seemed to change. And he couldn't hurt Kate. She had had enough pain in her life already.

She looked really excited to be going out, all flushed and alive. He supposed that *he* really should take her out sometimes but she wouldn't go in pubs and he certainly wasn't going to watch "Oklahoma".

'We'll be back by ten,' she said. 'Make sure Jimmy's in bed by seven.'

The door closed and they were gone. Billy turned the wireless on. A boring quiz programme. Well, he supposed he could sort his shed out. That would give him something to do. He got up and opened the back door. Jimmy was coming out of the shed with something in his hand. 'What you got there son?'

'Just the torch dad.'

'What for?'

'Just need it for a bit.'

'Well don't lose it. Oh and by the way has Legs told yer about ... you know ... how babies are made?'

'Yeah. I know all about sex now dad.'

Billy smiled to himself. 'An' there ain't nothin' you need to ask me?'

'No thanks dad, I think I get it.'

Jimmy started making his way out towards the stairs.

'Where are you off to? I could do wiv your help clearing out me shed.'

Jimmy looked at his dad, yawned in a very exaggerated manner and took a deep breath. 'Nah, I'm going to bed dad. I'm a bit tired.'

Billy looked at his watch. It wasn't even seven o'clock. Puzzled, he began to walk out to the shed. No, he thought, that kid's up to something. Since when did he volunteer to go to bed early on a Saturday night? He walked up the stairs quietly and into his son's bedroom. Jimmy was in bed, in his jamas and banging his head on the pillow.

110

What you doing that for? 'Billy asked him. 'There's something wrong wiv you tonight. You ain't right.'

'You should knock when you come in me room dad.'

'Don't you be giving me no lip son. Just make sure you wake up in a better frame of mind.'

Jimmy turned his back to Billy. 'Night dad.'

'Night son.'

Billy went back slowly downstairs. God, it wasn't just the shed that needed sorting out in this house he thought.

Chapter 16

It was just past midnight on Sunday morning. Churchill Street was quiet. It was a cold and windy night but the sky was clear as the four friends made their way towards the den. Jimmy was at the front with the torch and Josie carried her bundle of holy equipment. Legs struggled with the large bottle of sherry which he had hidden under his bed for two days. Jimmy had half a loaf of stale bread which his mum had left out for the birds. Del lagged behind. He hadn't brought anything. He didn't see any point. It was all a load of rubbish. Still, it was an adventure just being out this late he supposed.

They all wore their plimsolls so there would be no sound. They were ready. The torch wouldn't work properly though and Jimmy kept having to shake it.

As they reached the end of the road there were no more street lights and it was very dark. They made their way carefully across the wasteland towards the den. The thin beam of the torch didn't seem to shine far enough ahead.

'It's as black as hell,' said Josie dramatically. Scared but excited like they all were. None of them had ever been out this late before.

'Hell's red,' said Legs nervously. 'I seen it in a picture.'

The torch flickered and died just as they approached the den. Somewhere, an owl hooted. It sounded far away.

'I don't like owls,' said Legs. 'I think I might not stay long.'

'Owls can't hurt yer,' said Josie.

'What do you get when you cross an owl wiv a mouse?'

'It ain't the time for jokes Del.' Josie sniffed.

'A dead mouse,' Jimmy answered. 'I seen it in the Beano an' all.'

'Well, we're 'ere now,' said Josie as they groped their way into the den and found the candles. They seemed to light alright even though the wind was getting up.

'Right,' said Legs. 'Are we all here, only I can't stay too long.'

'What sort of question is that? You're still asleep mate,' Del said. 'We all just walked up the road together.' He cuffed Legs round the head.

Josie placed the candles at the furthest end of the den and put the statue of the Virgin Mary in front of them. The light shone on her face and somehow she looked sort of alive and warm.

Even Del felt a bit impressed. 'She weren't bad looking. Quite pretty,' he said quietly.

They all felt at peace somehow with the silence and the candlelight. And each other. Josie poured some water into a bowl. 'It's holy water,' she said reverently. 'Jesus has blessed it.'

'Must be old then,' said Legs.

'I ain't drinking old water,' said Del.

'You don't drink it stupid. I'm just going to do the sign of the cross on yer forehead wiv it and say a prayer.'

'We can drink the sherry though can't we?' Legs pulled the bottle out from under his mac.

'Not till we've done the baptisms,' said Josie. 'We've all got to be quiet now, while I'm doin' it. You'll have to baptise me Jimmy, so watch what I do.'

'You're a bleeding bossy boots tonight,' Del muttered, taking the bottle from Legs and having a swig out of it. Josie glared at him.

'D'you wanna be protected from the witch or ain't you bothered? Cos God won't be well pleased wiv you. An' no swearing an' all. He don't like it.'

Del giggled quietly and took another gulp of sherry. Josie coughed. 'Now, we all 'ave to close our eyes an' put our hands together. Let us pray.'

Del passed the sherry to Jimmy before he closed his eyes.

'Hail Mary, full of grace, the Lord is with thee and blessed is the fruit of thy womb Jesus.' Josie's voice was soft and hypnotising. The silence in the den was almost overwhelming. She brought the holy water, first to Del. 'I baptise thee. In the name of the Father, the Son and the Holy Ghost. Amen. You all have to say Amen now,' she prompted as she made the sign of the cross on Del's forehead with the holy water. It trickled down his cheeks and into his mouth but he hardly noticed. The most strange

113

feeling was coming over him. Like his whole body was being filled with everything he liked. Smarties, fish an' chips, Davy Crockett, coca cola. As if everything magical was now inside him and filling up all his empty spaces. He felt completely at peace. It was a feeling he had never had before. Was this God? He asked himself quietly. He turned to Jimmy. He was having a swig of the sherry.

'Is this what God feels like?' he asked him.

'Nah,' Legs answered. 'It'll be the sherry Del.'

'Come on, stop nattering,' Josie nagged. 'You all 'ave to say Amen together.'

'Amen.' They all spoke quietly. Josie did the same again with Jimmy and Legs. 'Can you remember the words Jimmy?' she asked. He shook his head. 'Well, I'll say the words for meself but you'll have to do me water.'

All had been still during the baptisms but now the wind blew up again and they heard the owl. Closer this time. It hooted twice. Legs jumped up.

'I don't like this now, let's go.'

'Here, Legs, have a drink of sherry. Pass it to him Jimmy.'

Jimmy had sipped a few mouthfuls. He didn't like the taste much but it was making him feel all cosy inside. Legs took one mouthful and spat it out.

'Ugh, that's horrible.' He passed it back to Del.

'Well, I ain't drinking it neither,' said Josie.

'Me an' Jimmy will just finish it off then,' Del laughed.

As the two boys carried on drinking, the wind began to rock the den. The candles suddenly went out.

'The witch is angry,' said Legs. 'She's out there. I know she is. We need to get home now.'

'We ain't done our Communion yet,' said Josie.

'Well, we're doing our best wiv the sherry,' Jimmy giggled.

'An' the bread ain't no good, it's mouldy. Anyways, she can't hurt us now an' we don't need no commu ... no commu,' Del laughed, 'whatever the word is.'

'You two are getting drunk,' said Josie crossly. 'You're disgustin.'

Jimmy and Del could not stop laughing. Tears were rolling down their cheeks. Del tried to stop but his mouth wouldn't go back to where it belonged. He put his arm round

Jimmy. 'You're me mate,' he said. 'I ain't forgot that you give me a penny.'

'An' you're my mate an' all. An' Legs. An' Jose.'

'Yeah, we're all mates. For ever and ever. Amen.'

The two boys started laughing uncontrollably again. The owl hooted. It sounded very near.

'We need another prayer,' said Josie quickly. 'Come on Legs, *we'll* have to do it.'

'Then can we go home?' Legs asked tearfully.

'Our Father who art in Heaven please protect us an' everyone else from the witch. She is evil. Please do this and we will love you for ever and ever. Amen'

'That weren't a proper prayer,' Del slurred. 'You made that up.'

The branches on the trees and bushes were making a dreadful noise. The children held on tightly to each other in the dark. Branches began to hit their corrugated iron roof and the wind howled through the den.

'It'll be alright,' said Josie. 'She'll go away in a minute.'

'Try the torch again Del,' said Legs. 'This dark is horrible.'

Del fumbled around and found the torch. His head didn't feel right now, it was spinning around. He pressed the switch and the torchlight came on. Only just, but at least it was something. He shone the light on the Virgin Mary, only it wasn't her any more. It was the owl. She stared at them. Unblinking. Her eyes wild and dangerous. And then she hooted. Three times.

'Get out!' Josie screamed. 'She's in our den. The witch is in our den!'

They ran and stumbled out onto the wasteland. All except Del.

'Where is he?' Josie shouted. 'We can't leave him in there. Not wiv the witch.'

'I can't get him,' Jimmy cried, 'I ain't well.'

Josie looked at Legs. Why were boys so bloody useless?

'Well, I ain't goin' back in there,' said Legs predictably. Josie ran back into the den. The witch had gone and Del had collapsed in a heap. He was groaning and had been sick all over his school mac.

'Ugh,' said Legs who had followed Josie in reluctantly. 'He's thrown up.' He picked up the flickering torch and helped Josie to drag Del outside.

'It's that sherry,' said Josie. 'We'll have to get him home.'

'I don't feel well neither,' said Jimmy. 'I think I might be sick an' all.'

'Well, keep away from me then,' said Legs.

They scarcely noticed that the wind had died down. Jimmy looked up. The stars seemed to be jumping up and down. He just about managed to stumble across the waste. Josie and Legs had to drag Del across the rough grass. He was still clutching the bottle of sherry.

'I can hear voices,' said Legs. He switched the torch off and they dived to the ground. All except Jimmy, who didn't care what happened to him now.

'Jimmy? Is that you son? Are you there?'

'Yeah, I'm here dad. I'm proper poorly.'

'Get down,' Legs hissed but Jimmy didn't hear him. He wanted his dad. He wanted him to tuck him up in bed and take away the pain. They all blinked in the light of a powerful torch. Oh no, it wasn't just Jimmy's dad but mad Mick Tyler as well. Del would really be in for it now.

'Get up Del,' he said menacingly. Del tried to stand but he collapsed into a heap at his dad's feet.

'He's bin sick,' said Josie. 'He ain't well. Don't hurt him.'

'I ain't well neither,' said Jimmy starting to cry.

'I'll knock seven bells of shit out of you when I get you home,' Mick Tyler growled. 'Sick or not sick.' He grabbed Del by the collar and pulled him up. The bottle of sherry fell to the ground, the last dregs spilling onto the grass.

Del looked up at his dad, his eyes soft and glazed. 'You can't hurt me now dad,' he slurred. Cos I got God.'

***

'I can go in on me own,' said Josie sulkily as Billy dragged Jimmy through her gate.

'I'm just making sure you get there,' said Billy. 'I don't know what you lot have bin up to but for some reason I don't trust you Josie. Your mum'll be worried sick.'

116

'She won't care,' said Josie defiantly. 'She don't care if I'm 'ere or not.'

God, what a night, Billy thought. Kate had got up to go to the toilet and then he had heard her scream. 'Billy! Billy! Jimmy's gone! He's not in his bed.'

'Don't be daft. Where else would he be?'

'Well come and see if you don't believe me. Oh my God, perhaps someone's kidnapped him!'

'Who on earth would kidnap a kid round here Kate, this ain't America,' he had shouted as he ran into Jimmy's bedroom. Empty bed. Covers flung back. No Jimmy. Little bugger. Where's he gone then, this time of night he had thought. He wondered if this had anything to do with the torch. 'Don't worry love. I'll go and find 'im, I'll bet they're all missing. Probably having a midnight feast or something.'

Then they had heard thumping and banging on their front door.

'That'll be 'im now.' Billy had run downstairs, pulling his dressing gown on over his striped pyjamas. He opened the door. Mick Tyler stood there looking remarkably sober.

'Is your Jimmy missing?'

'Yeah.'

'So's our Del. Maggie's doing her nut. I'll kill the little bleeder when I get hold of him.'

'Well at least we know they're together. Hang on Mick; I'll get me trousers on. I think I know where they'll be.'

Kate had been sitting on their bed crying when he had gone back upstairs.

'It's alright, he's wiv Del.'

'Oh and that's supposed to make me feel better is it? I might have known. It's always Del that gets him into trouble.'

'All I'm saying is that at least he ain't the only one missing. An' I'll bet Josie and Legs have gone an' all. Think they're the Famous Five or something. It's all them books you read him. Giving him ideas.'

'We just need to find him Billy,' she said tearfully.

He had supposed that he should have given her a hug or something but she was just getting on his nerves now. She had started to get clothes out from the drawer. 'You ain't coming wiv me Kate. It's blowing a gale out there

117

tonight. You just stay 'ere. We'll be five minutes. You could put the kettle on though; I'll need a cup when we get back.'

'What if he's hurt? Lying somewhere. We need the police.'

'We don't need no coppers. We'll find 'im and I think I know where.'

Well, it hadn't taken them long to find them. Billy knew they had a den on the waste but they weren't prepared for what they found. Del and Jimmy pissed out of their heads and going on about God. He didn't think that was the sort of thing that the Famous Five or the Secret Seven got up to. They had dropped Legs off with George who had not been very amused and now, here he was at Sally's house with a drunken, crying son and a stroppy female. He wouldn't be surprised if it was all Josie's idea. People underestimated girls sometimes.

As he knocked loudly on Sally's door he realised that this was the first time he would have seen her since last Saturday. He was suddenly glad that he had the kids with him. The lights came on and he saw her outline through the frosted glass.

'Who is it?' she called nervously.

'It's alright Sal, it's only me. Billy. I got someone belonging to you 'ere.'

'I told you she don't care,' Josie whispered. 'She don't even know I ain't in.'

'What the ... Why ain't you in bed?'

Sally's eyes opened wide when she saw her daughter standing at the back door with Billy and a very poorly looking Jimmy. She stood in the doorway, hands on her hips. She had no make-up on and her blonde hair was in large, wiry rollers. Her dressing gown smelt of baby sick and Billy could hear crying sounds from upstairs. He still fancied her. Now how could he think about that with all this going on?

'Dad, I need to get to bed. I'm gonna be sick.'

Sally spoke at last. Billy saw the tiredness and the anger etched into her face. 'Where the hell have you been Jose? You've woke the babies up now, you selfish little girl. Get in 'ere this minute.'

'I hate you,' Josie cried. 'You don't care. You wouldn't care if I was dead!'

118

Sally slapped her daughter then. Hard on her right cheek. 'Get up to bed now. I'll deal wiv you in the morning.'

As Josie ran past her mother sobbing, Billy saw tears in Sally's eyes. He smiled at her. 'At least she ain't pissed. Kate will go mad.'

Sally tried to smile back. 'Thanks for fetching her home Billy and you'd best get Jimmy to bed now or he'll be throwing up at my back door. That's all I need.'

Then she did smile, as she closed the door. His stomach churned as he smiled back at her. Their eyes locked, just for a couple of seconds and Billy knew then that she felt the same about him as he did about her. What on earth was he going to do?

***

Sunday was another grey, drizzly day. Jimmy woke up. His head was throbbing. He groaned. Everything came back to him. He had been sick and all over his dad's chair. How could his dad drink every night? He must feel like this all the time. He screwed his eyes up then closed them again. How could he get rid of this pain?

He was surprised that his dad hadn't hit him last night; he can't have minded that much. Perhaps he had got away with it. Precious had climbed into the bed with him. She was purring loudly. Jimmy buried his face in to her soft, warm fur. He wondered how the others were getting on.

'Wish I was a cat,' he whispered to Precious. 'You ain't got no worries.'

He could hear movements downstairs. Muffled voices, music on the wireless. His mum would be the problem. She wouldn't understand at all. He heard her soft footsteps coming up the stairs. Tears would be the best bet, he thought, as the door opened.

'Mum, I ain't well,' he wailed. 'I feel sick again.'

'I should think you do,' she said sharply. 'You deserve to be sick.'

She drew the curtains back aggressively. Jimmy closed his eyes. The light had made his headache a thousand times worse. 'Now get out of bed. Your dad wants to see you. Downstairs.'

So he hadn't got away with it. As his mum left the room, Jimmy's tears were genuine. He was in deep trouble. He knew that his dad was going to hit him. God might help,

119

he thought. Now that he had been baptised again. He put his hands together, they were shaking.

'God, I know I shouldn't have drunk that stuff but please don't let it be a slipper job.'

Jimmy's legs shook as he walked slowly down the stairs. His dad stood at the bottom, the hard, black slipper in his right hand. 'Get in the kitchen,' he said coldly.

'Don't hurt me too much dad, I ain't well,' Jimmy whimpered as he walked through.

'Just pull your jamas down and bend over.'

Jimmy held on to the back of his dad's chair. He could still smell the sick from last night, even though his mum had taken the covers off. He gagged. His dad walked slowly towards him. Jimmy looked at the slipper fearfully. How could people think slippers were cosy things? Things to keep your feet warm. They had obviously never been hit on the bum with one. He clenched his fists.

'Now you know why I'm doing this don't you son?' As he spoke, he brought the slipper down hard. Jimmy's body jerked with the pain. I hate you, he thought. When this is over I'm going to support Millwall. That will hurt you more than anything else in the world.

'Did you hear me?' his dad shouted as the slipper came down again. Jimmy nodded his head vigorously and bit his bottom lip. It never hurt as much after the first one and he wouldn't cry. His dad always hit him even harder if he did. Men must all be like that. Del said that his dad always hit his mum more if she cried. It would be over soon. He listened to the clock ticking on the mantelpiece and tried just to think about that, it usually helped. He had lost count but he had had more than usual. It was only the fourth time that he had had the slipper but this one was lasting the longest. Getting drunk must be the worst sin of all. Blood was trickling down his chin. He had bitten through his lip.

'That's enough Billy.'

His mum had come in from the garden. She never stayed when he got the slipper. As Jimmy straightened up, he saw that she had been crying. Her eyes were all red and puffy. She was crying a lot these days. Maybe it was the witch and that apple she had eaten. She looked away from him quickly as he straightened up and pulled his pyjamas back up.

120

'That's not the end of it,' she said angrily. 'You're having no roast dinner today and no pocket money for three weeks. Perhaps then it might just sink in what you've done. The whole street will be talking about us. You've not been brought up to behave like that.'

'But mum, that ain't fair ...'

She smacked him hard across the legs. 'Don't you dare answer me back like that after what you've done. And, there's something else.' She stopped and took a deep breath. 'You're never to play with that Del Tyler again. Not ever.'

'What do you mean mum?'

'I mean exactly what I say. He's going to turn out just like his dad. As long as you play with him you'll always be getting into trouble.'

'But mum. He's me mate.'

'*My* mate, not me mate Jimmy. How many times do you have to be told?'

'He's *my* mate mum. It weren't his fault. It weren't even his idea!'

The tears that Jimmy had managed to hold in check before, rained down his cheeks.

'I think you're a bit out of order there Kate,' his dad spoke.

'Del's a bad influence Billy. Jimmy wouldn't do something like that of his own accord.'

His dad sighed. 'They're all the same love. My dad belted me when I was out of order. I didn't get no luxury like slippers but he knew I was as bad as the others. No, Jimmy ain't no angel. Wouldn't want him to be neither. Don't want him turning into one of them pansy boys.'

Jimmy tried to stop snivelling. They'd forgotten he was there. He'd caused all these arguments. No, it wasn't him. It was *her*. The witch. She had caused all this trouble and all they were trying to do was to make the world a safer place. Stop people eating her apples. Try and get God to help them. But there was no point trying to explain that to grown-ups. They just didn't understand.

'Well, I'm sorry Billy but I know my son and I'm going over to see Maggie tomorrow. I'm not having Jimmy turning into some sort of hooligan. He's only nine years old and he was blind drunk last night. Molly is right you know ...'

Jimmy could have sworn that his dad was trying not to laugh. They both looked at him at that moment. 'Get upstairs now Jimmy,' said his dad. 'An' just stay there for the rest of the morning.'

Jimmy ran up the stairs and sat at the top. He needed to hear what else they were going to say. If they expected him to give up his mate they would be very disappointed.

'Well, thanks for supporting me there,' his mum was saying sarcastically.

'Look Kate. Don't you think Maggie has an' 'ard enough life without you going banging on her door complaining. Just leave it. He's bin punished enough.'

'And I suppose you'll all be having a good laugh about this down the King's Head won't you? Well that's my son you'll be laughing at and I don't want him growing up like ...'

'Like me?' his dad asked.

'I didn't say that,' his mum answered.

'You didn't need to,' he heard his dad say. Then he heard the slamming of the back door. And his mum crying. Again.

Chapter 17

Sally looked out of her kitchen window. The babies were fed and changed. The house was reasonably clean. That had been Josie's punishment this morning. Cleaning the house. She hadn't done a bad job and at least she hadn't been drunk last night. Poor Jimmy and Del. They were going to get it this morning. She looked at Josie now, sitting at the kitchen table, drawing. Sally could see the mark where she had slapped her. She hadn't meant to hurt her daughter but she could say such nasty things. She would love to be close to her but she couldn't see that ever happening. Josie hadn't spoken to her all morning.

Sally sighed and looked out the kitchen window again. She saw George next door, coming out of his shed. Billy appeared and the two of them were laughing. They would probably be off down the pub now. Have a joke about it all. It was so easy for them. She knew that Kate would be mortified.

Why were those two together? Sally couldn't work it out. Laugh a minute cockney Billy with a woman who thought she was better than everyone else. It wasn't just her that said it either. No-one liked her at work except dippy Pauline who wasn't the full shilling. She looked at Billy, laughing in the winter sun. As if he didn't have a care in the world. God, he was lovely, she thought.

When he had been at the door last night she had just wanted him to take her in his arms and make her feel better. Take away all the bad bits. The babies teething, the sleepless nights. Bread and jam for dinner on Thursdays because the money had always run out. Having to put nail varnish on your laddered stockings because you couldn't afford new ones. Living with an angry daughter who wanted to be a boy.

'Josie,' she turned to face her daughter. 'Don't never do what I done.'

Josie ignored her and got up to leave the room. 'I mean it love. Don't never have babies before you get married. And don't marry a man unless he's a good 'un. If that's the only bit of advice you listen to, that'll do me.'

Josie stopped in the doorway. 'How long did it take to make me?' she asked. 'You know. Sex an' stuff. Del says it takes about half an hour.'

Sally couldn't help smiling. 'Where do you get all this stuff from?' she asked. 'I think we need to have a talk.'

'I don't need no talk, Legs has told us everything. And I ain't never going to do it, it's disgustin' so don't worry about me. You never do anyway.'

'Don't you want to know about your dad then?'

Josie shrugged her shoulders but she didn't move. Sally sighed. 'Come an' sit down an' I'll tell you all about it.'

'I don't want to know about all the kissing an' stuff.' Josie sat back down at the table.

'I certainly ain't gonna tell you about the kissing an' stuff,' Sally laughed. At least she had her daughter's full attention. 'I loved your dad. He made me laugh. He weren't that handsome but that don't always matter. An' if you love someone Jose it ain't disgustin', the kissing and stuff.'

'Was he really ugly then?'

'No,' Sally laughed, 'an' stop interrupting.' She could feel herself blushing. 'He had a lovely smile. Just like yours.'

Josie rolled her eyes and clucked in disapproval. Sally carried on. She knew her daughter would be embarrassed by the sloppy bits but they were a part of real life. You couldn't just ignore them. 'And he was an airman in the war. He flew planes.'

'I ain't stupid. I know what an airman is.'

'Well, his name was Rory.'

'What sort of name is that?'

'Do you want to hear about your dad or not?' Josie sighed again and nodded. 'He was ... is an American. He worked at an air base and we met at a dance.'

'You mean, he was an American like Bill Haley and Davey Crockett?'

'Well ... yeah, I suppose so ...'

They were interrupted by a wailing sound from upstairs. Sally got up and patted her daughter on the head.

'What about *them*?' Josie signalled upstairs with her eyes. 'What about *their* dad?'

'No, that'll be another story for another day. Your dad ain't their dad. Your dad buggered off back to Kansas. He had his reasons.'

124

Like a wife and two kids, Sally thought to herself. No need for Josie to know that. She wasn't ever going to meet him anyway.

The crying upstairs became more insistent. Josie was smiling for the first time all day. Sally looked back at her as she made her way to the stairs.

'I'm an American,' she was whispering to herself, still smiling. 'Like Judy Garland.'

Oh well, Sally thought. That went better than I expected. At least someone's happy.

***

'I'm going out,' Billy shouted, slamming the door behind him. 'I need a drink.' He jumped over the fence in to George's garden. He guessed he would be in his shed this morning.

'How's your Clive?' Billy asked, standing in the doorway.

'Don't ask,' George laughed. 'Why do you think I'm out here? You'll have to make your shed a bit cosier Billy. It's a good place to hide.'

'Thought you northerners were always the boss.'

'Let me tell you something Billy. In my opinion women will always be the boss. They might let you think that you are but that's just them being clever. They knock spots off us.'

Billy looked around George's shed. There was a cosy, battered armchair and an old kettle for brewing up. Pictures of Blackpool Football team and one of Stanley Matthews. There was even a bit of carpet on the floor. An old Calor gas fire was giving out a good heat and his pipe and baccy were on a shelf next to the kettle.

'Blimey, when are you wallpapering?' Billy laughed. 'Don't suppose I can drag you away to the King's Head for one, can I?'

George looked at his watch. He didn't usually go to the pub Sunday lunchtimes. Still, he had an hour before roast beef and Yorkshire. 'Come on then,' he said. 'Let's get away from all these women.'

George opened his back door and they both trudged through. 'I'm off out love,' he gave May a peck on the cheek as he passed her closing the oven door. 'I'll be back for my dinner.'

May looked flushed and tired. 'Oh there's a surprise,' she glared at Billy. 'Very easy for you men to run away isn't it?' The two men beat a hasty retreat through the front door.

'She didn't get much sleep,' George explained. 'I did peel the potatoes for her though.'

'More than I did,' Billy laughed. 'Anyway at least your lad weren't pissed.'

'Ah yes but it was him that stole the sherry. Stealing is worse than getting drunk in May's eyes.'

'Did you never get caught drinking when you was a kid?' Billy asked him as they walked into Montgomery Road.

'No, but my dad caught me smoking once. Suppose I were about Clive's age. Couldn't sit down for a week. I remember that.'

'Have you given Legs ... sorry ... Clive a belting for last night?'

'No,' George said quietly. 'I've never hit any of them.'

'What ... never?' asked Billy, amazed.

'No. I had enough of that when I was a kid to know it doesn't work. Never stopped me doing owt.'

'Never did you no harm though did it?'

George stopped and lit his pipe thoughtfully. 'I don't know', he said. 'I don't think I ever really forgave him.'

As they walked past the big old house they saw the front door open and then close again quickly.

'Bloody German cow,' Billy spat on the ground outside her gate. 'She was coming out then. Till she saw me.'

'What have you got against her Billy? It's not like you.'

'She tried to get at Kate; you know when she was poorly after she lost the baby. Putting silly ideas in her head. I reckon it was 'er that was making her worse.'

He stopped to light a cigarette. 'I had to drag her out of there one day. We had a bit of a shouting match. Anyway I don't think our Kate will ever go back there again. Don't say nothing will yer George. Ain't proud of shouting at an old woman, you know what I mean?'

They ambled along companionably. Billy kept thinking about what George had been saying.

126

'I 'ate having to use the slipper on Jimmy,' he admitted. 'See that hate in his eyes. Has to be done though George. Well, that's what I think anyway.'

George shrugged his shoulders. 'We'll agree to disagree Billy and your Jimmy's a good lad. You've done well there, you and Kate. Anyway,' he changed the subject, 'I saw Mick earlier. He's more angry that the sherry made Del throw up. Tylers have always bin able to hold their drink George, he said to me. That boy has let me down.'

They both laughed.

'Er – Billy, I'd forgotten. There's something I need to ask you about,' said George.

'Oh wait till we're inside, we're here now. Sun might be shining but its still taters.'

'It'll keep mate. It'll keep.'

'Bleeding hell, it ain't even December an' they're all singing Jingle Bells,' Billy laughed as he pushed open the door. All the regulars were stood around the piano singing raucously. 'Hey,' said George. 'Look who's on the old Joanna.'

It was Old Bones, thumping away at the out of tune keys.

'Well I never,' said Billy. 'I didn't even know he could play.'

'He used to play in a band,' Arthur said as he passed them their beers. 'They was good an' all. I just asked him to come an' do a bit today. Cheer everyone up. You know what I mean?'

'He don't drink though does he?' Billy asked.

'Nah. Something bad happened. He was a bit of an alky you know. It's only rumours but he was married once, lived over Dagenham way. Only had one kid an' she died. He ain't touched a drop since then. The marriage broke up. That's all I know.'

'Anyway George,' said Billy, breaking the uncomfortable silence. 'What was it you had to tell me?'

'I don't know that I want to say anything after that. This won't cheer you up either.'

Billy looked at his neighbour. George looked nervous. 'Come on then mate, spit it out. This weekend can't get no worse.'

'Well, it's just rumours but I think you should know. People are saying ... well they're saying there's something going on. Between you and Sal.'

Billy felt stunned. As if someone had thumped him hard on the back. 'What the bloody hell do you mean?' he shouted angrily.

'Hey, what's all this? 'Arthur came over. 'What you having a go at George for?'

'Keep out of this Arthur, ain't none of your business. Just bugger off to the other end of the bar, its private.'

'Well, that's very nice being told to bugger off in me own pub,' he muttered as he moved away.

'Listen Billy, it's just people talking, you know what they're like,' said George. 'You walked her home last Saturday night. You left here, on your own with her and it was noticed. That's all.'

'And what is that supposed to mean? Oh I don't believe this.'

'Look Billy, I told you that you wouldn't like it. I'm just warning you that there's gossip about that's all. I know you wouldn't do anything but if I've heard it then I'm not going to be the only one.'

Billy slammed his drink down on the bar. 'It ain't no crime to look at other women is it George?'

'No. We all do that Billy but I know you haven't had it easy with Kate and sometimes temptation happens. And this one's a bit too close to home. You know how people talk.'

'Right, you've spilt beer on me bar now Billy Potter. I know what your trouble is. Too many women. God, one's enough for me. I don't know ...'

'Arthur.' George put his hand on the landlords shoulder. 'Just shut up eh.'

'Oh, no,' said Billy. 'Let him carry on. I think there's a few over in the corner who didn't hear that. Perhaps you'd better shout a bit louder next time Arthur.'

Arthur moved to the other end of the bar, muttering under his breath.

'That man is a bloody moron,' said Billy. 'He's a worse gossip than an old woman.' He lit a cigarette and took another swig of his beer. 'Nothing 'appened George,' he said quietly. 'Well, we 'ad a bit of a kiss that's all. I was just a bit pissed. It just felt exciting. It's like ... it's like if West Ham was

128

playing in the Cup. You know against a First Division team. Man United for instance and we're losing but just by the one goal. We set up an attack. We're all screaming, shouting, trying to make it happen for the lads but we know really, deep inside. That it ain't gonna go in. They're in the First Division, there's no way we could ever beat 'em ...'

Billy stopped. What was he doing talking to George like this? He just couldn't seem to stop himself. 'Anyway. That's what it felt like. That's how I feel about her. It was just exciting that's all. It's alright George. Ain't going to happen. It can't.'

'Blimey,' said George. 'I think that was our first discussion about feelings Billy.' He clapped Billy on the back. 'Come on. One more for the road eh? Do you know there's a tribe in Africa, they still get married for life, but three times a year, special holidays like, they can do it with whoever they want. The men and the women. Seems to work for them.'

Billy relaxed. 'We'll book an' holiday there then,' he laughed. 'Just the two of us eh? Where do you get all this stuff George?'

'Down the library. You want to get yourself down there Billy. That would stop you needing all that excitement, a bit of learning.'

'Are you two having another or is my pub meant to pay for itself?' Arthur had rejoined them.

'Anyway, what are you on about now? At least you've cheered up a bit.'

'Anthropology Arthur,' said George. 'You should try it some time.'

'Sod off,' Arthur replied. 'I don't need no 'ologies. There ain't nothing wrong wiv my 'ead.'

Chapter 18

'What did you get?' Jimmy asked on Monday morning in the playground. Del turned to look at him. He had two black eyes.

'That ain't all,' he sighed. 'Me bum's like a battlefield.'

Jimmy laughed. 'Mine's sore an' all.'

Legs came sauntering across to join them. None of them had been allowed out yesterday so this was the first chance they had had to talk.

'Bet you ain't bin hit,' Del smirked, eyeballing Legs.

'My dad don't believe in it,' he said. 'I ain't allowed out though. Not all week and no pocket money until I've paid for a new bottle of sherry.'

'That could take years,' said Jimmy. 'I'm glad I just got hit. I ain't allowed out neither though this week. And ...,' he looked sheepishly at Del, 'I ain't supposed to play wiv you Del, never again.'

Del's eyes almost popped out of his head. 'Why me? What have I done?'

'Dunno but I ain't taking no notice anyways,' said Jimmy. 'We're mates, we always will be. We ain't letting 'em split *us* up.' The three boys spat on their hands, shook on it and moved around the playground, kicking stones.

'Heard all about you.' It was John Baxter. Mr. Colour Televisions.

'What do you want?' Del growled at him.

'I done a lot more than that you know,' he smirked, 'an' I got away wiv it an' all. I was only three when I first got drunk.'

'Yeah, yeah,' said Jimmy. 'We know you've done everything better than anyone else.'

'So, what *was* you doing? Out that late at night on the waste ... wiv a girl? I'll bet I know.'

'You don't know,' said Del, 'so piss off an' leave us alone.'

John Baxter looked indignant. He glanced over to where the teacher stood about to blow the whistle. It was old Gutty. He made his way towards her. Jimmy, Del and Legs followed. 'I'm gonna tell old Gutty you swore at me Del

130

Tyler,' he sneered. 'Anyways, I bet I've had more girls than you have. And prettier ones an' all.'

'Oh, not more trouble,' said Legs. 'God ain't helping us much so far is he? Everything just seems to be getting worse.'

They could hear John Baxter whining to old Gutty.

'Stop telling tales Baxter,' she shouted. 'Stand up for yourself. Be a man. Sticks and stones boy. Sticks and stones.' She looked over to where the three boys were standing, whistle to her lips, and winked at them.

They laughed. 'Good old Gutty,' said Del. 'She hates 'im an' all.'

They had a reasonable day in school. Some of the kids seemed to have a new sort of respect for them somehow. Word had got around quickly about their night time escapade and drinking session. 'We have to be very careful now,' said Del. 'They'll all want to be in our gang.'

Del had been summoned to the headmaster's office. Miss Parsons had not been entirely convinced by his explanation of how he had acquired two black eyes.

'So Derek,' the headmaster opened the conversation wearily. 'Miss Parsons tells me that you met a sabre toothed tiger over the weekend. Is this correct?'

'Yes sir.'

'I didn't know they could throw punches like that. Where exactly was this ... sabre-toothed tiger hiding out?'

'In the woods sir. Down the park. Its bin there ages It just jumped me sir. I didn't see it coming.'

Mr. Cummings put on his most frightening face and began to shout. 'Enough Tyler! Just that name gives me the shivers. How many more of you must I cope with?'

'Three sir,' said Del. 'There's three more to come. Mind, me little sister Marilyn starts next year. She's the worst of all of us.'

The headmaster took a deep breath. 'Get out Tyler. Get out now before I kill you.'

'Yes sir.'

Jimmy and Legs were waiting outside the door for him. 'How did it go?' Jimmy asked.

'Alright. I think he believed me. He is seriously thick.' laughed Del.

***

131

Sally glared at Dianne across the conveyor belt. 'I want words wiv you at break time,' she said angrily. She had to shout to make herself heard over the noise of the machinery.

There was a chorus of 'ooh's' from the girls working close by. 'What you done Di?' one of them laughed. 'Pinched her new boyfriend or what?'

Dianne kept her head down. Sally kept glaring at her but she didn't look up. She bloody knows what she's done, Sally thought.

It seemed a very long morning, waiting for the bell for break-time.

'Well, what did you tell me for then,' Dianne shouted at Sally later on, in the toilets, 'if it was meant to be a secret?'

'I thought I could trust you. What a silly cow I am.'

'But you never said it was a secret. Ain't my fault. Everyone knows he walked you home anyway. They all saw you leaving the King's Head. It was heaving in there.'

Sally took a deep breath. She felt so angry with Dianne, she could have hit her. 'Oh, I wouldn't have minded so much if you'd told the truth but you had to go that little bit further didn't yer. Make it a bit more interesting.'

Dianne smirked. 'I was just using me imagination that's all. The teachers at school always said I had a great imagination. It was the only nice thing they ever said.'

Sally began to pace up and down. It took quite a lot to upset her. She knew what the end results could be in this situation. She had been here before.

There was a knock on the door. 'Can we come in yet Sal?' asked one of the girls. 'I need to do me hair.'

'Yeah, is there a lot of blood?' asked another. 'My bet's on you to win Di.'

There was raucous laughter outside. 'Just shut up all of you. Give us five minutes,' Sally shouted back. 'According to Julie Tyler,' she turned to face Dianne, 'the rumour she's heard is that me an' Billy are having it away every night.'

'Well I never said that!' said an outraged Dianne. 'On my life, I never. I never said that you went all the way. Just that you nearly did. Honest Sal, I only exaggerated a little bit. That Julie Tyler's just saying that out of badness. Little grass.'

'But that ain't true Di. We only kissed. Once.' Sally sighed in exasperation. 'And what about Kate? Have you thought about 'er? What happens if she 'ears these rumours? '

'Oh shut up going on Sal. I reckon you want her to know. That's why you told me.'

Sally banged her clenched fist against the wall. Tears sprang into her eyes. 'You're a cow,' she said quietly. She didn't feel angry anymore. The tears slid down her face. Dianne put her arm around her shoulders but Sally pushed her away.

'I'm sorry Sal, I really am, I didn't think.' She passed Sally her hankie. 'And let's face it, you don't mind a bit of gossip when it ain't about you do yer?'

Sally wiped her eyes with Dianne's well-used hankie and tried to smile.

'Mates again?' asked Dianne. Sally shrugged her shoulders and walked out of the door to cheers from the waiting crowd. They were all relieved to be able to get into the toilet but quite upset that there had been no fisticuffs.

The trouble was that Sally recognised the truth in what Dianne was saying. She was right. If you didn't want something knowing you didn't tell anyone. And if she was being honest she really did like Billy. So did that mean that somewhere in the back of her mind she *did* want Kate to know? She would have to stay well away from Billy Potter. It was the only way. Oh, sometimes she really didn't like herself very much. She knew now why Dianne didn't have many friends. No-one liked the truth. It hurt.

***

'What on earth was that?' Kate jumped as she poured the tea from the pot into May's cup.

'Well,' May laughed. 'I don't know who that is banging at your door but you'd best open it before they break it down.'

Kate walked through into the tiny hall. 'Alright, alright, I'm coming. You don't have to break ...' She stopped as she opened the door and then moved back instinctively as she saw Maggie's furious face. 'Oh ... Maggie. I'm glad you've come, I was going to pop over to see you later.'

Maggie's body was rigid. Her face red and contorted. Her fists were clenched and on a level with her

133

pendulous breasts. She looked like a cat, ready to spring. 'I ain't coming in,' she shouted. 'I just want to know what the hell is goin' on.'

Kate had heard about Maggie's temper but she had not really seen it until now. She took a deep breath and looked straight into the older woman's eyes. 'I don't know what you're on about Maggie,' she said, 'but I'd rather you didn't shout like that in the street.' She glanced towards the bottom of the stairs where Jimmy was standing. 'And I don't want you shouting in front of my son. You'd best come in if you've got something to say.'

Maggie moved into the hall and slammed the door behind her. She looked as if she were about to explode. She coughed and spluttered trying desperately to get her words out. 'Oh well. Excuse me, Mrs High n' Mighty for shouting in front of your sweet, sodding little boy who's too good to play wiv mine anymore. Oh an' sorry I ain't dressed for an' 'ouse as posh as this but –'

'Maggie!' May had squeezed herself into the hall, behind Kate. 'For goodness sake, what's all this about?'

'Oh, so you're 'ere an' all. Talking about my Del I suppose. All ganging up on him now are you? Well you can sod off the lot of you.'

'Go outside Jimmy,' Kate said quietly.

'But Mum, you said I weren't allowed ...'

'Get outside now,' she snapped, pushing him past Maggie and through the door.

'Come and sit down Maggie,' said May quickly. 'I'll get you a cup of tea and we can all talk about this sensibly. It's no use all shouting and getting upset.'

'Cuppa tea? Cuppa tea? You bloody think that sorts everything out don't yer. I ain't sitting down an' I don't want none of your fuckin' tea.'

Kate could feel herself shaking and energy coursing through her body. '*I* wasn't offering you a cup of tea,' she glared at May, 'and I do not like *that* word being used in my house. Just get out Maggie.'

'Oh no lady, not till I've said what I've come to say. All I know is that when my Del come home from school today he's told me that your Jimmy ain't allowed to play wiv him no more. Right or wrong? That's all I wanna know. Because if it's true an' I tell my Mick you'll have a lot more to worry about than people swearing in your 'ouse believe me.'

'Oh, I do believe you Maggie,' Kate retorted. 'I believe you alright, because your husband is an animal. It's not Del's fault he's like he is, it's his father. That's who I blame. Oh, no-one will say that to your face, they're all too scared, but that's what he is. An animal.'

Maggie moved suddenly towards Kate, pulling her clenched right fist back, ready to strike. 'You bloody cow!' she screamed, inches from Kate's face.

'No Maggie!' May shouted and forced herself between the two women. 'No!'

Maggie took a step backwards and looked straight into Kate's defiant eyes. 'You wanna take a good look at your bleedin' old man,' she said quietly, 'before you start slagging mine off you toffee nosed bitch. At least mine don't mess around wiv other women.'

There was a stunned silence in the hallway. Kate would have felt better if Maggie *had* struck her. She felt like she'd been hit. By a massive truck. Head-on. She couldn't breathe. And the pain. Deep inside. It filled her whole body so that she couldn't move. What did Maggie mean? What was happening?'

'You're out of order Maggie,' said May quietly. 'You'd better go.'

'I'm only saying what she'd hear from anyone down the pub or at the factory that's all. An' I know whose side you're on now May Pattinson. It's alright to slag my husband off ain't it but I ain't allowed to tell *her* the truth. Don't worry I'm going, an' it'll be the last time I come inside this 'ouse.'

Kate wanted to tell her that at least they agreed on something but she couldn't speak. She let May lead her through to the kitchen. They heard the front door slam, Maggie's last act of defiance.

'Come on Kate. Just sit down at the table for a minute. Your tea's still hot.'

Kate sat down automatically. So it had only been a few minutes since she had poured her tea out. Since her life had been bearable. It hadn't even gone cold and everything had come crashing in on her again.

'Why didn't you tell me?' she glared at May.

135

'Its rumours Kate, that's all. He wouldn't do that to you, not Billy. You mustn't listen to gossip. Now, come on. Maggie was just trying to get back at you.'

And, she's done that alright, May thought. She had never seen Kate look so devastated. Well, yes, just the once. After the little girl died, that was when she had last seen her like this. There was no colour in her face, no life in her eyes. She almost didn't look like a human being and then a light seemed to go on. She closed her eyes for a few seconds.

'No, I'm alright May now. That was all just a bit too much for me. I don't like scenes like that. I don't like confrontations, not really. And I've never seen Maggie that angry before. Anyway, I must get to the shops before they close. Billy will expect his tea on the table.' She tried to smile.

May put her arm around her friend's shoulders. 'Listen love. Please don't believe what Maggie said. It isn't true. You must believe me.'

'I do believe you May. You're right. It's too silly even to think about.'

I should ask her now, Kate thought. Is it someone I know? Is it just one woman? Is it serious? Her head was screaming for the answers but she couldn't bring herself to ask the questions.

'Well, if you're sure you're alright ...'

'I'm fine May.'

Have they had sex? What colour is her hair? Is she young? Is she married?

'Well, if you're sure. If you need me you know where I am.'

Is he going to leave me? Is he going to leave me and Jimmy?

'Thank you May.'

Kate heard the front door close. She took some deep breaths. Calm, she must try and stay calm. He wouldn't go with other women. Not Billy. Hadn't May just said that? And May knew. May was wise. Maggie was just a liar. And jealous. When Billy came in tonight she would ask him, straight out. He would probably just laugh and ask her what she'd been drinking. No, it wasn't even worth asking him. It was too ridiculous. She would just forget it. She picked up her shopping bag and walked quickly along Churchill Street. As she reached the footpath through to Montgomery Road Kate had to stop.

She was dying, she couldn't breathe. Her legs felt like lead. Everything outside of her head became a blur. There was just her, there. Trying to breathe. Trying not to die. Falling, she felt herself falling but she wasn't. She began to shake all over. Panic. She had been here before and she knew that she had to calm down. Breathe deeply and it would pass. Kate held on to the wall to her left for what seemed like hours. The shops. She must get there. It was shepherds pie tonight and she'd run out of potatoes. Slowly, very slowly, she returned from the edge. Her body was still shaking but she could breathe, she was back in control.

It wasn't until Kate reached the shops that she realised that her purse was still on the kitchen table.

Chapter 19

The four friends were gathered in the den. It was Saturday morning and Josie was putting tinsel on the branches.

'So, do you reckon that Bill Haley might be your dad then Jose?' Jimmy asked her.

'Not unless his real name's Rory,' she answered.

'Could be Davey Crockett,' said Del. 'He's an American an' all.'

'Yeah, but he ain't real,' Josie answered.

'I'll bet there's hundreds of Americans,' Legs chipped in. 'You'll never find him.'

'I will one day. An' then I'll go an' live wiv him in America and eat 'amburgers and chips all day.'

'Yeah,' said Jimmy excitedly. 'You can go to drive-in movies an' shoot all the red Indians on the prairie.'

'You could be a film star, they all live in America an' all,' said Del. 'James Dean, that's who I'd like to be.'

'He's dead Del.'

'Well, I'll be Roy Rogers then an' shoot the Cherokees.'

They all looked at Del and laughed. Since the witch had come into their lives they hardly thought about cowboys and indians anymore. It was quite good, thought Jimmy, remembering stuff from the past.

'Your mum alright about us now?' Del asked him.

'Yeah. She ain't tried to stop me going out anyway. She ain't well this week.'

Josie's eyes widened. 'You don't think ...'

'Dunno.' Jimmy shrugged his shoulders. It had crossed his mind that his mum could be under the witch's spell. It was like she wasn't really there half the time. She had burnt his porridge twice this week and yesterday she just hadn't got out of bed. His dad had been shouting at her to go to the doctor but she wouldn't. His dad had made the tea last night. Baked beans on toast and he hadn't done *that* right, the beans had been cold. It was all very unsettling and she *had* eaten a *whole* apple.

***

Billy had come in from the early Saturday shift expecting to find his wife busy in the kitchen. She hadn't been good this week but surely she would have got them something to eat before football. The smell of burnt toast pervaded the air. It was Jimmy in the kitchen, not Kate.

'Where's your mum?'

'She's still in bed. She ain't well again dad.'

Billy sighed and made his way slowly up the stairs. She was lying on the bed, curled, foetus-like, into a ball. The bedcovers lay on the floor. She was shivering and crying. He couldn't stand all this again. He had felt angry with her when he was downstairs but when he saw her like this...

He picked up the stripy sheets and blankets and put them over her. 'Are you alright love?' he asked.

'Nellie's dead,' she whispered. 'Nellie's dead.'

'Kate, that was ages ago. You didn't know her that well.'

'She was mum's friend. My mum's friend.'

Billy passed her a hankie and she blew her nose noisily. He took a deep breath. He knew he must try not to get angry. He felt the familiar despair rising in his gut. Helplessness. He wanted to lash out. He didn't know what else to do.

'Now look Kate.' He sat down on the bed next to her and tried to hold her hand. She pushed him away. He could feel uncontrollable rage careering through his body.

'Right Kate, I've had enough of all this now. You're ill again, like you was before, and you need to see the doctor. It ain't fair on me an' Jimmy this. And I'll tell you something else; I can't go through it again. I won't go through it again. Now me an' Jimmy's off to football. We'll get a pie when we get there an' I'll bring back fish an' chips so you ain't got to cook today. Just stay in bed and rest. If you're better tomorrer, that's fine but if you ain't, you're going to the doctor.'

He stood up and walked slowly towards the door. He felt like he was a little kid again. He wanted to cry.

***

As he closed the door behind him, Kate had a moment of clarity. So that was it. He had said it. He wouldn't go through it again. So he *was* going to leave them. She didn't even have to ask him now. She knew. She curled herself up again and closed her eyes but dreadful things were happening in her head. The babies. Always the dead

139

babies. She was walking to the shelter with her mum and little Shirley again. And then they were playing in the park, on the swings. Laughing.

'Push me higher Kate. Go on, please.'

And then, the clouds came over and Shirley had disappeared. She scrambled around the park, trying to find her. She looked under all the bushes. Where was she?

'I'll help you find her.'

Then *he* was there. Smiling but it wasn't a kind smile anymore. Not like it had been before. 'I'll find her for you if you'll just do something for me.' He began to undo the zip on his trousers.

'Me shoelace is undone,' Shirley wailed. Kate could hear her little sister but she couldn't see her.

He was still stood there, smiling. 'I think you liked that an' all didn't you Kate?'

He was carrying a bundle in his arms. It wasn't moving. Kate knew it was dead.

NO! She heard herself screaming. She couldn't stop the noise and her world turned black. Again.

***

'Is she alright?' Jimmy asked fearfully, as they wrapped themselves in their claret and blue scarves and walked out through the gate.

'No, she ain't son. I just got angry wiv her. I shouldn't have done that. I just can't cope wiv all that again.'

'Like after the dead baby dad, when she bought me that doll?'

'I'd forgotten about that.'

Jimmy put his hand into his dad's, like when he had been little. His dad squeezed it really tight. 'She'll be alright dad. She got better before.'

His dad nodded and put his arm around Jimmy's shoulders. 'You're a good kid son. I'm sorry I hit you so hard. You know that don't yer?' Jimmy nodded.

He always felt proud walking to football with his dad. It was what they did together, just them. He supposed that was what love was.

'Hey Billy, should be a good game today.'

'Yeah, see you in the chicken run Shorty.'

As they got nearer to Plaistow Station the pavements were a sea of claret and blue. Just a few girls out shopping in their hair rollers. Jimmy was still thinking about the doll. 'She kept playing wiv it,' he said. 'The doll. I wanted a train set.'

His dad patted him on the back. 'Look son, she'll be alright but it ain't just the dead baby you know.'

'Oh, I know that dad. I know what's making her ill.'

'Well I ain't never told you about it. Who's been saying things?'

Jimmy didn't know what his dad was talking about but he had better be careful. He couldn't tell him about the witch. It was nothing to do with the grown-ups. It was up to the gang to sort *her* out.

'Hey, Billy. Is Malcy playing today?'

'Dunno Dave. Manager ain't consulted me this week.'

'Ain't got no chance this afternoon 'ave we,' Loopy muttered. 'Leicester's doing well.'

His dad's mates all gathered together on the station platform, a few kids of Jimmy's age with them. He was just about to move over to join them when his dad put his hand on his son's shoulder. 'When we get home Jimmy, we'll talk about this. You need to know a bit more now. About why your mum gets ill.'

Jimmy nodded. 'We could always ask Leg's mum to get her to go to the doctor dad,' he said. 'She ain't a gossip, she won't tell no-one.'

His dad laughed as he went to talk to his football mates. Good, Jimmy thought. I think I've made him feel better.

***

Sally had dozed off in the chair and the babies were asleep. Josie was out doing the shopping. She had taken her shoes off, made herself a cup of tea and the next minute there was a banging on the back door. 'Come in,' she shouted, still half-asleep.

It was Julie Tyler. She came in and plonked herself down on Sally's settee. She looked awful. Her pale face was ghostly, her lank, greasy hair tied back. The roots were showing and even the ends looked too greasy to be called blonde. She was chewing her gum as if she was trying to grind it into her teeth. My God, Sally thought, she's only

141

fifteen and she looks forty today. 'Bad in your house today? You having a cuppa?'

To Sally's amazement, Julie began to cry. Racking, heaving sobs. Up until today Sally wouldn't have believed that anything could have made Julie Tyler cry. She was the hardest little cow she had ever met. Sally rushed over and put her arms around Julie's shaking shoulders. For a few seconds her body was rigid and unyielding. Then she clung to Sally and wept.

'You ain't as tough as you make out are yer?' Sally stroked the young girl's hair. 'Is it Freddie? Has he gone back off leave? Are you missing 'im love?'

Julie pulled away abruptly and wiped her face on the sleeve of her dilapidated black leather jacket. 'It ain't Billy,' she snuffled. Sally fetched her hankie.

'Ta Sal.' She blew her nose noisily.

'Right,' said Sally, sitting down next to her on the settee. 'Why don't you tell me what this is all about?' As she spoke, she knew what the answer was going to be. She had been there herself. Twice.

'You bloody know,' said Julie viciously. The hardness was back in her face, the vulnerability gone.

'You're pregnant.'

Julie nodded. 'I wanna get rid of it,' she said. 'I thought you might know someone.'

Sally took a deep breath. 'It ain't always the best thing Julie. You need to think about it.'

'You must know someone Sal,' said Julie, desperation in her voice. 'Freddie says he'll finish wiv me if I 'ave it. He says he don't wanna come home to a screaming brat. And as for me dad ... well you know what he's like. He'd bloody kill both of us.' She looked close to tears again.

'But what do *you* want Julie? D'you want the baby?'

Julie shrugged her shoulders. 'I ain't old enough Sal. Not for babies. No, I don't want it.'

'Well don't take no notice of what that Freddie says,' Sally said angrily. 'If he cared about you he wouldn't have said what he did. He's just an arsehole.'

'I know he's an arsehole Sal but I love him. Ain't never loved no-one before. And what about me dad?'

Sally really didn't want to think about that one. It would not have a happy ending. 'Look Julie,' she said

142

impulsively. 'You could always move in 'ere. Your dad's a bit – well scared of me. You'd be alright.'

'I don't want it Sal,' she was shouting now, getting hysterical. 'I want rid of it.'

'Alright, alright, calm down Julie.'

There was silence in the room, apart from the ticking of the clock. Eventually, Sally took a deep breath. 'As it 'appens I do know someone.' She went over to the sideboard and took out some paper and a pen. Sally didn't like this at all but at least this one was safe. She hadn't killed anyone yet. 'Are you sure this is what you want?' Julie nodded. 'An' you know it can be dangerous don't yer?'

'Yeah, I know all that.'

Sally watched Julie's face as she read the name and address. She was so alone. Just like she had been. 'Do you want me to come wiv yer?'

Julie nodded. 'Would you Sal? You're a mate. I ain't never gonna forget this.' She smiled then.

'You should smile more often,' said Sally. 'It suits yer.'

'An' I will, once this is done Sal. I'll be laughing all the time. Do you want me to babysit tonight? You ain't bin out much lately.'

'Nah, too tired these days. Pop round for a chat if you want. Dianne's coming round.'

'No ta, can't stand Dianne. I know she's your mate but ... you won't say nothing to her will yer Sal? It'd be all round the factory by Monday morning.'

'Course I won't but you're wrong about 'er you know.'

'It was 'er that told me that you an' Billy are 'aving it off.'

'I know Julie and we've sorted it now but her heart's in the right place. She didn't mean no harm. She just don't think.'

Julie shrugged her shoulders. 'Right well, it's your life. I'll be off. Ta Sal,' she waved the slip of paper, 'for this.'

As soon as Julie had gone Sally made herself another cup of tea. Her mind went back in time to when she was pregnant with Josie. The hot baths. The gin. The fear and guilt. Sometimes she swore that Josie knew. They had never really got on. Wouldn't it be nice, she thought, to live

143

somewhere where babies were always wanted. Everything seemed wrong here. Different to how things were meant to be.

Or was it fairy stories that were wrong? Were we all brought up to believe in things that could never come true? A self-pitying tear trickled slowly down her cheek as she walked upstairs and into the babies' room. The boys were lying there, sound asleep in their cot. She stroked Peter's hand with her finger and he clutched it and opened his beautiful blue eyes. Then he smiled and she knew that she wouldn't change anything.

***

'You bin cryin' our Julie?' Her mum wiped her nose on her sleeve as she mashed a mountain of potatoes for tea. She didn't wait for the answer as screams from the living room filled the air. 'What you two doin' to that baby? Get in there an' sort 'em out Julie.'

Julie came back carrying the screaming baby. Her mum wiped her hands on her pinny and took her.

'They was playing catch. Dropped her on her 'ead.' said Julie.

'It weren't me,' little Marilyn wailed. 'I ain't done nuffink.'

'It *was* you,' shouted three year old Stuart sticking his tongue out at his elder sister. 'Stinky poos.'

It took a while to quieten the screaming baby. She clung frantically to her mother, kicking her little legs in the air. Her mum looked at the baby's head. There was a small bump, just above her eye. 'Get us a wet cloth Julie. She'll be alright.'

She turned to Stuart and Marilyn, who had begun to spit at each other. 'That's it for you two now. No Father Christmas this year. No presents. I'm fed up wiv you all fighting. Other people's kids ain't like this an' I've 'ad enough. The two children looked at their mother, their eyes filling with tears.

'Well, it's too late now cos I'm telling 'im not to come. Julie, finish them spuds for me will yer?' She picked up the baby's dummy where it had fallen onto the floor and dipped it into a crumpled bag of sugar that stood next to the kettle. She stuck it, none too gently, into baby Ava's mouth.

144

'I be good now,' Stuart sniffed. 'I be good for Farty Chrisnus.'

Marilyn dissolved into fits of giggles. 'Farty Chrisnus, Farty Chrisnus,' she chanted, laughing at her little brother.

'Shut up, shut up Malin. Bloody shut up.'

Their mum dumped the baby, now sucking happily on her dummy, onto the floor and hit Stuart hard round the head. 'I ain't having you swearin' at your age. I've 'ad enough of all of you. Now Father Christmas ain't comin' an' that's it. Julie, watch 'em for a minute. I'll have to sit down an' have a fag now.'

Stuart had started to scream, his hands over his ears. As their mum disappeared through the back door to sit in her 'smoking seat' in the shed, the front door opened and slammed shut. Julie felt her body tense. She had to get away from this house.

'What the 'ell's going on? What's all this noise?' Their dad rolled into the kitchen. Julie looked at his eyes. That was always the giveaway. They looked soft today. Not always a good sign but at least it meant he'd be alright for a bit.

'Dad, dad.' Marilyn ran over to her dad and threw her arms around his legs. Stuart stopped crying.

'How's my little princess?' He patted Marilyn on the head.

'Mum says we ain't havin' Father Christmas this year'

'No Farty Chrisnus,' Stuart added.

Julie had started plating up the baked beans and mash.

'Right, well. Just get off me now kids. I need me grub an' a bit of a kip so I don't want no more noise.'

'An' if we don't make no more noise can we have Father Christmas?' Marilyn asked fearfully.

He sat down at the table and burped. 'Ain't no such thing,' he slurred. 'Ain't no such thing as Father Christmas.'

'Dad!' Julie exclaimed. 'That's cruel.'

Marilyn and Stuart looked from one to the other, bemused. 'Ain't no Father Christmas?' Marilyn asked. 'But I want presents.'

'Well you ain't bloody getting any. We ain't made of money you know.'

He glared at his eldest daughter. 'An' don't you be answering me back neither. You ain't too old to be put over me knee. An' where's Del an' Paddy got to? And where's your ... oh there you are.'

Their mum came in and shouted Paddy and Del who came bounding downstairs. They all crowded around the table to eat their tea.

'There,' said their dad, burping as he finished his meal and looked around the table at his family. 'Life ain't so bad is it Mags?' Julie felt sick as she saw him fondling her mum's knee. 'I think me an' your mum might have a little rest upstairs now. Julie, get that washing up done an' look after the kids. We won't be long. No fighting you lot.' He smiled at his wife lustfully as he shuffled through the door and up the stairs.

'Mum?' Julie stopped her as she got up from the table. 'He's just told the kids there ain't no Father Christmas.'

Stuart and Marilyn were looking at their mum. Watching her expectantly. She laughed. 'Well, it ain't the worst thing he's ever done is it? You know what your dad's like.'

'There is a Farty Chrisnus mum, ain't there?' Stuart pleaded.

'Yeah, course there is darlin'. Your dad was only joking. Won't be fetching much this year though. He don't bring much to kids on council estates.'

'Why?' asked Marilyn.

'He just thinks we ain't good enough, that's all.'

'I'll be good now,' said Stuart seriously. 'I be very good.'

They all heard their dad's voice bellowing from upstairs. 'Maggie, get up to this bedroom now.'

Her mum moved faster than Julie had seen for a long time. It was disgusting at their age, she thought. She closed the kitchen door and turned the wireless on loud. She would go over and have a chat with Sal later. Anything to get out of this house.

146

Chapter 20

May walked slowly down the stairs to see Jimmy and Billy standing nervously by the fire. They obviously didn't know what to do about Kate. Nor did she, not really. The doctor had just prescribed some pills and sleep and he had told Billy that Kate was having another kind of breakdown. May had just given her the pills, sat with her and held her hand while she cried. She was tossing and turning but her eyes stayed closed.

'Molly is on her way,' said Billy. 'She'll stay till she's better.'

'Does she have to?' Jimmy asked. 'She makes me wash about an' hundred times a day.'

Billy and May laughed. You had to, even in the worst of times.

'Me an' George are taking Clive up town to see the Christmas lights tonight Jimmy,' said May. Would you like to come?'

Jimmy looked at Billy. 'Can I dad?' he asked.

Billy ruffled his hair. 'Yeah. Yeah you need a treat if we're gonna have your Auntie Molly 'ere for a bit.'

'Can we go to Hamleys an' all?' he asked.

May smiled. 'Yes, we'll be going to Hamleys. See what Clive wants from Father Christmas.'

May patted Billy awkwardly on his shoulder. 'Don't worry Billy,' she said. 'It'll be fine. She just needs some sleep. Try and get her to eat some soup or something to keep her strength up. I've baked you a steak an' kidney pudding for your tea, I'll pop it round.' She looked at Jimmy's peaky face. 'And we'll pick you up at six o'clock young man. And,' she laughed, 'make sure you have a good wash.'

Billy helped May on with her coat and saw her out the door.

***

'You was gonna tell me dad,' said Jimmy, 'about what you thought was makin' mum poorly. You said I was old enough to know.'

Billy turned and looked at his son. He saw the confusion in his face; he had probably been too young to remember much before. He took a cigarette from the packet on the mantelpiece, lit it and sat down in the armchair.

'There is things you need to know about your mum son. She will get better though, as long as she keeps taking them pills.' He took a drag of his cigarette, the smoke swirling into familiar patterns. 'It ain't just the baby Jimmy. It was the war.'

'Hitler an' the Germans?'

'Yeah. Yeah. Hitler an' the Germans killed nearly everyone in your mum's family.'

'Did the 'ouse get bombed by the Luftwaffe? We done that in school.'

He sat down in front of the hearth and looked up at his dad.

'No, the house weren't bombed son. Your mum's dad, you know your Granddad. He was already dead, ambushed in Norway by the Germans. Your mum and her sister had been evacuated when the war started, like most of the kids were. By 1943 most of us were back though there was still bombing after the Blitz. Still nights when they was going down Bethnal Green Station. It was the nearest air raid shelter. Your Grandma, your mum an' her little sister.

It was weird down there son. Like another world. Sleeping in a tunnel. Ain't natural is it? Everyone crowded on the platform together. Oh people sang an' cracked jokes about Hitler, they even put shows on sometimes just to hide how scared they was. I went down a few times. It was 'orrible. I'd rather have taken me chances in the 'ouse. Anyway, no-one talks about that night much. Not them who was there. Even now no-one knows what really 'appened. Your mum don't talk about it so I only know from me mate who was on the anti-aircraft guns in Bethnal Green Gardens. He told me what really went on that night but he ain't supposed to. Even now. Everyone thought it was a German bomb. The government just let 'em believe it.' He inhaled deeply on his cigarette.

'Anyway, that night they was all going down to the shelter. Air raid sirens had gone off but there weren't no panic. Most people had got used to it and a lot of 'em just stayed in their own houses. They were the lucky ones. There'd been rumours though as well that there might be a raid soon. We'd just bombed Germany a couple of nights before that an' all so people was expecting something to happen. Anyway, the searchlights went on that night, after

148

the sirens started an' suddenly, from nowhere there was a huge explosion, well that was what it sounded like anyway an' a weird, whooshing sound. Then the ground started shaking.

Me mate said that it was a new kind of rocket battery, fired somethin' like an' 'undred rockets an' it was in Victoria Park, just up the road. There hadn't bin no warning about it. An' you got used to the sounds you see Jimmy, all the different ones. They'd never heard that before though. They probably thought it was a new kind of German bomb. Everyone who hadn't already got down onto the platforms started to run. They ran down the street to the station an' there was only one way they could go down. One tiny little stairway. They was all pushing and shoving and people started falling over and treading on each other. Sorry mate. I know it's horrible but it 'appened. It's the truth. Nearly two hundred people got crushed to death that night. Your mum survived it but your Nana and your Auntie Shirley didn't. That's what she can't forget son. That's why her nerves are bad an' that's why I get so angry when she won't go to the doctor.'

He stopped then, his voice was cracking. He looked up to see Auntie Molly standing in the doorway. They hadn't noticed her coming in. She was looking at Billy in a way she had never looked at him before. Almost kindly and tears were welling in her eyes.

'So now you know Jimmy,' she whispered 'I'll look after you both until she gets better. I'm the only family she's got left.'

Jimmy stood up and took her coat. 'I'm goin' up London tonight,' he said slowly, 'but I've already had two washes today.'

'And a third one won't do you any harm then will it? You'd best get up those stairs and we'll find something nice for you to wear. And I'll tell you something, you could do with a haircut. You're beginning to look like a yeti.'

Billy smiled. He felt an incredible weight falling off his shoulders. Much as he hated to admit it there were times when Auntie Molly was the most wonderful woman in the world. And now was definitely one of them.

***

Jimmy went on tiptoe into his mum's room. She was sort of asleep. Tossing and turning, whispering things he couldn't make out. He sat on the bed and, as he did, she opened her eyes. She looked really scared and grabbed his hand tightly.

'It's all right mum, it's only me. Just going up town wiv Mrs. Pattinson and Legs. Goin' to see the lights in Regent St.'

She held his hand even tighter. 'Not the trains,' she whispered. 'Don't go on the trains. Don't go down the station. Promise me Jimmy.'

'Yeah, I promise mum. We'll get the bus.'

He felt her relax the grip on his hand and moved it quickly away. 'I come to give you your pills mum. Auntie Molly says you've got to take 'em.' He opened the bottle she had given him and took out two blue pills, and then he picked up the glass of water on the bedside table.

His mum closed her eyes. 'I don't like pills Jimmy,' she said slowly.

'They made you better last time mum. Go on. Please.'

'It wasn't the pills,' she replied. 'It wasn't the pills that made me better.'

She took them from his hand and put them in her mouth. He passed her the glass and she took a few sips of water, then she turned her back to him.

'I'll ... I'll be off now mum then. See you later.' She didn't answer.

'Jimmy!' His dad was shouting from downstairs. 'Legs is 'ere.' Jimmy ran down the stairs excitedly. He had never seen the Christmas lights before. He couldn't wait.

'Alright mate?' Legs gave him a playful punch on the shoulder. 'Mum's outside.'

His dad and his Auntie Molly came into the hall from the kitchen. His dad gave him a two shilling piece. Jimmy saw Leg's eyes widen.

'Wow, thanks dad.'

'Well, you'll probably be getting some hot chestnuts or something an' you need your train fare. Now go on, 'ave a good time an' don't be showing me up.'

150

The two boys ran up the path where May Pattinson was waiting. 'Now you two,' she said sternly, 'no running off. It will be packed with people and I don't want to lose you.'

'John Baxter's allowed into town on his own,' said Legs.

'I very much doubt that John Baxter is allowed anywhere on his own,' May Pattinson laughed. 'It's not as if I'm putting you on reins or asking you to hold my hand or anything Clive.' The boys looked at each other and made a face. They laughed.

'You used to love holding my hand when you were a little lad,' his mum teased. 'How's mum Jimmy? Nice to see Molly there. She'll sort her out.'

Jimmy wanted to forget all about that now. He just wanted to enjoy this. Just for one night he wouldn't think about his mum and the witch and his Auntie Molly making him wash. Why did grown-ups not understand that? Did they never need a bit of different excitement?

They made their way quickly towards the station. Jimmy loved Plaistow Station. It always signalled adventure, travel. One day he would go around the world. It wasn't just a dream. He had always known that it would happen. He always thought about it, when he saw the square, squat building, standing at the top of the hill. Mustn't tell his mum though. That he had been on the underground.

The train was crowded, not as bad as when they went to Upton Park. He understood now why his dad always told his mum that they went to football on the bus and why she had always been frightened of the underground trains. It was all boys and men when they went on Saturday afternoons. Manly talk and masculine smells. Full of grown-ups and kids puffing away on their fags.

Tonight was different. Families. Excited kids. Girls giggling and parents nagging. Trying to get them to sit still. Christmas in the air. How would his mum be at Christmas? There, these thoughts kept coming into his head even though he tried to stop them. It had been horrible what his dad had told him about Bethnal Green but he knew that wasn't why she was ill. He knew it was the witch. Two weeks to Christmas. Would the witch let her get better or ... no he wasn't going to think about that anymore. He looked out of the window as they emerged from the dark tunnel.

MILE END

'We change here boys. Come on. Get your skates on.'

The next train was busier, wouldn't be able to sit down on this one. The boys laughed as they hung on to the seats.

BETHNAL GREEN

Bethnal Green. The signs flashed before Jimmy's eyes as the train slid to a halt. This was where it had happened. All them years ago. His Nanna and his Auntie Shirley who he had never known. Everything seemed to stand still. He couldn't hear any sounds and he searched in vain for some sign. Some recognition of what had happened here. There was nothing.

He looked up at May Pattinson. She was staring at him, sort of funny. 'Why don't it say nothing about all them people dying Mrs. Pattinson?'

She put her hand gently on his shoulder. 'It will, one day Jimmy. I'm glad they've told you about it.'

'That ain't right,' said Jimmy. 'People should know. What happened.'

'Yes,' she agreed. 'It isn't right. Now, come on you two. I think I've got some spangles somewhere in my pocket. Won't be long now.'

When they left the tube at Regents Park, everything else was forgotten. The lights were dazzling. 'Wow,' said Legs. 'This is better than rock n' roll.'

The boys had never seen anything like it in their lives.

'This must be like America,' said Jimmy.

Lights seemed to be everywhere. They could only shuffle along because there were so many people 'oohing' and 'ahing' and stopping every time they saw something new. Enormous lighted Christmas trees and baubles were strung across the road. All the shops were full of lights and tinsel. Everyone was laughing and happy. It was impossible not to smile, it was infectious.

'This is great,' Jimmy laughed. 'America couldn't be better than this.'

Legs let out a Red Indian whoop as they saw the sign Hamleys above a magnificent shop window display. Father Christmas sat, right in the middle, waving to all the

152

kids. Surrounded by little elves in green who busied themselves picking up toys and showing them to the rapturous audience in the street.

'Come on then boys,' said May Pattinson. 'Let's go and have a look inside.'

'Are we allowed in?' Jimmy asked in amazement. 'Don't they know we ain't posh?'

They spent a wonderful hour in Hamleys. So many toys that they could only dream of.

'There's me train set!' Jimmy said excitedly. The enormous box he was looking at was snatched away by a boy who looked about six years old.

'I want this one mummy,' he said to the tall, sophisticated woman who stood behind him. 'Of course you can darling but what is the magic word?'

Jimmy and Legs giggled. 'She talks like the bleeding Queen,' Jimmy laughed.

He watched as the woman took the box and added it to a pile of toys in her basket.

'Bloody hell,' said Legs, 'that must cost hundreds of pounds.'

Jimmy felt a moment of raw anger. It wasn't fair, but then that was what his mum always said. Life wasn't fair; you just needed to appreciate what you had. He looked at the boxes of train sets. Five pounds and fifteen shillings. There was no way he was going to get one of them for Christmas. Just for a moment, he thought he might steal one but this wasn't the local sweet shop and a couple of gobstoppers, this was the biggest toy shop in the country. Anyway it would never fit under his school mac. He glared at the boy who had everything and stuck out his tongue.

'Mummy, mummy. That boy is being rude to me.'

The Queen looked over to Jimmy. He quickly changed his expression to a smile. She smiled back.

'There Jonathan, he's smiling,' she lowered her voice. 'He's just a poor boy. You have to be kind. Father Christmas probably won't be bringing him very much.'

As they moved away, Legs looked at Jimmy. 'She's talking about us as if we were starving kids in Africa.' He laughed. 'Posh gits. He can keep his toys.'

'Yeah,' Jimmy agreed. 'Wouldn't wanna be him. Would you darlin'?'

The boys were still laughing when May Pattinson appeared back from her secret mission, carrying two bags. 'Well done lads,' she said, 'for staying where I told you. I think it's time to get some roasted chestnuts. Hungry?'

The boys nodded and followed her out on to the crowded street. Jimmy had smelt the wonderful aroma since they had emerged from the tube station. They found a chestnut seller up a side street. Standing in front of his brazier, little bags of chestnuts piled up waiting to be bought. Others were on the fire. The smell was overpoweringly delicious. Jimmy took deep breaths and put his hands over the fire for some warmth. In all the excitement he hadn't realised how cold the night had become. They ate hungrily as they walked back down to the station.

'Ta Mrs Pattinson,' Jimmy said, smiling up at her. 'That was the best night I've ever 'ad in the whole of me life.'

Chapter 21

'Sure you'll be alright you two? The kids are all asleep and the bottles are in the fridge if the babies wake up. Just give Josie a shout if they cause any trouble.'

Sally looked at Julie and Freddie sitting on the settee. She knew what they'd be up to the minute she went out the door, he couldn't keep his hands off her now.

'Just want to say Sal,' Freddie spoke. 'Ta, you know. Ta for sorting it. He patted Julie, none too gently, on her stomach. 'Much too young for sprogs me,' he laughed.

'You're still alright to come wiv me ain't you Sal?'

Sally nodded. 'Yeah, I'll meet you there. Thursday two o'clock.'

'Hope I'll be alright for Christmas and me turkey roast. Mind you last year we never got none. Me dad threw it out the window.'

Freddie sniffed. 'Glad I won't be at yours for Christmas dinner then. I like me Christmas nosh, not as much as I like me women though.' He grabbed Julie and started kissing her.

'Right, well I'll be off then,' said Sally putting her coat on. 'There's biscuits in the larder and help yourselves to a cuppa. S'pose it's a bit late to tell you to be careful.' She smiled.

'What no beer? Good job I've brought some wiv me then ain't it.' Freddie guffawed. He had an ugly laugh, Sally thought. She hoped Julie wouldn't stay with him but it was her life. He'd be back to the army on Monday. She shuddered as she walked out through the gate. Wouldn't fancy him on my side in a war, she thought.

Billy was stood outside his front door, smoking a cigarette. Sally laughed.

'You got to smoke outside now Billy?'

'Kate's auntie's here. She just moans every time I light up, it ain't worth it.'

Sally stopped at his gate. There was something about his tone of voice.

'Is everything alright Billy only Kate ain't been at work ... ?'

'No,' he snapped, throwing his cigarette butt onto the path, 'but it ain't got nothing to do wiv you.'

155

Sally was stunned. Why would he talk to her like that? What was the matter with him? 'Billy ... I didn't mean to ...' Too late. Billy had disappeared through the door and slammed it shut behind him.

'West Ham must 'ave lost.' The voice came from nowhere and Sally jumped. She turned round.

'God Bones, you nearly gave me 'eart attack then. You're always creeping around. How's Chuck?'

'Off on his travels again I think. Ain't seen him since this morning. He always comes back now so I don't worry no more. Ta for bringing him home though, the other week.'

'I've still got the scratch marks. I'll just leave him be next time then,' Sally laughed. 'What's up wiv Billy, Bones? He don't usually snap like that.'

Bones walked companionably beside her. 'Kate's poorly.' He patted his head, 'up here.'

'Oh dear. That must be hard, well for all of 'em. I've heard she 'ad a breakdown, lost a baby. We wasn't 'ere then.'

'It's the worst thing,' said Bones. 'The very worst thing.'

Sally looked at him. As they walked under the streetlight, she could have sworn she saw tears in his eyes.

'Anyways, I'm alright. I've got Chuck, well most of the time anyway.'

Dianne was approaching them at a rate of knots. 'Sorry I'm late Sal. We'll still get the bus if we're quick. We can always go up the Palais instead.'

'Oh, come on Di, I've bin looking forward to "Oklahoma" all week. We'll make the bus if we run. See ya Bones.'

The bus was just leaving as they got there. The conductor grabbed them both and pulled them on board. 'Only just made it girls,' he laughed. 'Must be worth a kiss at least.'

'Bog off Soapy,' Dianne retorted.

'You've bin telling me to bog off ever since primary school. Wait till I'm famous that's all. I'm gonna be in a rock n' roll band y'know. I just can't decide what instrument to play.'

156

'Well,' said Dianne. 'Why don't you phone Bill Hayley an' ask him if they need any more musicians. Ask him what he's short of an' then that's the instrument you can learn.'

Soapy's face lit up. 'I hadn't thought of that,' he said. 'Ta Di. Nah. Put yer money away. My treat.'

As the girls left the bus at Stratford, Soapy whispered to Dianne. 'Just one thing,' he said seriously.

'An' what might that be?' Dianne asked sarcastically.

'I ain't got Bill Haley's telephone number.'

'Bog off Soapy,' Dianne and Sally shouted as the bus pulled away. They dissolved into fits of giggles on the pavement.

'You're 'orrible to him Di. He worships you an' he ain't bad looking now his spots have gone. Why's he called Soapy anyway?'

'Never washed did he? Used to stink. An' I should know cos I used to sit behind him in primary school.'

'Well,' said Sally, 'I know he ain't the brightest spark in the box but he's a good bloke an' he loves yer.'

Dianne grimaced. 'I will never, ever be that desperate Sal. Now come on, let's go an' watch this sloppy film you wanna see then we can get down the King's Head before closing'. You ain't bin for ages. I know why but you can't hide from him forever.'

Sally sighed. Billy wouldn't be down the pub tonight anyway so she might as well. It was obvious what he thought of her now. That was good. Wasn't it? 'Yeah alright. I'm just going in for one though. That's all.'

The two girls walked into the cinema linking arms.

Two hours later they were having a drink at the Kings Head. 'Good film girls?' Arthur asked.

'Blimey,' said Dianne. 'Has he had an' 'ead transplant. Is he talking to us Sal?'

'Oh, very funny,' Arthur replied. 'I'm just trying to be sociable that's all an' what do I get for it? A load of abuse. '

He glared at Sally. 'An' if you're looking for Billy his wife is *very* sick.'

Sally felt like she had been punched, her cheeks were reddening. This wasn't fair.

The next second she saw Arthur, covered in shandy, spluttering and choking. Dianne had thrown her drink all over

157

him. 'How dare you,' Dianne snarled. 'How dare you accuse my mate. There ain't nothin' going on wiv her an' Billy ...'

'Di, come on.' Sally tried to pull her friend away.

'No Sal, they need to know. I made it up. I made it all up, it was lies. Alright? You all got that now?' She slammed her glass down on the bar. There was silence throughout the crowded pub. 'We ain't staying where we're not wanted. Come on Sal.'

'You certainly ain't staying,' Arthur boomed, 'but it ain't your choice, it's mine. You're both barred.'

Dianne flounced out, followed closely by an embarrassed Sally. When they got outside, Sally suddenly saw the funny side. 'I don't believe this,' she laughed. 'We've bin barred. From the King's Head.'

Dianne's anger soon melted at the sight of her friend taking it all so well. They both dissolved into giggles. 'Ooh dear,' Dianne snorted. 'I'm goin' to wee meself in a minute.'

'Well, you'll have to go over behind the hedge. Can't go back in there.'

'Oh, I'll hold on till I get home. Sorry Sal if I showed you up.'

Sally put her arm around her friend's shoulder. 'You was sticking up for me Dianne. You put 'em right. Ta.'

'Well, I felt a bit bad. Spreading stuff around like that. You know what my mouth's like. I'll pop in tomorrer yeah? I'll have to get home before I wet me knickers.'

Sally watched her friend as she walked away. She wasn't sure yet whether Dianne's display had been a good or a bad thing. Only time would tell. She strolled home slowly, there wasn't a soul around. As she walked up Churchill Street she looked up at Billy's house. He was framed in the front window. She put her head down and walked quickly. His door opened.

'Sal,' he whispered urgently, 'I'm sorry.' He ran up to the gate. 'I'm sorry I was rude to yer. I didn't mean it. It's just ... It's just hard at the moment that's all.'

Without thinking, she put her arm on his. His face looked so full of pain she couldn't help it. Oh, she wished she hadn't drunk those three Babychams. When he put his arms around her and pulled her towards him it seemed like the most natural thing in the world. Oh, this was what she wanted. This was what she needed so much. He kissed her then and for a few seconds she was in another world.

Then he pulled away. 'We shouldn't be doing this,' he said. 'I just can't. I'm sorry Sal.'

'Not good enough Billy Potter,' she smiled. Her lips trembled. She could feel tears pricking at the back of her eyes. 'Please don't stop now.'

As he walked slowly away she whispered urgently after him. 'Give me half-an hour, let me get rid of Julie. I'll leave the back door open.'

***

Billy sat down at the kitchen table and lit up a cigarette. He looked at the clock. Just gone half-past ten. He was stunned. He couldn't believe what had just happened. And what could happen in half-an hour if he let it.

All he could hear was the ticking of the clock. It seemed to bore into his head. And then he heard Auntie Molly snoring. Quietly at first and then growing to a crescendo so that the walls almost rattled. It was as if she was trying to tell him something. And what would George say? Think on lad, be careful. Don't do 'owt rash. Billy recognised, as the minutes ticked away, that this was some sort of test. He knew that if Sally had dragged him instantly into her house he would have gone.

He closed his eyes. Oh, just to have a willing soft and beautiful body under his. She wouldn't be shy or cold. She would love him with every bone in her body. Didn't he deserve that? After all these years. Was this it now for the rest of his life? But did he really want to lose Kate and Jimmy because that's what would happen. Kate would never put up with him being unfaithful. But his body, well, that was sending a different message through altogether. His brains had gone into his trousers. That was what his mum had always said about his dad. He watched the hands of the clock and just thanked God that he hadn't had a drink. He looked up towards the door. Molly was stood there in her dressing gown. Her hair in rollers. She sighed. 'I can't sleep,' she said.

You could have fooled me, Billy thought. 'I'll make us a brew then shall I Molly?'

She smiled at him. 'You're very domesticated all of a sudden Billy Potter.' She sat down in his armchair. 'This can't be easy for you Billy. I know we've not always got on and I never thought you were good enough for Kate, I admit that. I think I might have changed my mind.'

Not if you knew what I was thinking about right now, he thought to himself. 'You're not so bad yourself Molly,' he said, passing her a cup of tea. 'I don't know what I'd have done without you today.'

'She'll be alright you know but she does need to see someone. Oh, she'll get better for now but she needs to talk about everything. I'm as bad. We never talked about it. That night. Of course I was already down in the shelter when it all happened. When we came out in the morning there was no sign of anything.

We didn't have many bombs in Ilford. I was just staying with them for the night. As soon as the wireless went dead we knew there was going to be a raid. I got down that shelter like a bat out of hell; I suppose I wasn't used to it like they were.

'*We'll be there in a bit Molly,*' my sister said. '*There's no rush.*' Those were the very last words she ever said to me.'

Billy passed her his hankie as he saw her eyes start to fill up. 'I had to identify them. Her and Shirley. It was ... horrible. They had all been asphyxiated. They were purple Billy. Purple and swollen.'

Billy swallowed. He got up and patted her on the shoulder. He couldn't give her a hug. Not Auntie Molly.

'Why don't you get back up to bed Molly?' he said gently. 'I'm just going out for a fag. I'm gonna sleep down here. I don't want to disturb Kate.'

Molly nodded and walked slowly towards the door. She turned and smiled through her tears. 'You're not a bad man Billy. She could have done worse.'

Guilt flooded through his body because he knew exactly what he was going to do now. God, he only had one life. There could be another war tomorrow and he could be dead. He just needed something good to happen. All this talk about people dying and everything else going on. Why shouldn't he? As he looked at the clock he realised that he had failed the test. It was just coming up to eleven and, after checking that his cigarettes were in his pocket, he opened

160

the back door quietly. Over George's two fences and he was standing outside Sally's door.

He deserved this.

***

Sally watched the hands on the clock go up towards eleven. So, he wasn't coming. She was sitting here on her second or third hand settee. She had dimmed the lights and the wireless was playing soft, late night music.

'Bastard,' she muttered under her breath. 'Bloody bastard.'

She stood up and threw a cushion across the room. It hit the fireguard and bounced off sending sparks flying from the dying embers. Then he was there. Standing at the door.

'Billy?'

'Sal.'

They moved towards each other and fell, together, onto the settee. They couldn't stop. Their hands were everywhere. Touching, kissing, caressing. Billy started trying to pull off her blouse, kissing her breasts hungrily as he did.

They didn't see Julie come in. She hadn't knocked. Until she coughed, they had no idea she was there. They saw her walk across the room in front of them to where she had left her purse on the rug by the fire. Sally pulled her blouse back on and tried desperately to do the buttons up. Billy stood up and coughed.

'Sorry Julie,' he muttered. 'You shouldn't have had to see that.'

'Ain't me your hurting is it Billy?' Julie said as she walked towards the door.

'Please Julie,' Sally said tearfully.

'I ain't gonna say nothing,' said Julie. 'Ain't my business.' Billy followed her out of the door.

'Where are you going Billy? Please don't go,' Sally pleaded.

He looked at her. 'I'm sorry Sal. I ain't cut out for all this sneaking about. It ain't right. It ain't meant to happen.'

'Well I ain't giving up,' Sally smiled. 'Maybe it'll be third time lucky.'

As she heard the kitchen door slam, Sally felt tears threatening. Billy was a good man. No, it was Kate's fault.

161

Her and her depressions. Making his life hell. Well, she wasn't going to give up, not now.

She suddenly felt empty. Empty and sad. Tears erupted from her eyes as she slowly walked to the back door and locked it. She opened the larder door and reached for the top shelf. Sherry was the best mate you could have sometimes. Her head was going to be bad in the morning. She looked at the clock. Eleven fifteen. Forty five minutes ago she had thought her life might change. Now it felt like it was over and nothing had even begun.

Chapter 22

Kate looked over to the bedside table and waited for the clock to come in to focus. Seven o'clock. Morning or evening? She wasn't even sure what day it was. It was those pills. The other side of the bed was empty. Where was Billy?

He had left her. That was what had been happening. She remembered now. It was all coming back to her. And where was Jimmy? How long had she been lying in bed?

The door opened. It was Auntie Molly. What was *she* doing here? 'Oh Molly,' she cried, 'please tell me what's happening.' Molly was carrying a tray, on it a steaming bowl of porridge and a mug of tea. Kate's eyes were drawn to the bottle of pills. No, she thought. No. I won't be drugged anymore. They're all out to get me. To stop me thinking, to stop me feeling. Molly put the tray down on the bedside table and smiled at her niece.

'You're looking a bit better this morning,' she said. 'Bit of colour in your cheeks. You'll be alright Kate.'

'But what day is it and how long have I been lying here? Where ... where are Billy and Jimmy?'

Molly sighed. 'Billy's gone to work. Jimmy's downstairs having his breakfast and its Wednesday. You've been poorly for quite a long time but ... Kate what are you doing? Get back into bed you can't ...'

Kate struggled to stand, she felt so weak, and her legs were like jelly. She fell back on to the bed.

'I have to get to work,' she said. 'I'm on earlies on a Wednesday. I can't stay here forever.' Molly helped her to sit up in bed.

'The doctor has signed you off Kate. You're not going to work today. You've hardly eaten anything for a week.'

'Don't you tell me what I can or can't do Molly,' Kate snapped. 'This is my house. I'll eat my porridge and then I'm going to work. I'll be fine. Now just get out and leave me alone.'

'You are *not* going to work Kate and you *must* take your pills. They're the only thing that ...'

Kate interrupted. 'Keeps me quiet and asleep? Not causing any trouble? That's what you mean isn't it Molly? You're all in on this, all trying to destroy me.' She burst into tears and cried into the pillow. Racking sobs shook her whole body.

'What's going on?' Jimmy was at the door. When Kate saw her son's troubled face she tried desperately to stop crying.

'Sorry Jimmy but I need you to go. I don't want you to see me like this. Both of you. Please.'

They left but as Molly looked back from the doorway she whispered. 'Promise me Kate, you'll take those pills. I'll be back in half-an hour.'

Kate nodded. So, she had half an hour. Her mind suddenly became perfectly clear. She had half an hour to get herself ready and get out of this house. She ate her porridge quickly, greedily, dropping bits on her nightie. It would give her the strength. She managed to stand and walk across the room to the chest of drawers, on tiptoe so that no-one would hear. They would try to keep her in this room if they could. If she went to the bathroom they would hear her. She would have to wait until she got to work. Kate got dressed as fast as she could, found her handbag and crept out on to the landing. She could hear Molly nagging Jimmy for slurping his hot milk. She didn't have long.

She reached the bottom of the stairs. The door through to the kitchen was closed so they wouldn't hear her opening and closing the front door if she was careful. She felt like giggling. Bubbles of laughter were rising in her throat. She would beat them. They wouldn't stop *her*. She tried to walk fast down the road but after a few steps her legs were dragging. The cold air invaded her lungs and she was finding it difficult to breathe. When she reached the corner of Churchill Street she felt the panic rising again. Her body shook, her heart thumped. She couldn't breathe. But she knew it would pass. She held on to the wall and breathed deeply. Slowly, her body returned to normal. After a few seconds she walked on.

The bus was crowded, worse than usual. Still, at least she had got a seat. She was so tired. Smoke wafted down from the top deck, choking the air. She had to show them, she couldn't give in. They were probably all gossiping up there, about Billy and his tart. Perhaps she even worked at the factory. Well, she would show them.

164

'Hello Kate, are you feeling better?' Sally Evans had sat down beside her. That's all she needed this morning. She really *was* a tart. Kate smelt her perfume. It was a smell she recognised from somewhere else. Roses. She couldn't remember where she had smelt it before.

Kate glanced sideways at Sally. How could she look so pretty and fresh when she had three children? It wasn't fair. 'I'm fine,' she answered finally. Frostily.

She could feel Sally looking at her. Perhaps she was on their side as well. Perhaps she had been sent on the bus to take her home. She didn't usually sit next to her.

Kate closed her eyes. That would get rid of them all. Gossiping, laughing sluts.

Sally was talking to her. What was she saying? Kate opened her eyes. Sally was looking at her strangely. Waiting for an answer. 'Sorry, I – I must have nodded off. What did you say?'

'I was just saying that I don't know why Maggie puts up wiv Mick that's all.'

'Well, you wouldn't understand, would you? You've never been married. It's not all fun and sex you know. For better or for worse, that's what Maggie's doing. Marriage vows Sally. Something you should have thought about before you gave birth to three illegitimate children.'

She saw Sally's arm go up but she scarcely felt the slap on her cheek. Good, she was glad she had told her what she thought.

'Hey,' the conductor shouted. 'Ain't having no fights on this bus girls. What's going on?'

Everything seemed to go quiet as the factory gates loomed in front of them. Sally had jumped out of the seat and was glaring at Kate. One of the other girls was holding her back. Kate held her gaze defiantly.

'You don't deserve what you've got, you cow,' Sally hissed angrily. And then she was gone.

Kate couldn't move, there was no energy left. The young conductor tapped her on the shoulder. 'Ain't you working today darlin'?'

'I'm tired,' she cried, tears running down her cheeks, 'I'm so tired.'

'Alright love, we'll drop you back off at the depot if you like. Ain't far from the estate. You can always get the 25 from there if you need to.'

She took her hankie from her pocket, wiped her eyes and blew her nose. 'Yes. Yes I'll do that. Thank you.'

It felt wonderful to be on the bus on her own. All that space, no people. Just the gentle rumble of the engine. She wished she could stay on here for ever just like this. Peaceful, alone and free. The conductor helped her down from the platform as if she were an old lady. Kate laughed suddenly. She was only twenty seven years old.

She walked slowly past the park railings and saw children playing on the swings and slides.

It was then that she heard Shirley calling her.

'Push me higher Kate. Higher, higher. I want to fly!'

She walked, faster now, through the park entrance and in to the playground. Energy seemed to be pumping through her body. There were quite a few children playing and mums sat chatting on the benches but Kate scarcely noticed them. Her eyes were locked on to the little girl sitting on the swing. She had her back to Kate. Her long blond hair streamed out behind her as she swung. She was laughing. It was Shirley. She knew it was. She had come back.

Kate ran over, grabbed the swing and stopped it. The little girl turned around. It wasn't Shirley. Of course it wasn't Shirley. Shirley was dead and she, Kate, had killed her.

'Hey, what you doin? What you doin' to my kid?'

The little girl had started to cry, had jumped down from the swing and was running towards her mother.

Kate stood, tears drowning her face, still holding the chains on the swing.

'I'm sorry,' she wept. 'I thought she was someone else.'

The woman came up close to her. 'You ain't right in the head,' she hissed.

And then someone else came. Kate heard a kind, warm voice.

'Come on Kate. Come and sit down for a minute.'

'I – I can't sit down. I have to go.'

Kate looked in to the lined and lived-in face of someone she had known for a long time. She had taken the pain away before. She let her old friend take her hand and lead her slowly towards the park bench where they sat down together. Her friend held her hand and waited until Kate began to talk.

Kate told her about the panic on the day Shirley had been born. How she had helped her mum to deliver the baby because the midwife had been held up. How Shirley had smiled first at Kate, even before her own mum and dad. And that she had followed Kate around everywhere. Everything Kate did, Shirley copied.

And then she talked of Bethnal Green. And so, for the first time, she began to talk about the night that had become one of her greatest secrets. That dreadful night when she had let go of Shirley's hand in the crush on the stairs down to the station.

Greta stroked her hand. 'None of this was your fault Kate,' she said. 'Who knows what we are all capable of in times of stress? We have no more control over it than a leaf in the wind. Let me take you back to my home. You know I can help you. You must release your guilt or you will never move forward.'

Kate nodded and they walked slowly up the road together.

The old house looked forbidding today. Grey, drizzly clouds in the sky above. Kate shivered as her last memories of the house invaded her mind. Billy, angry. Shouting at Greta. Dragging Kate out from her healing session. She had to be careful. People, including Billy, thought you were daft, believing in things like that. Frightened of powers that they didn't understand. She supposed that was why he had been so angry.

As they walked slowly up the path three black cats came towards them.

Greta took her key out and opened the front door, Kate followed her in.

'Thank you,' she whispered as the door closed behind her.

***

Jimmy kicked the tin can over the wall in the playground.

167

'What did you do that for?' Legs shouted at him. 'What's up with you this morning anyway? Thought you'd be happy now you've seen the lights.'

Jimmy shrugged. 'Yeah, they was good.'

'What was that about at that station when me mum was talking to you?'

Jimmy took a deep breath. 'It's where me Nan died and me auntie. In the war. Me dad reckons that's why me mum's poorly.'

Legs pulled a face. 'That was years ago. I don't see that Jimmy. Do you?'

'Nah. It's definitely the witch, I know it is.' Jimmy said angrily. 'I don't know what else we can do. There ain't no more apples and we've bin baptised.'

The bell rang and they all got into line. Del came up behind them, late as usual and out of breath.

'Perhaps we could drive her out of town,' said Legs.

'Or we could just kill her,' Del gasped. 'Ooh, I got a stitch now.'

'No talking in the line boys. How many times do I have to tell you?' The headmaster glared at Del. 'And what is the excuse for your lateness this morning Derek? '

'Well sir ...' Del began.

The headmaster put his hand up. 'On second thoughts I don't think that I really want to know. Get inside all of you. And walk!'

Miss Parsons had just finished taking the register when the headmaster walked into the classroom. 'Morning class.'

'Morning Mr.Cummings sir,' the class replied in a bored, monotonous tone, all standing up reluctantly and scraping their chairs noisily back as they did so.

Jimmy gave Del a look. Surely he wouldn't be caning Del for being ten seconds late in the line. That was usually what it meant when he came in this early.

'Jimmy. Jimmy Potter. Follow me please boy.' Jimmy felt his face go red and his legs starting to shake. He hadn't done nothing yesterday. Nothing anyway. 'It's your mother Potter,' Mr. Cummings boomed as they walked along the corridor.

'But she's in bed sir. She ain't well.'

'Well, she's managed to go somewhere. Always a drama with you lot in Churchill Street isn't there? Promise me you'll never move to Chigwell, Potter. That's where I live. I couldn't cope with that. Ah, there's your Auntie. She's in a bit of a state and she'd like a word with you about the aforementioned problem but don't be long. You can't afford to miss your schooling.'

'Oh Jimmy, she's gone out.' Auntie Molly emerged from the headmaster's office, wringing her hands. 'I didn't know what to do. I went to May's house to phone the factory and she hasn't turned up for work, though they said she had been on the bus. The conductor said she seemed a bit tearful and they dropped her off at the depot. Can you think Jimmy? Think of anywhere she might have gone?'

Jimmy was stunned. It took a lot to shake his Auntie Molly up like this. Where would his mum have gone? He didn't have a clue. He didn't know what she did except that she went to work and she cooked and cleaned. He shook his head slowly. Two boys passed them in the corridor and stared curiously.

'You can sit in my office now Miss Walker,' the headmaster came out carrying a sheaf of papers. 'I shan't be needing it for a few minutes. Try not to keep the boy for too long.'

'He's full of compassion isn't he?' Auntie Molly said loudly as they moved into the stark, grey painted room. 'Worse than in my day and that's saying something.' She slammed her handbag down on his desk and plonked herself into his chair.

'You can't sit in Mr. Cumming's chair Auntie Molly, he'll go mad,' said Jimmy fearfully.

'I'll sit wherever I like Jimmy. Now, just try and think. There must be somewhere she goes. I've asked in the shops on the way here but they haven't seen her. No-one in the street has either. She's just completely disappeared.'

'We'd best get me dad. He might know something.'

Auntie Molly sighed. 'Well, it's either that or I'll have to call the police. We can't have her wandering around the streets in the state she's in.'

'Perhaps,' said Jimmy thoughtfully, 'she just wanted to go for a walk. She ain't bin out all week.'

'Don't be ridiculous Jimmy. Why would she want to do that?'

'Well,' he answered, 'she ain't never gonna forgive you if you call the coppers out.'

Auntie Molly sighed, stood up and collected her bag. She did look very worried, Jimmy thought. 'Yes, well, I'll try and get through to your dad at work. He might have some ideas. Now don't you worry Jimmy. You just get back to class.'

Mr. Cummings entered the room looking rather irritated.

'I want to come home wiv you,' Jimmy said quietly. 'I can look in lots of places that you can't get to.'

'For goodness sake,' Mr. Cummings said. 'Is the poor woman not allowed to set foot outside the door without having to organise a search party?'

Auntie Molly pulled herself up to her full five feet and two inches and marched over to where Mr. Cummings stood. She glared at him and spoke quietly but forcefully. 'My niece is a very sick woman,' she barked. 'She has had a nervous breakdown. I am *not* one of your pupils and I will *not* be spoken to in this way. Now get out of my sight before I punch you on the nose.'

Jimmy's eyes almost bounced out of their sockets. No-one he knew had *ever* stood up to Mr. Cummings before. Cor, he would really have something to tell the gang now. Good old Auntie Molly.

'Come on Jimmy, you can come with me. Get your coat and your satchel.'

'But you can't just take him ...'

'I think you'll find that I can actually,' said Auntie Molly as she flounced through the door.

As Jimmy went to follow her he turned to look at Mr. Cummings who had removed his glasses and was wiping his forehead. His hands were shaking. 'Don't ever let that woman come near me again Potter.'

Jimmy grinned at him as he followed his aunt out of the room. 'I'll try me best sir. See you tomorrer.'

***

Kate looked around her friend's front room. Cobwebs hung from the ornate ceiling but apart from that the

170

house was spotless. 'Spiders have a right to life too you know.'

'You read my mind,' said Kate.

'No Kate,' she laughed 'I just followed your eyes. Now, I'll get you a cup of tea. You just lie down on the chaise-longue and try to relax.'

Relax, Kate laughed to herself. Her mind felt like a box of fireworks. Thoughts exploding in her head. One after the other. Dead babies, blonde sluts, the bang bangs of the bombs and an air raid siren wailing. All these thoughts crashing through her head. Spiralling, out of control. She had to hold on. She had to. Greta would make it better, she did before.

She laid her head back on the green, chintz chaise-longue. Green. Green was peaceful. Green was space and trees and grass. Before the war, she remembered Victoria Park. Running on the grass with Shirley. Just running and laughing and being free in the summer sunshine. Now she was running but she couldn't stop. Couldn't stop.

'Here you are Kate.'

Tea, tea. That's what they always do. Have a cup of tea. Oh, your house just got bombed. We'll have a cup of tea. That'll make everything alright. Your baby just died but have a cup of tea and everything will seem better. Your husband is screwing a blond tart. Have a bloody cup of tea.

'Sometimes tea really does help Kate. It's a constant, a tradition, something predictable. And it brings people comfort. It's not the tea itself that makes you feel better; it's the fact that someone is making it for you, showing you a kindness. That's what I think anyway.' She laughed. 'It doesn't work so well for men I'm afraid. They're used to having tea made for them but us women ...'

'I'm frightened,' Kate whispered. 'I'm frightened that I'm going mad. I was so angry then that I wanted to ...'

'I know.'

Greta put her hands lightly on Kate's forehead. 'Now, just try to relax, close your eyes. Would you rather sit?'

Kate shook her head. Every muscle in her body felt taut, tense. Old memories attacked her brain in short, stat-taco bursts. Like gunfire. She had to try to keep her body still. She could feel it twitching.

171

She felt the hands lightly placed on her head and heard the clock ticking. And the birds singing outside. Something was happening in her head. It was trying to get in. Her brain was crackling, like pins and needles. The tension, like before a thunderstorm, was alive like electricity. Then it came, slowly at first, into the jumble and the pain. It was a light, a green light. That peaceful green of childhood memories. She so badly wanted it to come in but it was struggling to get through. She moved her head from side to side, felt tears on her face, tried to cry out but couldn't. And then it was there. Washing over all the bad things, drowning them in its beautiful serenity. It flowed through her whole body until she felt nothing but relief at the absence of pain. The healing hands were still there but she barely felt them. She never wanted to leave this place. Never again.

Kate opened her eyes and still felt calm. The healing hands were above her head now. Sweat was forming on Greta's forehead. Her eyes were closed and screwed up tight. Kate was suddenly filled with a great love for this woman and tears fell from her eyes as she saw again the numbers tattooed on her wrist. 41579. She remembered them from the last time. She knew now what they were. Old Bones had told her but she must never tell anyone, it was her secret. Kate also knew that whatever *she* had been through was nothing compared to the sufferings of her friend. 'Thank you Greta,' she whispered.

Greta smiled and sat down at the end of the chaise-longue. She looked exhausted. 'You need to go now Kate. People who care about you will be worried. Just sleep. That's what you need and it *will* be a peaceful sleep. Then come back and see me again.' Kate nodded.

'And talk to Billy, tell him everything. He needs to understand. I know what you've been through. He doesn't. So, when you're strong enough.'

She opened the front door for Kate. 'And tell that boy of yours to behave himself,' she laughed. 'He has a good heart but a vivid imagination.'

As Kate walked back slowly into Churchill Street the world seemed different somehow. Less complicated. God, she was tired though.

'Mum, mum. Where have you bin? We've bin looking for you everywhere.'

172

Jimmy ran up to her. She saw Auntie Molly standing at the gate.

'I just need to sleep now Jimmy.' She tried to raise her hand to ruffle his hair but the effort was too much. 'I just went for a walk.' And then she fainted.

***

When Kate came round she was back in bed, Billy was holding her hand. The muscles on his face were taut, his eyes angry. 'I'm guessing where you've bin Kate. It was the next place I was coming to look, an' you know what I think. I've got a good mind to go round there and tell her ...'

'No Billy, no. She's helping me, like she did before. She's my friend.' Kate could scarcely get the words out of her mouth. The tiredness was overwhelming.

'She didn't help you. Not over the baby. It was the pills.'

'I took the pills,' Kate said slowly, 'for two weeks Billy. After that I chucked them down the toilet. They made me feel ... bad, much worse. Someone told me about a healer so I started going to see her. That's when I began to get better. That day ... when you dragged me out of there I had already seen her three times.'

Please Billy, don't keep arguing, Kate thought. She closed her eyes. 'We'll talk about everything but I must sleep now. There was a roaring in her head and then the green flowed through and everything was calm and peaceful again.

***

'How is she?' George put the paper down as his wife came in the back door.

'Well, she's still sleeping. She seemed much calmer when she came back from wherever she had been.' May sat down at the table. 'Do you know George Pattinson,' she said. 'There are times I wish we'd never left Blackpool.'

'It was certainly a bit more peaceful up there,' George laughed.

'Just found something else out as well,' May sighed. 'Kate was on the bus this morning and I've heard that Sally slapped her.'

'What?' George's eyes bulged. He put his head in his hands. 'The gloves are off then I'd say. Bugger.'

'But Billy wouldn't ... It isn't true is it George? These rumours?'

173

George shook his head. 'I hope not. I'll have another word. He's vulnerable at the moment May and if Sally goes after him ...'

'Oh, that's right, always blame the other woman.'

'I'm not blaming anyone May but she shouldn't have lost her temper with Kate. She knows she's ill. I think its best if we don't get involved in this one though or we'll end up falling out.'

May sighed. She hated it when friends fell out with each other and it seemed to happen a lot round here. She had never been able to take sides like others did. She had never seen the world in black and white. Sometimes she thought it might be easier if she did.

Chapter 23

'So is your mum alright then now?' Josie asked Jimmy, who had just arrived out of breath at the den.

'Nah. She's bin asleep for three days,' said Jimmy. 'Me Auntie Molly is doing me head in.'

'You won't have no Christmas then,' said Legs. 'It's only seven more days. She won't be able to cook or nothing. Who's gonna get your Christmas presents?'

'Father Christmas,' Del laughed. 'Don't be silly Legsy.' He punched Legs playfully.

'What we doing today then?' Jimmy asked. 'It's freezing in 'ere.'

Josie reached into the box and took out her red catechism. 'We need to start wiv a prayer this morning. For Jimmy's mum.'

Jimmy bit his bottom lip. He could feel tears coming now. He just didn't want to think about it. He just wished they would all shut up. Then again, he thought, if it helped his mum...

They all closed their eyes and said the Lords Prayer.

'We might need even more prayers soon,' said Del. They all looked at him.

'What do you mean?' Josie asked. 'Ain't we got enough to worry about?'

'Just saying, that's all. If you don't wanna know, ain't gonna tell yer.'

They all sat in silence for a few seconds. 'Well, I want to know,' said Legs.

'Ain't telling you now. That's it. Cor, you're right Jimmy. Cold enough for snow today. That's what me mum said this morning and that ain't all she said neither.'

They all looked at him again. He always did this, Jimmy thought to himself, Del. When he wanted to tell you something he wound you up until you were desperate to know. It was never anything much anyway, Jimmy thought. I ain't gonna rise to it.

'Oh, come on Del,' Legs pleaded.

Jimmy and Josie tried to look disinterested.

'You ain't gonna like this,' said Del, looking at the two of them. 'Anyways there's more trouble coming. Grown-up trouble. Nothing to do wiv the witch this time.'

They were all getting curious now. No-one spoke.

'Well, alright then. I ain't sure exactly but I think ...' He looked straight at Jimmy and smiled. 'Your dad and Sally have bin doing sex.'

'No they ain't,' said Josie quickly.

'How do you know?' Del asked her.

'Because you have to do sex in bed an' Jimmy's dad ain't never bin in our 'ouse. Me mum ain't bin in yours neither has she Jimmy?'

Jimmy shook his head. What a Christmas this was going to be, he thought.

'Well,' Del continued to impart his unwelcome gossip. 'I heard me mum an' Julie talking'. Me mum saw 'em snogging Saturday night. So there.'

'They ain't doin' it,' Jimmy shouted. 'Me dad don't even kiss me mum and he's married to her. He don't kiss no-one.'

'If they do it to get babies,' said Del, 'that must mean ...'

Jimmy took a deep breath and tried to stop himself shouting again. 'Well, me mum can't have no more babies,' he said quietly.

Del thought for a minute and then looked excited. 'That must be it then. Perhaps your mum an' dad don't do sex if they can't make babies so your dad has to do it wiv someone else instead.'

Jimmy punched Del then, straight on the nose.

'No!' Josie shouted. 'Stop it you two. Remember the Code. We've got to stick together now.'

Blood was seeping from Del's nose, tears rolling down his face. 'Sorry mate,' he said to Jimmy. 'I didn't mean nothing. Just thought you should know.' Jimmy jumped up and walked out of the den, tears stinging his eyes.

Legs had withdrawn into the furthest corner.

'Just you get out there,' Josie almost spat at Del 'an' say you're sorry again. We can't fall out wiv each other, not now. Jimmy's got enough on his plate. You're a worse gossip than an old woman.' She dug deep into her pocket and pulled out her hankie. 'Here, stick this up your nose an' stop blubbering. I'll go an' talk to 'im.'

As she followed Jimmy out of the den the first light snowflakes fell from the overcast sky. He was standing with

176

his head back and his mouth open, letting the snow in. 'Snowing Jose,' he said excitedly. 'We can get the sledges out.'

'It ain't true you know Jimmy. What Del said. He is sorry and he ain't even angry that you hit 'im.'

'We'd know wouldn't we Jose, if that really was goin' on?'

Josie nodded and put her head back. The snow tasted fresh and clean and magical. Del came up behind them.

'We gonna get the sledges out then?' he asked quietly. He spat on his hand and held it out to Jimmy. Jimmy stared at him for a few seconds. He had made a right mess of Del's nose. They giggled as they shook hands and then they were both laughing and rolling around in the snow. Josie looked at them in amazement.

She would never understand men.

***

Billy marched straight from work and strode purposefully through Sally's gate. His mate, who had relieved him on his shift, had told him about Sally hitting Kate on the bus this morning. After all the trouble losing Kate this morning he couldn't believe that Sally had done that. How could she? What was she thinking? God, he thought, I've had a lucky escape there. If it hadn't been for Julie coming in the other night ...

What had shaken him up even more had been his anger, his reaction. He had wanted to kill Sally. The anger was like a ball of fire in his stomach. He just didn't know where it had come from. He had gone to sit in the park on the way home to try and hold it together before he confronted Sal. He hadn't moved from the park bench until his temper had cooled down a bit.

He went to the front door and knocked loudly.

'Billy!' she exclaimed. She looked at his face. 'I take it you've heard then.'

He moved into the hall and slammed the door behind him. 'I don't know what the fuck you think you thought you were doing, hitting a sick woman like that Sal. I can't believe that of you. You didn't did yer?'

'I did Billy. I did slap 'er. She said some very evil things.'

177

'She ain't well Sal. She don't know what she's doing when she's like this. I can't believe you done that.'

'Well, I'm sorry Billy but it was only a little slap. I didn't punch her or nothing. I was just ... just jealous I suppose. I don't know. I couldn't help meself.' She moved towards him, tears in her eyes.

'Don't you come near me. How can you be jealous? You ain't 'ad a life like she 'as. You've brought all your trouble on yerself. Kate's bad luck has just 'appened to her. You ain't fit to lick her boots.'

He turned towards the door and pulled it open. 'I'm going now,' he said, 'before I could say something else I might regret. Don't you never come near her again.'

Sally looked stunned but as he went through the door she pulled him back by the shoulders. 'You talk to me Billy Potter, about hurting her. How do you think she'd feel if she'd known what you was getting up to the other night. Or don't that count?'

Billy's face had turned bright red. 'Don't you think I don't know that,' he snapped. 'It ain't never going to happen Sal. Not now. Not never. She's my wife. And she always will be.'

***

They had all had a brilliant day in the snow. There had been about four inches. Sledging until they were breathless and building snowmen all the way down the street. Of course the best snowman had been the one Old Bones made. It always was. He had even made a snow ferret for it to hold. Jimmy really hoped that it would still be there tomorrow. After all the fun and excitement today he should have been shattered but he felt wide awake lying in bed.

He had sat beside his mum for a bit tonight. She had slept for almost three days. His Auntie Molly had just woken her up to give her food and today she had even eaten some shepherd's pie. Auntie Molly had said that was a very good sign. She wouldn't take her pills though, just spat them out. Auntie Molly had given up on that one. His mum looked really peaceful now when she was sleeping, not like before when she was tossing and turning all the time. She had opened her eyes tonight for a few seconds and smiled at him.

'Give her a kiss,' said his Auntie Molly.

He had said 'No' and run into his bedroom. He didn't know why he had done that. He didn't like himself much sometimes.

Now, he put his hands over his ears. Auntie Molly was sleeping on the camp bed in his room and she was snoring like hell. Jimmy switched his bedside light on. Perhaps that would wake her up. Instinctively he looked up.

The spider was directly above his head. It was an enormous one. He hated spiders, especially ones with long, hairy legs. For a few, terrifying, seconds Jimmy thought that it was going to drop right on his head. He couldn't move. Anything he did now could make it fall. Slowly, it began to crawl away, in a straight line, towards the other side of the room. He wished his Auntie Molly would shut up snoring. The vibrations could make the spider fall. His eyes were drawn towards it, as if it had some sort of power over him. He could feel sweat on his forehead. He needed to move, he was getting pins and needles but his body seemed frozen. The spider had reached just above the bottom of his bed when it changed direction. It was heading straight back to him now. Jimmy stared at it. Its eyes were wild. Wild and dangerous. That wasn't right, thought Jimmy. Spiders didn't have eyes, well not that you could see anyway.

The witch! Of course, it was the witch! She was here to attack his mum again.

'Mum!' he screamed as he leapt out of bed and ran into her bedroom.

'Jimmy, what the hell's going on? You'll wake your mum,' his dad whispered angrily.

'She ain't dead is she?' Jimmy whimpered.

'No. I'm not dead Jimmy.' The bedside light went on. Jimmy sank on to the bed beside her and passed out. When he came round his mum was mopping his face with cold water.

'What was it Jimmy, a nightmare?'

Jimmy nodded. His dad came into the room with a glass of water. 'Here you are son, what happened?'

'Dunno. Me head just went all funny.'

'Well,' said his mum, 'if you're not better on Monday, I'll take you to the doctor.' He looked at her in amazement.

179

She looked ... well ... different somehow. Sort of relaxed and warm and she was even smiling.

'You look much better now mum.'

'I feel much better Jimmy. Perhaps I just needed some sleep.'

'Well, you take it easy,' his dad said. 'No rushing back to work.'

'Oh no,' she smiled, 'I won't be rushing back to work.'

His dad moved towards the door. 'I'll get you a cup of tea love an' you get back to bed Jimmy. It's two o'clock in the morning.'

'Are you alright now then mum?' Jimmy asked quietly.

'Yes. I feel better now. In my head. It all seems clear.'

Jimmy coughed. Embarrassed. 'I prayed,' he mumbled. 'We all did. Del an' all.'

He saw tears come into his mum's eyes.

'That must be what did it then,' she whispered. 'Go on now, off you go to bed. I'll see you in the morning.'

Jimmy climbed back into his bed smiling and turned the light out. Auntie Molly was still snoring but it didn't bother him anymore. He looked up to where the witch had been on the ceiling.

'You don't always win,' he whispered as he felt himself slipping happily into sleep.

He never heard Maggie screaming over the road. Or the ambulance bells echoing in the snowy, dark streets.

Chapter 24

Jimmy rubbed his eyes as he walked slowly downstairs in his pyjamas. Auntie Molly was putting some toast onto the table for him. The marmalade with bits in was next to his plate. She always brought that with her from Ilford. 'Me mum ain't still in bed is she?' Jimmy asked. 'She was much better last night Auntie.'

'No Jimmy and it's not 'ain't' it's isn't. Do you know, your grandmother would be turning in her grave if she could here the way you talk.'

Jimmy started putting the bits from the marmalade on to the side of his plate. Usually Auntie Molly told him off for that but she seemed a bit preoccupied this morning. 'So where is she then?' he asked with his mouth full. 'Me Mum.'

'Oh honestly, all these questions first thing in the morning. She's just gone over the road. I told her not to get involved but she won't listen.'

'Over the road where?'

Auntie Molly moved over to the sink. Her back to him. 'There's been a bit of an accident. Over at Maggie's. Can't say I'm surprised. Anything can happen with people like the Tylers.'

'What sort of accident? Del ain't hurt is he?'

He saw Auntie Molly take a deep breath, as she sat down at the table and poured herself a cup of tea. 'Your mum will tell you when she comes back.'

Jimmy noticed that her hands were trembling.

'But it's not Del, he's fine. I'm more worried about your mum. She seemed so much better first thing this morning and this isn't going to help her. Now, come on Jimmy, just get yourself ready for school. There's nothing you can do about anything.' She crossed herself. 'The Lord giveth and The Lord taketh away.'

What was she on about, Jimmy thought. Why won't she tell me what's happened? You'd think he was a little kid the way she treated him.

'Just tell me Auntie Molly,' he said defiantly. There was a bad feeling coming over him. Filling his whole body. Something awful was happening again just as he thought things were alright.

'Don't you be so rude Jimmy Potter. I don't know where you get it from but it certainly doesn't come from your mother's side.'

Just then his mum walked in through the front door. There were tears in her eyes.

Auntie Molly jumped out of the chair and guided her into it. 'Now Kate, just sit for a minute and have a nice cup of tea. You mustn't make yourself poorly again.'

His mum sat down at the table and tried to smile at Jimmy. She put her hand on his head and ruffled his hair gently.

'What is it mum?' he asked quietly. 'What's happened?'

She moved her chair closer to his and put her arm around his shoulders. 'There was an accident last night,' she began. 'Over at the Tyler's.'

'Did he beat Del's mum again?' Jimmy interrupted.

'No. No this was nothing to do with Mick. I can't really believe what's happened myself. It ... It was Julie. She was really poorly Jimmy, in the night. They called an ambulance but she died. On the way to the hospital.'

Jimmy could barely breathe. This couldn't have happened. 'But ... but she ain't even old. How can she be dead?' He knew the answer, before he even asked the question. He had got it all wrong. They all had. It hadn't been his mum that the witch had been after. It had been Julie Tyler. She must have ate an apple as well.

'It sometimes happens Jimmy, I don't know why. I don't know why she's dead but she is. Now, you be nice to Del today if he goes to school. Tell him you're sorry.'

'Yes Jimmy,' Auntie Molly added. 'Now, let your mum have a bit of peace. Go up and get dressed. Last day at school today. Come on chop, chop.'

I'll chop, chop your bloody head off in a minute, thought Jimmy. 'Where's Del?' he asked his mum as she followed him upstairs.

'Next door at May's. All the kids are there.'

When Jimmy had got himself dressed he ran downstairs to the hall and grabbed his coat and his satchel. He could hear his mum and Auntie Molly talking in the back.

'Right, I'm off,' he shouted. He shot out the front door quickly. He had a funny feeling his mum might have tried to hug him this morning.

Del, Legs and Josie were waiting for him at the gate.

'Where the bloody hell 'ave you bin?' Del shouted at him. 'Ain't you heard what's happened to our Julie?'

Del's face was white and pinched. There were huge dark shadows under his eyes. He looked awful. Jimmy shuffled uncomfortably and looked down at the pavement. 'Sorry Del,' he said.

He spat on his hand and put it out towards his mate. Del shook it. His grip weak and limp. Josie was crying. Jimmy had never seen her cry before.

'Have we got time to go to the den before school?' Jimmy asked.

'Ain't no point,' said Del, bitterly. 'Ain't no use praying or nothing now is there?' He glared accusingly at Josie.

'Was there a lot of blood?' Legs asked suddenly.

'Shut up Legs,' said Josie.

'Yeah,' said Del, not offended. 'It was all down the stairs.'

Jimmy felt sick. The taste of the marmalade with bits in kept coming back into his throat.

'We have to tell the grown-ups now,' said Legs in a panicky voice. 'We have to tell them about the witch. We're just kids.'

'Oh no,' said Del. 'She'll get away wiv it if we do that. No, we know what we 'ave to do now.'

'What?' asked Jimmy. 'What can we do? Legs is right Del.'

'We 'ave to kill 'er,' said Del. 'We 'ave to stop 'er.'

Legs was about to argue when May Pattinson came out. 'Come on you lot,' she said. 'Off you go to school. Del, you come in now love. You needn't go in today. I've phoned the headmaster and explained.'

'Ain't staying 'ere,' he said, moving closer to Jimmy. 'I wanna go to school.'

Jimmy looked at him in amazement. This wasn't like Del at all. May came over towards them and put her hand gently around Del's shoulders. He shrugged her off.

'You're tired Del and you've hardly had any sleep.'

183

'I'm alright,' he mumbled, 'I ain't tired.'

May sighed. 'Oh, go on then, off you go. Perhaps it's for the best. And it *is* the last day of term. Look after him the rest of you.'

They all nodded and walked slowly down to Montgomery Road where Josie left them to catch her bus to the convent. 'I'll pray for you Del,' she said, looking down at her feet.

'Fuck praying,' said Del angrily. 'We'll see you in the den after school. I'll have made all the plans by then.'

'We can't kill her Del,' said Josie quietly. 'It ain't the law.'

'We have to,' said Del, 'an' it's up to us. She's our witch an' we ain't telling the grown-ups nothing.'

He looked at Jimmy for support. 'We can't Del. Josie's right.' said Jimmy. 'Anyway, how would we do it?'

'That's what I'm thinking about now,' said Del. They watched Josie as she ran down the road.

'Fire or water,' said Legs suddenly. 'That's what it has to be. That's how you kill witches.'

***

Kate had not hesitated for a second when Billy had come rushing back in to the house and told her what had happened to Julie. She had been sitting quietly at the table, just thinking how much better she felt. She could hear Molly still snoring upstairs. She would tell her to go home today. She would go and see Greta. The old lady had helped her again and she felt almost reborn.

'Kate, Kate,' Billy had come rushing into the room.

'Thought you'd gone to work.'

'I did but Mick come running out ...'

Then they had heard the ambulance bells. Kate had shivered. Not again. 'He's not hurt Maggie?' she had asked, standing up quickly.

'No, it ain't Maggie. It's Julie. I think she's dead, at least that's what Mick's saying.'

Kate had taken a deep breath. 'Oh, my God, poor Maggie, what's happened?'

Billy had shrugged his shoulders and run back out to the open door. 'They're putting her in the ambulance. May's over there an' Mick an' Maggie's getting in the ambulance now an' all.'

Kate had grabbed her coat. 'You ain't goin' over there Kate. You ain't well.' Billy had held her by the shoulders.

'Billy, I'm alright. They might need me to do something.'

'Well, I know I can't stop yer but just take it easy. We've only just got you back.'

Kate nodded and smiled at him.

'I'll wake Molly up,' Billy had called after her. 'I'll 'ave to get into work.'

The ambulance was careering out of Churchill Street, bells ringing and lights flashing. Curious onlookers stopped on their way to work and shivered. It was six thirty in the morning.

There was mayhem in the house when Kate had walked through the door. The kids were crying, May was crying. 'Oh, thank God, Kate,' she said. 'Thank God you're here.'

Kate took one look round the kitchen. It was where they had all gathered.

'Where mum gone?' asked little Stuart.

'She'll be back soon love,' said Kate, scooping him up in her arms. He clung to her. May was busy making a bottle up for the baby. The older children just looked stunned.

'There's loads of blood,' said Del sobbing and nodding towards the door, 'out there.'

Just then George came through the door. 'Right kids. I think you should all come over to ours. Come on, I'll get you all some breakfast.'

'We'll fetch all your clothes over, just keep your jamas on for now,' said Kate.

'Ain't going,' cried Marilyn. 'Wanna see Julie, ain't goin.' She stamped her feet and her blonde curls bounced.

'Oh yes you are,' said George assertively. He picked her up, kicking and screaming and carried her out through the front door. The others followed.

'We'll keep the baby here,' said Kate, 'and try and sort things out a bit.'

'And George,' May called after him. 'Phone Maggie's mum. Get her to come over.'

The two women watched the little group of waifs crossing the road. They had no shoes on and some of their feet were covered in blood. Marilyn clung to her teddy and turned to look back at the house. A frozen photograph that Kate knew her and May would never forget. Those poor, poor children.

'Why have they got blood on their feet?' Kate asked May.

'It's all down the stairs. She must have tried to get out ... or something. Oh Kate, I'm going to find Maggie's medicinal brandy. She won't mind. Tea just isn't enough for this somehow.'

Kate followed her friend back into the kitchen. May put the baby into the high chair and gave him his bottle. He picked it up and started drinking greedily. Kate put her arms around May's shaking shoulders. 'You sit down May. I'll find the brandy.'

They clung to each other for a few seconds and then May pulled away.

'It's in the second drawer down I think, under the tea towels. We're not helping them by being like this I know,' she said, 'but it's so awful.'

Kate found the brandy and two chipped teacups. She poured them both a generous measure. She drank hers in two gulps and though she coughed and spluttered, the warmth spread through her bones. 'So ... is she dead May?'

'The ambulance men said she's in a sort of coma. She's lost an awful lot of blood. They told Maggie she may not survive the journey to hospital.'

'But what was it?' Kate asked. 'She's just a young girl.'

'I think she's had a miscarriage Kate, judging by the questions they were asking.'

Kate gasped and sat down. 'But ... but ... did Maggie not know?'

May shook her head and took another sip of her drink. 'No, she didn't and I'd say it's lucky for Freddie that he's gone back to the army off leave. His life will definitely not be worth living if he comes near here. Julie was always Mick's favourite.'

The two women started trying to clear up. 'I'll clean the stairs,' said Kate. 'At least that's something I can do.'

186

'No Kate love,' said May. 'You're not well ...'

'I feel much better now May. Honestly, I can do this.'

It was about half an hour later that George came running in. He stood at the front door. Kate looked up from scrubbing the stairs. She took one look at George's face and she knew. 'She's dead isn't she?' she asked. May came out into the hall.

George nodded, put his arms around his wife and held her very close. 'Maggie wants us to tell the kids,' he said finally, tears in his eyes. 'I need you over there love.'

May nodded, picked up the baby and headed for the front door. 'I'll just try and get this all cleaned up,' said Kate. 'They can't come back and see it all.'

'God help us. How are we going to do this George?' May squeezed her husband's hand.

'Just tell them she's gone to heaven,' said Kate quietly. 'It's all you can do.'

'What sort of God let's this happen eh?' said George in a rare moment of anger. 'What sort of God is it?'

***

Del sat quietly at his desk. The headmaster came in. They all scraped their chairs back.

'Morning Mr. Cummings.'

He whispered something to Miss Parsons and immediately she looked over to where he was sitting. He could feel himself going red. Mr. Cummings was telling her about Julie. He still felt angry but in a more calm way. He wanted to cry but he couldn't. Not here. He watched the two grown-ups, heads together. Talking quietly. Miss Parsons looked up at him again. She looked like... she looked like she might cry. She pulled a hankie from her sleeve and blew her nose. And then she carried on with the lesson. He never listened much in class. It was all so boring and what was she talking about now? Logarithms. What the fuck were they?

The bell rang for break-time. Miss Parsons stopped him as he walked towards the door.

'Can I have a word Derek?'

'I ain't done nothing wrong miss,' he said, as he shuffled over towards her.

'No, I know you haven't Derek,' she said kindly. 'I just wanted to say that I'm very, very sorry about your sister.'

187

'Yeah, alright. Can I go now miss?' Del turned towards the door.

'I do understand Derek. A little anyway. I ... I had a sister who died.'

Del turned and faced her. 'Did someone kill her?' he asked aggressively.

Miss Parsons looked a bit shocked. 'Well, yes, it was during the war. A bomb fell in the garden and ...'

'So it was Hitler then?' Del interrupted.

'Well, in a roundabout sort of way. Yes, it was.'

'Someone should've killed him then shouldn't they miss?'

'Well, he did die Derek. He killed himself.'

Del looked down at the floor and shuffled his feet. He looked at the holes in his shoes, the laces that were missing. His dirty legs. He never usually noticed things like that about himself. 'Yeah, but that ain't the same. He'd killed all them people by then hadn't he?'

'I'm sure,' she answered, 'that he would have been sentenced to death for war crimes if he had lived.'

'No!' said Del angrily. 'Someone should've killed 'im before shouldn't they miss? Before he killed all them people? They should 'ave killed him after the first one.'

He looked hard into his teacher's face. He knew this was important. That she had been through the same as him. He saw her face contort. She was biting her lip and she was angry. She was angry like he was.

'The bomb fell after the all-clear sounded Derek. Mandy had just been putting the cat out. She didn't stand a chance. She was the kindest person you could ever meet.' Del could hear her voice breaking but he couldn't stop. Not know. He had to know.

'Yes Derek,' she answered finally. 'Someone should have killed him a long time before the war started and if I'd had the chance I'd have done it myself.'

Tears were coursing down her cheeks. 'Outside now Derek. Go on!' she shouted. She never shouted. Not Miss Parsons.

'Sorry miss,' he said as he walked slowly to the door. 'I didn't mean ...'

'Alright Derek just go now please.'

He turned back to see her, sitting at her desk. Her head in her hands.

***

This date would be etched on Sally's mind forever. December 20th 1955. The day Julie Tyler died. And it was all her fault. Oh yes, she had told her to go to the doctor after she'd had the abortion but she hadn't checked whether she did or not. She had just deserted her and Julie only fifteen years old. She couldn't cry, she just felt dead inside. Self-loathing consumed her.

The twins were playing on the rug by the fire. She had no recollection of washing or dressing them. She had certainly fed them by the state of their faces.

She thought about the aspirins in the bathroom. How many would it take, she wondered. And then she looked at the boys, laughing and gurgling.

She had heard the ambulance, seen Julie on the stretcher and knew straight away what must have happened. She had seen the sad little group of children crossing the road to May's. May was the only person she could have talked to but she couldn't. Not now. The time came and went when she should have got the babies ready for nursery and herself off to work. Josie had come downstairs earlier, muttering and moaning something about Reverend Mother. She had got her own breakfast, given Sally a funny look and hadn't even said, 'Bye Mum' as she went out the door.

She had come back though. To tell her the news. Julie was dead.

Sally forced herself up from the settee and looked out of the window. The twins were both asleep now, curled up on the rug, sucking on their dummies. A Ford Poplar pulled up outside the Tyler's house. She watched from behind the curtain as Maggie's mum got out of the car and helped her daughter out. Maggie's head was bowed as the two women walked slowly towards the front door. She saw Maggie fumble in her pocket for her keys. Sally took a deep breath. She had to go and see her. She had to confess, tell her what she had done and it had to be now. She grabbed the twins, put them in their pram and marched across the road.

189

'Hello Sal.' Maggie sat; her tired face blotched with tears. She tried to smile at Sally. 'Here love, sit yourself down an' have a brandy. I'm glad you've come to see me.'

Sally's mind screamed silently. Please don't be nice to me. I've just broken your heart.

Instinct took over and she put her arms around Maggie and hugged her.

'Did you know?' Maggie sniffed. 'Did you know she was pregnant?'

'No,' Sally said quickly. The first lie.

'Get Sal a brandy will yer mum?'

'Where's Mick?' Sally asked. Maggie's mum snorted.

'Gone to find a fucking drink I should think,' she said.

'Mum, leave it. Not today eh? He's still at the 'ospital. They wanted to ask more questions. I couldn't stay there Sal, I 'ad to come home.'

Sally took a sip of brandy. God that felt better. She felt the warmth seeping into her bones.

'You'll never guess who's cleaned up me house for me,' said Maggie. 'Mrs. Snotty Nose herself.'

Sally took a deep breath. Up until this morning all she had been thinking about was Mrs Snotty Nose and that she shouldn't have hit her. She had been distraught after Billy had confronted her and it had been the talk of the factory for the last three days. It paled into insignificance now. Maggie's mum poured them both another drink.

'Everyone's got a good side Mags,' she said to her daughter. 'When these sorts of things happen, brings people together.'

Sally didn't know how much longer she could sit here. She knew now that she could never tell Maggie the truth.

There was a knock at the door and May came in. She put her arms around Maggie and hugged her hard. 'Oh, I'm glad you're back love,' she said. 'The kids are all fine. George is reading to them. Mind you I think the Secret Seven is a bit old for Marilyn.'

'I don't fink our Marilyn ain't never seen a book before,' said Maggie, trying to smile. 'Our Julie never did neither. They said she was quite clever at school though if she'd not messed about ...'

190

Maggie broke down halfway through the sentence and started to sob on Sally's shoulder. Sally put her arm around her.

'I hate to say it Sal,' said May, 'but your babies are screaming in that pram out there.'

Thank God, thought Sally, I have *got* to get out of here. May took her place on the settee.

'Why May? Why would my little gal just die because she's lost a baby? I've lost three an' I'm all right.'

Sally left the Tyler's house while she could still move one leg in front of the other. The worst thing was that she knew that this was just going to be the beginning of the guilt she would carry with her for the rest of her life.

***

Del walked slowly out into the playground. Jimmy and Legs were waiting for him. 'What did Miss Parsons say to you?' Legs asked. 'You've been in there ages. It's nearly time for the bell.'

'She says,' Del said slowly, 'that we should kill the witch.'

Legs glared at him, disbelieving. 'Yeah,' he said. 'What teacher is going to tell you to kill someone?'

'Are you sure?' Jimmy asked. 'And what was you doing telling her about our witch. We ain't supposed to be telling the grown-ups nothing.'

'Well, I still think we should,' said Legs.

'Shut up both of you and listen. I didn't tell 'er nothing. I ain't that stupid. Hitler killed 'er sister. She said that someone should've killed him right at the start. She wished that she 'ad. That's how I know she thinks we should kill the witch.'

'Yeah,' said Legs. 'Millions of people would have been saved.'

'There wouldn't have bin no war,' Jimmy added.

'That's right,' said Del. 'This ain't just about my Julie.'

'No,' Jimmy said slowly. 'This is to save the world.' The three boys ran into Churchill Street.

'I need to get some food,' said Jimmy, 'before we have our meeting.'

'Good idea,' said Legs. 'I'm starving.'

191

Del looked over towards his house. Jimmy patted him on the back. 'I'll make you a sugar sandwich in ours if you like.'

Jimmy's mum was chatting to Auntie Molly as the boys came into the kitchen. They stopped talking as soon as they saw Del. 'Hello you two? How are you Del? How was school?' Jimmy's mum looked flustered.

Del shrugged his shoulders. 'Alright, I s'pose.'

'I just come in to make us a sugar sandwich mum.'

'Good idea love, that'll keep you going. Would you like to come here for your tea Del? Your brothers and sisters are still at May's house but you're very welcome to stay.'

'Where's me mum an' dad?' Del asked.

Auntie Molly sighed and went to get a loaf of bread out of the bin. She began to cut large doorstep slices.

'Well your mum's at home and your grandma is there,' said Jimmy's mum. 'She's looking after her. I'm not sure where your dad is to be honest.'

Jimmy's mum sat down at the table. He thought she looked weary but she seemed alright. This time yesterday, she was still in bed.

Auntie Molly had sprinkled a teaspoon of sugar onto each sandwich. 'There you are boys,' she said. 'You'll all have rotten teeth when you grow up though.' The boys grabbed the sandwiches hungrily and ran back out again. Legs was waiting by the gate.

'Don't know how you stand all that noise in your house Del,' he said. 'They're all driving me nuts. Let's get to the den. We can wait for Jose in there.'

They ran on to the waste and into the den.

'Right,' said Del, once they had all sat down and finished eating. 'Josie ain't gonna like this but ...'

'We need to wait for 'er coming,' said Jimmy with his mouth full. 'Ain't right to start without 'er.'

Jimmy noticed that Del's face couldn't seem to sit still. It was twitching and he kept wringing his hands like his mum did when she was poorly. He couldn't believe how happy he had felt this morning when his mum seemed so much better and now all this was going on. Happiness didn't last long in this life, he thought to himself. He suddenly had a dreadful thought but he couldn't stop himself thinking it. He

192

wished he had given Del sixpence to see Julie Tyler's titties. He would never see them now.

As they finished their sandwiches they heard footsteps approaching. Josie came in like a hurricane. Out of breath. 'I've bin runnin' all the way from the bus stop,' she gasped.

As she flopped down in the den Del began to speak. 'Most important thing,' he said, 'is to remember our Code. We can't tell the grown-ups nothin'. Agreed?'

They all nodded solemnly.

'Whatever happens now, we ain't tellin' no-one about the witch. We deal wiv her on our own. Right? We're gonna sort it.'

'How are we gonna sort it Del?' said Josie. 'We're just kids. We have to tell the coppers at least.' Del glared at her.

'She don't know yet,' said Jimmy. 'She don't know what Miss Parsons 'as said.'

'What?' Josie asked. 'What did she say?'

'That we should kill the witch,' said Legs quietly. 'Like someone should have killed Hitler.'

Josie's eyes opened wide. 'You can't just kill people,' she said. 'It ain't right. We have to tell a grown-up.'

'How many more people will she hurt then?' said Del angrily. 'She's made Jimmy an' his mum ill. She's killed Mrs Bransome an' now she's killed our Julie. We ain't waiting no longer.'

'I ain't being funny Del but there's no way a teacher would tell us to kill someone,' said Josie determinedly.

'Has to be fire or water,' said Legs again. 'I keep telling you. That's what you do to witches. That's how you kill them.'

'We got paraffin in our shed,' said Del. 'That'll do it. We'll stick a flaming' old rag through her letterbox.'

The other three all looked at each other. They all looked uncomfortable. Unsure. Jimmy felt sick.

'I can't do it,' said Josie. 'God would never forgive me.'

'I ain't asking *you* to do it,' Del screamed. '*I* wanna do it. If it was one of your twins you would.' You just have to come wiv me that's all. Just keep a lookout.'

193

'I ain't sure Del, neither,' Jimmy said. 'We could be put in prison or get hung.'

'Don't understand you mate,' Del said quietly. 'Your mum's sister was murdered by Hitler an' all. Thought *you'd* understand.'

Jimmy swallowed and coughed. Yes, he thought. Maybe Del's right.

'Tonight,' said Del. 'I'll do it tonight. We have to stick together Jose cos it's in our Code.'

Jimmy looked at Josie. He could see tears in her eyes and she was biting her lip. 'I think we need to pray,' she said. 'Then something bad will happen to her an' we won't 'ave to do nothing.'

'Don't work though does it?' said Jimmy quietly.

'I can't believe you Jimmy Potter. I can't believe that you're agreeing to kill 'er.' Josie was crying now. Tears running silently down her cheeks.

'Well, if Miss Parsons says ...'

Josie put her hands together and began to pray. 'Dear God, please ...'

'We'll all meet here at eight o'clock. Stay awake an' sneak out. There won't be no-one about then,' Del interrupted her. 'And you Jose. Don't let us down.'

Josie still had her eyes closed and her hands together. The boys left her. Jimmy impulsively put his hand on her head and ruffled her hair. She was only a girl. She couldn't help it.

Chapter 25

Josie didn't know how long she had been praying for in the den but it seemed like an eternity. She was suddenly very cold and she just didn't know what to do. She was on her own now. 'Please God,' she whispered. 'Please tell me what I can do about everything. I'm really scared. I don't want Del to be a murderer an' go to prison. Please, please help me.'

As she finished she heard a rustling sound at the other end of the den. Chuck the ferret came bounding over towards her. She picked him up and held him tightly while he tried to wriggle free. Josie gasped. This must be a sign and God had sent her a message. Old Bones. That's where God was sending her. Telling her where to go. He wasn't like a grown-up, not really. She would talk to him and tell him everything. He wouldn't grass them up and he would know what to do. 'Come on Chuck,' she whispered to the struggling ferret. 'You're going home.'

Old Bones opened the door cautiously. 'Oh, ta Josie. You needn't have bothered you know. He finds his own way back now,' he smiled his toothless smile.

'I ... I need to talk to you Bones,' Josie said quickly. 'God has sent me.'

Bones chewed noiselessly on his baccy and scratched his balding head. 'God eh? Must be important then. He ain't never sent mc no messages before. Still, first time for everything I s'pose.'

He turned and looked at Josie's tear-stained face. 'Josie, don't you think you should be talking to your mum about whatever it is?'

'No, I can't. I just can't. It ain't in our Code. We ain't allowed to tell grown-ups nothin'. You ain't a proper grown-up. Not really.'

Old Bones beamed. 'Ta Jose. Nicest thing anyone's said to me all year. You'd best come in then, it's a bit of a mess I'm afraid.'

It *was* a mess. It was worse than when the twins had a food fight and the smell invaded Josie's nostrils but after a few seconds she didn't smell it anymore. Bones lived in a one bedroom maisonette but with the fire roaring in the grate and Chuck firmly ensconced in front of it washing himself, Josie thought how cosy it was.

'Lemonade?' Bones asked.

Josie nodded. She would need refreshment; she had a long story to tell.

He didn't interrupt her like most grown-ups would have done. She told him everything about the witch. From when Jimmy ate three bites of one of her apples and was poorly. About how she had killed Mrs. Bransome with the apples and made Jimmy's mum really ill and now, worst of all, that she had killed Julie Tyler. She told him how they had all got baptised but that it hadn't seemed to help anything and she told him that the teacher at the primary school had told Del that they should kill the witch. And, last of all, she told him when Del was planning to set fire to the witch's house.

When she got to the end bit she did notice that Old Bones had begun to look alarmed but he carried on listening anyway. When Josie had finished she felt such a sense of relief that she felt herself smiling which didn't seem very appropriate but she couldn't help it.

Old Bones looked at her quite seriously. 'You done right Josie,' he said slowly, as if he was thinking hard about every word he said, 'telling someone about all this.' He coughed. 'Of course you know that really she ain't a witch don't you?'

Josie's stomach sank into her shoes. She realised what she had just done. So, Bones *was* a grown-up. Maybe in disguise, but he still was.

'She's had a very hard life you know, Mrs Broncowiez,' Bones was saying. Have you heard of concentration camps Josie?'

'Yeah. We done it in school. But she's a German. She's a German witch. That's even worse.'

'She ain't a German Josie, she's a Polish Jew. She lived 'ere until 1939. She went back to Warsaw just before war broke out. Not a good time to be a Jew in Poland. She was in Auschwitz. She saw some dreadful things Josie. It's made her go a little bit funny in her head perhaps but she ain't a witch. She helps people. She's a medium an' a healer.'

So, he *would* tell the grown-ups. He would have to. Josie could see that now and she should never have come. 'She *is* a witch,' Josie said defiantly. 'We know she is.'

'Listen Josie you're a kid, you've got amazing imaginations. That's why I love dustbin lids. You're all great but some things ...'

He got up and poked the fire. 'Some things, you don't quite get right.'

She would be out of the gang. First thing Del had said. We don't tell the grown-ups nothing. She had really done it now.

***

'Where have you bin all bleedin' day,' Maggie screamed at her husband, although she knew the answer to that as soon as she saw him.

'Sorting things out,' Mick Tyler slurred. He got hold of her roughly by the shoulders. 'Why didn't you tell me, you stupid, fucking whore?' He slapped her round the face. Hard. Maggie reeled backwards.

'You're pissed!' she shouted. 'Don't start Mick. Please, not today.' She burst into tears.

'Shut up bawling woman,' he shouted. 'My little girl's dead. What do you want me to do? Drink a fucking cup of tea?'

'It ain't my fault she's dead. D'you think I ain't upset an' all?'

'Well, that's where you're wrong because I think it bloody is your fault. You must have known. Someone must 'ave known an' you're 'er fucking mother.'

'I never knew, honest to God Mick. I never knew she was pregnant. Not until this morning.'

'I ain't talking about her being pregnant,' he screamed, slapping her again. 'I'll tell you what I'm on about as if you didn't know. What the doctors told me, shall I?'

He stood over her, his body swaying. The whisky on his breath stunk. Maggie pushed her hands back into the wall as if that might help. He had never frightened her this much before. Julie had always been his favourite. She usually tried to fight him, to taunt him but she couldn't cope with anymore today. She didn't really care whether he killed her or not. She stood, shaking and numb.

197

'Now,' he spoke quietly which was even more intimidating. 'Just tell me Maggie. Who was it stuck the knitting needle up her eh? Cos the coppers are gonna be round 'ere soon an' you'll have to tell 'em.' He shook her shoulders roughly. 'Just tell me who done it, cos some fucker has.'

'Oh no,' Maggie's face crumpled. She slid down the wall and buried her head in her hands. 'Not that, oh no. Oh, the stupid little cow.'

He kicked her then. Right in the stomach. It seemed to knock all the breath out of her body. 'So who done it?' he was shouting. Who killed my little girl?'

'I ... I don't know,' Maggie sobbed. 'I don't know.'

'I know,' said Del. He was standing at the door, tears pouring down his face.

His parents both stared at him incredulously. Forgetting Maggie for a moment, Mick began to stumble towards him. 'You what?' Mick screamed at his son.

'If you promise to leave me mum alone I'll tell you,' Del sobbed. 'I'll tell you who killed our Julie.'

Chapter 26

And so Del told them. He didn't tell them she was a witch because they wouldn't have believed him. She was a German and she had killed his sister. That was good enough for his dad. 'I wanna do it dad,' he said. 'I wanna kill 'er.'

'Oh an' how are you planning on that then son?' His dad seemed to have sobered up a bit since he had heard this revelation.

'I'm gonna set fire to her house.'

His dad looked at him and laughed in his face. 'You? You an' who's fucking army eh? This is a man's job son but your idea ain't bad I'll give you that...'

'No Mick ...'

His mum tried to get up. His dad punched her in the stomach again. 'In fact,' he said, 'there's some paraffin out there in the shed ain't there?'

'You'll end up in prison again,' his mum shouted. 'Leave it to the coppers.'

'Not till I've got to her first, they can 'ave what's left. Go an' get that paraffin for me Del. Right now.'

Del ran out to the shed and found the can of paraffin on the shelf. *He* should have been fetching that. *He* should be doing this. Why had he said anything? Well, he knew why. He was trying to help his mum but it hadn't stopped him hitting her and now he had broken the Code. He would be out of the gang. Especially after it was he, himself who had told them all to say nothing to the grown-ups.

His dad snatched the jerry can out of his hand and headed for the door. 'Not a word to no-one you two. Understand?' And then he was gone, slamming the door behind him.

Del helped his mum up off the floor. 'It ain't bin a very good day 'as it mum?'

His mum sat down on the chair, holding her stomach. Del looked at her bleeding mouth and her bruised face as if he had never seen them before. She was quiet for a long time. Just looking at him.

'I've 'ad enough now,' she said wearily. 'I ain't putting up wiv him no more. Long as I've got you kids,' she said to Del, 'we'll get through. We can do without 'im. He ain't never gonna hit me like that again.'

199

Del was amazed. He had never heard his mum criticise his dad before. She *always* stuck up for him. Always.

'No mum,' he said grimly, 'we *don't* need him.'

She smiled at him then and hugged him close to her and even though he was nearly ten years old he didn't mind at all.

***

Greta knew that she was in danger. It was all around her. It was in every bone in her body. She didn't know why they were out to get her. Why they would want to harm her but she sensed with every breath she took that her life was under threat. The cats were agitated, they couldn't keep still. Up and downstairs they roamed, meowing constantly. 'Alright my pretties,' she whispered to them. She would save the cats at least, but who would take care of them? She must give them the choice. Walking slowly towards the front door, she began to feel much calmer.

'What will be will be,' she whispered as she opened the door. It was snowing again, lightly. All was still. The cats ran out towards the gate and stopped. They sniffed the air, turned and looked at her.

'Off you go,' she said.

The cats did not move. They sat, huddled together by the unopened gate facing her. Waiting.

The old lady sighed. It had been a long life and a hard one. The talents she had been born with had isolated her and kept her apart. Her husband had certainly never understood and when his secretary had fluttered her eyelashes it hadn't taken him long to respond. 'You're weird,' were his last words to her, forty years ago. 'You give me the creeps.'

She had walked out of their comfortable home in Warsaw and moved to East London to live with her brother in this dilapidated old house. He understood her and left her alone to do what she was born to do. All her pleasure in life had come from her work, her healing powers. She read tarots and hands to earn a little money but she only charged for healing if people could afford it. People who believed in her skills were her only friends .

When her brother had died in 1939, she took him home. Home to Warsaw to bury him. It had been his last wish. Had he known what would happen to her he would

200

never have asked it. Of course she *had* known. When she had boarded the plane to Poland, there was a moment, like now, when she knew that her life was in grave danger. She knew she should have disembarked. That she should not have returned to her homeland and the worst six years of her life. But it was done.

And it would be done now. Why should she run away? This was her house. Where would she go? No, she would stay, follow her instincts and let fate decide.

The cats were scratching at the door to come in. She opened it slowly and they weaved their bodies around her legs, purring loudly. They weren't going anywhere either. She heard the gate creaking open and footsteps on the gravel. She shivered before closing the door again quickly.

'Come along my pretties,' she whispered. 'Let's get you some milk.'

***

'I'd best go an' see what's happening mum,' said Del when he had fetched her a bowl of water to clean herself up.

'Not so fast Del,' she said. 'How do you know it's 'er. How do you know its Mrs Bron ... whatever her poxy German name is? How do you know what's happened? You ain't old enough to understand. D'you even bloody know what an abortion is?'

Del shook his head. 'Dunno mum. What *is* a borshun?'

Maggie suddenly realised the enormity of what had happened. Not just losing her daughter. All this as well. Mick had gone off to probably kill someone. A dotty but harmless old woman who their nine year old son had declared guilty and Mick, pissed and angry, had just believed him. Oh my God.

She jumped up from the settee and grabbed her son by the ears. 'Now you just tell me the truth,' she shouted, 'an' I mean right now. Why d'you think she done it? Why d'you think she killed our Julie?'

'Mum, you're hurtin' me.'

'Then tell me the fuckin' truth.'

'Alright, alright.' He put his hands up and Maggie released her grip.

'She's a witch. The old lady. It was 'er what killed Mrs Bransome an' all. We know. We all know she done it.' He was sobbing now.

'Oh my God.' His mum put her bruised head in her hands. 'So this was all one of your silly games.'

'It ain't a game mum. It's the truth. She *is* a witch. She poisoned all them apples. She ...'

Maggie slapped him round the face. She barely heard the sharp, insistent knock on the door. 'We'll have to phone the coppers now!' she shouted at Del. 'Just get out of my sight.'

'You won't need to phone us Mrs Tyler. We're here. How's that for service eh?'

The second policeman dug him in the ribs. 'Not appropriate Sergeant,' he hissed. 'Sorry Maggie. I know it's a bad time love. I'm sorry about Julie. Let's sit down and chat about this shall we? We need to find out who did it.'

'Well I can tell you who didn't do it, but try telling that to my bloody husband.'

'Where is he Maggie? Where's Mick?'

'Oh I'll tell you where he is alright but that won't help you catch who done it. That's who you should be looking for.'

Maggie closed her eyes. If Mick did what she knew he was capable of doing they would be looking for him soon enough.

'You stupid, stupid man,' she muttered under her breath.

Chapter 27

The King's Head was buzzing tonight. All the talk was about the Tylers. News had travelled fast about the botched abortion and opinions were, as ever, divided.

'Should learn to keep their knickers on these gels,' said Arthur predictably. 'Can't blame the men for trying, that's natural ain't it.'

'That's a bit harsh Arthur,' George replied.

'Wouldn't need no abortions if they did.'

'You're worse than a load of old women,' George grumbled.

'What do you think then George if I'm so wrong,' Arthur asked as he pulled a pint for Billy.

George lit his pipe and thought about it for a few seconds. 'Legalised abortions,' he said finally. 'Done by proper doctors. That's the only way.'

'They'll all be at it like rabbits then,' said Arthur. 'Is that what you want to see?'

'Well I'll tell you what,' George replied angrily, 'you didn't have to tell those Tyler kids that their sister was dead did you? I wouldn't want to have to do that again.' His voice broke.

Billy came up behind George and clapped him on the back. 'That must 'ave bin horrible George. Don't envy you mate, don't know how you did it.'

'Alright, alright,' Arthur put his hands up. 'It's an' awful business an' I ain't trying to make light of it but something 'as to change, I know that.'

'They should be hung for murder them women what does it,' said Loopy, 'cos that's what they are. Bloody murderers.'

'Social need round here though ennit eh?' Billy spoke. 'Most of 'em survive it. Julie was just unlucky.'

'Nah,' Loopy was getting angry now. It had been a closed doors session in here all afternoon because of all this drama and he had already drunk twice what he normally had in a week. And he wasn't the only one. They had seen Mick Tyler crying into his whisky. Crying. Mick Tyler. Unheard of. A lot of the regulars were fired up.

'Well I expect the coppers will catch 'er,' said Billy. 'That's all I can say.'

'They ain't bothered,' said Arthur. 'Coppers ain't bothered. They think we're all filth down 'ere anyway.'

The doors opened and Mick Tyler walked in. He was carrying a jerry can. Silence descended on the King's Head. It was like the moment in cowboy films when the man with the loaded gun barges through the swing doors. After the amount he had drunk earlier everyone was amazed that he was still standing, let alone striding in like he owned the place.

Everyone in the pub turned and looked at him. It seemed an eternity until he spoke. 'I know who done it,' he shouted. 'I know who's killed my little girl,' his voice cracked with emotion. 'It's 'er in the old house, the German. She's the one what done it. Now I'm going up there,' his voice broke down again. 'I'm going up there right now an' I'm gonna sort her out. How many other kids is she gonna kill eh?'

There were some mutters of agreement around the bar.

'Fucking Kraut. They deserve all they get.'

'I seen loads of women going in there. Now we know why.'

'She's weird. Tell you something when I was a kid, we'd have thought she was a witch.'

'You can't do that Mick,' said George slowly. 'If you think it's her then you tell the police. They'll sort it out.'

'Yeah, come on Mick mate, I'll pour you a whisky,' said Arthur. 'Don't wanna be getting yerself into trouble do yer. George is right.'

'No he fucking ain't,' Loopy was shouting now. 'Mick's right. I'm coming with you mate. Let's sort her out. Anyone else or are you all just gonna let this go on?'

Mick turned his back to the bar. Loopy followed him. Before long, half the men in the King's Head had formed a posse. They were drunk, noisy and angry.

'Phone the coppers Arthur,' said George. 'And be quick. That's a can of paraffin he's got in his hands.'

'I can understand 'ow he feels,' said Billy. 'If something happened to Jimmy but ...'

'But what?' George asked as he watched Arthur dial 999.

'Well, I can't stand the woman, you know that George but Kate won't hear a word against 'er an' she just

204

wouldn't be friend's wiv an abortionist. No, it ain't her. I just know. An' I think we need to get up there,' said Billy, 'before they fucking kill 'er.'

***

Del ran across the road. Jimmy was outside his gate. 'Ain't eight o'clock yet,' said Jimmy.

'There's bin stuff happening,' said Del, his voice breaking. 'We need to talk. Right now. Jimmy, I got something to tell you ...'

'Hey, there's Jose,' Jimmy shouted. 'We need to get to the den. You can tell us when we get there. Get Legs Del.'

Jimmy ran over to Josie's gate. She stood there silently. She turned her head away from him.

'What's up Jose?' He put his arm around her shoulders.

Josie turned to look at him. She was crying. 'I dunno. I dunno what's happened but I've got a real confession.'

'Come on,' said Jimmy. 'Here's the others. Let's get to the den quick, before our mums come out.'

All four of them ran as fast as they could towards the waste. Only then did they slow down. 'I got a stitch,' said Legs.

They walked slowly towards the den. They were safe here. The den was covered in a light dusting of snow. Josie's tinsel made it look magical. They had all forgotten that it was nearly Christmas

Josie was sniffing and blowing into her hankie as they sat down in the den.

'Where's the paraffin Del?' Legs asked suddenly. 'Thought you were bringing it.'

Before Del could speak, Josie coughed. 'We can't kill her now,' she said. 'The grown-ups know.' There was silence.

'You mean you told 'em?' said Jimmy angrily. 'After all we said? I know you didn't wanna do it but I don't believe you've grassed us up. Not you Jose.'

Josie sobbed. 'It just 'appened. I was scared.'

'Well, someone's got to stop her,' said Legs, who was secretly hugely relieved that they wouldn't have to take any part in a murder and end up in prison until they were old age pensioners.

205

'Don't have to worry about that,' said Del quietly. 'Me dad's gonna do it.'

The other three gasped.

'Who the bloody hell told him?' asked Legs eventually, glaring at Del. Del couldn't look him in the eye. 'So you've both grassed us up.'

'It's all right for you two!' Del shouted. 'You got normal families. Ain't our fault.'

'I just thought Bones would be alright,' said Josie, trying not to cry again.

'An' I thought that if I told me dad he'd stop hitting me mum,' said Del.

'Did he?' Legs asked.

'Did he fuck.'

'So your dad's gonna kill our witch now?' Jimmy asked.

Del nodded. 'He's got the paraffin.'

'Well, that's better for us really isn't it?' said Legs. 'We're only kids.'

'I s'pose so,' said Jimmy.

Josie took a deep breath. 'You just don't get it you lot do you?' she said 'You don't realise what we've done.'

***

The men walked towards the big old house. Mick Tyler led the way. There were fifteen of them and most couldn't even walk in a straight line. They were very drunk and very angry. A lot of them had daughters.

'Lights are on,' said Loopy. 'She's in.'

'She'd bleeding better be,' Mick grunted. 'Now, shut it you lot, we don't want no witnesses. Just nice an' quiet like. You stay here. I'll go in on me own.'

The men all stood or swayed behind the hedge. Away from the glare of the street light. There was no-one about.

'Give us a shout if you see anyone Loopy,' Mick slurred.

He stood at the gate and removed a large piece of white material from his pocket. They all watched him while he poured the paraffin over it. The smell pervaded the air and made some of them feel sick. The snow had stopped. The gate creaked as he opened it; all the lights downstairs seemed to be on. He knew she would probably try to escape, but he'd be waiting for her and he wasn't going anywhere until he knew she had suffered. He fumbled in his pocket for the matches and lit one as soon as he got to the porch. The flames were immediate and he almost dropped the material. His hands were burning but he managed to push the flaming mass quickly through the letterbox. For a few seconds he thought that it hadn't caught and then, suddenly, he saw the flames leap up. He could make out something else catching light in the hall. This was going to work. Bitch.

He ran quickly back to join the others behind the hedge. 'It's caught,' he said 'She ain't gonna be able to put that out.'

'We'd best get out now Mick,' said one of the men.

'You go,' he slurred. 'I'm waiting here. For when she comes out.'

'You ain't gonna kill her Mick are yer?' asked Loopy.

'Nah but I'm gonna hurt her. I'm gonna make her pay for killing my Julie.'

As they talked, the flames began to take hold. They could see them licking around the front door.

'Go on,' said Mick. 'Piss off all of you. I'll sort it now.'

One by one they trudged off, shaking Mick's hand when they walked past.

'An' don't forget,' said Mick. 'None of us was 'ere tonight.'

He managed to crawl through a hole in the hedge and got into the back garden. He would wait for her there. She wouldn't be long now.

***

'I'm going outside for a pee,' said Legs. 'Back in a minute.'

Josie was trying to make them understand. She needed to tell them everything that Bones had said.

'Quick, out here!' Legs was shouting.

They stumbled over each other in their attempts to get out. What they saw made them gasp with horror. The old house was on fire. There was no mistaking it.

'Oh my God,' Del whispered. 'He's bloody done it. Me dad's set fire to her house!'

'Is she in there?' Josie whispered.

Del knew he should have felt happy, this was what they wanted but he just felt sick. Sick to his stomach. He looked up into the night sky. And saw something. He knew he did.

'No look,' he exclaimed. 'She's on her broomstick! Look behind them clouds. There she is again.'

The others looked. 'Yeah, I think I saw her an' all,' said Jimmy. 'So she ain't dead.'

'She won't come back to Plaistow though,' said Del. 'She ain't gonna bother us again.'

'No Del!' Josie shouted. 'Don't you get it? Any of you? She ain't a witch. She ain't up there on a bloody broomstick. She's probably gonna die now an' it's all our fault.'

'An' how do you know, Miss Clever Clogs. Miss Grass.' Del spat on the ground.

'Right, everyone just shut up now,' said Jimmy. 'Just tell us what you know Jose.'

So Josie told them everything that Old Bones had told her. When it got to the bit about Auschwitz, she cried.

'We done that in school an' all,' said Legs.

'I still think someone should 'ave killed Hitler,' said Del.

Jimmy sighed and took a deep breath. 'So we're all gonna be in real trouble now.'

'We ain't gonna get no Christmas presents,' said Legs. 'An' I'll probably never be allowed to watch the new television.'

'I won't get me train set,' said Jimmy.

'You ain't never gonna get your train set Jimmy.' Said Del. 'You've wanted one since you was five.'

'So what are we gonna do?' asked Josie. 'She won't die. She'll get out. Someone will rescue her won't they Jimmy?' They kept staring at the flames, leaping now into the dark sky.

Jimmy nodded. 'Yeah, I reckon someone will get her out,' he said, 'but I think the only thing we can do is to go off for a bit.'

'What do you mean?' asked Legs.

'Well, we're all in real deep trouble ain't we?' They all nodded.

'Where are we gonna go?' asked Del. 'We ain't got no dosh.'

'Let's go back to the lights,' said Legs. 'They were good and you and Jose haven't seen them Del.'

'Well, I don't wanna go home,' Josie agreed.

'I don't mind so long as we can come home tomorrow. When we get hungry,' said Legs.

'It could be our greatest adventure,' said Jimmy.

'I know where me mum keeps some money,' said Legs.

'Right then, we're sorted,'

They turned their backs to the flames and ran back down Churchill Street. As they raced down the road the fire engine came struggling up the hill, bells clanging.

'They'll get her out,' said Josie. 'They *will* get her out.'

'Course they will,' Jimmy smiled at her. 'It'll be alright but we do need to get away. Right now.'

As they ran Jimmy could feel his whole body shaking. He could scarcely breathe.

Chapter 28

When George and Billy reached the house it was well alight. A small crowd was gathering on the other side of the road. 'Where's the coppers and the fire brigade?' George shouted. 'They must have got Arthur's call.'

'God help her if she's still in there,' said Billy. Then, looking around, he realised that there was really only him that could try and get her out. It would kill George. He was coughing now, just with the smoke.

'I'll have to go in George,' he said. 'Ain't no-one else.'

'Billy, no!' He tried to pull his friend back. 'Wait for the fire brigade. You'll only end up dead.'

'I'll have a look round the back; the flames might not be so bad.'

Billy disappeared round the corner just as Old Bones came running up the road.

'Bones!' shouted George.

'What's 'happening?' Bones could hardly speak he had been running so fast. 'Ain't supposed to have started yet. Eight o'clock Josie told me.'

'Bones, what are you on about? Did you see Mick start it?'

'Mick, what's he got to do wiv it?'

'Bones, is she in there? Billy's gone round the back to try and get 'er out.'

Old Bones looked horrified. 'She ain't there George. She's round my house, she's safe. Oh my God, we'll have to get 'im out.'

As they ran around the side they could hear timbers crashing from inside the building.

***

When Billy tore round into the back garden he saw a dark shadow appear in front of him. 'What the fuck are you doing here Billy?' Mick growled. 'Just let me get on with this will yer. When she comes out I'm gonna ...'

'No-one ain't gonna come out of there you stupid bastard. She didn't even do nothin' Mick.'

'How do you know that?'

'I just know,' Billy shouted 'Who told you she did?'

'My Del did. He knew. Them kids know everything.'

Billy put his head in his hands. He didn't believe all this was happening. 'Just fuck off Mick an' if I was you I'd fuck off a long way cos if she is in there an' she ain't done nothin' they'll lock you up an' throw away the key.'

Mick didn't hang around. He crashed through the hedge and sprinted up the road faster than he had ever run before.

Billy turned round and saw the flames everywhere. The heat was intense.

Only seconds after Mick had disappeared George and Bones turned up. 'Billy! Billy!' George was spluttering and coughing as he ran up to him, closely followed by Bones.

'Billy, she's safe.'

'I've got the cats an' all,' said Bones.

Billy laughed, mostly with relief. 'Well I weren't gonna go in there to rescue any fuckin' cats Bones.'

They moved away from the house and back round to the front. Quite a large crowd had gathered now and the sounds of a fire engine and police car bells filled the air.

Sally came running towards them, she looked grief-stricken. 'Billy, what's going on?'

'Mick thought she'd done the abortion that killed Julie, he set fire to the house,' he said quietly.

'No, no!' Sally screamed. 'It weren't her. It weren't her Billy!' And then she collapsed.

'Sal, it's alright, she ain't dead. She ain't there.'

George felt for her pulse. 'She's fainted,' he said to Billy. 'Go an' tell the firemen that the house is empty.'

Billy just couldn't believe what was happening. Sweat was pouring off him as he ran to talk to the nearest fireman. And, he thought to himself, he knew the next person he was going to look for. His son. These kids had something to do with this.

***

The crowd grew outside the house as the firemen fought to control the blaze. Thank God, Sally thought. Thank God no-one else has died. She stood next to George as they watched Billy come back.

'What did you tell 'em?' George asked.

'Nothing, they don't need to know. No-one's got hurt and hopefully Mick will piss off back to the Merchant Navy and we can all get a bit of peace.'

'He should pay for this,' George shook his head. 'Unless she *did* do it of course'

'She didn't,' said Sally, 'but I ain't tellin' no-one who did.'

They both looked at her. She was suddenly conscious of the state she was in. It must show on her face.

'We'd best get you home Sal,' Billy said. 'You ain't well.'

'Oh my God,' she cried. 'I've left the babies. I saw the flames, I couldn't find Josie and ...'

They moved quickly away and into Churchill Street. Everyone was standing outside their homes, just watching the flames.

'We need to find these kids,' said Billy. They've got something to do with this. I know they 'ave. When I asked Mick who told him it was Mrs Broncowiez that done the abortion he said that Del had told him. Del. How would he know about anything like that?'

'We never know what they get up to do we?' George sighed. 'They only come home to eat.'

'It ain't the kids fault,' Sally cried as she ran in her gate. 'It's mine. This whole mess is my fault.'

Billy went to follow her, but George pulled him back. 'Not a good idea Billy,' he said sharply. '*I'll* go and talk to her. You go and find these kids and,' he shouted, following Sally through the back door, 'see if your Kate's alright. She's a friend of Greta's; she'll want to know she's safe.'

***

Billy ran to his own front door. Kate opened it as he got there.

'Is she alright Billy?' she asked, tears in her eyes. She looked so vulnerable and lost. After all that had happened today and after being so ill.

'She's fine love. She's staying at Bone's flat. Even the cats got out.'

He put his arms round her and she clung to him and he knew in that moment that he did love her. It wasn't what he had felt for Sally. That had been different.

Kate pulled back from him and took a deep breath. 'And where's Jimmy? I haven't seen him. He's not been in for his tea and Legs is missing as well.'

'I think we'll find that they're all missing,' said Billy. 'They've got something to do with this Kate. I don't know how or why but I think they know they're in trouble. I'll get to the bottom of it.'

Molly came into the hall. 'You don't mean it was them who set fire to Mrs Broncoweiz's house, surely Billy?'

'No, that weren't them Molly but they're involved in it somewhere.'

Molly sighed. 'Well, when all this is done and dusted Billy you need to think about that boy. About where he's going to end up if he stays round here. Look at what's happened today. You need to think long and hard about emigrating and giving yourselves a new start. It's the only answer.'

'Not now Molly,' Kate said sharply. 'Let's just find Jimmy shall we?'

Billy gave her a grateful smile. 'I won't be long. You stay 'ere an' they'll all be back when they're hungry. Just then May burst through the door. She looked at Kate.

'Has anyone found them yet?' she asked tearfully. They all shook their heads.

'Del's gone missing too and Clive has raided my housekeeping tin. There was five pounds in there,' she cried. 'He's never been a thief, not our Clive. Well, apart from the sherry. What's been going on Billy?'

All three women looked at him as if he should know the answer. Well he didn't but he was bloody well sure he was going to find out.

***

George couldn't believe what he saw when he walked into Sally Evan's house. Suitcases out in the hall. Three of them. Bulging and packed in a hurry. Little bits of material sticking out here and there. He called out from the hallway. 'Are you there Sally? Are they alright?'

She appeared at the top of the stairs. George could see that she was shaking and crying. 'They're fine,' she whimpered, 'they're still asleep. Oh George, what have I done?'

213

George wasn't sure how much more he could cope with today. He knew he wasn't the only one but at his time of life he felt that another day like this might kill him. Too much emotion. He wished he didn't think so much sometimes. Why couldn't people be more predictable? He just didn't understand how they thought. What made them do the things they did. He would have to get some psychology books out from the library.

Now he looked at Sally, as she walked down the stairs towards him. She could have done something with her life, she wasn't daft. He looked again at the suitcases and back to her. 'Shall I make us a cuppa?' he said kindly.

She nodded and followed him through to the kitchen. He sat her down at the table, made the tea and poured it out. Sally laughed through her tears.

'You'd make someone a good wife George. Why didn't I ever meet a man like you eh?'

'You're only young Sal. You've got your whole life ahead of you and by the looks of it you're not going to spend much longer round here so what's going on? What are *you* running away from?'

Sally sighed. She told him everything. About Julie getting pregnant and having the abortion and how guilty she felt. How she couldn't tell Maggie and she just didn't think that she could face her friends in Churchill Street knowing what she knew. Also how she had really thought that Greta had died in that fire and been blamed for something she never did

They had to go away and leave all that guilt behind. She was just waiting for Josie and they were going off to Dianne's mum's house, the only real family she had ever known. Just until they could find somewhere else to live.

'And what about Billy? Is that all over?' George asked quietly.

'It never started George. Nothing 'appened really. Just a bit of snogging that's all.'

'Sometimes that's all it takes. Not even that.'

George put his hand over hers.

'I would have though George. I still would, if he wanted me. What does that make me?'

'Life isn't fair Sal. We can't always have what we want. You're probably not very lucky in love that's all. It will

214

happen for you though. You're a good girl, I know that. And I know you feel guilty about what happened to Julie but that isn't your fault. If you hadn't tried to help her, someone else would. There's only me and Billy that knows anything and we'll keep quiet.' He laughed. 'We're not like women, we can keep secrets.'

'You're a funny bugger George. I don't understand half of what you say but you've made me feel a bit better. I'd love to marry someone one day an' be like you an' May. How do you find that George?'

George laughed. 'That's easy,' he said, 'that was just luck. Right person. Right place. Right time.'

'And ain't you ... ain't you never bin tempted?'

'More than my life's worth Sal,' he laughed. 'She'd cut off my balls and have them for breakfast.'

Chapter 29

The four friends ran as fast as they could up the hill towards Plaistow station. It was busy. People coming home from work or going uptown to see the lights.

'What station we going to?' Jimmy asked as they ran into the entrance.

'Dunno,' said Del, 'but we ain't paying. Follow me.'

They all ran after him as he slipped around the side of the ticket collector and jumped over the barrier. 'Hoy! You bloody kids!' the ticket collector shouted as he saw them legging it over the barriers. 'Come back 'ere!'

The four jumped into the waiting train, laughing and breathless. The doors closed and they were off. 'You got the money Legs?' Josie asked.

He put his hand in his pocket and brought out five, crumpled pound notes. They all looked hard at it. 'I ain't never seen that much money,' said Jimmy wide-eyed.

'I think we should all take one,' said Del, 'in case we lose each other.'

'No,' said Legs, quickly folding the notes and putting them back in his pocket. 'You'd spend it all on rubbish.'

'What we gonna buy wiv it then Legs?' Jimmy asked.

Legs shrugged his shoulders. 'We could have some hot chestnuts.'

'Yeah,' said Jimmy. 'They was smashing.'

'Can we go to Buckinham Palace?' Josie asked suddenly. 'I ain't never bin.'

An elderly man was sitting next to Del, reading his paper. Del looked at him and nudged him in the ribs. 'What station do we get off for Buckinham Palace mate? You know, where the Queen lives.'

The man smiled. 'You'll need to change at Mile End and get on the central line. Change again at Holborn and get the Piccadilly line for Green Park.'

Del looked at Josie. 'Can you remember all that Jose?' She nodded.

'Can we go and see her?' Legs asked. 'The Queen I mean.'

'Don't talk stupid,' Josie said 'you'd 'ave to phone first. You can't just walk in. She's the Queen ain't she?'

216

'Well, is Oxford Street near there?' Del asked the man, who was trying to keep a serious face, 'only we need to see the lights later an' all.'

The man delved into his pocket and produced a London street map. He showed them how to get to the lights from Buckingham Palace.

Del turned to Legs as they got on the central line train at Mile End. 'We'll need some food Legs, wiv your money,' he said. 'There's a lot of walking.'

'Hey,' Legs said excitedly, 'we could get American burgers. There's a caff called a Wimpy Bar. We saw it, didn't we Jimmy?'

Jimmy nodded. The train was pulling in to Bethnal Green again. 'This is where your Nan and your auntie died,' Legs said, looking at him, 'isn't it?'

Josie gasped as the train stopped. 'We must say a prayer,' she said, crossing herself. She put her hands together. The boys looked at her as if she were mad.

'Dear God, please remember Jimmy's nana an' auntie an' keep them safe in heaven ... '

'Shut up Jose now,' Del whispered. 'We ain't in the den, we're on a bloody train.'

Jimmy smiled at Josie. He felt strangely warmed by her prayer. The people around them all stared. Some smiled, others shuffled their feet.

All four piled off the train at Green Park and managed to evade the ticket collector there as well. Before they knew it, they were strolling up to the front of Buckingham Palace.

'Wow!' Josie exclaimed.

'That's a very big house for one person,' said Jimmy.

'The kids live there an' all,' said Josie.

'Yeah, and all the servants,' Legs added. 'I haven't ever seen a house as big as that.'

'Look,' said Del excitedly, as they crossed the road to the gates outside the Palace. 'Look at them guards in the sentry boxes. Just like in the pictures I've seen.'

They approached one of the sentries and stared at him. He was unmoved and kept perfectly still. 'Hello mate,' said Del. 'Any chance we could get in like ... you know, to have a butchers at the Queen?'

217

The sentry stood completely still. Not a muscle moved on his face. Josie elbowed Del in the ribs. 'They ain't allowed to talk Del. They 'ave to keep properly still.'

'Well, I just think he's rude,' said Del loudly.

'He ain't much fun,' Jimmy agreed.

'He could be,' Del laughed. 'Watch this.'

He swaggered towards the sentry who remained unmoving. 'I think you're a bit of a pillock. You look like one in that stupid hat.'

'Del!' Josie exclaimed. 'You can't talk to 'im like that, he's the Queen's soldier.'

The others laughed. This was really good fun. They all gathered around the hapless sentry. 'Can we look at your gun mate?' Legs asked. 'We like guns.'

'Bet you can't shoot it, bet it's just a pretend one,' Jimmy laughed.

'Are you cold?' Josie asked. 'I'd be cold if I had to stand out here for hours an' hours.' She shivered. There was a thin layer of snow on the ground.

Del was still talking to the sentry. 'I think you're a real plonker. You ain't right in the head. An' I'll bet you're a nancy boy. Me dad says you all are.'

Josie gasped. 'Del stop it. Right now.'

The others were laughing so much that Jimmy thought he might wet himself. He looked at the man's face. It was beginning to twitch and he seemed to be breathing very heavily. Suddenly he glared at Del. 'If you little shits don't move on I will show you just how well I can shoot,' he hissed. 'I will show you four times. So just fuck off.' His lips had barely moved.

'Well, that weren't very nice,' said Josie as they sharply retreated. 'I'll bet 'Er Majesty don't know you swear. I'm gonna write her a letter when I gets home.'

The boys were running back across the road. Josie was behind them. She was still hurling abuse at the immobile sentry and forgot to look both ways before she ran after her friends.

'Jose!' Jimmy screamed. They watched as it all happened in front of their eyes in slow motion. The black cab swerved and screeched to a halt in front of their very eyes but not before it had hit Josie. The impact sent her flying

218

through the air to land in a crumpled heap, outside the front gates of Buckingham Palace.

***

The pub was a mess. Because he had been open all day, Arthur had not had any time to clean up. He had asked Bones to do a bit of glass collecting now. The posse had headed up to Greta Broncowiez's house and returned minus Mick Tyler. Arthur had been blackmailed into telling the coppers that they had all been in the Kings Head since six o'clock and that he hadn't seen Mick all day. He was a bit miffed about that but, as they all reminded him; he did on odd occasions deal in stolen goods. He certainly didn't want the coppers sniffing around for too long.

Everything had quietened down a bit and then suddenly all hell broke loose again. Billy came rushing in, grabbed Bones by the throat and lifted him off the ground.

'Hey, Billy, put him down,' Arthur roared.

Billy dropped Bones unceremoniously on to the floor. Two of the regulars helped him up, another two held Billy back.

'Right,' said Arthur, 'here's your pint Billy. Orange juice Bones. Just the two of you come over 'ere an' talk about whatever it is.'

'I'm past talking,' Billy shouted. 'Our kids have all gone missing an' he knows something about all this. An' what sort of man drinks fucking orange juice anyway?'

Old Bones walked over to the bar and picked up the juice. He took a swig and glared at Billy. 'I'm the sort of man who drinks fucking orange juice Billy Potter cos I used to need a drink so much that I left my little girl to die. To choke on her sweetie while I nipped out to the pub. 'Here you are,' I said. 'You have these sweeties. Don't tell your mum I went out, I won't be long ...'

His voice broke. Billy gasped. He put his arms around Bones and held him while he sobbed.

'Right,' said Arthur. 'Seems to me that someone needs to take charge 'ere. I ain't seen so many men cry since we ran out of beer in 1937, so just shut it now all of you. I've had enough of all this doom an' gloom. Seems to me like we need to find these kids.'

219

He brought out a street map from under the bar while all the men gathered round. The posse were the first ones there.

'Yeah,' said Loopy. 'Let's find the little buggers an' bring 'em all home.'

Bones told Billy all he knew. About the kids thinking Greta was a witch, and that they thought she had killed Nellie Bransome and Julie with the apples.

'They thought your Kate had been poisoned an' all. I'm sorry Billy that I didn't come straight an' tell yer. I just wanted to get her out the house. It was the kids that was planning on doing it. I'd have stopped *them*. I didn't want to grass 'em up.'

'They're kids Bones.'

'You wouldn't grass *your* mates up Billy. They're my mates. I like 'em so let's go an' find 'em. They think they're in trouble, that's why they've gone.'

'They *are* in bloody trouble,' said Billy, 'but we just need to know they're safe for now. That's all that matters.'

Arthur had organised all the men to search different streets and areas and they all set off. 'Any ideas Bones?' he asked. 'Where they might 'ave gone?'

Bones shook his head.

'Well, I've looked in the den,' said Billy 'an' they ain't there. Come on Bones, we'll do Montgomery Road. They could be hiding somewhere.'

'I'll go an' get Chuck,' said Bones.' He might sniff 'em out'

'They ain't rabbits Bones,' said Billy.

'Someone *will* find 'em Billy.' Said Arthur. 'If we ain't got 'em in an hour I'll call the cops.'

Billy shook his hand. 'Thanks mate. For all you're doing.'

'Oh, fuck off,' said Arthur.

***

It was very overcrowded in May and George's house, bodies everywhere. All the women and children had gathered. May and George were the only ones in Churchill Street who had a telephone. George had poured all the women a sherry before he'd gone out to join the search. 'They've only been gone a couple of hours,' he said. 'They'll be alright. They're all together.'

220

'But it's dark,' Maggie sniffed, trying to force the bottle of milk in the grizzling baby's mouth.'

'Here you are Maggie,' Sally took the baby from her. 'She just needs a bit of winding I think. I'll feed her for yer. You've had enough today.'

'It's so cold out there,' said Kate, shivering, 'and he hasn't got his cap.'

'They'll be fine,' said George. 'We'll find them.'

After he had gone the women all sat in silence for a long time, trying not to think about the worst that could happen.

'We know nothing about their lives at all do we?' Sally said. 'We know what they have for breakfast an' tea an' what time they go to bed an' that's about it.'

'Posh families take their kids to places I s'pose,' Maggie agreed.

'We try taking Clive out but he never wants to go,' said May tearfully.

'They won't have any idea that they've caused this much upset,' said Auntie Molly. 'I'll put the kettle on girls shall I?'

She walked through to the kitchen. She didn't really approve of them drinking alcohol at a time like this. Not women all drinking together. It wouldn't happen in Ilford and she was sure it would never happen in Australia.

When the telephone rang, about an hour later, they all jumped. Fear and hope permeated the room in equal measure. For a few seconds they all looked at the phone. Eventually, Kate grabbed it. 'Hello . . . Yes . . . Oh, thank God ...'

Everyone in the room relaxed. They had found them, someone had found them. They were safe.

'Why?. . . Yes she's here . . . I'll pass you on to her now.'

Kate looked straight at Sally. They hadn't seen each other since the morning on the bus. It didn't seem to matter now. 'They want to talk to you. It's a doctor and he's phoning from St Thomas' hospital, up in London.'

Sally grabbed the phone and a few seconds later let out a long, low groan. May rushed over to her. 'It's Josie,' she cried. 'She's bin run over. She ain't good. I need ... She looked around the room in despair.

221

'Come on,' said Auntie Molly. 'I'll drive you.'

'I'll come too,' said Kate. 'We can bring the others back. They're all there.'

'What about ...'

'I'll look after the babies Sally, 'said May. 'You just get off. Quick as you can.'

Maggie quickly poured herself another sherry. 'What the bloody 'ell are they doing up town?' she asked as the three women ran out the door.

***

Kate sat in the back seat of Molly's car with Sally. Sally seemed to be in a state of shock. She was staring straight ahead and breathing deeply.

'What did they say Sally?' Kate asked quietly.

'They just said to get there as soon as I could. She's unconscious an' she's broke 'er arm. Oh Kate, I don't know if I can stand anymore today.'

She cried in Kate's arms as Molly drove like a maniac. This car had never done more than thirty miles an hour before today.

'I'm so sorry Kate,' Sally was sobbing. 'I'm so sorry. I never should have hit you the other day.'

'It's not important now,' Kate replied.

Sally's perfume filled the car. Kate recognised the smell. Roses. And she remembered when she had smelt it before. Before the bus, before everything. Sally's tears mingled with her own. It didn't matter now, Sally was suffering enough.

***

The men were pouring back into the Kings Head, shaking their heads.

'Ain't nowhere,' said Loopy. 'Them kids have disappeared off the face of the earth.'

'Don't be so bleeding dramatic Loopy,' said Arthur, walking over to the phone.

'Now I'm phoning the coppers. If any of you is carrying anything or doing anything illegal you can piss off for a bit.'

As he reached to pick up the phone it rang. Arthur just stared at it for a few seconds.

He picked it up just as Billy came running in with Bones. 'Can't find 'em anywhere,' said Bones.

222

'It's George for you Billy,' said Arthur passing him the phone. Everyone gathered around. Billy held the phone to his ear. There was silence in the King's Head.

'It's alright,' Billy shouted at last. 'They're alright. They went up town. Come on George, get yer harris down 'ere,' he was shouting down the mouthpiece. 'I'll get you one in.'

There was a collective sigh of relief around the whole pub.

'Ain't you going home Billy?' Bones asked.

'Nah. Think we all need a drink first after the day we've 'ad,' Billy laughed.

Arthur stood behind the bar grinning. A rare sight. 'Now then lads,' he shouted above the cacophony of noise which had erupted. 'I'm gonna take the very unusual step of standing you all a drink.'

There was silence again and then cheering broke out from every corner of the pub.

'Blimey,' said Loopy, 'you should tell them dustbin lids to get lost more often Billy.'

'Come on,' Arthur shouted. 'It's Christmas in a few days time. Get on that piano Bones. Give us a bit of 'Jingle Bells.''

As the whole pub erupted into song, Billy laughed. The smile soon left his face when he saw George walking in. He didn't look happy.

'What's up George?'

'It's Josie Billy. She's been hurt bad I think. Got run over outside Buckingham Palace. Unconscious so they said.'

'So, what about Sal? Does she know?'

'Yeah. Molly and Kate have gone with her to the hospital.'

'Kate's gone wiv Sal? Bloody hell George. George nodded and lit his pipe.

'Yeah. They're all at the hospital. The other kids are just a bit shocked. Seeing it all I suppose. Molly and Kate will bring them all back but Sal's in a right state.'

'What the 'ell were they doing up there?'

'Getting away from us I should think,' George smiled. 'And Billy, please promise me you won't hit him. When he gets back. It was just all in their imaginations. They weren't doing anything deliberately.'

223

'He's my son,' said Billy grimly. Ain't nothin' to do wiv you George. Now drink your bloody beer. They won't be back for a bit yet. And Arthur's bought it for you. It's on the house.' Billy looked into his beer for a moment, a frown on his face. 'How did Sal know?' he asked George. 'That it weren't Mrs Broncowiez what done the abortion? She seemed pretty sure.'

George told Billy everything he knew about the part Sally had played in the drama that had been going on all day. 'Her bags were all packed Billy. She was moving out. I think I've talked her out of it but don't say anything will you. Keep it to ourselves.'

Billy nodded. 'It ain't her fault,' he protested. 'She shouldn't feel guilty.'

George was giving him a funny look. 'I nearly did it,' said Billy. 'The other night. It could have happened. It won't now so don't worry. I'm just a boring old fart George at the end of the day.' They both laughed.

George turned to Arthur and held up his pint. 'Cheers Arthur,' he said. 'Drinks on the house, didn't know you had it in you. I think I'm going to need it mind. We've got Sal's twins to look after.'

It was ten o'clock at night and the pub was full of punters who could barely stand. Some of them had been drinking for twelve hours. They had formed a posse to burn someone's house down and then another one to find four lost kids.

'I think,' George said, to no-one in particular, 'that this has been the longest day of my life.'

'It certainly ain't one we're gonna forget,' Billy agreed.

'Well I know which bit I'll remember most,' Loopy laughed. 'Arthur buying us all a drink.'

And from the tears and the traumas of the day, laughter echoed around the King's Head.

Chapter 30

The waiting room at St Thomas' Hospital was full. It was a busy night.

'Thanks for staying wiv me Kate. I don't deserve it after what I done to you. '

'To be honest Sally, I don't remember much about it. I know I probably said some unkind things.'

'Yeah but you was ill. I should have thought.'

Kate couldn't quite bring herself to touch Sally again but she managed a weak smile. Jimmy was safe and Molly had taken the three boys home. That was all she cared about now.

A doctor had been in to see Sally. Josie was no longer unconscious but they were worried about her. They were doing tests to see if her head was alright and her arm was broken in two places where the taxi had hit her, so she would have to stay in. Sally hadn't been allowed to see her yet.

This was a horrible place, Kate thought. The antiseptic smells in hospitals always made her feel sick. She shivered and looked around the room. There were a couple of drunks in the corner; one had been sick all over the floor. Even though it had been cleared up quickly the awful smell still hung in the air. Their brother had been trying to climb a lamppost and had fallen. They had been told that he would probably have to have serious surgery. He was only twenty four. A worried looking middle-aged woman was clutching her hankie and shaking. Her mother was ninety two and had just had a fall. There were others. Some agitated, some trying to crack jokes but the tension in the room crackled with despair and hope in equal measure.

The door opened. Everyone looked at the young doctor. He was smiling. This must be good news.

'Mrs. Sally Evans?'

***

As Billy walked home from the pub he felt exhausted. What a day. What a week. Just seven days ago life had been very different. Kate had been really poorly and he had been in despair. Since then he had almost been unfaithful, Sally had hit his wife, the kid over the road had died after a botched abortion, his mate had set fire to a house and their kids had all gone missing. You couldn't make all that up if you tried. He should write a book or at least an episode of The Archers. Well, he would if he could write. Perhaps Jimmy would. No, he couldn't write very well either. As he went in his front gate he looked over to Sal's house and was glad that he just felt nothing at all.

Now he walked slowly up the stairs and tiptoed into Jimmy's bedroom. When he was asleep, his son still looked as vulnerable as when he had been a baby. Little shit, Billy laughed to himself. He, himself had got up to all sorts when he had been a kid but nothing like this. Jimmy's bedcovers had fallen off. As Billy picked them up off the floor and put them back over him, his son's eyes flickered.

Billy suddenly felt a warm rush of love for his little mate. He was so glad at that moment that things had worked out right.

'You ain't gonna hit me are you dad?'

Billy tried to look stern. 'I dunno son but whatever 'appens we're gonna have a very serious talk in the morning.'

Jimmy nodded and was back asleep in seconds. Auntie Molly was snoring in the corner on the camp bed. How his son could sleep through that Billy didn't know.

He made his way into the bedroom. Kate was sitting in bed reading.

'He's alright,' said Billy. 'I don't think they'll run away again in a hurry. What a day.'

Kate seemed very calm, very in control. He couldn't believe how ill she had been just a few days ago.

'I thought we'd lost him Billy. I really did.'

He put his arms around her and she snuggled into his chest. 'Everything's alright now love. It could have been a lot worse. And Josie's gonna be fine. Hey, have you bin drinking Kate Potter?'

'How do you know?'

'I can smell sherry that's why.'

'It was medicinal,' she said, 'and it was hours ago.'

He laughed as she pulled away from him. 'Turn the lights out Billy.'

Billy leapt out of bed. Well, it was all happening today. He climbed back in and put his arm around her.

'It's just that I have to talk to you about ... everything and I don't think I can do it with the lights on.'

'Oh,' Billy felt like he had just had a cold shower. Still, he probably wouldn't have had the energy after everything that had happened.

'You want to talk ... now?'

She nodded into his chest. 'I need to Billy. I have to tell you everything. I just don't know where to start.'

'Well I reckon Bethnal Green might be the best place,' he replied. 'You ain't never talked about that night.'

She was right, he thought. It *was* easier to talk in the dark.

She told him about the searchlights and the sirens. The fear when they heard the explosions.

'We just ran Billy. Me and Shirley. Everyone did. We just needed to get off the street. We got to the entrance and there was a wall of bodies in front of us. I couldn't breathe. We were being pushed forward all the time. I shouted at Shirley. *We're turning around, we're not going down there!* but it was too late. We couldn't turn back; we were just being carried along. There was scarcely any light on the stairs and everything seemed wrong. The steps were soft, like you were walking on pillows and we were too high up and then I realised. We were treading on bodies. I just went mad Billy, I had to get out. I – I let go of Shirley's hand and –'

She stopped and took a deep breath. Billy squeezed her hand. 'That's enough now,' he said.

'No Billy, I need to tell you. I pushed, I kicked, I screamed. I fought like I'd never fought in my life. I don't know what happened after that but I got out and there were dead babies Billy. I saw them. I can't ever forget that.' She cried then as he held her close.

Kate told him that she didn't remember how long she had stayed in the tiny recess in the wall. Probably for hours because when she came out, there was nothing there. No dead children. She had thought that perhaps it had all been some dreadful nightmare but then those two men, the ARP wardens had come running towards her. She remembered screaming and screaming. One of them slapping her to try and make her stop. And most of all she remembered him telling her never to say a word about what she had seen. It was a secret. And Kate was good at keeping secrets.

227

The other one had taken her down the escalator to the platform. Most people were asleep but she heard little whispers. Anxious whispers. Family members who were missing. Consoling words.

'Be alright love. They'll have gone somewhere else. We'd know if something 'ad 'appened. Anyway what *could* have 'appened?'

Someone had pulled on her coat. 'Has something gone on up there love? You look like you seen a ghost.'

Kate had shaken her head furiously and then she had spotted her Auntie, lying in a bunk. Snoring. She had run over to her and thrown herself onto Molly's body.

'Kate is that you? I was waiting for you. Where are the others? Kate? Where's your mum and Shirley? Has something happened?'

Kate had shaken her head. 'No,' she had said. 'Nothing's happened. They're just ... somewhere else.'

'Well, get in here with me then and keep yourself warm. We'll go home soon.'

***

Billy had been stroking Kate's hair while she talked and wiping her tears away with a hankie.

'And I thought it was all my fault you see Billy. Everything. Thought I was being punished and that I'd killed my little sister and then when Dawn died I just knew it was God, getting his own back for not helping all those babies. For treading on them, trying to get out. For letting go of Shirley's hand.'

'None of that was your fault Kate,' said Billy. He felt tears running down *his* face too.

'I know that now,' she sniffed. 'Greta has helped me to see that Billy. I know I couldn't have changed anything.'

'And I want you to promise me that you'll go to the doctor Kate. You need to talk to someone professional like. I do believe you now that Greta 'as been a good mate to you but she ain't a proper trained person.'

Kate sniffed again. 'I *will* talk to the doctor but no pills Billy. They don't help me. I feel much stronger now but I will go because I want ... I want to be a better wife to you ... you know in *that* way. You'll just have to be patient, that's all.'

Billy smiled. 'Well, I've waited ten years I'm sure a few more days won't hurt me.'

'Oh Billy.' But she was laughing through her tears as she picked up her pillow and hit him over the head with it.

'One thing though,' Billy laughed. 'I ain't going to Australia.'

***

'Where's Auntie Molly?' Jimmy asked as he came downstairs.

'She's gone home Jimmy. She'll be back for Christmas Day. Come and have some breakfast, although it's actually nearer lunchtime.'

'Why?' Kate asked her son when he was sitting eating his toast. 'Why did you run away like that?'

Jimmy bowed his head. 'We was in trouble,' he muttered. 'It was all the witch's fault.'

'She isn't a witch Jimmy.'

'Yeah I know now.' He shuffled his feet and kept looking at the floor.

'What happened wasn't your fault either you know,' Kate said. 'You didn't mean any harm, you just didn't understand. You're just a little boy.'

Billy was sitting in his chair with his paper. 'By rights son, I should give you a bloody good hiding,' he said quietly.

Kate stood up from the table and glared at him. 'Don't you think there's been enough violence round here this weekend? You touch one hair on his head today and I will bloody kill you!'

Billy and Jimmy gasped in shock. Kate never swore. Never.

'Alright love,' said Billy, slowly reaching out towards her. 'I didn't say I was going to did I? Just that he deserves it that's all. Making us all worry like that. Ain't no need to shout. You've got hangover wiv all that sherry, that's what it is.'

'Because I'm angry? After all that happened yesterday. A young girl dead. My friend almost burnt to death by hooligans. Worried sick over my son who just runs off to God knows where. How am I supposed to feel after all that? Tell me that Billy. Am I not allowed to shout and scream because I've lived in Ilford? Too posh for all that? Is that what you think?'

229

Jimmy began to cry then. Heaving sobs. 'Just shut up shouting,' he cried.

Billy put his arms around his son and held him tightly. He couldn't remember the last time he had done that. Apart from at football of course when the Hammers scored.

Kate gasped. 'Oh Jimmy, I'm sorry,' she said quietly, ruffling his hair. 'You're still in shock after everything. I won't shout anymore, I promise. And Josie's going to be alright. She's broken her arm but they think she was just concussed, she'll be home soon.'

She walked past them both and got her coat down from the peg.

'Where are you goin' now?' Billy asked.

'I need some fresh air,' she answered as she opened the front door. 'I need to walk and think. And actually I *have* got a bit of a headache.'

'I knew it,' Billy laughed.

Kate smiled weakly at them as she went out of the door.

'Well,' said Billy, sitting himself down at the table. 'Well, well,' he said again. 'I think we can safely say that your mum is feeling better son.'

Jimmy was wiping his runny nose on his sleeve. Suddenly he laughed through the tears. 'That was funny when she sweared dad, ain't never heard her swear before.'

Billy laughed as well. 'Looks like we're gonna have to get our own grub before football.'

'We can get a pie at the match dad. It's only a reserve game. They won't have sold out. It don't matter.'

'Yeah son, that'll do. Get us a cuppa will yer?'

'Dad? Can I ask yer a man question an' don't shout at me.'

Billy laughed. 'I ain't gonna shout at yer son.'

Jimmy turned to face him. 'Are you doing sex wiv Sally?'

Billy couldn't believe he was hearing this. 'No I'm bloody not!' He shouted.

'You said you wouldn't shout.'

'Just get me that tea will yer. We ain't got all day.'

'That's all right then,' Jimmy said quietly.

There was a long silence while he concentrated on preparing the tea.

230

'D'you fancy moving to Australia then?' Billy asked his son as he eventually brought him his drink.

'Dunno,' said Jimmy, shrugging his shoulders. 'There's sharks an' crocodiles. We done it in school.'

'Not everywhere there ain't,' Billy laughed

'What about me mates?'

'Well, we ain't taking' them wiv us an' all. You'd make new mates. Probably.'

'Nah,' said Jimmy. 'I don't wanna go nowhere.'

'Nor do I son,' Billy agreed. 'Nor do I.'

***

Kate sat quietly knitting and listening to the wireless. She was amazed that she felt so much calmer. She had no idea why she had snapped at Billy like that this morning. Well, she did really.

She knew that she would have to ask him about Sally. Last night with everything that was going on it didn't seem to matter and when they had been in bed and she had told him about Bethnal Green she had felt so close to him. But when she had woken up this morning and he wasn't there, little doubts had kept niggling in her mind. For a terrifying moment, she thought he had left her. Then she had heard the toilet flush. It wasn't her imagination. Not this time. She had smelt Sally's perfume on him one night. She knew she had.

She had been to see Greta today at Bone's house. She had laid her hands on Kate's head again and peace and calm had been restored. After everything that had gone on in the last two days, Kate was proud of herself. Proud to have survived it all and not been ill again.

Greta had read her tarots as well. Strange cards that Kate had never seen before. Wise cards, the old lady had called them. When the death card was turned over, Kate gasped. 'Don't worry Kate, it doesn't mean you're going to die. It signifies change. A great change in your life. A new life.'

She had turned more cards over and was silent for a long time, studying them. 'The hard times are behind you and you're going to grow stronger. You have a decision to make, but whichever path you take it will work out. Your pain is all in the past.'

231

Kate had told Greta that Billy thought she should talk to someone and Greta had agreed.

'I don't know everything Kate,' she had said. 'And there's something else that you've never told me about too isn't there?'

Kate shook her head and looked down at her feet.

'And have you told Billy?' Kate shook her head.

'I do want to be a *proper* wife to him Greta. I know that's important now.'

Greta watched her friend, her eyes flickering and dancing around the room. 'Look at me Kate,' she said. 'Look into my eyes. If you want me to help you with this all I can do is listen. You can tell me whatever it is if you want to but you *must* tell Billy. It will help him understand.'

Kate looked into the old lady's eyes. 'You know don't you?' she asked quietly.

'I can guess,' Greta replied.

'I knew him,' Kate began quietly. 'I'd met him before. He was there at Bethnal Green, that night. He had been kind to me. And he was only young. He'd been injured in France, that's why he was working as a warden.' She stopped and took a deep breath. 'His name was Pete.'

'I was just running through the park. It was only a week before we moved to Ilford. I'd been to the shop for Auntie Molly. It was getting dark, there wasn't anyone about. And then I saw him. He was walking towards me.

'Hello,' he said. 'It's Kate isn't it?'

'I looked closer and then I remembered who he was. I felt a bit of a lump in my throat especially when he asked me if I'd found Shirley. I started crying then. He put his arm around me and took me over to sit on a bench. I just couldn't stop crying. He kissed me then. I didn't mind, I just thought he was being kind really but then. . .

***

'He began to touch me Billy, all over. He was really rough. I tried to push him off but he was too strong. I tried to scream but there was no-one about and he put his hand over my mouth. I kept trying to lash out at him and to kick him but then he started trying to strangle me. I thought I was going to die Billy. I knew I had to choose. Either I carried on fighting and he would kill me or I could stop and just let him - do things to me.'

232

Billy couldn't believe what he was hearing now. All these secrets seemed to be pouring out of Kate like a tap that drips for years and years and then suddenly explodes.

They were lying in bed; Billy had his arm round her shoulder. He could hear the normal night-time sounds. The barges on the river, a wireless playing too loud, someone shouting their dog to come in. He moved and sat on the side of the bed, his feet on the floor, clenching and unclenching his fists. He had his back to her now.

'He raped you didn't he?'

'No. No he didn't in the end Billy. Oh, I just seem to be talking about awful things to you all the time. I'm sorry.'

'*You're* sorry? What have you got to be sorry for?' He still couldn't look at her. She put her hand in his and he gripped it tightly.

'He just ... made me do things to him. To make him feel better, he said. Oh Billy, I didn't want to die. It was ... awful.'

'An' I don't suppose you told no-one did yer?'

She shook her head. 'He begged me not to. He was crying and I just wanted to forget it. I ran home and told Auntie Molly that I'd fallen over in the park and that's how I'd lost two of the buttons off my coat. They were blue buttons, I remember. She told me off because I'd been a long time. She was worried, with the blackout and everything. And then we had egg and chips for tea.'

'You don't like egg an' chips.'

She put her head down. 'No, I know.'

Billy jumped off the bed and walked across the room over to the window. He clenched his fist and hit the wall so hard that it hurt. 'Bastard,' he hissed. 'Bloody bastard. If I ever get hold of him ...'

'He's dead Billy.'

'Good. I hope he suffered.'

'He hung himself. It was in the papers.'

Billy came slowly back towards the bed.

'Everyone suffered in the war, I don't hate him anymore.'

Billy held her very tightly. 'Is that everything now?' he asked. She nodded.

'Thank God for that,' he laughed suddenly, 'I'm thinking of getting a job as one of them agony aunts.'

233

'Oh, Billy,' she dug him in the ribs. 'Will we be alright?'

'Course we will,' Billy swallowed. 'We'll work it all out. Now that I know.'

***

Kate was glad she was alone now. Billy and Jimmy had come back from football, ecstatic and starving, after a West Ham win. Jimmy was asleep, worn out. Billy would be back soon from the pub. He had bought a Christmas tree on the way back from football. It was standing next to the fire, waiting to be decorated. They could all do it tomorrow. After roast beef and Yorkshires. She was *almost* completely relaxed. She just had to know this one thing. When she heard the door open and close she felt herself tensing.

'Sorry love,' he mumbled. 'Couldn't get away, people kept buying me drinks.'

He walked over and kissed her on the cheek before going over and putting the kettle on. 'You're up late love. Thought you'd be in bed after your night on the bottle.'

'You're never going to let me forget that Billy are you?'

'Not for a very long time. D'you wanna cup?'

She nodded. 'I'm still up for a reason Billy. I need to ask you something.' She could feel her voice shaking.

He passed her the tea and sat down in his chair. He looked at her. 'Let me guess. Am I having an affair wiv Sal?'

Kate gasped. 'How did you know I was ... ?'

'Because every other bugger except you has asked me, including our son. And the answer which I've told 'em all is no. No, I'm not having an affair wiv Sal.'

'You thought about it though. Didn't you?' Kate forced herself to ask.

He nodded and looked down at the floor. 'I kissed 'er, he said, 'a couple of times. That's all.'

Kate took a deep breath. 'Did ... did you really want her Billy?'

'Yeah,' he said getting up and putting his cup in the sink. 'I'm sorry Kate but I'm trying to be honest wiv you 'ere.'

'So why didn't you?' Kate was trying to keep the anger and hurt out of her voice.

'I don't want to talk about it any more now Kate. I'm no good at all this stuff. You know that. I can't do sloppy stuff

234

but we're still 'ere after ten years. Must mean something. It's finished wiv Sal now anyway. It never really got started.'

Well, Kate thought. That was probably all she was going to get out of him. And she believed him. That whatever had happened, it was over.

'We could decorate the tree now love,' he said quickly lighting up a cigarette. 'Be a surprise for Jimmy in the morning.'

'What, now?' she laughed. 'It's eleven o'clock at night.'

Billy knelt in front of her and took her hands in his. 'Kate, we ain't fifty yet. We don't 'ave to go to bed early. We're still young. Never know I might just take you rock n' rolling down the Ilford Palais next week. Now, I'll get the box of decorations down from the loft an' you can make us another cuppa.'

Chapter 31

The den seemed really empty without Josie. The boys all sat round trying not to get wet. The snow had given way to a cold drizzle. 'We could go an' see her in hospital,' said Del. 'Pinch some flowers from the park.'

'Ain't no flowers in December,' said Jimmy. 'Anyway she's comin' out soon. Me mum said.'

'Never thought I'd miss a girl,' said Legs.

They all nodded in agreement. Church bells rang in the distance.

'Perhaps we should pray for her,' said Jimmy.

'She ain't gonna die,' said Del. 'She's only broke her arm.'

Legs stretched and yawned. 'We could have some biscuits now she's not here to ration them.'

They tore the lid off the box and Jimmy handed out two each. They munched away happily for a few seconds.

'Wonder what our next adventure might be,' Legs laughed.

'I don't want no more adventures yet,' said Legs. 'That was horrible.'

'There was some good bits though,' said Del. 'Some exciting bits. London was good. Well, until Jose got hurt of course. I wonder if the Queen has bin to see her,' you know, being knocked down outside her house. She might 'ave.'

'Bet *she* could get flowers in December,' said Jimmy.

'Nah,' said Legs, 'she'll be too busy at Christmas I expect. Bet her kids will get good presents.'

They all nodded. Jimmy put on a posh voice. 'Now darling Charles would you like another horse for Christmas or shall I buy you a new servant?'

They all laughed. 'Bet he don't have no mates though,' said Del, 'in that big house all alone wiv a poncy sister.'

'That would be funny if he come an' joined our gang for a bit wouldn't it,' Jimmy laughed.

'We could teach him swearwords an' stuff.'

'We could write to the Queen,' said Legs excitedly. 'Tell her about the accident and ask her if we can borrow Charles for our gang, we don't want the girl. Just till Jose comes out of hospital.'

236

The voice came from nowhere but it was outside their den. 'Jimmy, Del, Clive. Come out here now please.'

'Mum?' said Jimmy. 'What are you doing here?'

They all scrambled out of the den. Jimmy's mum was standing there with her rain hat on looking very serious. 'We're going on a little visit boys. Follow me.'

'Where are we going mum, we're really busy,' Jimmy muttered. Was she trying to show him up or something? Were they in trouble again? What was she doing marching over to their den? Their territory.

'You're all coming with me to apologise to Mrs. Broncowiez. For all the trouble you've caused.'

'Who's she?' Legs whispered.

'The witch,' Jimmy hissed back.

'Oh, I'm sorry Mrs Potter,' Legs stuttered. 'I can't go, I've promised my mum.'

'Your mum knows all about it and so does yours Del. We're all in agreement. You've said some dreadful things about that woman. I know you're only children and you didn't mean any harm but you have to be accountable for your actions and learn from your mistakes.'

'What does all that mean?' Del asked Jimmy. 'I don't know how you can understand a word your mum says.'

'Now, come on boys, keep up with me and Jimmy ...' She handed him a brown bag. 'You're to give her this cake. When you apologise.'

The boys all sighed and muttered but they followed. They didn't think they had much choice. Jimmy's mum led them past the witch's old house. Blackened windows, the door hanging off. Part of the roof had collapsed in the fire as well. It was a mess. Jimmy shivered. Surely it hadn't all been their fault.

'Is your dad back home yet?' Legs whispered to Del.

Del shook his head. 'Nah. Me mum said it's best he don't. She don't want him no more. She says we're better off without 'im.'

'He was scary,' said Jimmy. 'Even more scary than the witch. I don't wanna do this.'

Jimmy's mum knocked on Bone's front door. They heard scuffling sounds and Bones swearing. He opened the door looking even more unkempt than usual. His hair was sticking up everywhere.

237

'The boys have come to say something to Greta. If that's alright with you that is.'

Bones looked at the boys and winked. 'Yeah, she's out the back doing her spells wiv the cauldron.' The boys all giggled.

'Come in Kate.' The boys heard her voice calling from inside. 'Oh.'

She stopped when she came to the door and saw the boys.

They couldn't believe that this was the same person they had believed to be a witch. Yes, she was very old. Sixty five, Leg's mum had said but her hair was all brushed and shining, she was wearing a skirt and a woolly jumper, even though it was on inside out. She just sort of looked like an ordinary old lady. And she was smiling, actually quite a friendly smile. She had loads of wrinkles of course. The boys couldn't believe their eyes.

'It's alright Greta,' Jimmy's mum was saying. 'We don't need to come in. The boys just want to say something, don't you boys? And Jimmy ...' She nodded at the cake.

Jimmy stepped forward and held out the bag. 'It's for you Mrs Bron ... Mrs ...'

'Just call me Greta boys, it's easier.'

'We're sorry,' Jimmy blurted. 'Sorry we caused trouble.'

'Yeah an' I'm sorry an' all,' said Del.

Jimmy elbowed Legs in the ribs. Legs had gone into some sort of trance when he had seen the transformation of their witch. 'Er yeah. I'm sorry too,' he said eventually.

'I can't pretend I'm not cross with you,' said Greta. 'You have all done some very hurtful things but it's not the worst thing that has ever happened to me. I accept your apologies. And I have one of my own too.' They all looked at her.

'I want to say that I'm sorry for spitting at you all. It wasn't a very ladylike thing to do. I always wanted to spit at the Germans in Auschwitz you see but I never dared.'

'Well, now that's all done,' said Bones. 'I think you should all come in and 'ave a drink of squash. I think we've got some ain't we Greta?'

'Yes and we could cut the cake too.'

They smiled at each other. That sort of smile, thought Legs that his mum and dad did sometimes. No, surely not. Not the witch and Old Bones.

'Well, I think I'd best get home,' said Jimmy's mum, 'but I'm sure the boys would like to stay.'

'Do we 'ave to?' Jimmy hissed at her.

'Yes. It's the least you can do,' she whispered to them all.

At the thought of a piece of Jimmy's mum's chocolate cake Del nodded. 'Yeah, I'll come in. Can I play wiv Chuck?'

And so the boys all trooped in to have drinks and chocolate cake with the witch and Old Bones.

'Wish Jose was here,' said Jimmy sadly. 'She just would not believe it!'

They walked home slowly from Bone's house. 'We just had tea wiv the witch,' Del laughed. 'That is funny.'

'What I don't get,' said Legs, 'is how she doesn't even look like a witch now. She hasn't got a big nose or warts on her face, at all.'

'She don't even talk funny now neither,' Jimmy added.

'Praps she's had an operation or something,' said Del.

'Nah.' Jimmy looked up at the sky. 'I think it was just our maginations.'

Del looked up too. The clouds were low and heavy but there was nothing else. No witches on broomsticks. They were just clouds.

***

Sally swallowed hard as she opened the door to see Kate just standing there in a ridiculous plastic rain hat. Her stomach seemed to fall to her feet. She must know, Sally thought. She braced herself against the onslaught she thought was bound to come.

'Oh, it's you Kate. You'd best come in.'

Kate followed her in silently and sat down on the chair in the kitchen.

'Cup of tea?' Sally asked breathlessly.

'No. I won't be staying that long; I'm just on my way to see Maggie. How's Josie?' she asked.

'She's – she's coming out tomorrow. I'm just off there now. May's got the babies –'

'Then I'd better say what I've got to say,' said Kate. 'I know ... I know. Oh dear, this is all so difficult.'

Sally nodded. 'You know about the rumours? About me an' Billy? They ain't true Kate.'

'I know they're not true but I know there was ... something. If I thought Billy was in love with you Sally I would let him go.'

'What?'

Sally couldn't believe what she was hearing. You certainly didn't do that where she was from.

'You mean you wouldn't fight for him Kate? You wouldn't fight for your kid's father? You would just let him go?'

Kate nodded. 'We're very different Sally. I don't see the point in holding on to someone at all costs.'

'If I had bin you Kate, I would have punched me. That's what I expected when I saw you at the door. That's what I deserve because I wanted him Kate. It weren't just him that did all the running. I'd 'ave understood that. If you'd hit me. I don't understand what you're saying now.'

'We have to live with each other Sally. We're neighbours. Our children are best friends.'

'You were very kind to me on Friday at the 'ospital Kate.' Said Sally, 'I ain't never thanked you for that, not properly. You and Molly ...'

Sally could feel tears threatening and she wanted Kate to go now. 'I really thought she was gonna die. She let me give her a hug you know in hospital. That ain't 'appened for years.'

'Its all about them really isn't it?' said Kate. 'The children.'

'Yeah, I know you're right, but I need a man an' all Kate. I just sometimes get lonely. An' I'll tell you what; you need to look after Billy. If you ever let him go I'd be the first in the queue. And I mean that.'

Kate laughed. 'You don't have to live with him.'

'D'you know you're really pretty when you smile Kate. You could do wiv wearing a bit of make-up an' some modern clothes though. An' get rid of that curly perm. It makes you look about forty.'

240

Kate shook her head as she got up to leave. 'When we win the pools perhaps. Look Sally, I know we'll never be friends but I just think we can still be good neighbours. I just wanted to say that really.'

'Well, I'm glad you did. I still don't understand the way you think though Kate. I still can't believe you ain't scratched me eyes out.'

As she closed the door after her, Sally smiled. Oh well, as Dianne's mum would say. 'It takes all sorts.'

***

The three boys stood at Sally's door. 'Can we come in an' see Jose?'

'Yeah, yeah, come in boys,' said Sally distractedly.

'I got her some chewing gum,' said Del. 'It's only bin chewed a little bit.'

'An' I got a catapult,' said Legs, 'and Jimmy's found some good stones.'

Sally smiled at them. 'She's in the bedroom, just resting but she'll be glad to see you. Up you go. Josie!' she shouted up the stairs. 'Your mates are 'ere to see you.'

Josie was just sitting on the bed, looking sad. She had a plaster on her left arm and it was in a sling. Jimmy went and sat next to her and Del and Legs sat cross-legged on the floor.

'You alright?' Jimmy asked gruffly.

'Yeah,' she sighed. 'I suppose so. Pissed off wiv this arm though. You can write your names on the plaster if you want.' She handed them a red wax crayon.

'You ain't got a Christmas tree up Jose,' said Legs.

'Nah, we're going to Auntie Dianne's for Christmas.'

'Ooh,' Del laughed, 'how's Father Christmas gonna find you then Jose?'

They all laughed. It felt good. All being back together again. They told Josie about their meeting with the witch and how they thought that her and Old Bones were in love with each other.

'He wouldn't do that,' she said. 'Old men don't do sex. Witches might I suppose but they ain't real are they?'

'They'd be too old to have sex anyway,' Del agreed. 'They just hold hands probably.'

241

'Well,' said Legs. 'I didn't get told off much. My Mum says that we're only young. She doesn't blame us for believing stuff like that, you know, witches and things.'

'My Mum said it could've bin worse,' said Jimmy. 'I can't believe I never got the slipper.' They all laughed.

'We'll have to make sure our next adventure don't hurt people,' said Josie.

'Aliens,' said Del, excitedly. 'I read about 'em in me brother's comic. There's loads of people who are really aliens. They just look like us but they ain't. Bet there's some round 'ere.'

'What about that new family?' asked Legs.

'The wogs you mean?' Del asked.

'No Del. The ones at number 53. They look a bit weird,' said Josie, 'an' don't use that 'wog' word. It's 'orrible. You sound just like your dad.'

'I miss me dad,' said Del suddenly.

'Why?' asked Legs. 'He was nasty.'

'At least I had one,' he said quietly.

Josie put her good arm on his shoulder. 'You'll be alright Del. We'll look after yer.'

Josie wanted to say how much she had missed them all without sounding like a girl. 'Can you wait till I get back from Auntie Dianne's then?' she asked, 'before you start another adventure? I've missed ... I've missed ... our adventures.'

'We ain't doing nothing till after Christmas,' said Del. 'Wooooooooooooh, it's Christmas!'

They all laughed and jumped up and down on Josie's bed.

'Oi, watch me arm!' she screamed. 'Silly buggers.'

The Chicken Run ... Christmas Eve 1955

Chapter 32

It was a beautiful day. Christmas Eve. One of those crisp, winter days. Blue sky. Excitement and anticipation in the air. There were West Ham supporters with tinsel stuck to their bobble hats, even old men with tinsel round their caps. Everyone was laughing and joking in the chicken run.

'D'you wanna go down the front son?' his dad asked him.

Jimmy shook his head. 'Nah. I'll stand wiv you now dad. I ain't a little kid anymore.'

'Oh, think you're a man now do yer?' His dad laughed. 'Hey Loopy. My son's too old to go an' stand wiv the kids now.'

His mates all grinned. Loopy pulled Jimmy's bobble hat off and ruffled his hair. He wished they would stop doing that now he was nearly ten. Grown-ups. He joined in the laughing with them though. The banter, the team talk. Who Ted Fenton should play and who not. Might win today, he thought. Swansea weren't much better than the Hammers.

There was a roar around Upton Park as the teams came out. Everyone started singing 'I'm Forever Blowing Bubbles.' It echoed around the ground. Jimmy felt the familiar excitement, the churning in his stomach. He looked at his dad and grinned.

'We're gonna win today son,' his dad shouted. 'I can feel it in me water.'

It wasn't long before they were all jumping up and down and hugging each other as West Ham scored. Even Loopy gave him a hug.

'You brought us luck young Jimmy. You'll have to stand wiv us all the time now. Ain't that the best feeling in the world? Come on You Irons!'

His dad lifted him up on his shoulders. Jimmy protested. 'Dad, I'm too old to sit ...'

'You're never too old son. Now sing.'

'I'm Forever Blowing Bubbles' reverberated around the ground and Jimmy joined in. Up on his dad's shoulders he felt like he was King of the Chicken Run and if he jumped off his dad's shoulders right now he would be quite happy to drown in the sea of claret and blue scarves and hats beneath him.

***

The King's Head, on Christmas Eve was packed with punters. Loopy punched Billy playfully on the shoulder. 'Five one Billy. I can't bleedin' believe it. Five one. We was all over 'em! What a great Christmas this is gonna be.'

'You lot are mad,' George laughed. 'None of you have stopped talking about it all night. And you haven't stopped grinning Billy Potter.'

George and Billy were in their usual places.

'Well Billy,' George had to shout over the noise. 'May's told me your Kate's pretty set on Australia after everything that's happened. One West Ham win won't change all that's gone on you know. Come on, I'll get you another pint.'

'I wouldn't be happy out there George,' said Billy lighting up a cigarette and taking a long swig of his pint.

'Why don't you just go and try it, give yourself, I don't know a couple of years. You've got one life Billy. Two years is nothing.'

'It's all right for you George; you're used to moving around. It's the other side of the world for God's sake. It takes six weeks to get there. And I ain't good on boats neither.'

'When did you ever go on a boat?'

'Down Southend. One of them fishing trips. Sick as a bloody parrot I was.'

George couldn't stop laughing. Arthur came over. He had a sweat on tonight and his face was ruddy and glistening. 'Good to hear you lot laugh after the week we've had. One Hammers win an' you're all back to normal. Well, if any of you *is* normal.'

'Yeah, come on Arthur give us a hand,' George laughed. 'I'm trying to persuade Billy to go to Australia.'

'Yeah, fuck off Billy. I might get a bit of peace if you go. In fact you can take the rest of Churchill Street wiv yer an' all.'

'Ta very much Arthur. I love you too mate.'

Arthur moved away to serve another punter chuckling to himself. Just then Bones started playing 'I'm Forever Blowing Bubbles' on the piano.

244

'Bad timing Bones,' George muttered as the whole pub started singing. Not a good time to persuade Billy to leave his West Ham heroes. Their team had won this week and one day they would be back in the First Division. At eleven o'clock in the pub on a Saturday night there wasn't a man in there who didn't really believe that was going to happen.

'Last orders ladies an' gents,' Arthur was shouting as he rang his bell which had been purloined from a German U Boat. 'Last orders. Now drink your drinks and fuck off.'

Everyone rolled out of the King's Head singing 'Jingle Bells'. Loopy had started a conga winding up the road.

'They used to say getting pissed was the quickest way out of Manchester,' George laughed as they walked up the road.

'Who said?' Billy asked.

'The people in Manchester of course. Sometimes I wonder about you Billy, I really do. Get yourself off. Sunshine, plenty of work out in Australia. Wish I was your age again. Just think you'll regret it if you don't give it a go.'

They came in to Churchill Street. Somewhere a dog barked.

'What you got Kate for Christmas?' George asked.

'I just give her a bit of dosh,' Billy replied. 'Mind you it's a bit tight this year wiv her being off sick from the factory.'

'You'd have oodles of money in Australia,' George laughed. 'They're giving it away out there.'

'Yeah, yeah. Night George. Dinner tomorrow at yours eh? Hope May survives it.'

'Night Billy. See you tomorrow. Happy Christmas mate.'

Christmas Day 1955

Chapter 33

This was going to be a great Christmas Day, Jimmy thought. He had woken up very early as usual and when he moved his leg he could feel the weight of his Christmas stocking. He jumped out of bed and ran across the cold lino floor to switch on the light. There it was. His stocking. Knitted in claret and blue of course. He didn't know where it went to for the rest of the year because he only ever saw it on Christmas morning. Sat on the top was his usual tangerine. He took it out slowly, savouring the tangy smell. He always lingered over the presents in his stocking. He had a long time to wait before his presents round the tree. His Cox's apple was next.

At first he recoiled from it, remembering the witch. Then he laughed at himself. That was when he had been young and didn't know any better. He knew it wouldn't hurt him now. He took a large bite. Wow, a new West ham rosette and a tin whistle. He thought perhaps he had best not blow it yet. The clock said it was just past four. Next was a packet of marshmallows, a ping pong ball and, right at the bottom, two tin soldiers. This was the brigadier and the major. Great, he had the whole set now. His mum always put a load of newspaper in his stocking to fill it out a bit but even so that was more than he had expected.

This was what had first alerted him to the possibility that Father Christmas was actually a made-up thing. It was always the Daily Mirror in his stocking. That alone wouldn't have convinced him but, combined with lots of other little signs; it built up a list of parental errors. By the age of six, him and his mates had all realised that Father Christmas just did not exist. It had been a sad moment for them all.

Precious jumped up in to the bed and climbed under the covers.

'What you doing in?' he asked her. 'That must be your Christmas present Precious. A night in.'

Back in bed, under the covers, it wasn't long before he drifted off to sleep again.

246

He was woken by his mum, pulling back the curtains. 'Happy Christmas Jimmy,' she smiled, 'I see you were up early as usual.'

She wasn't cross though. She was never cross on Christmas Day. He had come downstairs in his jamas to the smell of bacon and eggs. A rare treat. His dad was sitting on his chair. He looked a bit empty without a paper.

'Morning' son,' he smiled at him. 'Happy Christmas.'

Jimmy's eyes were drawn to the tree in the corner, decorated now with tinsel and baubles, the branches groaning under the weight. And, underneath, loads of presents had magically appeared.

'What time's Molly coming?' his dad asked as they sat down at the table for breakfast.

'Any time now I think,' said his mum.

'Well I ain't having no more washes today,' Jimmy grumbled.

'Do we have to go to May and George's for our dinner?' his dad moaned.

'Well, if you don't want to starve, yes.'

She wiped her hands on her pinny, before taking it off and sitting down with them. 'It's the first time Del's older brothers have missed a Christmas here and I think she wanted to do something for Maggie as well. It'll be alright. George has got you a jug of beer from the off licence.'

'And don't you be going on the sherry again Kate,' his dad laughed. 'No. It's just all those kids All the noise. Still can always go an' sit in George's shed, it's like a little palace out there. Bet he's decorated it an' all.'

'He has,' Jimmy laughed. 'We helped 'im the other day.'

Apart from Sally, Josie and the twins, all the neighbours were there. Auntie Molly, Old Bones and even the witch were all crowded into the house as well. Jimmy supposed that he would have to start calling her Greta but he knew that she would always be *the witch* to him.

It had been a brilliant day so far. Turkey and roast dinner, plum pudding and trifle. Jimmy felt stuffed but in a happy way and they had all pulled crackers except that little Marilyn had got a bit frightened when they banged. She had climbed up on to his knee and just wouldn't get down again.

'Ah, look at her,' Maggie smiled. 'She loves you Jimmy.'

The little girl planted a wet, sticky kiss on his cheek, which made everyone laugh. She was quite sweet, Jimmy thought. He secretly hoped that he would be a dad one day. And have a little girl like Marilyn.

May and George had bought all the Tyler children a present and there were squeals of delight from them as they ripped off the paper excitedly. Maggie, who had been a bit heavy on the sherry, had started crying. Not surprising really. They hadn't been able to have Julie's funeral yet so no-one minded her shedding a few tears.

All of them had moved into the sitting room and May Pattinson had lit all the candles on the tree. They didn't last long but everyone, even the youngest Tylers, gazed in wonder for a few seconds, no-one saying a word.

After the presents, Bones had started playing the piano and they all sang carols. He was great, thought Jimmy. He didn't even smell anymore now he was in love with the witch. The witch was all smiley and happy as well but the funniest bit of the whole day had been when Auntie Molly had let out a piercing scream from her chair. She moved faster than Jimmy had ever seen before and started shaking herself all over. 'Something horrible and furry has just run up my skirt!'

Chuck, the ferret had followed Bones down the road and had managed eventually to find an open window and join the party. He was so traumatised by Molly's screams that he leapt from the chair on to the tree which immediately gave way and fell on top of Marilyn. Everyone laughed so much. Jimmy thought he might even wet himself. Even his dad laughed then. He must have got over not having a Daily Mirror to read. And Sally, Josie and the twins had turned up near the end, just to have a cup of tea.

Then they made their way home. There was still one more present under the tree. They had taken all the others to May and George's.

'There you are son,' said his dad, putting some more coal on the fire . 'You can open it now.'

Jimmy removed the green paper with red Christmas trees on and there, in his hands, was a large box. **HORNBY TRAIN SET** written on the top. The box looked quite old so it wasn't new but Jimmy didn't care about that. How many years had he been waiting for this? And even though he knew he was probably too old for it now, it didn't matter. 'Ta mum, ta dad,' he said excitedly. 'I think this really is the best day of my life.'

***

It had been a good day next door but it was better to be back home, Billy thought. The fire was roaring and he had his comfy slippers on. He might just have a little doze now. Jimmy had just gone up to bed and Kate was pottering around. And he had seen Sally today. It had been alright. They had been laughing in the kitchen with George. When George had gone into the other room it had felt awkward for a moment.

'Sorry Sal,' Billy said. He didn't really know why he had said it. Just that he seemed to have hurt her somehow without knowing.

'Oh, it's alright Billy. Worse things have happened this week.'

'You will meet someone you know,' he blurted out.

'Just not you,' she said quietly.

'Yeah, just not me.'

Just then George had come back in. 'I'd keep out the way if I was you Billy. Molly's on about Australia again. The application forms have come through.' He laughed.

'I ain't going George so don't you start. I ain't going to bloody Australia an' that's the end of it.'

Chapter 34

Jimmy had looked around the house once more before they had left. Walked into each room and stood, just for a few seconds. He had lived here for nearly all of his life. He didn't want to go. It hadn't seemed real up to now. Even when everything was being packed into big boxes his life had carried on much as usual. No, it was just today, they were off to Australia. His whole life was going to change.

He suddenly felt frightened. It felt like when he had nearly drowned at the baths. He had only been seven and had just jumped in the deep end. Del had dared him. Would probably have been alright if he had been able to swim. But that feeling, that he was probably going to die. Trying desperately to touch the bottom, crying out and no-one hearing him. Del's face. Laughing and then changing as he realised. Sometimes, those few moments came back to him as he was drifting off to sleep. But he wasn't drowning now so why did he feel like this, just because he was going to Australia?

He had sat, for a few minutes, on his bedroom floor. It wasn't the same, without the furniture. It was just a room. Just a room in a council house in Plaistow. He felt empty and homeless. No-one even cared what *he* thought about it. Apart from that one time when he had told his dad he didn't want to go.

They were going from Southampton on the *SS Arcadia*, P&O Lines. The Piss & Off Line Del had called it. Quite a new ship, Auntie Molly had told him, so it shouldn't sink.

Mind you, she had said to his mum, they said that about the Titanic. You could tell Auntie Molly was really excited. She didn't usually say anything funny.

'Come on Jimmy,' his mum had shouted, 'the taxi's here.' The taxi was taking them to Waterloo Station and the train to Southampton. That had caused a bit of a row. Auntie Molly wanting to go from Southampton instead of Tilbury.

'We'll just see a bit of the English countryside for the last time,' she had explained. His mum hadn't been very impressed. Tilbury was only up the river from here.

He had walked slowly down the stairs, for the last time. Everyone had gathered on the street to wave them off. Jimmy had never seen anything like it, except when there was weddings and funerals and once when the old couple from number eight had won the pools and went to Spain for a holiday.

Maggie Tyler grabbed him as soon as he came through the gate and kissed him all over his face. It made him feel quite sick. Del said that she laughed a lot more now, since his dad had gone. She was working at the factory and said she was much better off without him. Del still missed his dad though. Jimmy didn't really understand why.

'Oh, I'll miss you Jimmy,' she cried. 'You was always the sensible one. Say goodbye to your mate Del. You ain't never gonna see him again.'

Del had stood looking down at the ground.

'See you mate,' Jimmy had said. He hadn't known what else to say. They spat and shook hands. Legs moved towards him and they did the same. He was wiping tears from his eyes.

'Shut up Legs, you're soft,' Del muttered.

'I'm not crying Del,' Legs sniffed. 'It's my hay fever. Don't let them sharks get you Jimmy.' He punched him on the shoulder.

Jimmy had looked around. Everyone was kissing and crying. Sally Evans was crying on May Pattinson's shoulder. He had sometimes wondered whether his dad had loved Sally a little bit but he said he hadn't and he didn't tell lies. He was a grown-up. Well, apart from the Father Christmas one. Oh, and God of course. That couldn't be true. He had been really good since Christmas and God was still sending him to Australia.

Sally had a new boyfriend now. Legsy's older brother Joe had moved down to Forest Gate, only a couple of miles away and they had fallen in love. Well, that was what he thought. Del said that it was probably just sex. Anyway, they seemed to be quite happy together and Josie got on alright with him.

He looked around. Where *was* Josie? She said she would be here. To say goodbye.

'Come on now,' said Auntie Molly. 'Let's get away or we'll miss the train.'

251

Jimmy had hung back, just in case she came running up the road. She wasn't there. They had got into the taxi, his mum wiping her eyes with a hankie. Everyone in the street was waving and cheering them as the taxi set off. Then he saw her, just turning the corner. She was waving.

'Stop!' shouted Jimmy. 'It's Josie. Stop the car!'

'Well, I don't think we've got time ...' Auntie Molly began to speak.

'Let him say goodbye Molly,' his mum had sniffed. 'She's his best friend.'

Jimmy had jumped out the car almost before it had stopped and ran up to meet her. They stood looking at each other. Then looked away, embarrassed.

'Just went to the shops to get you this Jimmy,' Josie said, pressing a small bag into his hand. Jimmy opened it. It was the new West Ham badge. 'I'll never forget you. I'll write to you an' all. I'll let you know how the Hammers get on. And I'll look after Precious, I promise.'

She spat on her hand and held it out to him. He did the same. He had felt his face crumple as he looked at hers and then she threw her arms around him and hugged him so tight that he thought he might run out of breath.

He heard a few 'Aah's' from the crowd and they had all cheered as Jimmy got back in the taxi.

'See ya later alligator!' his mates all shouted in unison.

'In a while crocodile!' he shouted back. He wondered whether they had rock n' roll in Australia yet. They had probably never even heard of Bill Haley out there. 'I'll come back,' he shouted to Josie as the taxi drove off. 'When I'm older, I'll come back.'

His mum had put her arm around him and they had sobbed together. 'Why are you crying mum?' he had asked her. 'I thought you was glad we was going.'

'It's just hard saying goodbye sometimes that's all Jimmy. We've all been through a lot together. And it's not 'we was going', it's 'we were going'. The Australians are never going to understand you if you don't speak properly.'

Jimmy grinned instinctively. Some things never changed, he thought. Auntie Molly was sitting in the front seat, next to the driver. 'Oh Jimmy, she had said, 'this is such an adventure. Stop crying now. You'll make lots of new friends.'

'I don't wanna make new friends,' he had muttered.

He hadn't spoken much after that and now they were on the train to Southampton. He looked out the window. It was a lovely summer's day. Blue skies.

He had been on a proper train once before when they had gone to Southend for a holiday. He had been about six and he remembered it mainly because it was the first time he had ever seen cows and sheep. Oh, he had seen them in pictures but not in real life so that had been exciting. He looked at all the houses when they passed them and wondered who lived in them and whether they had lived there all their lives. There were so many people in the world. He wondered if Australia would be the same.

'Do you want an egg sandwich Jimmy?' his mum was asking him. 'You're very quiet. Aren't you just a little bit excited?'

Jimmy shrugged his shoulders. He did feel excited, even though he didn't want to. It was like there was a feather tickling all his insides and he was finding it difficult to control. Just being on a proper train was exhilarating and different. Still, he was determined to sulk for a bit longer yet. He wasn't going to make this easy for them. He took a sandwich from his mum and started chomping on it. He was hungry, he hadn't eaten any breakfast but the gang had put their pocket money together and bought him a packet of chocolate digestives. He had them in his satchel.

He was looking forward to seeing his dad at Southampton station. He had gone on ahead with all the luggage and had stayed in a B&B last night. Said he would rather miss out on all the goodbyes. He had looked a bit sad then.

Jimmy knew his dad would really miss West Ham and his mates, just like he would, but his dad had changed his mind about going. Jimmy thought it might be his fault. They wanted to get him away from here, where he always seemed to be getting into trouble. Jimmy hoped that they sold the Daily Mirror in Australia or his dad might get really depressed.

'You'll learn to read and write properly out there Jimmy,' his Auntie Molly had said. 'Miss Parsons thinks

253

you've got it in you. If you were just in a smaller class. Then you'll get a good job. It's important Jimmy. For you to get the best chances in life.'

He just wanted to be with his mates.

'Come on then everyone, this is where we get off.' Auntie Molly lifted the bags down from the overhead rack. She and his mum had been chatting to the three other people in their compartment. They were all going to Australia as well. Jimmy had been so busy thinking that he hadn't really noticed them. There was a boy about the same age as him. He looked miserable an' all, he thought.

'They have shark nets now,' Jimmy said to him as they got off the train, 'so they can't get yer.'

The boy looked at him as if he was mad. 'Piss off,' he hissed at Jimmy.

'Only trying to make you feel better,' said Jimmy. '

'Oh look,' his Auntie Molly was saying, 'Jimmy's made a friend already. He'll be fine Kate. Don't fret about him.'

His dad was stood waiting at the barrier. They were in a massive shed. There were bags, boxes and suitcases everywhere. People running around shouting and directing.

His dad put his arm round his shoulders. 'Kate, you an' Molly go an' line up at the desk,' he said to them, 'number ten it is. I just want to show Jimmy something. Come on mate.'

For someone who didn't even want to go to Australia, his dad was acting as if he was really quite excited.

'Where are we going dad?'

'Just round this corner son.'

They had walked the full length of the shed. There was an open door at the end.

Jimmy stood in the opening and was transfixed. There she was. Right in front of him. The name in huge letters on the bow.

ARCADIA

She was white with a yellow funnel and she was an enormous ship. It took his breath away. Everything bad he had been feeling just seemed to melt away. This was a *real* adventure. Not a made-up one like the witch. He was going to sail to the other side of the world. A real explorer. There was a blast from the ship's funnel, it made him jump. His dad laughed.

'Wow,' he said. 'It's big ain't it dad?'

There was all sorts going on. People running up and down gangways with food and cases. Lots of sailors in different uniforms. Banging and clanking. Smoke was belching from the funnel.

'Just wanted you to see it mate. We're gonna be living on there for six weeks.'

'D'you wanna go now then dad?'

'Nah, not really.' He looked sad again. 'We'll see how it goes. We can always come home once I've made me fortune,' he laughed.

Jimmy still thought that it was getting beaten by Spurs in the FA Cup 6th round that had really changed his dad's mind. At the end of the replay his dad had almost been crying. 'That's it,' he had said, throwing his programme on to the pitch. 'Might as well go to bloody Australia now. I'm finished wiv 'em.'

Of course they had both got over it and had carried on going to Upton Park for the rest of the season. That was what you did when you *really* supported a team. Jimmy couldn't believe how excited he felt now. He looked again at the ocean liner. He would never, ever forget this day.

It took hours, or so it seemed to Jimmy. Filling in forms, sorting out their luggage, finding out what cabin they were in but, finally, clutching their embarkation cards, they were walking up the rickety gangway. 'Welcome Aboard,' said a sailor in a posh hat as they reached the top.

'Are you the Captain?' Jimmy asked.

The sailor laughed. 'Wish I was mate. Wouldn't mind being on his salary.'

He looked at their card. E Deck. He pointed to a staircase. 'Two decks down. I'll probably see you around.' He smiled at Jimmy.

It wasn't long before the ship's hooter signalled their imminent departure. A very posh voice came on over the tannoy. ***"ss Arcadia will shortly be sailing for Vigo. Will everyone who is not sailing on board please disembark by the final gangway which is situated on E deck aft"***

'That'll be the Captain,' said Jimmy. They were all stood at the rail watching the band play them away on the quayside. Jimmy felt in his pocket for his West Ham badge and clung on to it tightly. He felt tears pricking the back of his eyes when he thought about Josie. He would come back and marry her one day. Never tell anyone that though. It would be his secret. Everyone would think he had gone soft. Imagine what Del would say.

He bit his lip and looked up at his dad. 'Ain't as good as the band at Upton Park are they dad? Do you remember that day I threw me orange peel down the trumpet. I might miss the chicken run a bit.'

His dad smiled. Jimmy was standing between them, just watching all the people waving from down below.

'We're really going now ain't we mum?' he asked as the anchors clanked and heaved out of the water and the ship began to pull away from the quayside. He looked up at his mum and dad. His dad had his arm around her. His mum's hair looked lovely now that it was wavy and down to her shoulders, he thought. They were looking a bit soppy at each other. A bit like May and George Pattinson sometimes did.

***

Kate gripped the ship's rail tightly and looked at England. The country of her birth. The country she had never left before and had seen so little of. One day, she would come back and go to all those places. She shivered. Even though it was summer it was still cold. Well, it wouldn't be cold in Brisbane.

Kate thought of all the things she would miss. All the people in Churchill Street who, in the last few months, she had come to understand. The kindnesses they had all shown her now that her mind seemed to be free. Free of all that guilt. She fleetingly thought of spring in Victoria Park. Before the war. Childhood memories creeping into her mind. Shirley, her mum and her dad. All that pain.

'It'll be alright, won't it Billy? We can always come back if we don't like it.' She leaned into his shoulder.

'Yeah,' he said, smiling at her. 'We'll give it a go. We ain't got nothing to lose. Everything's gonna be fine.'

Jimmy slipped his hand into his mum's and squeezed it tightly.

Kate wasn't so sure that everything would be fine. She knew life wasn't like that. No-one truly lived happily ever after. There were good bits and bad bits and you just had to get through them but they were taking a chance and that had to be a positive thing. It was George who had convinced Billy to give it a try. She would miss him and May. And Greta. Greta who had saved her life. Greta who had rescued her from Bethnal Green Station and that dreadful night. Greta who had given her the courage to talk to people who had helped her to change her life and save her marriage.

Tears welled in her eyes as the band played its last tune and the ship moved out into Southampton waters. The last streamers between the ship and the shore snapped and danced across the waves. Everyone was crying and waving and screaming as the ship's hooter sounded for the final time. And they watched and listened as the band played the very last tune. And everyone on the ship joined in the chorus.

"*Waltzing Matilda, waltzing Matilda, you'll come a-waltzing Matilda with me...*"

###

NOTE TO READER

THE BETHNAL GREEN TUBE SHELTER DISASTER

On 3rd March 1943 the siren sounded at 8.17 p.m. People made their way in the pitch dark of the blackout to file in an orderly manner down the steps to the unfinished underground station which had been used as a deep air raid shelter since 1940. Suddenly those waiting to enter were alarmed by the unfamiliar, deafening sound of a new anti-aircraft rocket battery firing nearby. They assumed that it was deadly enemy bombs exploding. At that moment a woman with a child fell at the bottom of the wet, slippery stairway and others fell on top of her. The crowd above continued pressing forward unable to see what was happening below in the dark. A complete jam of about 300 people, five or six deep, built up within seconds. It was 11.40 pm before the last of the 173 dead was pulled out – 84 women, 62 children and 27 men – and over 90 were injured. Many more suffered life-long trauma. This was the worst civilian disaster in Great Britain during the 2nd World War.

WHAT IS
THE STAIRWAY TO HEAVEN MEMORIAL TRUST?

It is a registered charity. The Trust aims to erect a fitting Memorial to those who died, were injured or survived this disaster. It will also honour the key role of the Emergency Services.

At the time of this book going to press, work on the memorial has begun but there is not enough money raised at present for it to be completed.

CAN I HELP?

Yes you can. You can find out more information about the tragedy and find out how you can make a donation here www.stairwaytoheavenmemorial.org

THANK YOU

ABOUT THE AUTHOR

Lynne Whelon lives with her cat Minty and several garden gnomes in a small village in North Lancashire but spent her formative years in Reading and Ilford, Essex.

She joined the Merchant Navy as a nursery stewardess and enjoyed herself seeing the world and gathering information for her future novels before being made redundant in 1986. She then began writing in earnest, attended many writing courses and workshops and has since had short stories and articles published in magazines. The Chicken Run is her first novel.

Lynne has been working at her local primary school for the last thirteen years.

ACKNOWLEDGMENTS

Thank you Jelly Friskers writing group who have helped and inspired me to improve my writing skills. Special thanks to Jenni Thornley in the group, who has helped an old technophobe on the computer and who also, designed my cover.

The tragedy at Bethnal Green in 1943 was the worst civilian disaster of the 2nd World War. I would like to thank Alf Morris and Sandra Scotting of the 'Stairway To Heaven Memorial Trust' for the information they provided me with about that terrible night.

Many of my family and friends past and present, at sea and ashore, have helped unknowingly. Little phrases they have come out with, that I have used in 'The Chicken Run'- thank you Tim Taylor and Helen Askew for your ideas and Wendy for Old Bones! Thanks to all of you.

Greatest thank you of all must go to friend and ex-workmate Gill Garbutt who has advised me brilliantly throughout the writing of 'The Chicken Run' and has kept encouraging me to get to the end. It has taken a long time.

And last but not least to all those who have lived or worked in the old East End. Only you know how its spirit enters your soul and never quite goes away again...

Lightning Source UK Ltd
Milton Keynes UK
UKOW052246050912

198521UK00001B/12/P